POLOSTAN

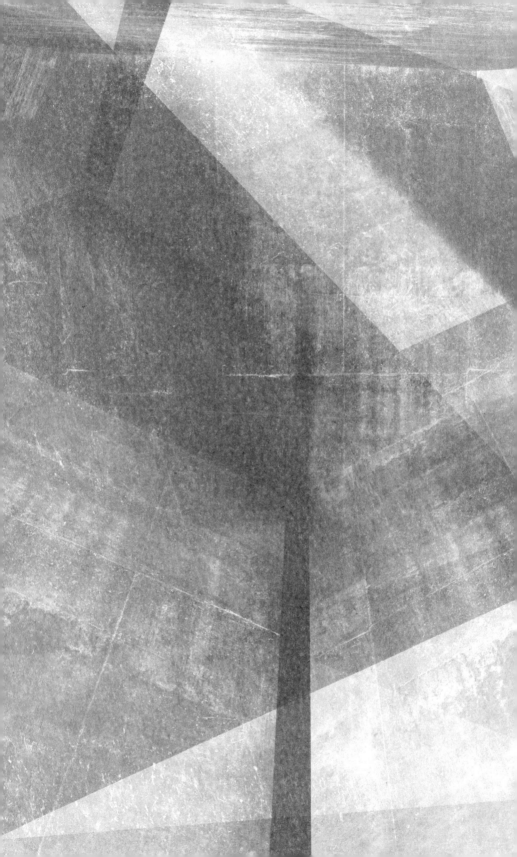

NEAL STEPHENSON

WILLIAM MORROW

An Imprint of HarperCollins*Publishers*

POLOSTAN

VOLUME ONE OF *BOMB LIGHT*

HarperCollins books may be purchased for educational, business, or sales promotional use. For information, please email the Special Markets Department at SPsales@harpercollins.com.

FIRST EDITION

Designed by Elina Cohen
Art courtesy of Shutterstock / Evannovostro
Endpaper art courtesy of Shutterstock / pascal_serwill

Library of Congress Cataloging-in-Publication Data has been applied for.

ISBN 978-0-06-233449-7

24 25 26 27 28 LBC 5 4 3 2 1

To Seamus

What men are poets who can speak of Jupiter if he were a man, but if he is an immense spinning sphere of methane and ammonia must be silent?

—Richard Feynman

THE GOLDEN GATE

OCTOBER 1933

The engineer hadn't ridden the rails hobo-style since his getaway from the massacre in D.C. more than a year ago. Back east, he'd hopped freights from time to time just to show that wearing a suit and tie hadn't put him on the wrong side of the class struggle. Out west, though, the distances were just too vast, the trains too few and far between. Getting stranded in the middle of nowhere could be fatal. So on the long-haul trips between Gary and the Golden Gate, he was happy to let the steel company buy him passage in a Pullman coach.

Consequently he lacked a hobo's ingrained knowledge of how California's railway lines were hooked up. He'd looked at maps. The steel company had plenty of those. The lines—twin filaments of metal, a ton of steel in every eight yards of track—drained down from the high wild reaches of Oroville, Calistoga, Fruto, Thrall, Bray, Weed, Raisin City, and Mount Diablo.

There was no guessing what such places might be harboring some offshoot of Dawn's weird, difficult kin. She could be coming from practically any direction. Eventually, though, the railways did converge on a few trunk lines that groped around the bay and tried to get as close to San Francisco as geography would allow. One swung through Vallejo in the north, sliced down through Marin, and terminated at Sausalito. From there, you had to take a ferry to Oakland or San Francisco.

The engineer was presently engaged in trying to put those boats out of business by constructing a mighty bridge across the Golden Gate. His work took him over to the Sausalito side all the time. He had agreed to meet Dawn there this morning. She'd got a telegram to him mentioning a time.

When he was a boy, he'd been kicked in the face while milking a cow. They'd put his head in a new kind of machine and shot a thing they called an X-ray, side-on. Looking at the film in the doctor's office through the one eye that wasn't swollen shut, he had been struck by the soft convolutions of the oral cavity, defended from the dirty world by wrapping systems of lips, jaws, and gums. Where it really mattered, though, teeth erupted from the flesh. People thought of them as the centerpieces of smiles. But the X-ray had made it obvious that they were weapons. Expensive and complicated ones at that.

So it was at the entrance to the bay. Scrub-covered hills, pleasant enough to look at, were the outward form of the bay's converging jaws. But humans had studded them with fangs: forts, bunkers, and gun emplacements embedded in the extremities of the Presidio and the Marin Headlands, zeroed on the Gate, ready to bite and crush any foreign fleet seeking to force the passage.

Other than that, those cold and wind-lashed points had attracted very little human activity until recently. But as the engineer walked down the slope and around the sweeping curve of Lombard Street, he came in view of a materials depot and a logistical complex that had sprung up around the old fort since January of this year. The country as a whole might be bogged down in depression, but it had somehow resolved to send a lot of steel and a lot of men to this one place to get a thing done. And as much as he hated the country and the people who ran it, his engineer's heart thrilled to see it.

Once you got past the army hospital and the little airfield, Lombard's pavement had simply been pulverized by the wheels of heavy trucks. It frayed into dirt tracks and fanned out into an earthen ramp that plunged into a crowd of jostling barges in the lee of the point where the old fort squatted.

He did not have to wait for ferries. In his billfold was a pass that empowered him to go through any gate, to climb aboard any of the small craft that continually shuttled across the Golden Gate on bridge business, darting between the heavy steamships bound for Yokohama, Manila, Anchorage, and Peru, and the smaller fishing vessels headed for wherever the black cod schooled.

He found space aboard one boat, crowded with workers. It stopped almost immediately at the site, just off the point, where they were working on the foundations for the south tower. At this stage that was all just underwater blasting and dredging. The men who disembarked here were mostly divers. In a couple of hours when the tide went slack they'd put on their big spherical helmets and go down to plant dynamite.

Beyond that, the boat ventured out into open water. Wind and tide were both coming in off the Pacific, so the ride was choppy, but nothing that would put any kind of scare into these daredevils—mostly riveters working the high steel of the north tower. All summer the perverse weather of San Francisco had given them cold, foggy days, but now that autumn was here it was glorious sunshine. So the workers happily sat abovedecks, smoking, bullshitting, enjoying the sunshine and the views. The engineer took shelter in the lee of the pilothouse so that the wind wouldn't peel his hat off. Alcatraz was a couple of miles off to starboard. This came in for more discussion than usual. It was a disciplinary barracks for the army prison, but the announcement had gone out, only a few days ago, that it had been acquired by the federal government. They were going to turn it into a penitentiary for the very worst sort of inmates.

Riveters disembarked at the foot of the north tower, slowly rising above its submerged foundation in a vertiginous three-dimensional maze of scaffolding and hollow steel structural pieces. Even from down here the cacophony of the pneumatic rivet guns was maddening. The last stop, only a short distance farther, was where the cable anchorage was rising out of the bedrock of the Marin Headlands. The engineer, in no hurry, waited for the carpenters to stream off the boat. They clambered up a mess of stairs surrounding the gray ziggurat of reinforced concrete that would one day haul back against the tension on the bridge's yard-thick cables. Their job was to dismantle the wooden forms from the last pour, wrench the nails out of the boards, and rebuild them a little higher. Holding back the pressure of all that wet cement required such structural might that forests had been felled farther up the coast just to supply the timbers.

No respecters of hierarchies, the carpenters would give him a tongue-lashing if he got in their way. So he skirted the work site by following the shore, then scrambled up-slope and strolled between the gun emplacements and through little neighborhoods of army housing until he found a path that descended into Sausalito. There, between the railway terminal and the ferry dock, he found a diner. He sat in a booth, drinking coffee and eating a slice of cherry pie—this being the season for cherries—and waited for Dawn.

Distinctive as she was, he didn't recognize her until she was almost at his table. She'd grown another inch or two and now, even in flats, was taller than the average man. But it wasn't just that. She'd been through things that had changed the way she held herself, the way she moved. And not for the worse. The coltish farm-girl enthusiasm of 1932 Dawn had been replaced by a cool self-possession, wary without being afraid.

They both knew there'd be no hugging or any other such display of mutual feeling. There were only so many circumstances in which a thirty-year-old bachelor engineer could be seen conversing with a girl who was still young enough to attend high school. The cover story they'd used in Indiana—that she was his country cousin in town for a few days' visit—wouldn't fly here. And the truth of the matter—that he had no interest at all in women—couldn't be spoken aloud, even in San Francisco. He rose to shake her hand, then gestured to the opposite bench. If anyone connected with the steel company happened to see them and asked questions, he'd say he was interviewing her for a secretarial position.

"Dawn's dead," she announced.

"I saw an article in the paper. From North Dakota. Fancied it might be you."

She raised an eyebrow at that. She was learning how to use her face—saying things without words.

"As soon as they figured out it wasn't Bonnie Parker, they lost interest," he added.

She nodded, then reached for the menu.

"So, what should I call you, young lady?"

"Av— Aurora." She stumbled over the first syllable, unaccustomed to saying her own name.

"Your dad used to call you that when you were speaking together in Russian," he recalled. "Pronounced it with that 'v'—'Avrora.' But Aurora it is." He shrugged and grinned. "I'm still just Bob."

The waitress came over and sized her up, giving Bob an excuse to do likewise. That summer in D.C. he'd watched her "bootstrap," as she called it. Starting out little better than a hobo, she'd scavenged, or hand-sewn, enough decent clothes that she wouldn't get thrown out of a beauty parlor. Eventually she'd climbed the ladder to the point where she'd been able to go full Cinderella at a ball with army generals and society matrons. Since then she'd been through a few cycles of boom and bust. Bob estimated she was about halfway to recovering from the latest crash. Midmorning sun coming in the diner's window revealed a streak of heavy foundation on one side of her face, covering something she didn't want seen.

She looked tired, stretched out, older than she was. But the eggs and hash she ordered would help her fill out that dress if she kept at it. He considered asking her when she'd last eaten a square meal but decided against it.

"Still have your violin?" It was a bit of a silly question, since all she'd brought in was a little suitcase.

"Lost it in the fire. Probably for the best."

"You're a real chip off the old block." Even as he said this Bob winced, thinking it was a little close to the bone. But she just gave him a wry look. He had to keep reminding himself that she was just eighteen.

She'd glanced toward the cash register a couple of times. Bob now understood she was looking at the newspaper rack. "I've been a little out of touch these last couple of weeks. Visiting family. No newspapers where they live. Any news about Bonnie and Clyde?"

He shook his head. "I'm afraid the Barrow Gang has been knocked off the front page by competitors. Dillinger escaped. Machine Gun Kelly got sent away for life. He'll probably end his days on Alcatraz."

"What's that?"

The food had started to show up. Bob understood that Aurora was, between bites, prompting him to talk so that she could shovel food into her mouth. So he explained the new management of Alcatraz, and what they planned to do with the place. He went on to fill time with reminiscing about what had happened in D.C. He filled her in on contacts he'd made with the International in these parts, mostly across the bay in Berkeley.

A man came in and sat down in the next booth. After that, Bob just talked about the bridge project. When Aurora was finished eating, which didn't take long, she showed no hesitation in letting him pay for her meal and then buy her a ferry ticket. These were prerogatives of womanhood that would never have crossed the mind of girl-Dawn in blue jeans but that she now accepted as her due.

The ferry wasn't crowded, so they were able to go abovedecks and talk more freely. Alcatraz was practically dead ahead. Now that Aurora understood what it was going to become, she kept a wary eye on it. A bank of fog was beginning to extrude through the Golden Gate, promising to turn the day gray and clammy.

"It's beautiful here," she said. "How do you like it?"

"It's better for . . . someone like me than Gary. Put my house on the market there, but no one's buying."

"Thinking of settling here?"

"Maybe. You?"

She shook her head. "I need to get out of this country."

He nodded. "Back to Russia, then."

"The Soviet Union," she corrected him. "From here you can get to Yokohama. From there to Vladivostok."

"My geography's a little rusty, but that's in the far east."

"Of course. The end of the Trans-Siberian Railway. So from there it's just a long ride on a train."

"To where? Where are you planning to get off that train, Aurora?"

The hard light of the sun sank into the looming cliff of the incoming fog bank and scattered back, making it seem more substantial than it would to an outbound mariner steaming into it. But Bob's eye snagged on a hard, straight edge, barely discernible. Then another, exactly parallel to the first, not as long. Then a third, shorter yet. All of the edges proceeded to a common end, where they turned a crisp right angle and went on until the fog swallowed them again. Something in the arrangement of those edges called to a memory. He'd seen them on paper. He'd *drafted* them on paper.

The blast of a horn came out of the fog and he saw that the whole construct was resting on a barge that was being towed in from the Pacific by a tugboat. He knew what this was: one of the hollow steel cells of the north tower, the parallel lines and crisp edges all obedient to the bridge's Art Deco aesthetic. It had been made in Pennsylvania and shipped through the Panama Canal.

"I did the structural calculations for that," he told Aurora. "They're taking it over to Alameda. It'll sit there until the workers are ready to hoist it into place and drive in the rivets."

She was more interested in him than in the rivets. "You love it," she said. "Designing a thing. Planning it. Then seeing it made real."

"That's what engineers do!"

"What if you could work on something bigger, though?"

"Bigger than the Golden Gate Bridge?!"

"Yeah. And build socialism while you're at it."

"What are you talking about?"

"You already know, because you told me about it!" she exclaimed, mock-scolding. "When I saw you last, you mentioned that your company had landed a contract with the Soviets. To build a new steel mill there. Bigger than Gary."

"The biggest in the world," Bob said with a nod.

He wasn't making the connection. Didn't get it until she looked him in the eye and held out her hands, palms up, as if to say, *How about it?*

"Oh no," he said.

"I'm totally fluent," she said. "I'll be your translator."

1

MAGNITOGORSK, SOVIET UNION

CHRISTMAS EVE, 1933 (ELEVEN WEEKS LATER)

When she closed her eyes, Aurora could almost believe she was back in Montana. Deep, dry snow snuffed out all sound, save the squeaking footfalls of thick felt *valenki*. Stung by the coldness and dryness of the air, her numb nose smelled nothing. The clenching of her empty stomach was familiar enough from her days spent roaming America. Only the swaying of the scaffold beneath her feet proved she was not on the hard-frozen earth of the High Plains.

She couldn't keep her eyes closed for more than a few seconds, though, lest they freeze shut. The steam escaping from her lungs—for clambering up the scaffold was hard work—puffed up out of the scarf wrapped around her neck and face to solidify on her lashes and brows. She had more in the way of the former and less in the way of the latter than the other members of the Workers' Shock Brigade, all of whom were men. In the quarter of an hour since they'd filed out of the warming shed and begun scaling the bird's nest of twine, lumber, and baling wire wrapped around the two-hundred-foot tower of Blast Furnace #4, those men's brows had become thick with white frost. The effect was mildly inconvenient and mostly comical.

Less funny and more perilous was the ice on the scaffold. The Industrial Lake—a dammed-up stretch of the Ural River—was of course frozen solid, and had been for months. Thick enough to host a sparse suburb of ice-fishing shacks. But near the reinforced-concrete plinth of the blast furnace was the cooling basin for the water that came boiling out of the open-hearth furnaces. Fat columns of steam rose from them when there was a heat under way, and when the wind bent them in this direction, ice grew inches thick on the ropes, boards, and bark-covered tree branches that constituted the scaffold. This had not been sturdy to begin with, for it had been built recently, in cold weather, when the labor force of Magnitogorsk pilfered trainloads of wood, or anything else combustible, from railway sidings and the open-air supply dumps that spilled out around them. Every stick of wood that made it up here unburned, and contributed its feeble strength to the scaffold, was a little miracle. But miracles no longer belonged in the Soviet Union, so ice and gravity were doing their best to tear it all down.

Any sane person would now be asking whether the shock brigade's collective weight might be the straw that broke this camel's back. Comrade Fizmatov had tried to reassure them on this point by performing a quick mental calculation of the total mass of ice on this structure and then letting them know that the brigade's mass—six underfed men plus one comparatively healthy and robust Aurora—was trivial in comparison.

The brigade had paused for a moment. Just ahead, the scaffold jogged up a rustic ladder and ducked through a sort of armpit where a ten-foot-diameter conveyor system angled up from below. This had captured an eddy in the vapor and so their way forward was blocked by a wall of icicles gleaming red in the light of a river of molten pig iron flowing out of Blast Furnace #3. Comrade Griaznov was going ahead, clambering up the ladder, then crawling on hands and knees to a place where he could lie on his back and hammer at the encrustation. The others—half a dozen workers strung out along a span barely wide enough to plant their *valenki*—leaned back against the riveted iron plates of the stack and lit huge cigarettes, which, before setting out, they had fashioned out of loose tobacco and old copies of *Pravda*.

Earlier this year, when Aurora had been pretending to live the life of a normal American teenager in Chicago, she and her then boyfriend, Dick, had gone to a couple of movies. Dick's taste ran to gangsters, so they saw a James Cagney feature. For Aurora, all of that tommy-gun action was a little too close to home, and so, to even the score, she had made Dick suffer through *State Fair*—a sunny tale of American kulaks. In any case, the features had been preceded by short animated films meant to amuse more punctual moviegoers as late arrivals filed in. The style of the artwork in these productions tended toward humorous exaggeration, with heads, feet, and hands drawn at double life size. Looking at her fellow shock workers in their big *ushanka* hats and big *valenki* boots, pinching their sausage-sized cigarettes in their bulky mittens and exhaling vast clouds of mixed smoke and vapor into the moonlight—all of this, combined with the rambling and improvised nature of the scaffold, put her in mind of those cartoons. It would have been funny had she not been here.

Fizmatov, who at his age shouldn't have volunteered, was laboring to catch up, snorts of breath bursting from his nostrils to be whipped away by the wind.

"That's it—chop-chop—move along smartly, Comrade!" Tishenko shouted down to him. "The brigade must stay in close formation lest we incur unnecessary casualties!"

Aurora glared at him, but even if Tishenko were the type to notice, the gesture would have been lost in the burst of vapor that escaped from her scarf as she let out an exasperated sigh. She took advantage of the respite to have a look around. She'd never been this high above Magnitogorsk, except for when she took a turn at the parachute-jumping tower, and when you were parachute jumping you had other things to be thinking about. She knew from maps that the Ural Mountains were off to the west, but in general they were not visible from here save as a white thickening of the horizon when the moon was in the east. This—the fact that they were east of the Urals—meant that they were technically in Siberia. But having recently ridden a train across Siberia she knew that many thousands of miles of it separated them from the Pacific, while Europe was only a short distance farther.

The Industrial Lake formed a hard western boundary to the complex—"city" seemed the wrong word yet. This occupied a four-kilometer-wide swath of former steppe between the Industrial Lake and the freak deposit of high-grade iron ore that gave Magnetic Mountain its name. The northern end of the swath was where the MMK, the Magnitogorsk Metallurgical Complex, was plugged into the rest of the Soviet Union—for, as inconceivable as it was on a night as cold as this one, most of the USSR lay well to the north. At any rate, up thataway were the airstrip and the railyard, including a "train station" that turned out to be an open-air siding out on the steppe where trains that carried people had been known to stop. To detrain there, as Aurora and her party of American pilgrims had learned, involved a bit of a leap of faith.

From there you could walk to the posh cottages of Magnitogorsk's revolutionary vanguard, if you didn't mind trudging through a fertilizer plant. The main rail line continued south, cutting through the huddle of huts and tents where the convicts like Fizmatov were obliged to live, then feeding an industrial complex modeled after Gary, Indiana, but bigger. For Gary was the world's biggest, and Comrade Stalin wanted to overtop it.

Even if, like Aurora, you came into Magnitogorsk not knowing a thing about steel production, you'd have a sense of how it worked by the time you'd followed the line down to the Socialist City at the southern end of the complex. Coal was brought in on trains from other parts of the USSR and delivered to coke ovens. There it was cooked to make the high-grade fuel demanded by the blast furnaces, of which Numbers 1, 2, and 3 were operational. A blast furnace worked on gravity, with iron ore and coke delivered into the top by conveyors. The material sank gradually into the base of the furnace, undergoing various transformations along the way, until it descended into the zone, down near ground level, that gave the blast furnace its name: superheated air was blown into it to complete its transformation into pig iron. This then flowed south to the open-hearth furnaces where it became steel, and thence to rolling mills, where it was shaped into whatever forms were deemed most desirable by the People's Commissariat of Heavy Industry, filtering its diktats down, like so much ore in a blast furnace, through the Main Administration of the Metallurgical Industry and the Magnitogorsk Metallurgical Complex. In any case, the row of blast furnaces was dead in the middle of the complex, the first thing the visitor's eye was drawn to, and so Aurora's vantage point, cold and precarious as it might be, gave her the best possible view.

A few low hills rose out of the steppe a kilometer south of the rolling mills, and that was where the State Institute for the Planning of Cities was trying to show its fine qualities. A welter of settlements—shantytowns improvised by various ethnic minorities and political prisoners in different phases of rehabilitation, plus a whole village that had walked here from Poland—was being shouldered aside by apartment superblocks designed by Western architects enthralled by the radiant promise of socialism. At this hour, the place was as close as it would ever come to a Christmassy "Silent Night" scene. Big machines like the blast furnaces and the open hearths ran at all hours, but very few people or vehicles were on the move down below. The most notable exception was a penal brigade of Russian Orthodox priests, supervised by a couple of rifle-toting boys no older than Aurora. The priests were working through the night, attacking a long mound of frozen dirt with picks and sharpened iron bars. This feature ran between a railway siding and a ditch that connected to the shore of the lake.

Fizmatov, seeing utter confusion on Aurora's face, had told her the story of it: two years ago, when Magnitogorsk was just getting started, some of the Western engineers who were planning it had ordered some turbines from Siemens, and paid for them with Soviet gold. The equipment had duly been shipped out here from Germany and hoisted up off of flatbed railcars and set down next to this railway siding, only to sit out in the snow and rain all through 1932 and 1933 as various delays meant that there was no place to install them. Meanwhile the requirement for this ditch had arisen and some newly arrived laborers had been put to work digging it. They had to put the dirt somewhere. Gradually the level of the earth around the Siemens turbines had risen until they had disappeared altogether. Now they were needed in order to get Blast Furnace #4 working, and so the job of digging them out had been assigned to this gang of gaunt, forlorn priests, jobless in the religion-free Soviet Union but stubbornly refusing to cut off their long beards and long hair. Those were frost-matted and swinging heavily as they drove their makeshift tools into the rock-hard ground. Aurora, who had actually been baptized into their church—against the wishes of her parents, but that was another story—felt some sympathy for their having to work on Christmas Eve. But they still followed the Julian calendar, so for them the holy night was still two weeks in the future.

Up ahead, Griaznov cried out and cursed. The rhythmic crash of his hammer stopped.

"What's the matter, Comrade?" Tishenko demanded. "We are all waiting for you."

"Hammer broke," Griaznov moaned. "I got a piece of it in the eye."

"Well, bring the head of it along in your pocket and we'll have it fitted to a new handle later."

"That's the hell of it," Griaznov said, "the handle is fine. The head is what's broken." He had been inching back along the catwalk toward the top of the ladder. He now descended this with great care, as the numbness of his hands and the thickness of his mittens made it difficult to really know whether he had a firm grip on the rungs. He handed the evidence to Tishenko, then took the extraordinary step of removing one mitten so that he could dab at his eye. One didn't want tears streaming down a cheek in these conditions.

"What did you hit?!" Tishenko demanded. "This damage can't have been inflicted by mere ice."

"Must have broken through to the frame of the conveyor," Griaznov answered. "Those big rivets are work-hardened." Then it seemed to penetrate his awareness that he was being interrogated. That he was under suspicion for being a wrecker. "It was an accident!"

Fizmatov had finally caught up, and now excused himself past Aurora with a courtly nod of his ushanka. He was twice as old as anyone else and had lost four toes so far to frostbite. "Comrade Tishenko, if I may?" he said. He had a gravelly voice, low and settled, with no trace of the defensive anxiety that men like Tishenko were accustomed to hearing. Aurora had learned to recognize his accent as Ukrainian.

Tishenko handed over some metal fragments after a short, irritable pause. "It could be a serious matter—a matter for the OGPU," he said, "if the conveyor were to be damaged by a careless blow—or a malicious act."

Griaznov stiffened.

"Not that I am making any such allegation," Tishenko continued, in what he probably supposed was a soothing and reasonable tone, "but others might. There's a saying nowadays, down there—" And his ushanka tipped to one side as he nodded in the direction of the Socialist City. But as everyone here understood, he was alluding to the OGPU headquarters, which loomed over it from the top of a hill. "In every backward department there is a wrecker!"

"Fortunately, the responsible authority in these parts is the Commissariat of Ferrous Metallurgy." Fizmatov chuckled. "And I can assure you, Comrade Tishenko, or anyone else who expresses curiosity on this matter, that what we have here"—he lifted the fragments of the hammerhead, pillowed on the palms of his mittens—"is a purely metallurgical phenomenon! I can express it using technical language, but in plain terms it is this: when steel becomes very cold, it becomes brittle. Comrade Griaznov, may I assume that this tool was stored out in the open overnight?"

Griaznov thought about his answer.

"In a very cold place?" Comrade Shaimat prompted him. He was standing between Fizmatov and Tishenko. A Tatar who had never seen so much as a ladder, let alone a blast furnace, when he had arrived in Magnitogorsk. But now, thanks to the Komsomol Campaign for the Liquidation of Illiteracy, he could read and write. And he could read people, and situations, better than most.

"Yes indeed!" Griaznov said. "Extremely cold, as we all know!"

"Meanwhile the vapor from below, condensing on the frame of the conveyor, warms it," Fizmatov said.

"Warms it?!" Tishenko scoffed. "You call that warm?"

"No, but if we bring a thermometer up from the assay lab, I can assure you it will read many tens of degrees warmer than this," Fizmatov said, again raising his mittens. "When the bitterly cold and embrittled hammerhead struck the warmer steel of the conveyor frame, it shattered, as glass would shatter if you struck it against an iron railing."

"You have me at a disadvantage, Comrade," Tishenko admitted. Which was putting it mildly given that Fizmatov had a PhD from the University of Paris and Tishenko was a jumped-up peasant. Fizmatov, of course, had the good sense not to point this out. Neither did he mention that the disadvantage, in a sense, went deeper. He'd already been sentenced to death. This had been commuted to ten years at Magnitogorsk. Tishenko might be asking himself: If the Sword of the Revolution had already made up its mind to spare Comrade Fizmatov's neck, who was Tishenko to denounce him?

"You believe that this . . . *theory* would pass muster with the OGPU?"

"I am quite sure of it," Fizmatov assured him, "if they really have nothing better to do than investigate a broken hammer."

"That's settled, then!" Shaimat exclaimed. He shouldered past Tishenko and Griaznov to the base of the ladder and began climbing it as if he were not freezing and it were not icy. "Myself, I never saw such a thing as a hammer until I came here! When we had to pound tent stakes into frozen ground, we used these! Cheaper than hammers, and plenty of them!"

He reached into the pocket of his coat and proudly displayed a rock.

IN A FEW MINUTES' VIGOROUS BASHING, SHAIMAT CLEARED THE WAY. TISHENKO FILLED the time by developing an analogy between their situation and things he had seen—or perhaps only heard about?—during the Civil War, when the advancing Red forces—they were always advancing—had encountered some barrier in the earthworks thrown up by the (always-retreating) Whites and been obliged to bide their time for a short while as they sent sappers ahead to clear the obstruction. Shaimat, of course, was, in this analogy, the valiant sapper. But the blockage to be liquidated was not merely a lot of ice but some entirely logical to Tishenko, but difficult for Aurora to make out, complex of foreign capitalists, cliquism, Jews, inherited rural backwardness, opportunists, hooligans, ineradicable counterrevolutionary tendencies in the Russian Orthodox Church, wreckers, diversionaries, kulaks, Petliurite scum, national deviationists, backsliders, actively malevolent foreign agents, ex-bourgeois and White Guard elements, and their witting or unwitting accomplices. Occasional mistrustful glances at Fizmatov during all of this, and imploring gestures directed toward Aurora, as if she were just on the verge of being brought around. For her part, she was bemused by the man's sheer energy, and beginning to suspect that all of this talking was really just a strategy that Tishenko made use of to stay warm. Tishenko was the Agitator: an actual job title here. You probably couldn't get that job unless you were agitated to begin with.

Mercifully, Shaimat broke through with a triumphant crash of shattering ice, followed by merry tinkling noises as falling icicle fragments chimed against bits of scaffolding far below. Probably the closest thing to Christmas bells that would reach Aurora's ears in 1933. "*Ura!*" Tishenko exclaimed, bolting toward the ladder, then seemed crestfallen when the others seemed more interested in finishing their cigarettes and idly rubbing snow on parts of their faces that had begun to show signs of frostbite.

"*Ura!*" Aurora shouted. "Let's storm the front, Comrades!"

The comrades in question had been taken aback when she had materialized in the warming shed at two o'clock in the morning, saying it was no place for a girl. But now that they were all up here they seemed to have accepted her as a sort of mascot or cheerleader, and so finally they grumbled out "*Ura!*" and made a collective move for the ladder.

This brought them up into the complex of massive plumbing and equipment that crowned the blast furnace. Part of it was there to dump very large quantities of heavy ingredients—coke, iron ore, various mineral additives—into the furnace, and part of it was to draw off the hot gases that erupted from the top while the thing was in operation. For to prevent those from setting fire to the conveyors and other material-handling equipment up here, they needed to be contained and diverted along ducts as big around as subway tunnels. The fabrication of those ducts, which had to be welded together from curved steel plates, had become a sticking point in the campaign to get Blast Furnace #4 back on schedule—hence Tishenko's remark about this being a "backward department," and hence the need to assemble workers' shock brigades at two in the morning. Of this brigade, half—Griaznov, Ivanov, and Myshkin—were welders. The others were there to support them.

They reached the "front"—the end of the duct, projecting out into space like a snapped-off tree limb, where the welding needed to happen—only half an hour behind the schedule that had been plotted out by their Agitator. But it was too late for one member of the previous shift who, as became immediately obvious when Shaimat tried to shake him awake, had frozen to death. In his last minutes he had embraced his electric welding machine, trying to steal some of its warmth. Now he had stiffened up around it. In trying to pry the body loose, Shaimat yanked a little too hard, tore the body suddenly loose, lost his balance, and began to slide down the duct toward the unfinished end. He let go of the body and saved himself by grabbing the welder's power cable. A few seconds later the body made impact on the concrete foundation of Blast Furnace #4, where it broke up.

"SOMETHING SEEMED TO BE WRONG WITH AMERICA," AURORA SAID, "AND SO I CAME HERE."

"America must be very bad then," Shaimat said, looking around significantly at Dining Room #30 and then down at his serving of bread. "Fifty grams, Aurora. You have a card for the Engineers' Dining Room, don't you? There you could get a hundred."

"I'm not hungry," Aurora said with a long glance in the direction of Blast Furnace #4, where she, Shaimat, and Fizmatov had just spent half an hour collecting the remains of the frozen welder. Fizmatov had then trudged off to his lodgings in the penal colony. Run-of-the-mill prisoners would be lucky to get fifty grams there. Fortunately Fizmatov was so obviously important to the Magnitogorsk Metallurgical Complex that mysterious workarounds had been put in place enabling him to eat as well as any commissar.

Shaimat took her meaning, then nodded. "I was worried you had taken ill," he said, then pantomimed scratching in the vicinity of his armpit.

Aurora recognized the gesture, which transcended all linguistic barriers. She smiled and shook her head, indicating that she did not have lice—the carriers of typhus. The women's dormitory she'd been living in was relatively clean. "In America I got in the habit of sleeping on the floor if there were any questions about the bedding."

Shaimat nodded. "Some of the guys in the Kazakh settlement sleep outside on wooden benches."

Aurora raised her eyebrows—which had thawed, and which had enough sensation returning that she was pretty sure no frostbite had set in.

"It's not that much colder than indoors," Shaimat added reassuringly.

Having satisfied himself that this new arrival from America knew the ropes where basic typhus prevention was concerned, Shaimat began to spoon soup into his mouth. "Your Russian is very good," he remarked. "Oh, I'd have no way of knowing, since mine is so bad! But the others say that if they didn't know you came from America they would think you had been brought up in St. Petersburg."

It was called Leningrad now, but you could get away with using the old name in a historical context.

"But I *was*," Aurora said.

2

PETROGRAD

(FORMERLY SAINT PETERSBURG—LATER LENINGRAD)

1920–1923

She must have been aware of things before, since even dogs and babies are aware of things. But the first time she was *aware of being aware* of something—and perhaps that is the beginning of memory—was when she got it clearly fixed in her head that some things had two names. And she was one of them. She was Dawn. But if she was called that here, in the new place where she had gone with Mama and Papa, people would laugh and think it was the name of a river.

In the old place, Dawn was the sunrise. It happened every day.

In the new place, a special dawn had happened when she was a baby, in the month of November, or October as they called it here.

Rossvyote was what they called the rising of the sun here, but here Rossvyote was not a proper name for a little girl and so Papa called her Aurora, which meant something like Dawn but not quite. It was the name of a famous battleship, the ship that had started the Revolution. When Papa said it to grown-ups who were just meeting her for the first time, they would smile and say that she was a good little *oktiabriata*, October Child.

Then words came to her like the seeds of cottonwoods when the wind blows in the spring, so fast that she could not open her mouth to breathe without catching several upon her tongue. The new place was Petrograd or Saint Petersburg. The old place was America or the United States.

Sometimes you could tell what a person was thinking from which word they used.

Kommunalka was the name of the place where they lived. It meant something like *house.* But no one lived in those anymore. Houses were for Whites. Houses were bourgeois. Reds lived in kommunalkas. This one had been a house before, but the Whites who had lived there had gone to France and taken all of their bourgeois things with them. Reds had appropriated it and hung blankets up to make walls so that men and women could be separate. It was like camping out in America. Not real camping out, like Mama did in Montana, but play-camping. Papa and the other men lived on one side of the blankets and Dawn and Mama and the other women lived on the other. Mama could not understand as much pa-Roosky as Papa and so she did not know what the other women were saying about her.

When one of the other grown-ups was chasing her, Dawn could drop to her hands and knees and crawl under the blanket to the other side where that person could not follow; but Dawn was allowed to go every-where except when certain things were happening on the other side of the blanket. Then Mama would pull Dawn up onto her lap and hug her until she fell asleep.

Some parts of the kommunalka were for men and women both: the kitchen, and the room with the big table. But the men always sat around the table while the women stood in the kitchen. Once Dawn asked, "Did we run out of blankets?" thinking that there ought to be a blanket between those two rooms. Mama laughed in a strange way that did not make Dawn feel like laughing, too, and marched out of the kitchen into the room of the big table with water dripping from her hands. The men looked up at her surprised, and Mama said something about Dawn and blankets to Papa and said, "Out of the mouths of babes" in English. After that was a lot of shouting, the only part of which Dawn understood was that people were angry. She was told not to feel bad, but she did anyway.

The women said that Mama's pot had too many pieces of meat, which was bourgeois. Mama had to stand in front of her pot until it was all cooked or else it would disappear, she said. Dawn liked to be in the kitchen with her, but the other women were always telling her to get out of the way. One of them, Galina, even liked to kick Dawn. She would call, "Out of my way!" even though Dawn wasn't really in her way at all and then she would try to get close enough to Dawn to kick her. Dawn enjoyed the game, and nearly always won, until one day Galina came up to her without speaking and spilled boiling water on her from a pot and gave her a scald on the arm, a red blotch shaped like a star. Papa took Dawn away screaming and put butter on the scald, and not just Mama but all of the other women shouted at Galina.

After that Dawn spent less time in the kitchen so that she would not be *underfoot*, which was her new favorite word. She spent time in the room with the men, which smelled always of papers. For papers came into the kommunalka like snowflakes during a blizzard, to the point where they sometimes had to be shoveled out. But often the men would tell her to go and play, and she would crawl under the blanket and go to a cold, empty part of the house. There were no other children there, and she had no brothers or sisters. They did not bother with families, because families were bourgeois and sentimental.

One evening, when she had been sent to play, Dawn heard Papa on the other side of the blanket, talking about America and how things there were very bourgeois and sentimental and religious, so that getting a divorce from Mama was difficult, but here in the Soviet Union he just pulled off his gold ring and he was divorced just like that.

She thought she might have dreamed this, for the scald on her arm was making her sleep strangely. But the next morning she saw that the ring was gone from Papa's finger. She asked Papa what had become of it and he looked at another man, who made a funny face, and then he looked down at the table and said that he had given the gold to the People, to buy bullets to fight the Whites.

"Then why don't you pull out your gold tooth and melt it down too?" asked Antonio. He was Italian. He was always saying things like this. Sometimes the other men would laugh. Other times they would become angry and tell him not to say such things. This time, Papa became silent.

But what about Mama? Dawn asked. She felt as though she had tried to swallow a big piece of black bread without chewing it properly, though in truth she had not eaten anything since the night before.

"Mama is fine," Papa said. "She and I had differences."

Which made Dawn think she must not know the correct meaning of the word "difference" since it seemed that the entire point of a Mama and a Papa was for them to be different. The men at the table were very quiet for once, all looking at Papa, none of them looking at Dawn. Papa said in Russian, "It is not the same now, this whole idea of marriage, of man and wife; it was an invention of the priests, a form of bourgeois morality."

"Be a good small comrade, Aurora," said one of the other men, saying it the Russian way: Avrora. "Don't begin crying, think of the much worse suffering of our comrades who are fighting the Whites." Which only made her want to cry more, so she turned her face away from the men with their whiskers and eyebrows and spectacles, and stumbled into the kitchen. Mama was not there. Mama had moved to another kommunalka in the next building. She came and visited Dawn after that, and mostly talked about Montana. Then, one day, after the red splotch on Dawn's arm had faded, she came and hugged Dawn for a long time and cried without speaking, then stood up and smoothed her orange hair and walked out. Dawn went to the window and saw her climbing into a carriage. Her suitcase was in the back, all tied up with rope. She said something to the driver, who popped his whip and made the horse take Mama away. Feeling a hand on her shoulder, Dawn jumped up in surprise, but it was just Papa, on the wrong side of the blanket. In a soft voice he explained that Aurora should not feel bad because Aurora was an October Child, too young to have become bourgeois. "*We* must strive to alter our consciousness but not *you*, small comrade."

Papa walked with her to the United Labor School. She must learn the way by heart so that she could walk it alone. For Papa was busy translating the Twenty-One Theses of the Second Congress of the Third International into English, to inform the proceedings of the Red International of Labor Unions, which was preparing an ideological offensive to cleanse its ranks of naïve anarcho-syndicalism. She could see in his face that it was important. He took her into the school and told the teachers that her name was Aurora. Aurora Maximovna Artemyeva. Dawn protested. Her middle name was Rae. "But my name is Maxim," Papa said, "and so here in Russia your middle name must be Maximovna." Whereupon he exchanged a look with the woman who was enrolling Dawn, and she wrote it down thus.

The Whites were losing the war. Different parts of the Red Army came back and marched through Petrograd with people cheering and weeping. A man came to the kommunalka with a tape measure and did sums in his head, moving his lips and rolling his eyes, and said that they had too many square meters and that room must be made for the heroes of the Red Army. Two men moved in, and, on the women's side of the blankets, Veronika. Veronika marched in wearing black boots that came up to her knees. Her greatcoat was rolled into a long bundle and slung over her shoulder, with a copper pot dangling at the side. She spread her coat out on the floor and slept in it. She took her pot with her to the kitchen and cooked in it, and none of the other women dared make anything disappear, even when she had meat. She would not share her meat with the other women but she would give Aurora as much as she wanted. Veronika was a machine gunner in the Red Women's Death Battalion. In Siberia she had fought the White Cossacks with her machine gun and been awarded medals. Aurora sat on her lap and ate meat and listened to her stories. Much of these she did not understand. Kerensky had formed the Death Battalions. Kerensky was better than the tsar, but not as good as Comrade Lenin, and so Comrade Lenin had stormed the Winter Palace and defeated him in the October Revolution. Some of the Death Battalions had gone over to Lenin's side, and to prove their loyalty they now fought harder than anyone else. Aurora asked Veronika whether she, too, could be a machine gunner when she grew up, and Veronika said that it was not like being a regular soldier, it was technical, like operating a sewing machine, which was why women were better at it than men, and she would have to attend to her studies and become clever with arithmetic.

Staying up late doing her sums, Aurora would sometimes hear Maxim Alexandrovich talking about Mama, which was a thing he was more apt to do when he had been drinking vodka with the other men around the table.

In the days just after Mama left, he would say that she was an anarcho-syndicalist, which apparently was not a nice thing to call someone, but it did explain to the satisfaction of the other men why he had taken the ring off his finger.

After some time had gone by and they had begun to receive letters from Mama, mailed from Montana, his voice became softer when he spoke of her, and he said that she was more in the nature of an instinctive anarchist, with all of the best intentions but needing an infusion of Leninist theory and revolutionary discipline.

All of it just made Aurora want to curl up into a ball and suck her thumb, which was no way for a small comrade to behave, but she did it anyway, sometimes nestling with Veronika under the greatcoat. To her, Mama was a woman on a horse with long orange hair that blew in the wind. Aside from an image of a great blue lake in Chicago, this was the only memory of America that she still had.

Sometimes, after months had gone by, Papa would call Mama a cow-girl instead of an anarcho-syndicalist or an instinctive anarchist, and then make a sound like laughing, encouraging the other men to laugh with him, which they did. After that, it was always "cowgirl."

It rained. It rained more. It rained most of the time. It rained all of the time. As Aurora walked to school, mud would grow on her shoes, making her feet heavy until she stomped through puddles to wash it off. The best puddles were in the street. One afternoon she was doing this and she heard a bell ringing. She remembered a thing Mama had said once in English: *clear as a bell*. She had not understood its meaning until the sound of this bell, so sharp and close, came into her ears like an icicle. She looked up to see that it was the bell of a streetcar, which had stopped next to her. The conductor was pulling the bell rope with one hand and gesturing with the other. She turned around and saw an automobile coming. The driver, a clean-shaven young man in a black leather coat and a military hat, was looking toward her with his green eyes and so she assumed that he would go around, but his black leather fists on the steering wheel did not move decisively to one side or the other, making only tiny corrections to avoid potholes. She sidled up next to the streetcar, feeling the hum of its motor against her head, and the automobile whooshed past, hurling up a wing of brown water. In the instant before this collapsed over Dawn's head, she saw through the automobile's rear window where a man in black leather was holding up a lit cigarette in one hand and, in the other, a white page with a list typed on it. Someone had been drawing on it with red ink. The thought came into her head that this man must have a daughter who had used the paper for coloring. She wondered for a moment whether the paper was important and the daughter was going to be punished for using it so.

Then all went brown. She was gasping and rubbing the water out of her eyes when a hand grabbed the collar of her coat and pulled her aboard the streetcar. It was the conductor, very angry—but not at her. "I can see from your clothes that you are not some wild hooligan child—where are your parents?" he demanded. She said that one of them was in Montana and the other at such-and-such an address.

The conductor sat down slowly in the wooden chair at the front, where the levers and knobs were. He had a huge black mustache that reached out from his thin face like the parts of an insect that grab food. He put his hands over his eyes like a man weeping or praying, and the ends of his mustache fidgeted as his lips moved. He was almost silent but Aurora could hear him saying the names of streets. Then he took his hands away and blinked his blue eyes out the windscreen as if surprised to find himself there. "It can be done," he announced in a clear voice. He sounded happy but the people riding in the streetcar groaned, and one of them demanded to be let off "before you get up to any of your conjuring, Grisha!" Grisha did something with levers that caused the car to move forward. Soon he rid himself of the complaining passenger, and later of several more who did not approve of conjuring.

They came to an intersection of streets where the rails went every which way, like steel noodles flung onto a table. Grisha leaned forward, peering down at them and, wiggling his mustache-ends with further incantations, he then pulled on a lever that made the streetcar's lights go out and the whine of its motor sigh down to nothing. The little points in the rails before them moved, shifting sideways, and a moment later the streetcar veered left, gliding dark and silent onto a new course. Men snapped their newspapers, reading of Whites and Wobblies. Grisha heaved the lever again, the lights came on, the motor hummed, and the streetcar moved confidently to the next intersection of rails—where Grisha did it again and switched them onto another new track. After a while Grisha had to ask Dawn to leave off screaming whenever it happened, for she was very excited about how a tiny movement of the points could effect a shift in the course of the giant vehicle and all the people aboard, and her squealing every time was making it difficult for the other passengers to read their books and their newspapers.

"You see, there's one in that doorway, and a whole mob of them just disappeared into yonder alley," Grisha said, when not mumbling street-names. He was referring to small persons in bad clothing. Aurora saw them frequently in certain places and had learned to avoid such parts of town. "War orphans, runaways, peasants from the back of beyond. Imagine coming to a city to escape a famine! Those little ones don't go to school, do they?"

"No, they don't go to school."

"The Chekist driving that car—he mistook you for one of them, playing in the street—so he didn't care if you got run over," Grisha said. Then he turned his blue eyes on her and shook his finger. "Don't let yourself be mistaken for one of them!"

"What's a famine?" Aurora asked. "Can it come into the city?" She assumed it was some sort of monster.

In due time—having dropped off several of the original passengers and, after lengthy discussions, picking up a few more—Grisha got as close to the kommunalka as the streetcar lines would allow. He then took her by the hand and led her down the street. One of the passengers protested, but some women shushed him and said that he should be ashamed of himself.

Grisha took Dawn up the stairs and asked for Maxim Alexandrovich. By now it was late and so Papa was home, sitting around the table with the other men, reading their papers and eating kasha. Grisha asked Aurora if this was her father and she said yes. He asked Papa if this was his daughter and Papa said, "Who are you to ask?" and stepped around the table and picked her up in his arms and asked where she had been all this time. "Very nearly under the tires of some Chekist's automobile!" Grisha answered.

It led to Dawn's being sent to the other side of the blankets so that the men could talk. Dawn told the story to Veronika, thinking that she would be delighted. But instead her face went red and she stood up and began to stride back and forth across the women's half of the room and to stare out the window toward the street. Finally Veronika turned around and Aurora saw that she had tears on her face. "You must never let it happen again!" she cried. "Promise me."

"I will stay out of puddles."

"No, not that!" Veronika said with a strange laugh.

"I will look both ways and—"

"No!" Veronika dropped to her knees. It was cold in the room; she was wearing her greatcoat, which collapsed all around her and made Aurora want to climb inside of it. Veronika reached out and took Dawn's arm roughly. "You let him take you!" She said this in a whisper so harsh that it stung Dawn's ears like the bell of the streetcar. She wiggled Dawn's arm to show what she was talking about. "You just let a strange man grab you and take you away. To a place of his choosing. Never do it again."

"Because of the famine?"

"No."

"Then why?"

"I can't tell you, for you are too young. But some men will do a terrible thing to you. The worst thing. It is what Cossacks do." She was crying now.

"Does it ever get better?"

"Maybe a little. Not all the way. The only thing you can do for it is—"

"Is what?"

But Veronika had gone back to her usual way, which was not to look people in the eye. Aurora's gaze strayed to the sleeve of Veronika's greatcoat, the arm that was still reaching out to hold Dawn. There on the elbow was the colored patch with the yellow border that Veronika had embroidered on the sleeve, a little picture of a fat-barreled gun on a stand with three legs.

Papa with Grisha devised a new order of things, which was that each morning Dawn walked to a square just down the street where several streetcar lines converged, and presently Grisha's car came along and fetched her, always with other passengers aboard who were going other places. In due time he got her to school.

At school the teachers helped them strive to become good little Sovki. The students wore red kerchiefs and faced the Red Corner each morning and sang songs. In the old days, capitalists had forced the workers to stand at the capitalists' lathes, but now the lathes belonged to the people. Aurora told Grisha that she would one day know how to make parts to fix his streetcar, and she told Veronika that she would make a new barrel for her machine gun.

Veronika would come home after dark with flushed cheeks and tend to her uniform. Dawn asked her if she had been at the front, machine-gunning White Cossacks. Veronika laughed and said no, she had been rehearsing *The Storming of the Winter Palace*.

This was a thing Dawn had heard of in school, and she was perplexed and alarmed to know that it already needed to be stormed again. She had seen the Winter Palace—it was not far from the kommunalka—and the thought of its having been re-occupied by Tsarists and Whites kept her up at night. But Veronika just stroked her hair and told her that she would see and that it would be all right.

They played games at school, out in the yard. To play cowboys and Indians was bourgeois, the older girls said. Dawn cried because her mother was a cowgirl and her uncles were cowboys. Lidiya—one of the older girls, always sweet to the little ones—took her by the hand and drew her into the game of *razverstka*, which in some ways was like hide-and-seek. First they would gather up acorns from the schoolyard, which was bordered on one side by a wood of old oaks. The acorns were placed into a hat so all could see how many there were. Some of the children would then tie their red scarves over their faces and count slowly to one hundred. These were the Bolsheviks, or the Reds. The others, who were called Mensheviks or Whites or kulaks, would run all over the schoolyard hiding the acorns. When the Reds counted to one hundred, they would peel off their scarves and cry out, "Razverstka!" and one who was their leader would demand to know the location of the acorns (though he would call them gold, or potatoes, or ammunition) so that they could be distributed to the Workers' Committees. The Whites would say, "There are none, we swear it!" and this was the signal for the Reds to search for the missing acorns while the Whites counted to one hundred. All the acorns found were then thrown into the hat, and if the number was sufficient, the Whites would have to confess that they were bourgeois speculators and accept their punishment. This varied because the game was different every time. Sometimes it was running a spanking gauntlet, which did not hurt much through the warm clothes.

All of the good hiding places became known; the Whites couldn't win. Some of the older boys, who couldn't stand to lose, insisted on being Reds every time, and the girls, trying to be good, agreed to be Whites, saying that they didn't care who won. Aurora did care, but she was too small to argue against Lidiya and the other big girls. Andrei, who was not the biggest or the oldest of the boys, but the most furious, took on the responsibility of telling everyone how the game would be organized. For a while Dawn pretended to enjoy the game as she had once done, but when all of her secret places became known, and the big boys became quite loud in their triumph, she cried. The older girls had words with the boys. The teachers came out to see what was the matter. They made Andrei denounce himself. Andrei did it curtly, staring off into the sky, then wheeled around and stomped away cursing. He was angry at Lidiya and Lidiya was angry at him and Dawn reckoned they were enemies now and that was that. Yet they looked at each other all the time, Andrei staring like a dog and Lidiya pretending not to notice, Lidiya then watching Andrei sidelong when Andrei was so busy running or playing that he could not be aware of her gaze.

Veronika went to the station and returned with a tall, skinny old lady in a long black dress, like from an old tintype. This was Tyotya. She came from where Veronika had come from, in the east. She had only a small bag, and the one dress. She had come to watch *The Storming of the Winter Palace*. The other women in the kommunalka did not like her clothes, her manners—both of which were very old-fashioned—or the cross she wore around her neck or the way she pronounced words or her cooking or how she smelled.

The next day was the storming. It was wet but not too cold. They packed hampers with jars of herring, loaves of black bread, bottles of vodka. In the evening they all walked down toward the Winter Palace, quickly getting lost in a river of people, far more people than Dawn had ever seen in one place. Some of them carried great red banners and marched in groups.

They came out into a vast square in front of the Winter Palace, the biggest building she had ever seen. On the far side of the palace lay the river. Instead of going directly into the square where all of the people were gathering, Papa led her down the side of the palace to the water-front. A great ship of war was there, painted white, all lit up by powerful lights shining from the top of the palace. Aurora's name was painted on its prow. She was thrilled by that and spent a long while looking at it, but Papa would only look at her. In time he said they should get back to the square or else all of the good spots would be taken. As they walked hand in hand, Papa told her of how peasants in Massachusetts had once fired a shot heard round the world to fight the imperialists, and a little while later some workers who had heard that shot had stormed a castle full of aristocrats in Paris, but here in Petrograd the shot and the storming had happened on the same night, and they were about to see it. And that was why her name in this place was Aurora, not Dawn.

All of the other people who had come to see it stood in two huge groups cordoned off by ropes. Between those groups ran an open lane, and in the center of the lane stood a column, an old monument, covered for tonight with new work: a scaffold, a high platform, telegraph lines radiating from it to places around the square: a pair of huge stages at one end of the lane, the Winter Palace facing them at the other end, and busy, crowded works stuffed into the corners of the square and the surrounding parks where trucks and horses and artillery pieces were being readied by thousands of people—one of whom, she knew, was Veronika. Papa told her that the director was up on that platform, watching in all directions and telling people what to do by telegraph. Aurora wished to see the director, but he was sheltered from rain by a shed roof, walled off from the wind by canvas, warm behind glass, only the red tip of his cigarette visible in the dark.

For a long time they did nothing but marvel at the two stages, one all in white, the other red, the two joined by a bridge that arched over the lane. The white one was all flat slabs at different heights, like a sort of wedding cake, the red one was like a great machine-city with factories and a tall spire. Stray musical noises emanated from under the bridge, and when Papa took Aurora up onto his shoulders she was able to see that the lane between the red and the white stages was carpeted in musicians, all dressed in black and white and tuning up their instruments, the gleaming brass and the glowing wood.

Some signal must have gone out over the telegraph wires, for suddenly all went dark. "It's a blackout!" someone joked, and a few people laughed but others cursed him angrily. Then a great boom sounded from the river. "The *Aurora!*" Papa exclaimed, and then for a few moments all of Petrograd was saying it.

Under the arch of the bridge between the stages, a brilliant disk of light appeared around a man in a long black coat who called the musicians to order with a wave of his baton and then got them playing a great loud piece of music. Lights came on aiming at the White stage, which was suddenly crowded with men and women in fancy clothing: furs and jewels, uniforms, top hats. They applauded a man in khaki who was hissed and whistled at by the crowd. "Kerensky," Papa explained.

"For real?" she asked, suddenly feeling exposed up on his shoulders, but she could feel Papa's head shaking between her thighs. "Playacting," he said.

Play-Kerensky gave a speech. No one could hear it, but he was making all sorts of crazy movements that made him seem quite silly, and the fancy people up on the White stage adored him but the crowd in the square only laughed, and Aurora felt like a silly little girl for ever having been afraid of such a clown.

Lights came up on the Red stage. Workers emerged from factories, moving strongly. "You can tell they're dancers," Papa said in English. Some went to work beating anvils in synchrony with the music. A red flag was raised in a crossfire of light beams, and other workers gathered around it as cold people gather around a bonfire. The music changed and Aurora's ears picked out a tune that they sang every day at the school, "The Internationale." This grew louder and the lights grew brighter until they all, even the crowd, were singing it. Lenin came out and everyone screamed for him, stopping the show for several minutes. He spoke to the workers, who took up brilliant Red Guard banners and began to wave them gorgeously under the lights. They marched to the bridge and did battle with Whites above the orchestra, the White fighters a fearsome and yet comical menagerie of Cossacks, Savage Battalions, Germans in spiked helmets, Women Death Guards. Kerensky continued talking, trying to make the aristocrats ignore the Red Guards, but then they all fell down as the Reds fired their rifles, and scattered, scooping up bags of money and jewels and silverware. Things became confused. The telegraph must have been busy. Trucks loaded with bayonet-carrying soldiers issued from one part of the square, Cossack cavalry from another. A mock train rumbled along the streetcar track, firing cannons. Artillery pieces were dragged out of a park by teams of proletarian women pulling on ropes and began to make far too much noise. Kerensky was being defended by women; then he wasn't. People thought that funny. He climbed into a car with an American flag on it and drove down the lane between the two halves of the audience, careened around the base of the pillar, and made straight for the Winter Palace. No one knew where to look for a while; Aurora became drowsy. But then it suddenly seemed that the Red Guards were everywhere victorious, rushing toward the Winter Palace, the Cossacks and the Savage Battalions, the Women's Death Guard and the workers all merged into one great Red Army, searchlights sweeping back and forth across their multitudes as they converged. But one spotlight remained constant, steadily following a lone figure as he strode down the middle of the open lane, his bald head shining in the light: Lenin. He marched straight up the steps into the Winter Palace. Lights came on in the palace's many windows and now fighting could be seen, silhouetted figures acting out a panoply of looting, fist-fighting, chasing, bayoneting, suicide, cowardice, and surrender. The silhouette of a man grabbed the silhouette of a woman and held her to him even as she pawed at his face. As each of these little dramas concluded, the light in that window turned red. The entire palace had been limned in a fringe of white light, which Papa told her was made by searchlights on the *Aurora*, directly behind it. But when the last window in the Winter Palace had gone red, *Aurora* trained her searchlights up into the sky above it to reveal an enormous billowing red flag being run up. The music and the singing were very loud now, Aurora's eyes heavy. People in the front of the crowd laughed at something Aurora couldn't see. *Aurora* fired all of her cannons; Aurora screamed into the wall of noise and plugged her ears. Fireworks went off from batteries all around the square, and Aurora looked up into a bursting and writhing storm of red light. After it was over, black cinders rained out of the dark sky for a minute. Aurora flinched as one of them went down the back of her neck. Someone behind her flipped up the collar of her coat. She turned around and saw that it was Tyotya.

"I will be Aurora now," she said, but Papa didn't hear her.

She was asleep in Papa's arms before they got back to the kommunalka.

TYOTYA DID NOT GO BACK TO HER OLD HOME IN THE EAST AFTER *THE STORMING OF THE Winter Palace.* Aurora came to understand that it had never been the plan for her to go home, and that the other women in the kommunalka had seen as much from the very beginning. She would sit in a soft chair that she had shipped in from the country, and do needlework, improving the badges on Veronika's uniform, adding tiny details to the little picture of the machine gun on her sleeve. Veronika did not approve of the soft chair and called it *byt*, bourgeois comfort, but said it was all right for an old woman. Sometimes, though, when Veronika was away, Tyotya let Aurora sit in the soft chair for tea parties.

Tyotya would get up early in the morning and walk Aurora to the streetcar, and when Grisha brought Aurora home in the evening, Tyotya would be waiting for her. At the beginning of each week, Papa gave a bundle of tea to Tyotya, or sometimes an envelope, and she handed it to Grisha. Some of the other men in the kommunalka did not like this way of doing things and said that it was bourgeois, that Grisha was a speculator, but Papa said that he, Papa, was doing important work for the Revolution and that Grisha was assisting him.

Sometimes she got to school late, because of all the time Grisha spent talking to his other passengers. Some of them paid their fares with money but others brought tea, chocolate, cigarettes, gilt picture frames, Tsarist medallions, models of ships, pelts, table lamps, spoons. As the weather got colder, some brought firewood: chair legs, bundles of lath with lumps of horsehair plaster still a-dangle, molding, shrubbery. It piled up in the back of the streetcar.

Certain men Grisha did not wish to speak to at all. He would go far out of his way to avoid them, but sometimes they would blow whistles and come aboard the streetcar and demand money, tea, or whatever he had that was easy to carry away. Aurora asked if they were police. Grisha said, "Not exactly" or "It depends on precisely what you mean."

The morning mud became as thick as congealed kasha, then hard as stone, and the wheel ruts in the streets were floored with ice that glowed pink in the light of the dawn, like paint lashed across old leather. Steam covered the windows of the streetcar and it became Dawn's task to stand next to Grisha and wipe it clear with a rag so that he could see the points and look out for passengers, and the men with the whistles.

Snow began to fall. When they played razverstka now, and the Whites' hoarding was exposed, the punishment was a snowball firing squad. Once when Dawn was "shot," she lay on her back waving her arms and legs. When Lidiya came over to find out what was the matter, Dawn said that she had become an angel. She got up to show the wings and the skirts of the angel that she had made in the snow. Lidiya smiled a little bit but said that she should not talk of things such as angels, which were bourgeois superstitions created by the priests as a narcotic for the workers.

A deep snow fell and it became easy to hide the acorns. The Reds became frustrated, their gesticulations like those of the clownish Whites in the storming. Seeing the way Lidiya laughed and mocked him, Andrei announced that there would have to be an interrogation, and he tackled Lidiya into a snowdrift and sat on top of her and tickled her until, laughing and screaming with tears on her face, she told him where the acorns were—a big cache. She and Aurora had buried it together, their secret. Aurora got a sick feeling and almost threw up as she wondered what the penalty was going to be. But no penalty came to her or any of the other small children. All backs were turned, no eyes were on the little ones. Lidiya's penalty was to swear obedience to the Revolutionary Workers' Committee, and to kiss Andrei.

After that, Aurora never played the game again. It became all about interrogations and kissing. The smaller children were not invited. Some of the older girls had become sick of it, did not wish to go on being Whites every time, did not wish to be interrogated, and one of them slugged a boy in front of everyone and called him a Cossack. Which made Aurora remember what Veronika had told her about being grabbed and taken by men. Aurora tried to start another game in which the girls were all machine gunners and the boys were all Cossacks. It was popular for one day and then she could not get them to play it anymore.

TIME WAS TOLD BY THE SLOW WALK OF TACKS AND YARN ACROSS SCHOOLROOM MAPS: THE fronts where the Red Army was pushing back the remaining Whites, and the expansion of the revolutionary workers' state into the Caucasus, Siberia, the Far East. Veronika would come and go for weeks, months at a time.

She came back for Tyotya's funeral. Afterward she gave Aurora a locket that Tyotya had wanted her to have. The lid was engraved with a crest that was familiar to Aurora because she saw it on the gates whenever she visited Papa at work. It was the crest of the Smolny Institute for Noble Maidens, which had once been a boarding school and had since become the headquarters of the worldwide proletarian revolution. When the locket was opened, there was a cross on one side, in the queer Russian Orthodox style with the slanted crossbar at the bottom, the ramp from hell to heaven, and on the other a bust of a young woman in profile, carved in pink-orange stone, the color of the winter dawn.

The Ukraine became settled enough that Papa felt it safe to journey there in search of his cousins, even if only to bury them. For Papa had been born there and had emigrated to Pennsylvania in his fourteenth year. His trip was supposed to last for only a couple of weeks, but Aurora did not see him again for months.

The men around the table fell silent when Aurora was nearby. Antonio, the Italian, walked with her one morning to the streetcar and asked her about school, and whether she talked to the teachers or the other children about her father and what he did, and who he associated with, and what he said around the table, and the other men who lived in the kommunalka. He was speaking of these matters as an adult speaks to a child of how babies are made. But Aurora had seen how the daily flood of papers had been funneled down to one, which was *Pravda*, and she had picked up certain habits from the older children at school, who had become coy about what they said and whom they said it to—particularly after one of the teachers had, without explanation, ceased to exist, and the other teachers had denounced her, all using the same words and phrases.

"No," Aurora said, "I say nothing."

"Good," Antonio said.

A week later, he disappeared. All assumed the worst until he sent them a postcard from Rome.

There was shooting at night, not just small arms but machine guns. Lying awake, Aurora felt the same vague dread as when Grisha had spoken to her of the famine. But Veronika came home from the front, listened to it for a few minutes with the distracted stare of a doctor with a stethoscope, and said it could not be real fighting. It was like the Storming of the Winter Palace, she explained. But then, sensing that some of the other women were awake, she added, "during the Great October Socialist Revolution of 1917."

The Chekists—for it was they who did the nocturnal shooting—raided different neighborhoods on different nights, and in the morning the children at school would compare notes as to who had heard what. Some had not merely heard but seen, and these never wished to talk. Aurora did not understand why until the Chekists visited their neighborhood.

They shot sporadically from midnight onward, just frequently enough to make sleep impossible. Then, just before dawn, they came down the street in a flatbed truck, firing pistols in the air. Most of the women flattened themselves against the floorboards, but Veronika rolled up to her feet, strode to the window, and pulled the curtain aside. One of the other women screamed at her, but Veronika turned around with a look on her face that Aurora would always remember, and said, "If they wanted us dead . . ."

Aurora ran to the window, wrapped herself in the skirts of Veronika's greatcoat, and looked. The truck had already rolled past, but at a stately pace. Men in long black coats stood on its back with feet planted wide, gazing about like old statues of tsars. The truck went into the intersection where Aurora waited for the streetcar every morning. In its wake came automobiles, trundling along so slowly that Chekists were able to step out of them every so often and take up positions along the street.

"You'll be late for school," Veronika predicted.

They opened a jar of herring and breakfasted. Everything was silent, out on the street and inside the kommunalka where people were sitting near windows.

"It is all because Comrade Lenin is sick," one of the men said. "When he recovers—"

Another man told him to shut up, looking at Aurora.

"Everyone knows it!" the first man said. But now everyone shushed him. There was a general movement toward the windows. Aurora slipped along in Veronika's wake. At the last moment, the man who had looked at her noticed her and threw out an arm crying, "No!"

Aurora dodged under a blanket to the women's side. The windows were thronged. She went on to the lavatory and locked the door behind her. She stood up on the seat of the toilet and threw open the tiny window of painted-over glass that they used to let in fresh air. Directly below her the truck was passing by. Four Chekists stood at the corners of the flatbed, submachine guns slung from their shoulders. The bed itself was covered with persons, packed side to side, head to foot, like sardines, all facedown, their hands wired together behind their backs.

Cold air came in through the little window, which was of a perfect size to frame her face and shoulders, like the cameo that Tyotya had given her. The street was still, a few snowflakes drifting down, as if in the van of a blizzard. All of the other windows on the street were closed. Aurora knew that behind them people, hundreds of them, were peering. But hers was the only face visible. The faces of the Chekists on the near side of the truck swiveled to look at her, and she fancied she was illuminated by them as the faces of the actors at the storming had been lit by the sweeping beams of the searchlights. Lit, and warmed, for she felt blood wash into her face as she was seen.

One of the Chekists recognized her, and she him. He had been looking stern, but a happy grin flashed onto his face. "Aurora Maximovna!" he called, and took one hand off of his submachine gun to give her a cheerful wave.

She was about to call greetings back—for polite habits overrode all sense and circumstance—when the head of one of the prisoners moved suddenly, turning and then lifting off the truck's plank bed. A pair of blue eyes, rimmed in white, stared out from a face otherwise masked in red, unrecognizable were it not for the way frozen and clotted blood dangled from the long ends of the mustache. Then some instinct of shame or mercy made him close his eyes. Grisha banged his forehead down onto the boards and buried his face between the feet of the man lying next to him.

She was not sure she had even seen it. Her gaze went back to the young Chekist who had greeted her. He was still smiling but seemed crestfallen. "It is I!" he called.

"Good morning, Andrei Sergeievitch!" she called back.

3

MAGNITOGORSK

She told the story in bits and pieces over several days. Mostly she was telling it to Shaimat, as he was her most frequent companion at meals.

He was right that she could have gotten larger servings at the Engineers' Dining Room. Indeed, when she was really hungry, she would go take a meal there. But there, all conversation was in English. She would always end up at a table with Engineer Overstreet, as he was known here. And Bob Overstreet knew enough of her story that he knew better than to pry. But the other Westerners were as inquisitive as Shaimat. And in certain cases these men's endless verbal probing was clearly intended to lead to probing of a different sort. Even if Aurora had found these middle-aged middle managers attractive, she'd have avoided them as carefully as she stayed away from lice. It wasn't the fear of getting pregnant. The doctors in North Dakota had told her she'd never get pregnant again. It was all of the other stuff. But in Dining Room #30, mean as it was, Shaimat, the Tatar, had found ways—small, considerate gestures—to let her know that he wasn't interested in her that way. He kept going on and on about his sister in Akyar, who was the same age as Aurora, and she took his meaning well enough.

But others would drift by, meal tickets wedged between stumps of fingers, and occasionally, if some word or phrase in Aurora's story piqued their interest, they would sit down and listen. Aurora didn't mind. Of course they were curious about her. It was only natural. Better for her to take soup and bread with them from time to time and talk openly about her story than to act as if she had something to hide.

Which she did, of course. But she'd gone over this in her head during the voyage across the Pacific, the train ride across Siberia, and she was confident she could tell the story in a way that added up. No one here could gainsay her version, unless they put the whole resources of the OGPU to work digging up newspaper clippings and police reports scattered across half of America.

SHAIMAT, NORMALLY CAREFUL NOT TO MAKE THE SLIGHTEST CONTACT WITH HER, WAS kicking her under the table. As he was doing it with a valenok made of half-inch-thick wool, she didn't really take note of it for a while. Then she snapped out of it and looked down the table into the staring blue eyes of Tishenko. The Agitator. He seemed agitated.

"MANY OF THE COMRADES ARE FASCINATED BY YOUR STORY," TISHENKO SAID, SPEAKING clearly and just a bit deliberately, as he did not want to get ahead of the stenographer.

It was safe to assume that the cream of the Soviet stenographic crop had been skimmed off by important ministries in Moscow and Leningrad. Anyone holding down that job in the Special Department of Blast Furnace #4 in Magnitogorsk might not have won a lot of prizes and medals. That, and her fingers were cold; the Special Department's office was warmer than most places, but you could still see your breath. Tishenko was seated behind an item of furniture too humble to be called a desk. It was one cold night away from being kicked apart for kindling. But it had a lot of papers on it and conferred on him a kind of authority that he did not have when striding around in the open air yelling at people. The stenographer, a woman barely older than Aurora, was a column of blankets and scarves, steaming at the top, interrupted near the middle by two small red hands, one supporting a notebook and the other taking down shorthand with a pencil about an inch and a half long.

"As I understand it," Tishenko continued when the pencil stopped moving, "it all started when Comrade Shaimat expressed curiosity as to why your Russian was so excellent."

"Yes, that's true," Aurora said.

"He may not be aware that you work as a translator for Engineer Overstreet—at least, when you are not volunteering for Workers' Shock Brigade actions at two in the morning." The tone in which Tishenko mentioned this detail made it clear to Aurora that he found it a very odd thing for her to have done. So odd, in fact, as to be suspicious.

Now, Aurora had always known that she would at some point come under suspicion and be asked questions. In a way it was surprising that it had taken this long. She'd been here for weeks. Even so, the awareness that it was happening right now caused her scalp to burn.

But *everyone* came under suspicion at one point or another and was obliged to explain themselves. How could it be otherwise, when the Soviet Union was hemmed in by implacable enemies? Not just surrounded but infiltrated? She reckoned it was like having medical checkups. The doctors would ask certain questions, perform tests just to be sure that everything was normal. On *everyone*. Not just sick persons. Her mother had ignored a mole on her scalp until it was too late, and look where that had gotten her.

Every bureau in the vast apparat of Magnitogorsk had a "special department" like this one. Everyone knew that the job of the special department was to be the eyes and ears of the OGPU. Still referred to by many by its former name of Cheka. Aurora tried to settle herself down by thinking that this was like having a nurse in every school: not a doctor as such, and not sitting in a hospital or even a clinic. Just a representative of the medical profession who knew enough to keep an eye out for trouble. Everyone probably ended up explaining themselves to the likes of Tishenko from time to time. Obviously he'd talked to Shaimat, and probably some others.

"If he knew that you were an interpreter, and if he were capable of reading some of the glowing accounts of your performance that I have seen," Tishenko continued, resting a gloved hand gently on a neat stack of documents, "he might have asked a different question. Namely, why is your *English* so good? The story has become common knowledge of how you came to Russia as a toddler, almost pre-verbal, and were raised there. So it's not surprising that you speak Russian like a native. But how, during those years, could you have learned English so well?"

"It might help to explain that, Comrade Tishenko, if I could be so bold as to offer a slight correction."

"By all means, go ahead!" Tishenko sputtered.

"I was born in America in early 1916. My mother brought me to Petrograd four years later. I was already speaking English as well as any normal American four-year-old."

"Nineteen-sixteen, you say."

"Yes."

"But it was in 1917, during the February Bourgeois Democratic Revolution, that the crew of the battleship *Aurora* mutinied and took up arms for the Workers' and Peasants' Revolution." In his element now, rattling off revolutionary lore.

"Indeed."

"It has been assumed by everyone that you are named after that famous ship. That you must, therefore, have been born after February 1917."

"You might say it is a half-truth. When I was born—in 1916, in Montana—my mother named me Dawn." She said the word in English.

"Don? Like the river?"

Aurora spelled the word out for the stenographer. "It is an English word meaning daybreak. Like *zarya* here. And like Zarya, it can also be a girl's given name."

"I see."

"But when my mother brought me to Petrograd, they wanted to give me a Russian name. Zarya would have made sense—but because the memory of the Revolution was fresh in everyone's minds, they chose Aurora. So, I *was* named after the battleship in a sense—but I was born before it became famous."

The lengthy pause that followed wasn't just to let the stenographer catch up. Aurora got the impression that this was more new information than Comrade Tishenko was used to ingesting in a whole week.

"We'll have to correct your file," he said. "So, you are eighteen years of age. Not sixteen, as we had thought."

"In another few weeks I will turn eighteen, yes."

"And somewhere in a file cabinet in Montana there is a record of your birth under the name Dawn."

"Presumably."

"Last name Artemyeva?" For Artemyev had been her father's surname.

"Bjornberg. My mother's maiden name."

Tishenko raised his eyebrows.

"Complicated situation," Aurora said. "My full name was recorded on the birth certificate as Dawn Rae Bjornberg."

"So you're telling me that you have two altogether separate legal identities. Two sets of papers. Dawn Rae Bjornberg, an American from Montana, and Aurora Maximovna Artemyeva, Russian, from Leningrad."

"In a manner of speaking."

"What does that mean?!" Tishenko demanded. She got the impression that the man was exasperated not so much by the twists and turns in the story as by the sheer volume of explanatory paperwork that this was going to entail.

"Dawn's dead."

"What?!"

"I killed her off. So that I could come here. So that I could make a clean start."

A lengthy pause now caused Aurora to question whether she was really as fluent in Russian as was claimed by those glowing reports under Tishenko's glove. Had she miscommunicated? She raised her hands, pantomiming the operation of a tommy gun. "Dawn Rae Bjornberg died in a shoot-out with police. A bank robbery gone wrong in Fort Sickles, North Dakota. Her body was consumed in the ensuing fire."

Still Tishenko just sat there with his mouth open, displaying several gaps in his gums where the dentists of Magnitogorsk had applied the one therapeutic procedure they knew of.

"You know of Bonnie and Clyde?" she asked.

"*Da!*" exclaimed the stenographer, to the great surprise of both Tishenko and Aurora. She tucked her pencil stub into the palm of her hand and imitated the tommy-gun shooting gesture.

Tishenko, it was safe to say, had not heard of Bonnie and Clyde. His face reddened. He had made up his mind that Aurora and the stenographer were having a little fun at his expense. "We'll revisit the 'death' of Dawn Rae Bjornberg later," he announced. "I am more interested for now in making sense of your early life and your unusual fluency in both languages. You have explained to my satisfaction why your *Russian* is so good. But by your account you were only four years old when you left America. Your command of *English* can't have been very advanced at such an age. But I am informed"—his eyes darted down to another document—"that many in the American compound are under the impression that you are American born and bred."

"My mother spoke English to me for as long as she remained in Petrograd."

"But she divorced your father and returned to the United States in the middle of 1921." Another document. The man was more systematic than an Agitator had any right to be. Either that, or someone had fed him all of this stuff. Probably that. "You'd have been only five."

"For three years, it is true, I heard and spoke very little English," Aurora admitted. "But then"—she let her eyes wander curiously over his makeshift desk—"as you might be aware, my father was assigned to travel to America to resume his career organizing workers."

Tishenko nodded. "The two of you took the Trans-Siberian Railway to Vladivostok and from there traveled on a freighter to Seattle."

"Exactly."

"Beyond that, not much is recorded of your father's movements until the events of summer 1932 in Washington, D.C.—eight years and a whole continent away! He was in Chicago?"

"Yes."

"And you were with him."

"No."

"No?! You were only eight years old, who—"

"My mother. And her people."

"They organized workers in the American west," Tishenko said confidently.

Aurora's turn to sit with her mouth open, displaying fully intact dentition.

"Or—" Tishenko began uncertainly.

It was at such moments that Aurora was reminded that her face had considerable power over men's minds. She made a note of it.

"Is that what my father claimed?" Aurora asked.

She could just see it: Maxim Artemyev talking to a room full of Bolshevik theoreticians, trying to relate the story of how he'd spent his time and their money in places like Butte, Spokane, Telluride, and Tacoma in terms that they would understand. Of course he would call that "organizing workers." A bunch of riots and lynchings was more like it.

"There's a split," she said. "Chicago's in the middle. East of there, big cities, factories, steel mills. Work forces that came over from Europe recently. *Those* people you can organize, yes. They get orders from the International in Moscow and"—Aurora snapped out a salute—"that's how my father started. Before the war. But west of Chicago it's all different. Ranches, mines, timber camps, fishing boats. That's where people work. They are different. They are . . ." She spent a few moments trying to think how to get this through Tishenko's head. "Cossacks. And even when they are engaging in revolutionary struggle, they do it in the style of Anarchists. They don't take orders from anyone. My mother was one of those. She met my father when he was out west trying to get some women out of prison in Spokane." She decided to skip over some of the details, such as how they were being forced into prostitution.

"Before the war," Tishenko said. "Before he was inducted into the American Army."

"Yes. He did a few short jail stints and finally they shipped him off to the trenches hoping the Germans would finish him off."

"Very well. But let's get back to your story, Aurora. You're saying you spent the years 1924 to 1932 among the 'Cossacks' of your mother's people?"

"Yes. Eastern Montana and Wyoming."

"And they were doing what? Fomenting anarchy? Cattle ranching?"

"Robbing banks and playing polo."

"What?!"

"That's how I learned to play polo."

4

SEATTLE

1924

They stayed near the Pike Place Market, in lodgings that Papa insisted were "worker housing" but that his fisherman friends identified as flophouses. For Papa it was a good place because he could keep in touch with his friends in the movement, many of whom worked on the waterfront. For Dawn it was good because there was no place on Earth better suited than the Pike Place Market for running away from truant officers. She came to know its passages and bolt-holes well while avoiding the statutory requirement that a girl her age should be in school. Once she found herself hiding under a counter where some workers were butchering a cow-sized halibut. Two women were talking to each other in Russian. This led to a conversation, which led to her locket being noticed. Before she knew it she had escaped from school only to find herself in church: a neat little Russian Orthodox church, complete with onion domes, tucked up against the base of a steep hill. The offering plate was passed. A man fumbled for change and dropped a penny on the floor. After the service, Dawn requisitioned this surplus property in the name of the Red International and took it to the post office, where she bought a postcard and borrowed a pencil. She addressed it to her mother in Montana and covered it with a rambling childish update.

Some weeks later, Papa and Dawn boarded the train for Chicago. This took them north along the edge of the sea to Everett, where Papa pointed out the site where the five revolutionary martyrs—a Frenchman, a Swede, an Irishman, a German, and a Jew—had been gunned down by the police and their goons. There the train cut inland, climbing up over a great range of snowy mountains into the night. Sunrise greeted them on the steppe, which in time gave way to more mountains.

The passengers were mostly bourgeois. Dawn found that fascinating, like visiting a zoo, but Papa kept sighing and reminiscing about the old days riding freight trains around the west, organizing the workers. Whenever they passed a freight train on a siding he would gaze into the deeply shaded apertures on the box cars, speculating as to how many soldiers of labor might be concealed therein, cooking beans over Sterno and singing songs about Joe Hill. But Comrade Zinoviev had not sent him all this way and entrusted him with so much money so that he could take his daughter on a hobo adventure.

A few passengers, at least, had more of a rough, country way about them. One of these, a big, sunburned fellow wearing jeans and smelling of horse, seemed restless upon boarding and walked the whole length of the train two or three times before finally settling into a place at the end of their car. In his hands was a giant hat and over his shoulder was a half-ruined saddlebag. He made a stab at reading a discarded paper, then tossed it down and took to gazing out the window and twiddling the ends of his huge brown mustache. They were descending the eastern slope of the Rockies and there was plenty to look at.

Papa got up and went to the lavatory at the end of the car. The man with the mustache got up, ambled back, tried the lavatory door and, finding it locked, took up a vigil. When Papa emerged, the two of them struck up a conversation, which moved to the space between the cars and went on for a bit. Dawn guessed that Papa must be pleased to have been thrown in with an actual proletarian. But when he finally re-entered the car, he looked far from happy. The cowboy—for it had finally dawned on her that this was what the big man was—followed Papa down the aisle and sat right next to him, across from Dawn.

"Sweetheart, gather your things," Papa said. He had to say it loudly over the sudden strenuous blowing of the train's whistle. Something, probably cattle, must be on the tracks ahead; they were out in the middle of nowhere.

"I will see you again," Papa added in Russian.

"Now, what did I tell you about that?" the big man said mildly.

"Everything is fine," Papa said in English.

The train's brakes came on hard, disarranging people and goods throughout the car. Out the window was open country, broken here and there with outcroppings of rock and expanses of dark-green forest. The cowboy lurched to his feet and put the hat on. He stepped between Dawn and Papa so that he could lower the window sash. The air that came in smelled of sage. Dawn had forgotten that she had forgotten this smell, but now she remembered that she remembered it. Horses could be heard a-gallop. Papa maneuvered his head sideways so that he could see Dawn's eyes and said "I love you" in Russian. The cowboy reached into his saddlebag and pulled out a revolver. "Beg pardon," he muttered, cocking it. Papa's eyes went wide, thinking he was about to be executed for speaking in Russian but the cowboy thrust the weapon out the window and fired one shot into the air. The smell of gunpowder drifted in. The pounding of the hooves converged.

Dawn looked out to see—cowboys! Four of them, plus two saddled horses.

No, it was three cowboys and one cowgirl.

The cowgirl spun down off her mount, long orange hair flying around her like a cape, and stormed up the steps onto the carriage.

"For reasons having to do with the constabulary," said the cowboy, "it is desirable that you address her, loud enough for all of these witnesses to hear, as—"

"Mama!" Dawn shrieked, pounding down the aisle with arms outstretched, her vision already shattered by tears.

"That'll do," said the cowboy.

"Welcome home, Dawn Rae," said her mother into her ear.

5

MAGNITOGORSK

JANUARY 1934

One January morning, at breakfast in the American settlement, Aurora received a typewritten note with an official-looking stamp, letting her know that she'd been excused from her usual translating duties for the morning and inviting her to come to the infirmary for some reason. Ignoring it didn't seem like a good idea, given that she'd been under the eye of Comrade Tishenko, and hence presumably of the OGPU. So she dutifully walked down out of Berezka, the little town of cottages where Western engineers and high-ranking bureaucrats lived. She skirted the open-air prison of the Collective Labor Colony and began picking her way across a flat area, a couple of kilometers across, between the Magnetic Mountain to her left and the row of coke ovens and blast furnaces to her right. This was called Fifth Sector. Billed as a temporary improvisation while the new Socialist City was being erected, it showed every sign of becoming the real and permanent city of Magnitogorsk. Tens of thousands of workers lived here in nameless, numberless barracks—long, low buildings of wood tacked together and slathered with stucco. It was famously impossible to tell one from the next, and tired ironworkers were forever getting lost only a few meters from their own beds. Aurora had a vague notion that the medical block—yet another row of barracks, just like all the others—was in the southeast corner, near the big machines that crushed and sifted the ore coming down out of the gutted mountain. So she navigated by the sun and the fixed landmarks of the blast furnaces and the mine.

"May I assist you, Comrade Aurora?" This from a man who had been crunching along behind her for a while and then, as she stopped at a crossing of haphazard ways trying to puzzle out her next move, had begun to encroach on her peripheral vision. She'd instinctively been turning away from him. It was twenty below zero. She was peering out through a sort of gun slit framed by scarves and an ushanka. This style of dress created funny distortions in the usual etiquette that prevailed between men, who enjoyed looking at women, and women, who only wanted to be looked at in a certain way. There was nothing for a man to see unless he could maneuver around directly in front of you and peer through the aperture in the wool-and-sheepskin bunker that was keeping you alive. But this man had somehow recognized her.

She looked at him. It was Comrade Fizmatov. He kept a respectful distance and made a little suggestion of a bow—a bourgeois affectation that, if he kept it up, wouldn't do anything to shorten his prison sentence.

"I thought it was you!" he exclaimed. "I saw you walking by as they were letting me out the gate." Meaning, as she understood, the gate of the Corrective Labor Colony. "Oh, please don't think I've been following you. We seem to be headed the same direction, that's all."

"Where are you going?"

"The Mining and Metallurgical Institute, as usual. And yourself?"

"The hospital barracks."

"They are practically next door to each other. May I accompany you? It would be my honor."

Nobody talked like this. Had he picked up such manners during his studies in Paris? She nodded and smiled. Not that he could see her mouth, but perhaps it would come through in her eyes. With one mittened hand he indicated the direction they should go, and then fell in step beside her. "I trust everything is all right?" he inquired.

"Oh. You mean, why am I going to the hospital barracks? Nothing more than some kind of routine examination, I guess. You know how the bureaucrats are."

He did not make any sign of agreement but only walked beside her for a while, apparently lost in contemplation of whatever it was that PhD metallurgists thought about.

"So, what sort of name is Fizmatov?" she asked. For it seemed funny for him to catch up with her, introduce himself, and walk with her, but then to say not a word. "Ukrainian?" For he had that kind of accent.

"It is a totally made-up name!" he said. Amused, but not in a cruel way. "With your skills as a linguist, I'd have thought you could puzzle it out!"

"Now I feel stupid! But I'm afraid it means nothing to me."

"Physics and Mathematics," he said, turning toward her. "Phys-Mat. Fizmatov. You see?"

"You named yourself after physics and mathematics?"

He shrugged. "You must know that this was all the rage after the Revolution. People discarding their old bourgeois names, taking new ones. Naming their children after whatever they found inspirational in the new order of things. My old name had reactionary associations, especially strong in Kyiv, and so I renamed our family after the institute where I worked."

She already knew he was divorced, his ex-wife living in Moscow. "Your family," she repeated. "You have children?"

"Indeed, two boys."

"And did you give them inspirational names?"

"Most certainly! Proton and Elektron." He pulled up short in another intersection and turned to enjoy her laughter.

"You named your sons after subatomic particles!"

His frost-encrusted eyebrows went up. "Ah, you know about physics! You are well-informed."

"I went on some dates with a young man in Chicago who wouldn't stop talking about such things."

"Well," he said, "I'm afraid here's where we part company. The institute is that way, and the hospital barracks are just down there on the right." The mitten emerged briefly from the coat pocket to show her the way.

"Thank you, Comrade Physics and Mathematics."

"It was my pleasure, Comrade Battleship." He turned away and took a step, then turned back, his eyes serious. "I shall come and check on you later."

"Oh, it's as I said, I'm perfectly fine! It is just a routine examination or something."

He looked as if he were making a conscious decision to say nothing. Then he made his little bow again, turned his back on her, and walked away.

At the medical barracks, Aurora presented the typewritten summons to a nurse and was sent through to an examination room with an un-Soviet level of efficiency that might have made her suspicious. But sometimes Aurora had a knack—a knack that didn't always serve her well—of telling herself stories about what was going on. And the story that got her through the wait that followed was that, thanks to the information about her legal identities that she had provided to Comrade Tishenko, some decision had been made to transform Aurora Maximovna Artemyeva into a Soviet citizen in good standing. That certain rights, as well as responsibilities, went along with that. That among the former was healthcare, and so of course they would want to perform a basic examination and start a file.

The wait was long enough that she considered walking out of there, but they had all of her warm clothes. Finally a nurse came in, weighed her, and took down her blood pressure. Later a female doctor (for they had such things here) entered the room and chatted with her briefly, explaining that some routine tests and examinations were in order. And examine Aurora she did, thoroughly and invasively, muttering notes to the nurse the whole time.

She noticed the needle marks on Aurora's arms. They weren't particularly obvious, for the drugs had been administered by professionals under reasonably hygienic conditions. But you could see them.

"There is an explanation," Aurora said.

"I look forward to reading it," the doctor replied.

"Reading it?"

The doctor was washing her hands, obviously getting ready to leave.

"Would you like me to come back some other time, or—" Aurora began.

"No need," the doctor replied with a bright tone and a prim little smile. "We are going to admit you for further tests. Get your clothes on, I'm sending you over to a different clinic."

THEY PUT HER IN THE BACK OF AN AMBULANCE, JUST A WINDOWLESS SHEET-METAL BOX on the back of a truck, benches along the sides and a stretcher sliding and bouncing on the floor. In the front was a slit to allow communication with the driver. Peering out through it she saw a hundred or so Fifth Sector barracks pass by, then finally some hills and some new construction: the modern superblocks of the Socialist City. To the left, then, would be the mud-hut slums called Shanghai, a place she had been sternly warned against visiting even in the daytime. But she could only see what was dead ahead. The doctor had spoken of some other clinic. It must be one of the more modern facilities being erected in these new parts of town? But the ambulance drove straight through all of that, all the way to the shore of the Industrial Lake, just a perfectly flat strip of snow-covered ice dotted with fishing shacks. A pile of earth reached about a third of the way across and then they were driving over the top of the dam. This was a low structure, barely more than a levee made of concrete that had been poured in frantic haste by shock brigades a couple of years ago when the city was nothing more than tarps and tents. Nevertheless, it proved capable of supporting the ambulance's weight. As soon as they got to the west bank they turned south and fishtailed down a track of compacted snow into a tiny old town, Magnitnyi, which had existed before Stalin had decided to build the world's largest iron and steel complex across the river. This miserable huddle of mud huts had been improved with a barracks, exactly the same as the ones carpeting Fifth Sector. The ambulance pulled up in front. Out the slit, Aurora could see nothing but an old cemetery with the frozen river running along its edge. She already knew that the door at the back of the steel box wouldn't open from the inside. After a quarter of an hour, she heard footsteps approaching. The latch clattered, the hinges groaned, and the doors swung open, revealing a pair of very large men who had thrown winter coats over the white uniforms of medical orderlies. They gave her much unasked-for and unhelpful assistance in climbing out, then bracketed her during the brief walk through the facility's entrance, past a desk, and into another examination room. There followed a repeat of everything that had just happened at the hospital barracks in Fifth Sector: exchanging her clothes for a shift, waiting, being weighed, and so on. While she was waiting she noticed that in this facility there seemed to be rather a lot of shouting, dimly perceptible through the walls.

Nevertheless, it still did not penetrate her awareness until they pushed her through a barred door into a ward full of women, dressed in shifts like her, and locked the door behind her, that she had been committed to a psychiatric hospital.

"EXPLAIN THE NEEDLE MARKS ON YOUR ARMS," SAID COMRADE STASOVA. YET ANOTHER woman doctor. A psychiatrist. It had taken her two days to find enough time in her schedule to sit down and interview Aurora. So far, she had shown intense focus on two topics: polo and tommy guns.

Aurora could explain those easily. But now the interview was headed into more difficult territory. "I had a medical crisis," she said. "During my recuperation, I was given drugs. Morphine."

"A lot of it!" scoffed Dr. Stasova.

Aurora was beginning to perceive that not all psychiatrists were there to listen with a sympathetic ear. "These doctors were up to no good. They were trying to control me."

"So, when doctors give you medicine in a 'medical crisis,' would you say they are conspiring against you? Trying to control your thoughts?"

Aurora sighed. "You said yourself it was a lot of morphine."

"Depends on the nature of the medical crisis. In some cases, it might be warranted."

"I doubt this was one of those."

"What exactly was it?"

"I became pregnant. Out of my womb, they say, came a monster."

Dr. Stasova slapped her pencil down on the desk and sat back in her chair with such violence that it threatened to give way.

After a long silence she said, "I'm sending you back to the women's ward." She glanced up at a clock on the wall. "Later I'm going to show you something in the men's ward. It's okay, we'll be safe. Afterwards, we will resume this conversation."

Now, the women's ward was just a long room, a row of beds along each wall, the beds occupied by women, some of whom seemed normal, others in the grip of mental afflictions of which Aurora knew nothing except that they seemed to make the sufferers prone to making noise at all hours. The ones who weren't making noise all the time *never* made noise and wouldn't talk to Aurora. So she hadn't been sleeping well and she hadn't made any friends.

The men's ward, as she discovered a couple of hours later when she went in there with Dr. Stasova, was a whole different world of loudness and bad behavior. In thirty seconds she was exposed to the sight of more penises than she had seen in her whole life to this point, and she had been in some rugged places. She and the doctor were escorted by a burly man with a nightstick.

In the center of the lane running down the middle of the ward was a wooden table, not large—it might have seated four, or six in a pinch— but extraordinarily massive. Nearby was a wheeled cart where a man in a white coat was at work with tools of the druggist's trade: a mortar and pestle containing bright-yellow powder, a delicate scale, miscellaneous vials and jars. He was mixing up some amber concoction in a beaker.

The doors at one end of the ward burst open. In stormed the pair of extraordinarily large orderlies who had escorted Aurora from the ambulance into the building. They were holding a smaller man between them. Each of the orderlies was holding one of the man's arms twisted behind his back. They had him bent over, but he was craning his neck up to look forward, making it obvious that a cigar-sized dowel had been inserted horizontally across his mouth, secured behind his neck with a leather thong. He had a salt-and-pepper goatee, but the whiskers on his cheeks had been growing out for a while. His hair was cut somewhat long, as if he were in the habit of brushing it back from his high forehead. But it had not seen comb or brush recently. He was wearing pajama bottoms.

As soon as he saw the table, he planted his bare feet. The orderlies jerked him up off the ground and kicked his legs out from under him, and from that point he was just being dragged, the tops of his feet making a faint squeaking sound along the tile floor. The orderlies picked him up effortlessly and heaved him belly-down onto the table. Then they performed a neatly choreographed pas de deux in which each of them, while using one hand to keep the patient's arm twisted behind his back, pirouetted back and sat down on one of the patient's thighs. The combined weight must have been five or six hundred pounds. The only part of the patient's body still capable of movement was the lower legs, which were kicking. The orderlies soon used their free arms to trap the ankles in the crooks of their elbows and hug them against their bodies.

The druggist drew the amber fluid up into a steel syringe and approached the table. He jerked the waistband of the pajamas down to expose the tops of the buttocks. In quick succession he jabbed the needle in four times: once into each buttock and once beneath each shoulder blade. Each time he shoved the plunger down a quarter of the way.

The logic behind the dowel now became clear as the patient, who until now had only been trying to talk, began screaming. He was too thoroughly immobilized to flail around and had to settle for smashing his forehead into the tabletop, perhaps in an effort to render himself unconscious.

A couple of nurses—stocky women whom Aurora identified as peasants—entered the room. From under the table they dragged out a rusty washtub full of water. A big piece of canvas had been soaking in it. They hauled that out, dropped it on the floor with a heavy splat, and unfolded it. The orderlies heaved the shrieking patient up off the table. His whole body had turned as red as a boiled lobster. They dropped him along one edge of the sopping canvas and quickly rolled him up in it, like a human cigarette. They then squatted there, holding the free edge of the canvas in place, while the women got to work with curved needles and stout thread, sewing the canvas into place around the patient's body, leaving only the head exposed.

That looked like it was going to take awhile, and the shrieking, even through the gag, was becoming hard to take. Dr. Stasova plucked at Aurora's arm and nodded at the guard.

A few moments later they were sitting back in the office. The doctor picked up her pencil and examined it between her hands as if it were a dagger.

"The canvas will shrink as it dries," she said.

"That was the one part of it I understood."

"Pyretotherapy," Dr. Stasova said, looking Aurora in the eyes. "Developed in the West ten years ago, for syphilis. The drug causes the body temperature to go up—so hot it kills the spirochetes that are the cause of the disease."

"That man had syphilis?"

The skepticism in Aurora's voice was so clear that it caused the corners of Dr. Stasova's mouth to draw back a millimeter. "Later it was determined that these high temperatures can alter the chemistry of the brain in a way that is therapeutic for schizophrenics."

"It seems quite painful?"

"Sometimes Novocain is administered first."

"But not today."

"No."

"So that man is schizophrenic."

"He has been diagnosed as such," Dr. Stasova said quite slowly and distinctly, again looking Aurora in the eye, and then said nothing for a while, letting her think it all through. "It will be helpful for you to know that, here in the USSR, the science of psychiatry has advanced beyond where it is in the West. New types of schizophrenia have been discovered."

"And are being treated."

"As you saw."

"What are the symptoms of these newly discovered types of schizophrenia?"

"Oh, I don't think you need concern yourself with those. Your symptoms are easily covered by the old, well-known types."

"My . . . symptoms?"

"Hallucinations. Delusions of grandeur."

"Such as?"

"Claiming you are a polo player. That you are a tommy gun–shooting public enemy like Bonnie and Clyde. And that a monster came out of you."

"I can explain the first two."

"THE OLD WAYS OF MAKING A LIVING—SO EXPLOITATIVE, SO PRODUCTIVE OF REVOLUTION-ary fervor among the working class—were for the same reason unattractive to proud, energetic people who simply wanted to have food and stay warm."

Aurora had, at long last, come to understand that she needed to start talking like this in order to get out of this psychiatric hospital with her body and her mind intact. Fortunately she had grown up around Bolsheviks and got a refresher course in the most up-to-date Stalinist verbiage by spending time with Comrade Tishenko. She saw no trace of concern on Dr. Stasova's face as she launched into this. On the contrary, the doctor appeared to be relaxing.

Aurora continued: "Deprived of the opportunity for a genuine people's revolution, the men of my mother's family discovered that their skills had more lucrative uses. Some of them transported whisky across the border from Canada and put it on the railway, disguised as other goods. Some, it is true, robbed banks. Others allowed themselves to be exploited by the polo-pony industry, which—whether or not you believe it—is very lucrative in eastern Montana and Wyoming."

"Because of the cavalry units stationed there to suppress the Indians?" Dr. Stasova guessed. For even a psychiatrist knew that one could not maintain an effective modern cavalry without polo.

"That's how it got started. The big operations are all run by remittance men."

"I am not familiar with the term."

"Younger sons of British aristocrats. By law only the eldest son can inherit. The others are still rich and need never work. A monthly remittance is cabled to them, wherever in the world they may roam. Some spend it. Others invest."

"In polo-pony ranches?"

"It gives them an excuse to ride and play every day of their lives."

"I wouldn't think there'd be much of a market, out there—"

"They ship ponies all over the world. British cavalry officers in India ride ponies from Wyoming. American plutocrats take the train west, marry off their daughters to remittance men's sons, ride their ponies, and buy them for their stables in New York."

"Trading daughters for horses. The ways of the elite beggar parody. Tell me, though, what need did such men have of revolutionary outlaws?"

"They needed men who could handle horses. Who could ride. And play."

"Cowboys play polo?"

"Cowboys, and Indians. These remittance men living out in the middle of nowhere must have opponents—and good ones—or they will become bored and forget how to play the game."

"And is it really the case that you know how to play?"

She paused long enough to control the beginnings of a smile. "I spent four summers working on such ranches, mucking out stables at first. Then riding new ponies, teaching them not to fear the whirling club, the whack of the ball. It is ticklish business. If a new pony receives even a glancing, accidental blow from an errant club or a mis-hit ball, it may take months for it to lose its fear—a great waste of time and effort. If the club goes between its legs and trips it, the animal may be a total loss. So, the trainer must be able to control the club and strike the ball nearly as well as a player. Before I could even begin to work as a trainer, I had to . . ."

She noticed that Dr. Stasova was glaring at her, and she trailed off.

"Yes," she said, "I learned how to play."

This seemed to satisfy Dr. Stasova, at least as far as the first of Aurora's "delusions"—being a polo player—was concerned. "Now," she said, "as to the tommy guns and so on? I assume that there is some connection there to the members of your family who were engaged in criminal activities."

"That is true, but in a more roundabout way. As an adolescent girl I took no part in such operations. Oh, everyone in that part of the country is familiar with guns, and I was especially interested in automatic weapons because of the memories I had from childhood, of Veronika."

"The machine gunner who lived in your kommunalka."

"Yes. But an ordinary girl living on a ranch has no need of a submachine gun. Sometimes the men of the family would carry one if they were worried about wolves."

"Isn't an ordinary pistol or rifle sufficient to kill a wolf?"

"Yes, but not a whole pack. They told stories of wolf circles."

"What is a wolf circle?" Dr. Stasova had become sufficiently interested that she was forgetting to take notes.

"Sometimes in the wild places they would find the remains of a man, completely torn apart and decayed, but clearly human. Somewhere near him there would be a revolver, out of ammunition. And around him would be a circle of dead wolves. It was not difficult to understand what had happened."

"The man had been surrounded by a pack consisting of more than six wolves."

"Yes. So if they were going into a place where they knew there was a big wolf pack, and if they had a submachine gun, they might bring it along. But again, I rarely saw a tommy gun and never touched one until last year."

"What happened last year?"

"As I grew older, Mama and Papa worked out a deal. I'd ride the train to Chicago and see him sometimes."

"Passenger or—"

"The Comintern's records will show that he paid for passenger tickets. Which he did. I cashed them in and kept the money, then hopped freight trains instead."

"Alone?"

"With uncles or cousins who were going to Chicago on business."

Dr. Stasova nodded. "They repackaged Canadian liquor as freight, and transported it by rail—"

"With an escort. Which was necessary, especially during the last few miles."

"What exactly happened in the last few miles?"

"The line passed through the territory of the Westside O'Donnells, en route to the Cicero Hump. Once we got there, I would stay in the boxcar and keep my head down while the Bugs's men handed over the money and loaded the goods onto a truck."

"Bugs's men?"

"Agents of the primary customer. Have you seen *Scarface*? The North Side Irish gang depicted in that film is based on Bugs Moran's organization. They are credited with introducing the tommy gun to Chicago."

"So, when you say that you kept your head down—"

"I meant it literally. They were at odds with the Westside O'Donnells."

"Who apparently did a poor job of policing this thing called the Cicero Hump."

"It is a forty-two-track bowl. It's three miles long. No one gang could control it. But there would be skirmishes. Anyway, when the coast was clear, we would hike out and take the Cicero Avenue bus all the way up north to Belmont and then cut east toward the lake and get to where Papa lived."

"That is the district of Chicago where the headquarters of the IWW were also located?"

"He lived and worked in the same flop," Aurora said. "The Wobblies have fallen on pretty hard times."

"Yes. Perplexing, given the movement's success in Britain."

"He went to England around the time of the general strike, as you know, so I didn't see him for a while. Other than that, yes, everything ran smooth until three years ago when Mama got sick."

"Cancer?"

"A wart, she told me at first, when she had it cut off. Later they took out a piece of her scalp the size of a postage stamp and she had to cover the scar with her hair. She was hoping it would blow over. The next year she started to get other symptoms and came clean with me as to what it really was. We went into Chicago where she could get better treatment. They would poke a radioactive needle into her for a while, then pull it out. She never complained. I stayed with Papa and rode the El to the hospital, visited her every day toward the end. I know, bourgeois sentimentality. But after she died, it felt right to stay there with Papa for a time. Which is how I got caught up in the Bonus Army stuff."

"Rekindling the revolutionary fervor that had lain dormant during your exile as an impressionable youth surrounded by charismatic revanchists," Dr. Stasova corrected her, writing the words down.

"Exactly."

6

CHICAGO

By the time the Chicago Communist Party Central Committee mobilized, the bulls had given up on trying to stop veterans from hopping eastbound freights. Many of the bulls were veterans. All were patriotic. Anyway, it was unstoppable. Some of the railways had begun adding empty boxcars to eastbound trains just to clear frustrated Bonus Marchers out of their yards. For, following the example of their commander, Walter W. Waters, the men of the Bonus Expeditionary Forces had become expert at soaping rails and disconnecting brake lines. The economy was at a standstill. Idle rolling stock was about as useful as canoes in a desert. Sending a few boxcars east to clear a freight yard of such nuisances was more than worth it. So, far from hiding, Papa's band of Reds lit an open fire as they waited for their train to marshal, boiled up a kettle of slum, and played a madcap baseball game, tripping over rails and vaulting stacks of ties as they ran after long fly balls.

A cop and a bull strolled by to pass the time of day with them and pass out smokes. When they came to Papa—who was reclining in the shade of a boxcar, reading a book—their tone changed. Dawn, sitting inside the boxcar, sewing a hammer and sickle onto an expanse of red fabric, listened.

"Fellas are saying you're the leader," said the cop in flat Chicago vowels.

"Then I reckon I am," Papa said, "until they say somebody else is."

"What kind of accent is that?"

"American."

"Don't be smart."

"Polish," guessed the bull, and just from that one word Dawn could tell he was Irish.

"Good guess," Papa said. "Russian. Technically, Ukrainian."

"But it's all part of the same country now, eh?" said the cop.

"Not so much a country as an international movement, Officer."

"You part of that movement?"

"I'm proud to say I am."

"What's a Red Russian doing on a veterans' march?"

"I'm a Red American," Papa said, "and a veteran."

"Prove it."

Papers rustled. Dawn also heard the pop of a baseball into a mitt, a groan from one of the sides. "Why aren't you playing baseball like the others?" asked the bull. "You appear spry."

"Looks can be deceiving. My lungs have seen better days."

"Says here he's right," said the cop. "Says here he's on fifty percent disability. 'Cause of his lungs."

"Aw, that's a shame," said the bull. "Tuberculosis?"

"Gas," Papa said. "Half of my platoon bought the farm. I got my mask on a few heartbeats sooner."

"It's all in order," said the cop. "Just don't be raising any Red trouble around here."

Dawn knew what Papa was thinking, what he wanted to say: *The trouble's all being created by your paymasters; we're just trying to put a stop to it.* "Thank you, Officer. But if that was what I wanted, I wouldn't be hopping a train out of town, would I?"

"That smart mouth of yours is going to earn you a licking," said the cop. But he moved on.

"NOW YOU CAN SEE WHY I WAS INSISTENT ON ALL OF YOU HAVING YOUR PAPERS IN ORDER," Papa said later to the committee: half a dozen men and women, all card-carrying members of the Wobblies and of the Communist Party, and all bona fide veterans or war widows. The train had pulled out of the yard an hour earlier; they were meeting at one end of a car. "The only reason the Bonus Expeditionary Force is allowed to exist is that the forces of capital are afraid to be seen crushing a movement of men who fought their war for them. Commander Waters is savvy enough to know that if his camps in D.C. are found to have been infiltrated by poseurs, why, then it's all over. Comrade Browder tried to enter the main camp down in Anacostia and was turned away at the gates. Not because he's the head of the party but because he's not a veteran. That little shakedown? Just a dress rehearsal for what we can expect later."

"I heard otherwise," said Booker Pryor. "I heard tell Commander Waters is turning a little brown around the edges." Everyone looked at him curiously. "No, not brown like me! As in the Brownshirts. He's going fascist. Purging the Communists. That's what I heard anyway."

"I'm sure he's under great pressure from the Bureau of Investigation and other organs of the reactionary puppet government to make a show of being Red-free. Whether he is sincere, or just using a little common sense, is a thing I mean to find out. Our revolutionary comrades have scouted other locations in D.C., even closer to the centers of power, where we can lodge if there is tactical advantage to be gained by maintaining the appearance of separation from Commander Waters."

Later, after the train had curved east around the shore of Lake Michigan and the sun was going down over the prairie, Papa invited Dawn to clamber out onto the back of the caboose and enjoy the evening air. Seeing his union card, the engineers were happy to let them pass time there.

"A red sunset," he pointed out, inevitably.

"They're all red," Dawn said, "because of the dust, because of the drought." She loved him, but it made her weary that he was only capable of talking about one thing.

"Just let me be poetic for a moment, my dear young scientist." Papa didn't smoke, because it riled up his lungs, but he did chew. He had a wad going. His eyes watered and he leaned over the railing to spit onto the tracks. They were well clear of the city, passing through a cut lined with scrubby growth save where hobos had hacked it all down and built long, skinny shantytowns on the right of way, canvas roofs and clotheslines caressing the sides of the passing trains. The train was clacking along fast enough that neither hobos nor mosquitoes could catch it, slow enough that the wind wasn't a menace.

"You were born into a red dawn and now, even though I don't believe in superstitions, I think that these red sunsets mean something. The sun is setting on your childhood. You're a grown woman now. Only sixteen, I know, but you've experienced more than most women twice your age, and that counts for something. You're so big and strong, I can't believe you're my daughter."

I'm not, she might have told him. *While you were on a tramp steamer to Liverpool to organize dockworkers, you were cuckolded by a six-foot-four-inch stickup man named Jim O'Faolain, who was hanged a month after I was born.* She said nothing, though, letting him enjoy her. Being gazed at by men, she had learned, was as much a part of the natural order of things as gravity. More so when you were five foot eleven and freckled. She wore jeans; all she had was jeans. No one cared on the ranch. On the El, riding to the hospital to see Ma, women in skirts and pearls would look her up and down and make it clear that they did not approve. Men would stare in a way that, on a ranch, would have led to violence. Being gazed at, with affection, by a man who believed he was looking at his daughter, was quite tolerable by comparison, as warm as the low heat of the setting sun.

"So there'll be a short summer night and then a new dawn," he said. "It's going to happen in D.C."

"What is?"

"It's the Petrograd of America. Even the geography is the same—the rivers, the drawbridges, the palaces of capital, the military bases full of enlisted men toiling under the whip of the officer class, just waiting for their moment. It'll be the Great July Revolution or the Great August Revolution, depending."

So far, nothing she hadn't heard before—the same dreamy talk he would exchange with the men around the table at the kommunalka while the women cooked for them.

"It's time to talk about what your role is going to be."

"Making kasha? I forgot the recipe."

He laughed. "I always saw you as more of a Veronika."

This felt to her as a secret violated. Of course he'd have noticed Veronika, talked to her, thought about her. But Dawn had wanted her all to herself. Papa did not really know Veronika, what she had suffered, how it had made her. Otherwise he would never have uttered such a curse.

"Obviously," he continued, "I never had good relations with your mother's side of the family."

My only family.

"Now I need something from them. Because they don't like me, don't trust me, I need you to be a, a—"

"Go-between?"

"Agent."

"What is it we need from them?" The question was a formality; she knew the answer would be whisky. Whisky he could slip to D.C. cops and pols, trade for food, smuggle into the BEF's camps and flops and shantytowns to get in their good graces.

"Tommy guns," he said. "And, if possible, hand grenades."

She must have looked at him funny.

"Oh, I have money," he said.

AT FT. WAYNE, WHERE THREE GREAT LINES INTERTANGLED, THERE WAS A DAY'S PAUSE AS they awaited a Norfolk Western train bound south and east. The layout of the place and the manner of its workings would have baffled them were it not for the sages of the adjoining Hooverville: wizardly hobos who had nothing to do but squat back in the cover of the sumac jungle and observe. They knew every locomotive on the system and could recognize every engineer from miles away by his touch on the whistle. They could say which bulls were best avoided and which might look the other way as a platoon of revolutionaries clambered up into a string of boxcars.

They encountered half a dozen half-starved Kansas City Communists who had come in a few days earlier. They'd been part of a larger, mixed contingent that had convened a sort of tribunal, found them guilty of being Reds—which was true enough—and cast them out before boarding an eastbound freight. Papa and Booker spent the better part of an evening chewing the fat with them over a small campfire before accepting them. Their leader was Rusty Krieger, an old Arizona mining-camp Wobbly, known by reputation. The others were newer recruits from packing plants and railyards. One of these, a lad named Al Larson, was obviously too young to be a vet, even supposing he'd lied about his age. But he had papers proving that he was the only son and heir of a marine who'd fought at Belleau Wood and come home with a wound that had eventually killed him. Al had been making himself useful with his knowledge of railway lore and had become Rusty's chief deputy. So from then on, when Papa held meetings of his central committee, Al and Rusty participated.

A day later they were eastbound again on a Norfolk Western freight that would take them to within striking distance of the capital. Getting on a train had been more difficult than in Chicago, until it had suddenly turned easy. Papa confided in Dawn what she'd already guessed—namely that he had dipped into his stash to pay someone off. His hand strayed thoughtlessly toward the breast of his jacket, where Dawn saw cack-handed stitching and more bulk than her sunken-chested Papa could account for on his own.

"WHY DON'T YOU JUST ORDER TOMMY GUNS FROM SEARS ROEBUCK LIKE EVERYONE ELSE?" she'd asked him one evening, not long before, after she'd recovered from his surprising request for fully automatic weapons.

"You don't understand," Papa had said, "we need lots of them. You have to think about practicalities." He had paused for a moment, eyes watering, and she had known he was remembering the gas attack, when there'd been plenty of gas masks—just not handy. "When that red banner you sewed gets hoisted above the Treasury Building, or the Capitol, or whichever building we decide to use as our Winter Palace, we're not going to have time to break open the crates from Sears, wipe the grease off of the parts, assemble them, and then kill another half an hour shoving cartridges into magazines."

"Ordering a lot of them at once—"

"Would lead to General Robert E. Wood picking up his phone at Sears headquarters in Chicago and placing a long-distance call to the offices of the Justice Department's Bureau of Investigation," Papa had said with a smile.

"In Montana I've seen one tommy gun. One."

"But there's a place world-famous for having a surplus."

"Chicago, sure."

"And your relatives know those people. Deal with them."

"The people you're talking about like their tommy guns, Pop."

"Prohibition's done for. That era is passing. And you can bet they over-bought. That's the mentality. Why buy three tommy guns when you can afford thirty? Mark my word. They're sitting in speakeasy basements all over Chicago, and Bugs Moran is saying, 'The handwriting's on the wall; Rockefeller just came out for Repeal, Roosevelt's going to lick Hoover in a few months, what use are tommy guns to a legit operation?' It's a buyer's market, Dawn."

"You sound like a capitalist."

"We must use the human materiel and the goods provided us by capitalism to destroy it."

"How would we get them the money?"

"I hid it in Chicago. A down payment, and the balance, in separate locations. All we need to do is send a cable."

"Why didn't we do this before we left?"

"Do you remember last week, when I asked you whether any of your cousins happened to be in town?"

She nodded. The answer had been no. So it would all have to be done anyway through letters, cables, telephone. More important to get to D.C., to scout the battlefield, than to tarry at home fussing over logistics. Communists, outlaws, and gangsters all knew how to be discreet.

THE TRAIN FELT ITS WAY EAST, ALL THE TOPOGRAPHY CONSPIRING AGAINST IT. RUSTY Krieger made it clear, by his way of talking and his choice of topics, that he was a lonely man, more interested in camaraderie than revolution. It was well known that he had been a hellraiser of the first water during the Wobblies' salad days, and Papa made a point of paying homage whenever an opportunity arose. But there was something about his glib recitation of old slogans and his tiresome bids to get everyone singing old Wobbly songs that made the younger Chicago Communists exchange looks. They looked to Papa, too, but rather than meet their eyes he only gazed poker-faced at Rusty. Al Larson, by contrast, never got a word in edgewise, and soon had a nickname.

"Silent Al's sweet on you," Booker told her during a break on an Ohio Valley side track. "He got the wandering eye, does Al. Oh, he knows how to hide it. His mama raised him right. But Booker can see it."

She didn't doubt him; seeing things was Booker's job, and that's why Papa kept him around, invited him to meetings, talked with him afterward.

"He is a polite young man," she said, "I could do worse."

"Aww, you had me there for a second!" he said, after a double-take.

"I'm not altogether joking," she said. "Got to start somewhere. And if he has an eye for a hobo in blue jeans—"

"Let me tell you something, girl," Booker said. "I almost called you child, but this is not child talk. When it comes down to it, men *do not care*. They got an eye for *everything*."

"Then why do women—"

"Women dress that way *for each other*. You want to make friends with a girl, you go get yourself all dressed up. With a boy? Better think twice."

"Not even Silent Al?"

"Just don't sell yourself short, is all I'm saying. Just because you wear blue jeans." He nodded, a parting shot as he strolled away: "You gonna be turning heads in D.C." And then he disappeared into a swirl of orange campfire sparks, green fireflies, and blue-white stars.

ONE MORE TRAIN CHANGE GOT THEM INTO D.C. ON A FREIGHT ALL BUT EXPROPRIATED BY the Bonus Expeditionary Forces: swarming with thousands of veterans, widows, wives, children from all over, whites and coloreds mixed up like

Dawn had never seen. She had no idea where they were, but some of the men did, and as word spread up and down the train, they began to open suitcases and take out such odds and ends of uniforms as had survived the decade and a half since Armistice Day. Water was heated over Sterno, scraps of soap passed from hand to hand so that each man got enough to shave. A colored barber from Alabama set up shop in the open side door of a boxcar, flicking suds and whiskers off his straight razor onto the siding.

D.C. had little industry and did not spread into the surrounding country like Chicago. So it surprised them. A white spike and a white bubble were on the horizon, and all were looking at them, unwilling to believe that these were actually the Washington Monument and the Capitol dome. A rough chorus of "America the Beautiful" broke out, to the immense pleasure of Rusty Krieger, and then "Over There."

After their long hobos' journey, Dawn was expecting an improvised and helter-skelter progress through Washington, but in fact it was organized better than many actual military operations. A sort of honor guard was drawn up, waiting for them at the north end of the Potomac Yard, flags flying and drums rattling. Cops were there, too, ranked on motorcycles, and Glassford, the chief of police, known to be a friend of the Bonus Marchers. Flatbed trucks waited to convey women, children, amputees, and grizzled Spanish-American War vets. Dawn found herself shunted to one of these. Even though she was more capable of marching than many of the vets, she accepted the lift because she was burdened with bulky luggage such as the banner, which was all folded up in an army duffel bag. She and the other women of the Chicago contingent looked after that and the other big stuff—Dutch oven, canned beans, tools, tents—and cheered for the men as they fell in, formed ranks, saluted the flag, and began marching out, ten abreast, preceded by the drum-and-bugle corps and Chief Glassford, paced by motorcycle cops, and followed by the trucks.

They had been studying maps during their journey. Otherwise, she'd have been hopelessly confused. Senators might enter D.C. from the north, detraining at Union Station, but hobos, Bonus Marchers, and Bolsheviks approached from the west and jumped down from their boxcars in a huge yard on the Virginia bank of the Potomac. The first leg of their march, then, took them a couple of miles north up the bank to the first available bridge, which carried them northeast across the river and over some parks and waterways before bearing north in the general direction of the Washington Monument. Just short of the Mall they turned right onto a course that would take them along the southern front of the Capitol. It became a regular parade, complete with spectators lining the streets, waving flags, and holding up signs saying things like BONUS NOW and SUPPORT OUR VETS! Near the Capitol, fleshy, self-assured men in light summer suits were out shaking hands. Someone said they were congressmen. They paused at an intersection; Rusty let himself down off the truck, explaining that, as a non-veteran, he'd best go no farther. Laying a finger aside of his nose he said that he had a place to stay with some comrades. As the truck began moving again he reached out and grabbed the top strap of the duffel bag with the red banner, dragged it off, and slung it over his shoulder. Dawn was relieved to see it, and him, disappearing into the crowd.

Once they were past the Capitol, the neighborhood changed decisively. The sun told her they were bending south, her inner ear that they were canted downhill. The faces on the sidewalk became mostly colored, with the exception of one stretch that was all navy men, cheering them on—there was even a navy band playing. Water appeared in their way: a river, spanned by a bridge. Remembering Papa's remarks about Petrograd, Dawn took note of the fact that it was a drawbridge. She scanned for the control tower, which would have to be first stormed and then defended. Everyone was guessing that this was the Potomac again, but Dawn knew it to be Anacostia Creek. Plotted on a map, their route was a giant horseshoe, the destination almost directly across the river from Potomac Yard, where they'd first jumped off the boxcars. Ahead there was some indiscipline in the ranks as men in the left files craned and jostled for a view to the right; some broke ranks altogether, ran to the bridge's right-hand railing, and waved hats, flags, whatever they had. As the truck bumped out onto the span, Dawn and the other women saw why. On the creek's opposite bank, downstream along its gradual junction with the Potomac, was the biggest Hooverville she had ever seen: the usual improvised shacks and tents but laid out with precision on a grid of mud streets. A big green Salvation Army tent stood on the near end. There was a large open area spattered with lozengy puddles and engraved with the huge white glyph that, only in North America, meant baseball. Rising above the middle of the shantytown was a wooden platform that she first took for a gallows. But flags flew from it, and someone was on top, not being hanged but in a hortative posture, the apex of a large cone pressed to his lips. Of the drab groundlings below, some listened and others went on about their business. Much of this seemed to involve the relocation of large random objects: tree branches, automobile seats, sheets of cardboard and plywood. Following their trail down the bank, Dawn saw that much of this had been quarried from a dump that ran like a levee between the town and the edge of the water. To the extent that there *was* an edge; for in truth the boundary between river and bank was not as crisp as one might wish for in a plumbing-free development supporting tens of thousands of humans. Men were wading out, soap-clutching fists flailing above their heads, trying to find water deep enough to bathe in. Women gathered in little societies to launder clothes.

"No panhandling, no liquor, no radical talk" were the rules posted above the flaps of the big tent, which served as a sort of gateway to Camp Marks—as this whole place had been dubbed in honor of a local cop who had befriended the first Bonus Marchers. For the benefit of new arrivals who did not know how to read, or could not afford glasses, the same rules were barked out by the khaki-shirted myrmidons who were checking everyone's papers.

Papa had not gone in but had waited for Dawn, since she would need his credentials to be admitted. She found him reclining in a strip of shade alongside a tent, a wet bandanna on his forehead. She helped pull him to his feet. He made a remark about enjoying the nap, but she suspected that the long march in the July sun had knocked him flat. His breathing was labored, his sentences short. "No radical *talk*," he repeated as they made their way through the tent. It was warm in there and crowded, and smelled of unwashed bodies. There was a lending library where men were browsing, and dumps of donated clothing where ragged women appraised worn boys' dungarees and stained calico dresses at arm's length.

Papa led Dawn out into what she took for the main street of Camp Marks. The speaking platform was a hundred yards along. "Notice . . . it's not 'no Reds.' They just want us . . . to keep quiet. Fine. For now. Smart."

Dawn was of a mind that Papa might be reading too much into it—a common failing of Soviet intellectuals in America—but was distracted by a round of applause from the crowd of mostly new arrivals who had gathered around the platform. A speaker had just been introduced. At a distance Dawn took him for a senior military officer, but as they drew closer she noted that his khakis—though spotless, starched, and pressed—bore no insignia, and that they hung slack on a gaunt frame. His blond head was protected not by an officer's cap but by a fedora. "Gotta be Commander Waters," Papa said.

Waters was flanked by a couple of men also in khaki getups that did not quite rise to the description of uniform. They were junior, but they weren't young—few young men were in the camp since they were all vets of a war that had ended fifteen years ago. Younger dependents like Dawn and Silent Al were exceptional. Dawn could also see a cream-colored parasol up on the platform, and as they worked their way into the crowd she saw it was in the white-gloved grip of a tall lady who fanned herself from time to time with a copy of the *BEF News*. Perhaps because of this ladylike paragon, exposed on the platform; perhaps because of what Booker had said about turning heads; or perhaps because of the soggy warmth of the sun pounding the Anacostia Flats, Dawn felt the heat of many men's eyes on her. She was wearing a broad-brimmed straw hat, cowboy-style, which a man requested she take off. Not knowing how to take that, she instead moved laterally, skirting toward the edge of the crowd, and lost contact with Papa for a time.

"Commander" Waters (she understood now that the title was an affectation) gave a speech about how he had fought Pancho Villa and the Huns like every man jack here and found himself drifting around the Yakima Valley and Oregon doing honest work only to find himself jobless, and how he and a few hundred veterans had started the BEF in Portland only a few short weeks ago and ridden the rails from coast to coast, picking up supporters all the way, like a snowball rolling downhill. That part made for a good story. But then he wandered off into talk of how things were organized and who was in charge of what and when Congress was going to adjourn next. Dry-as-dust subject matter, strangely charged with emotion for him. She found her attention wandering. "He keeps resigning," explained an old-timer, "and refuses to come back until they give him his way."

"'Dictatorial powers,' I heard is what he asked for," said a new man.

"And was given. Only way to get anything done in an operation like this," said a third. This little debating society was quashed by rough, indignant voices. Waters talked of all the people who were helping them with food, clothes, and medical care, and introduced Mrs. Cahoon—the lady with the parasol—who stepped forward to applause and then addressed the small minority of women in the crowd, letting them know that there were actual proper houses where they could stay if they wanted to spare themselves and their children the rigors of Camp Marks, and telling them where to get donated clothes, of which they now had an embarrassment.

THEY HAD BROUGHT SURPLUS ARMY TENTS FROM CHICAGO. THEY PITCHED THESE AT THE limit of the camp, only to find themselves deeply embedded in it a day later as new arrivals continued to march in. Dawn awoke to reveille one morning and realized she'd already lost count of the days. For the feeling of the place was of a great thing happening, but nothing ever occurred. Yes, a bugler sounded reveille each morning. Some men fell in, out of habit, and did calisthenics and marched about. But they were an army with no guns, no chain of command, no enemy, and no mission. Between reveille and taps they consumed time with epidemics of rumor and the laborious framing of plans that were gradually forgotten as attention drifted to food. Small children were dying in the camp, and not from disease. Dawn had not been plump to begin with, but she had to borrow a leather punch to add some new holes to the belt she was using to keep her jeans from collapsing around her ankles.

The woman with the parasol turned up from time to time. Papa knew the correct spelling of her last name: Colquhoun. Maiden name Flynn. She was from a family of New York pols, Tammany Hall figures, who'd made a lot of money from Prohibition, and she'd married into a family rich from newspaper publishing. Papa, weak from a combination of hunger and the effect that the fetid atmosphere of the Anacostia Flats had on his lungs, kept sending Dawn on missions. "Try to get noticed by Ida Colquhoun," he said. So Dawn volunteered to help sort through the bales of old clothing that arrived from time to time at the Salvation Army tent, sometimes accompanied by Mrs. Colquhoun and sometimes not. The lady volunteers who staffed the place were known as Sallies.

Dawn's more important task took her across the drawbridge into D.C., where, in a Capitol Hill telegraph office, she penciled out the following cable to Montana: STRONG LOCAL DEMAND WOLF CIRCLE PREVENTION NEED MEN CHICAGO DELAY MORE EXPENSIVE THAN HASTE. She'd lain awake all night devising the wording. Seeing it penciled out on the Western Union form she feared it was too clever by half. The queer looks she was collecting from the men in their summer suits and the women in their pearls did nothing to ease her mind.

Just how ludicrously conspicuous Dawn was, was a thing difficult to explain to Papa. She entered into a sort of cosmetic bootstrapping project. Mrs. Colquhoun's donors were insensitive to Camp Marks's skewed sex ratio, and so there was a comic oversupply of women's attire. Dawn mined out a skirt that had probably been donated because it was unfashionably long. But on her frame it fell halfway between knee and ankle, which was the current style. She was no seamstress, but with a bit of work she was able to get it into a condition that, at least, would not cause fashionable girls to laugh at her from a block away. Then she found a blouse. It didn't matter that the sleeves were miles too short because she rolled them up in the summer heat anyway. Then a pair of shoes too small, but enough to get her to a shoe store, where she spent some of the Comintern's money on a pair that she could walk in. Thus attired, she returned to Western Union to collect the following return message: TWO MEN ON EB TOMORROW SAY HI BILLY BACH FORT MYER

"Who's Billy Bach?" Papa asked, back at Camp Marks, before feeding it to the fire. He'd already figured out that "EB" was the Empire Builder.

"Billy used to work in the polo stables around Gillette," Dawn said. "Local boy. A couple of years older than me, I think. I guess he must have enlisted."

"Politics?"

"Oh, his people are German Catholics, very traditional. The only thing we had in common was mucking out stables together."

"But your people stayed in touch with him."

"Yes." *It is what normal human beings do.*

"The economy *ist kaput,*" Papa said, filling in the rest. "The family dirt farm has blown off in the general direction of Nebraska. This peasant boy, his good judgment, if he ever had any, narcotized by some backwoods priest, enlists in the army as an alternative to starvation. It's discovered he knows everything about polo. Of course he would end up at Fort Myer."

Dawn's memory of Billy Bach was much more favorable than the picture that Papa seemed to be conjuring up in his head. She tried to let it roll off her back. "How does that follow?" she asked.

"Go there and you'll see. It's right across the Potomac. You can almost see it from here."

"Still. Aren't there other things I could be doing?"

By way of an answer, Papa let his gaze wander slowly around the camp. A black man and a white man were carrying the rusty hood of a Model T, obviously planning a shelter project. The white man slipped on some greasy mud and went down. Closer to the river, another man squatted over a slit trench, his anus bugling. "A tinderbox is full of fascinating potentialities," Papa said, "but until the spark is kindled, it is not such an interesting place."

"Okay," Dawn said, "but I'll be surprised if Billy remembers me."

"That's not why I want you to go. I want you to go because Fort Myer is the closest cavalry base to central D.C. and so that is where the counterattack will come from. I am asking you to conduct military espionage."

"I need a haircut," she blurted. "A brassiere. Kotex. I know you'll say they are luxuries. But I can't conduct espionage when other women are picking me out from a quarter of a mile away as some kind of vagrant." And she was ready with other arguments she had marshaled, but a switch went on in Papa's head and he cut her off with "Tradecraft."

"What?"

"Of course you can spend money on tradecraft. Hell, you might as well, since we can't spend it on food." He referred to the fact that all food at Camp Marks was prepared and served in a communal mess. A week earlier, some pork had come in from sympathetic New York City meat-packers; for the past three days, however, the Bonus Army had subsisted on cracked wheat.

"In fact, you might just want to move out of this place," Papa went on. "WESL has a decent squat at around Thirteenth and B Southwest." WESL was the unfortunate name of the Workers' Ex-Servicemen's League, the Red wing of the Bonus Army. "Rusty would take you in."

"If I get lice," she said, "then I'll move."

Pages of old *Washington Posts* drifted around camp, read and re-read until they were torn into strips and used for toilet paper. Papa had eyes only for the front pages, with their news of FDR's nomination, Hoover's desperate gambits to prop up the rotting corpse of capitalism. Red revolution in Peru and Brazil, the rise of the Steel Helmets in Germany. More popular, hence harder to come by, were the sports pages. Mostly these covered the deeds of Ruth and Gehrig on the first page, racing on the second. When polo was covered it was invariably on the first page, shouldering aside the minor baseball stories. But unlike baseball games, which happened every day, polo tournaments came and went; some issues of the *Post* were stuffed with information, others had nothing. Dawn assembled a pocket archive of polo coverage and studied it while on the streetcar, waiting for the hairdresser, getting soup and a sandwich at a lunch counter. These were all stages in the bootstrapping. The streetcar wouldn't stop for an obvious vagrant. A girl with lice in her hair would be ejected from the beauty parlor. The coffee shop might not serve a solitary young woman who wasn't up to a certain standard of grooming. The lingerie saleswoman looked askance at her but, seeing the fashionably short haircut, gave her the benefit of the doubt. Undergirded by the new brassiere, she did not feel out of place at Woodward & Lothrop buying a blouse that actually fit. There the scents and hues on display in Cosmetics caught her attention, but she thought better of embarking on any such experiments now, without a mother or a girlfriend to let her know when she was making a fool of herself. The objective—the reason this could be passed off to the Comintern as tradecraft—was to draw as little attention as possible. She felt she'd got it right when her next visit to Western Union earned her no looks save the kind any six-foot-in-heels girl had to get used to.

It was a lot of coming and going, and at Papa's suggestion she took advantage of it to familiarize herself with the other Bonus Army bases around the city. The two most important were Camp Glassford, named after the vet-friendly D.C. police chief, and the WESL squat, where most of the Communists were staying.

Camp Glassford was directly west of the Capitol on the south side of Pennsylvania Avenue. She had been told as much but, until she went there and saw it, could not believe how close it was. Other than a few hundred yards of trees and grass, nothing stood between the Capitol and the abandoned Ford dealership that served as Camp Glassford's HQ.

The WESL squat was distributed over a square block a short distance southeast of the Washington Monument, nearer the White House than the Capitol, and not nearly as conspicuous as Camp Glassford. In addition to those two there were several other buildings around town crammed with Bonus Army marchers.

From those yellowed *Post* pages she learned the names of the local polo teams: the Fort Humphreys Engineers, the Sixteenth Field Artillery. The 110th. Two War Department teams, the Blues and the Whites. The Quantico Marines. But the best teams were the Greens and the Yellows of the Third Cavalry, based at Fort Myer. She scanned the scores, read the stories to get a sense of who the best players were: Davis, Meany, Patton, Macphail, Truscott. Mostly captains and majors. The big matches and tournaments were held at Potomac Park, which was the tongue of land you looked at when you stood at the edge of Camp Marks and gazed across Anacostia Creek.

Fort Myer was farther up the river, synonymous to most with Arlington Cemetery. So it was there that she went on a streetcar mostly full of tourists, if that was the right word for widows and parents carrying flowers to lay on graves. Myer was a pocket pistol of a base, half planted in dead soldiers, so she'd really have had to work at it to get lost. Its back half supported the usual hierarchy of barracks and junior and senior officers' housing, skewed toward the top end since this was where the army's top brass lived. These surrounded open ground policed for stray leaves and litter by enlisted men. To one end was a whole equine civilization: massed stables combed by lanes where horses were being led to and fro by grooms. Some were cavalry mounts, others polo ponies. The latter, she figured, ought to be finished with their afternoon trot and should be getting groomed, munching a light snack of hay as amuse-bouche for their 5 P.M. graining. Unlike bigger mounts that could chow down a few big meals a day, polo ponies had small stomachs and required as many as half a dozen separate feedings of grain, with hay put down in between to tide them over. The Greens and the Yellows would each require two dozen ponies in tournament condition, plus several younger ones still learning the ropes and a few retirees for training new players. The feeding and the exercising and the grooming and the mucking kept a lot of men employed.

A walled pit with a wooden horse in the center anchored that part of the grounds devoted to polo. Beyond it Dawn saw the flimsy breakaway goal posts, the boards set down to delineate the field of play. A few helmeted officers cantered about whirling mallets, unwinding at day's end with an informal club chukker. Wanting no truck with officers, she found her way into the stable mews.

The only American army base she had visited before was a cavalry fort on the high plains, a relic of the Indian wars. There, an unescorted young woman appearing in the stables would have created a sensation, if not a riot. Here, it seemed to be an everyday occurrence to judge from the way the grooms reacted, or didn't. She approached a private leading a pony back to its stable but hesitated to ask about Billy, suddenly afraid that he wouldn't remember her. But before she could say a word, she heard a voice back in a nearby stable calling out, "Do my eyes deceive me or is that Dawn Rae, all growed-up?"

Billy Bach was all growed-up too. Probably six-three, and so much stronger in the shoulders and the jaw that she might not have recognized him. He stopped at attention three paces off and gave her a wondering look up and down. Perhaps her bootstrapping project had not altogether miscarried. She extended her right hand. He looked uneasily at his. "There's nowhere that hand could've been that would trouble me, you of all men know that, Billy," she said.

"Well, now that you put it that way," he answered, and stepped forward to shake her hand with greater than normal vigor and persistency. It was good—no, it was a joy—to see a man who was young, who was strong, not starving, not ragged, not devoting all his waking hours to grievance. Like being back on a ranch. Papa's voice in her head told her it was all founded on pitiless exploitation. But she needed a vacation from Papa's voice.

Billy's face shifted around. "Heard about your ma. I am more sorry than I can say. So young and all, so healthy."

"Thank you, Billy. I got some time with her. It was sweet."

"In Chicago."

"Yes."

"Dawn Rae, I don't know how to say it, but—this ain't Chicago."

This tripped her up for a moment and then she laughed in a way that drew glances from grooms and whinnies from their equine spectators.

"Billy, either I had forgot about your wit, or the army issued you some when you signed up."

"Army's a little short on that," he confided, "though there are some clever fellas in the Third Cav, I must say. Real aristocrats."

"Didn't know those two things went together."

"Not always. Remember that poor little viscount in Wyoming? But you'd be surprised by some of 'em."

Billy looked about, the first time he'd had eyes for anything but Dawn. Down the lane, an NCO was smoking a cigarette, looking at them curiously.

"I know I'm getting you in terrible trouble."

"Not so terrible if you don't mind my working while we chew the fat."

She ended up standing outside the stable door, watching him at a demure remove as he inspected the pony's feet. He bent down to sniff at one curiously, and she caught herself smiling. She gathered that these were the stables of the Yellows, currently the number-one team in the area, and as she could see, uncommonly well mounted. No army in the world would pay for ponies such as these; they must be the private property of rich officers.

"Some beauties in here," she remarked.

"I'll say," he said, looking right at her.

She answered sharply, "I'm in town with my pa. You never met him."

"Heard about him," Billy said.

"All lies," she joked.

"Bonus Army?"

"Yes."

"Well . . . not all of those Reds served their country when they were called. But your pa did though, didn't he?"

"Yes, and collected a Purple Heart for his troubles."

"So I reckon he's got as much of a right to his bonus as any other. I'm with the Bonus Marchers. Most of the men here are. As long as they keep the peace."

"They are ever so particular about doing that."

"Commander Waters? That the fella's name?"

"Yes."

"What sort of a man is he?"

"He's a man in an unusual spot," she said. "This thing kinda happened around him, in a freight yard in Oregon, and here he is trying to figure out what to do with twenty thousand hungry men on a mud flat."

"I wouldn't want to be in his shoes."

"Nor me."

"Shame there's no work for 'em."

"That it is." But this was verging on politics, which she was sick of, so she turned the conversation to Billy's family, and what had led to his ending up here. It was not a long conversation—perhaps twenty minutes. Mess call approached. He walked her to a shuttle bus that would get her back to the streetcar, and they parted with a handshake a little more decorous than the first. He had her address now, for it was possible to receive mail at the Salvation Army tent, and she had his. He said nothing of what might occur next, but if he didn't ask her out, she'd be shocked.

She was halfway back to Camp Marks before she realized that she had forgotten to collect any military intelligence.

IN THE MIDDLE OF THE NIGHT SHE WAS AWAKENED BY A BUGLE PLAYING A DITTY THAT SHE had heard before, in talkies and on the radio, but she knew not its coded army meaning.

"Assembly," Papa said, the word catching in his gullet. He sat up on the cot that he had improvised to keep his ass out of the Anacostia mud, reached for the beat-up saucepan they used for a chamber pot, and hawked something into it. "They're sounding Assembly."

They were all sleeping in their clothes anyway. They pulled on shoes and began shuffling toward the platform, which was vaguely lit by kerosene lamps. But as many were running back the other way as toward it. One of these practically knocked Booker down, and she had to grab him by the arms to keep him from splattering into the mud. "The Reds are coming!" he said as explanation and apology.

Neither Booker nor any of the other Reds in their group had an answer ready for that.

"Gonna fetch my hickory," the man continued, and ran into the dark. He was only one grain in an hourglass. In a dark, muddled process that would have been excruciating to anyone who actually was worried about oncoming Reds, most of Camp Marks assembled round the platform, armed with ax handles, canes, lengths of pipe, and bricks. Through it all Commander Waters stood above, first at attention, then gradually sagging to at-ease. From time to time he would check his watch or turn his head to receive a scrap of news from one of his khaki Praetorians. Sporadically one of these would boom down the steps and be engulfed by the more ardent men who'd pushed their way to the front. Deputizing a dozen or a score, he would lead them off toward some part of the camp's perimeter thought to be vulnerable. Papa, Booker, and Silent Al—the Red triumvirate—took it all in without comment. Nothing was ever explained. Commander Waters never found the right moment to address the crowd but slowly faded to an anonymous form in the sepia glow of the kerosene. The bugler never sounded Recall. "Drill," "False alarm," and "Ran 'em off with their tails between their legs" were the most frequently circulated verdicts. Each member of the Bonus Army made his own decision when to stumble back to his cot.

In the light of the morning Papa was most pleased with Dawn's work at Fort Myer. What she saw as a failure to attend to the matter at hand, he construed as shrewd cultivation of a source. He exhorted her both to follow up aggressively and to avoid seeming too forward. Dawn thought she hid her exasperation well, and took this as a cue to check the mail and visit Western Union. Passing the mess tent she noted a haggard Commander Waters in some sort of confab with his favorite men. No mail awaited her in the Salvation Army tent, but she got drawn into a shirt-sorting project, the objective of which was to pull out anything that was, or that could be made, khaki. After putting in a decent amount of effort she slipped out and took the streetcar across the bridge to the Western Union office she'd been using—by no means the most convenient to Camp Marks, but busy enough that, according to Papa, she might go unnoticed, and/or her connection to the BEF would not be scented. Tradecraft. She had her doubts. The staff already knew her and handed over a cablegram from Chicago before she identified herself.

APPOINTMENT WITH TOMS SON FRIDAY

She cabled back the address of the man in Chicago to whom Papa had entrusted the down payment, providing a false name, and then cabled that fellow to let him know to expect a visit from two gentlemen asking about Mr. So-and-So. Friday was three days out.

Then it was back to the Salvation Army tent, where the Sallies were conducting a scientific experiment to see if white shirts could be made khaki with tea, coffee, or some admixture thereof.

"It means 'dirt' in Urdu," Papa said. "How difficult can it be?" But having delivered this morsel of intelligence, Dawn was already slipping into the tent to read a letter that had reached her from Billy in the afternoon post.

The next morning she wrote him back, accepting his invitation to go watch *Scarface* in Dupont Circle on Friday evening.

QUERY SHIPMENT DETAILS reached her the next morning.

DONATIONS CLOTHING REQUIRED IN BULK URGENT was her answer. And then she was off to the Library of Congress to learn about Blackshirts and Brownshirts for Papa. Though their origins reached back to the close of the Great War, and as such were chronicled in books, their recent doings could only be gleaned from newspapers. So it was that she spent a few days scanning through back issues, looking for stories about the Sturmabteilung and the Stahlhelm, the Bund der Frontsoldaten and the Squadristi. Chicago, with all of its connections to Germany, had good coverage of doings in that country, and Italy was well reported on by London papers, maybe because journalists enjoyed being posted there. Even so, it was a needle-in-a-haystack project. Papa mightn't have been best pleased had he known how much time she spent reading polo scores from England or lurid crime reportage from the Hog Butcher for the World. Stories of kidnappings, railway mishaps, and drownings became her entertainment as she waited for the temperature to drop on the Anacostia Flats, for cables to come in from Chicago, for her date with Billy Bach. She read all of the stories about the Lindbergh kidnapping and about the exploits of Amelia Earhart and the latest high-altitude balloon records, and of a curious couple in the Midwest named Bonnie Parker and Clyde Barrow; the latter was at large and thought to be planning an assault on a Texas prison farm where he'd once been incarcerated, the former had lately been let out of jail after a jury had declined to indict her for something. She thought Papa would be cheered up by the splendid image of a mass jailbreak from a prison farm, a battalion of shovel-swinging shock troops for the Revolution.

YES TWO DOZEN read a cable in her pocket as she sat in the cinema next to Billy Bach watching *Scarface*.

This was the most interesting film she had ever seen, for a few reasons.

The North Side/South Side division, Italians on the south, Irishmen on the north, was amusingly simplistic compared to Chicago's actual turf map. But she had to admit it worked in the movie.

Scarface was in the habit of looking out his window at a big electric sign, shaped like a globe, emblazoned THE WORLD IS YOURS. It put Dawn in mind of the fact that she had been all the way around the globe before her eighth birthday and it caused her to wonder whether she might ever again journey abroad. Or would she settle down in Montana or Chicago, or—it was not too soon to ask—marry Billy Bach and live out her days as an army wife?

To her surprise—and, she suspected, Billy's—the movie depicted adult relationships between boys and girls in a way that she found uncomfortably direct. It was nothing she had not seen, or at least heard, in the kommunalka. But it was supposed to be different here. Bourgeois morality might be arbitrary superstition. But at least it was rules. If those were being waved off now, it raised the question of what would happen—how she and Billy would look at each other—when the movie ended and the lights came up.

But these concerns were minor compared to the movie's central theme, which was the Thompson submachine gun. Not just as a piece of hardware but as the subject of some men's obsession, and a catalyst and a symbol for abrupt shifts of power. "Hey, lookit!" Scarface exclaimed while lying on the floor of a restaurant being machine-gunned by furious Irishmen. "They got machine guns you can carry! If I had some of them I can run the whole works in a month!" The film showed a decent respect for the amount of time and manual dexterity needed to load magazines, good illumination and clean, level surfaces being of the essence. Dawn had forgotten the exact sequence of steps needed to ready the weapon for firing and was glad of the cinematic tutorial. All of the Communists would have to come here and watch this movie before two dozen of the weapons showed up at Potomac Yard concealed in bales of donated clothing.

Or so she thought through most of the movie. But at the very end, the tommy gun was overmastered by a weapon even more powerful: tear gas. Bursting fountains of it filling rooms, making the most potent gun seem toyish. Driven out of his apartment, Scarface died in the dark on a wet streetcar track under a crossfire of white lights, engulfed by cops who had not just tommy guns but Browning automatic rifles.

The lights came up and Dawn forced herself to look at Billy, expecting great awkwardness around the boy/girl material. But as they walked to the streetcar stop, it became clear that he had seen an altogether different movie. A movie about cars, and car chases, and running gun battles between cars that were chasing each other. "That's the future," he told her. "That's what I'm gonna work on, Dawn. Except better."

"What are you going to work on, Billy?"

"The *Landesjäger*." Which meant nothing to her; but the one thing she took back to Camp Marks was the look on his face when he said the word, and the way he pronounced it: in the high German that his parents spoke at home.

PAPA SIGHED AT THE NUMBER—HE'D BEEN HOPING FOR MORE THAN TWO DOZEN TOMMY guns, apparently—but gave her the name and address of the man who was holding the rest of the money. The next morning, Saturday, she went to Western Union and penciled that out on a form, along with the stipulation ASSEMBLED. For in the movie the guns had come out of their packing crates ready to fire, which was pretty much how Dad wanted it.

She set her pencil down and gazed out the window before sending the cable off to Chicago. It was very strange to have seen this world in a movie one night and be part of it for real the next day. "These fellas bootleg machine guns like they bootleg booze," the cop in the movie had complained, and she'd been glad of the theater's being dark, since her face had gone hot. She suspected that Papa had seen the movie and somehow convolved it with his plans.

Now her cousins were sticking their necks out in a Chicago infinitely more complex than the one in the movie. The cop had complained: "They had some excuse for glorifying our old Western bad men. They met in the middle of the street at high noon and waited for each other to draw. But these things sneak up, shoot a guy in the back, and then run away."

SEE SCARFACE, she added, then took the form up to the window.

The next morning, Private Bach came to Camp Marks to pick her up for a date. He did a fine job of making it mysterious, suggesting that she stand at the edge of the water at 0700 wearing "something nice." She did so, then ended up waiting for half an hour, giving her time to parse that remark in all of its possible meanings. How nice, exactly, did it need to be? Was she going to be compared against other girls wearing things that, in their world, were nice? Did Billy mean to imply that being nicely attired was out of the ordinary for her?

He emerged from the mist on the creek in an olive-drab rowboat, turning around every so often to get his bearings. When he caught sight of her, he began to row harder, and soon ran the thing aground. She took her shoes off and squished out to meet him, covering a hundred feet of stuff that was neither land nor water. Then she trailed her feet over the side as he rowed, letting the water clean them off, if it was correct to say that anything in contact with Anacostia Creek could ever be clean.

This was not obvious from water level, where everything was fore-shortened and commingled. But three channels, separated by two narrow points of land, came together before Camp Marks. From east to west, the three channels were Anacostia Creek, the Washington Channel, and the Potomac. The strips of land separating them were Buzzard Point and Po-tomac Park. Of these, the former supported Fort McNair, a small post, the site of the Army War College. Parts of it were all of a quarter of a mile from Camp Marks, and indeed Commander Waters might have chosen to site his primary bivouac on the Anacostia Flats precisely because it was within shouting, or at least bugling, distance of an army base. McNair had recreational facilities, including a little marina where soldiers could borrow rowboats and canoes. This explained the unusual and, Dawn had to admit, dashing style of Billy's arrival.

He did not, however, row her back to Fort McNair but rather swung round Buzzard Point and up into the Washington Channel, a waterway about a thousand feet wide running between army territory on the east and a golf course on the west. Half an hour's row up this took them to a little boat landing in Potomac Park, where Billy was able to berth the rowboat.

From there they walked to the polo grounds, where a tournament was under way. Private Bach, who was there in a supporting capacity, let her in through a side gate so that she could watch for free. Directly he was assigned tasks by shouting, red-faced men. There was no really appropriate place for an unescorted civilian to stand. Apparently Dawn's hat, which she had plucked from the Salvation Army dress-up box, made her look sufficiently respectable that she was mistaken for a paying customer who'd lost her way. A colored enlisted man showed her to the grandstand and extended his hand and would not leave off until she had gone up there.

She might have looked decent to him, but to most there, she was so far out of her league as to suppress conversation wherever she went. Not so much, though, as to be worth the fuss of ejecting her.

Polo, seen from the spectators' gallery, turned out to be exorbitantly social. Chukkers were separated by breaks long enough for the players to get fresh ponies and the fans to get refreshments. Her nose told her that Prohibition was being flouted, and the behavior of some confirmed it. Between matches were breaks long enough to get little sandwiches.

It was during one of these, as she was on her way into the ladies', that she came face-to-face with Ida Colquhoun, who was coming out, freshly powdered.

Dawn hid behind the brim of her hat and dodged round. But when she emerged Mrs. Colquhoun was loitering outside the toilet. "Ida," she announced, as if this would be news, and strode to the attack, extending her gloved hand. "You're the girl from Camp Marks."

"Dawn Glendive," she said, using the name of a town in Montana.

"I might not have recognized you, Dawn, save for that lovely hat. I spotted it in the tent the other day and I was saying to one of the Sallies what a shame its charms were to be wasted on the population of Camp Marks. I'm so pleased you had the good taste to pluck it out and make it yours—it does complement your eyes very nicely."

Dawn was armed against anything save pleasantness. She mumbled something. Ida took that as license to link elbows with her and begin powering back to her place in the grandstand. "I do hope you'll sit the next chukker at least with me; I should so like to hear your ideas on the present situation at the camp . . . oh my, the Sixteenth Artillery has some spirited mounts, don't they?"

Being on Ida's arm explained Dawn's being here: another daft char-
ity project. Mrs. Colquhoun seemed to swing a big enough stick that the
sorts who had been throwing bum looks at Dawn were suddenly trying
to converse with her. The Bonus Army would have been a difficult topic.
Dawn worked the conversation round to western polo ranches—never
mind what she did, or how she got, there. This gave them all they really
wanted, which was a way to break the ice and talk of polo. She was able to
sit back and let the men take over and talk of the very ranches where she
and Billy had worked, and the ponies they knew from there.

Once the men had wrenched the conversational steering wheel, as it
were, from the women and jammed the gas pedal down, Dawn felt a light
touch on her arm from Ida. "Do you play, Dawn?"

"Oh, no, I—"

"I mean, quite obviously there is no facility at Camp Marks. But your
duties at the ranch, as you've described them, included some riding. Some
use of the mallet."

"Yes."

"You might be interested to know that there are women's teams."

"I'd heard, but—"

"Barely. It can be difficult to field two entire sides. More often than
not they fill out their numbers with men who, I'm afraid, don't take the
women's game very seriously."

Dawn couldn't help glancing at the heavy, self-assured men who had
assumed responsibility for their conversation.

"Yes," Ida said, "you see the problem."

Dawn looked at Ida, who gave her a lovely smile and said, "Could you
play tomorrow?"

BLUE JEANS AND WORK BOOTS SUFFICED. HER JOB WAS TO FILL OUT A SCRATCH TEAM THAT
existed to give Ida's neighbor's daughter's side something to practice on.
They played in some other girl's "backyard" that easily accommodated a
regulation 300-by-200-yard grounds. Her teammates were a sixty-year-
old uncle suffering from Parkinson's but cheerful and game; a teenage boy

who had just begun learning the game three weeks prior and who was too paralyzed by the sight of girls' bottoms in riding breeches to be of much use; and Katherine, a well-bred young woman loaned to them from the other team, which was called the Lady Blues. The point was to give the Lady Blues some time playing together. Katherine was the least proficient, and, like most novices, bewildered.

The Lady Blues, to their credit, immediately scored six consecutive goals. Dawn gave up on ever making anything of her own side and tried to understand what the Lady Blues were after. She appointed herself to the position of back and began riding off their number one, who was aggressive and a dab hand with the mallet but lacked agility. Dawn's mount was a little hard-mouthed but a great runner, and so she was able to make a few good runs up on offense. The Lady Blues won 8–0.

Dawn had already resolved to walk straight to the horseshoe driveway after the match and climb back into the chauffeured car that had brought her. Not that she hated these people. But almost nothing was more pathetic than a girl in her station waiting to be noticed by the likes of the Lady Blues. The car, however, was driverless. Ida ran her down, fetched her back, and made her sit in a gazebo with all of the other players, being served lemonade and cucumber sandwiches by colored servants.

She sat next to their number two—the best player—who had scored seven of the goals. This was Adele, Ida's neighbor. Through mysterious preverbal signals in posture and glance, Adele and Dawn had determined that they liked each other, a state of affairs that would endure whether or not they ever had an actual conversation. Adele confirmed as much, and Dawn reciprocated, through microscopic shifts in posture and silent pacts as to what they would and wouldn't attend to. Across the table was Patricia, the number one, looking blown and battered since Dawn, who outweighed her by thirty pounds, had spent the last two chukkers riding her off. "My breeches!" she exclaimed, and made Dawn see several small holes in the fabric.

"Those hooks on your boots," Adele explained, glancing down. Dawn noticed that strands of beige stuff were dangling from the lacing hooks.

"We shall have to get Dawn proper riding boots for next time," Ida said.

This was the first Dawn had heard of the possibility of a next time. No one else seemed surprised.

Patricia—who lived here—still seemed a bit put out.

Since no one else was going to say it—and since she'd already been invited back—Dawn said, "Sorry if I hustled you too much. But listen. Your pony is beautiful. I know why you're in love with him. But he's too big for a number one. You're petite. Your game needs to be agile. If you can't slip the back, you're a liability to your side. If you were a man, you'd have been told this. I'm telling you."

BACK AT CAMP, PAPA WANTED TO KNOW ALL. FATHERLY PRIDE, ANTHROPOLOGICAL FASCINA-tion, and political outrage were hustling one another inside his head, producing results she found tiresome. Small children were starving to death within a hundred yards of this campfire. Rich women were looking to her to get their polo team sorted. And she was embroiled in a plot to ship two dozen submachine guns to the nation's capital, where they would somehow topple the government. She would do anything for Papa but accept responsibility for how he was feeling.

"I am going back on Wednesday afternoon," she said. "They are practicing for an exhibition game Saturday, and they have a long ways to go."

"Well, it'd be a terrible shame if they made a poor showing," Papa said.

She did not care for his petulance. She knew how this looked: that she was a shallow girl, distracted, insufficiently attentive to the requirements of the global workers' proletarian revolution. But there was no getting around the fact that the interactions she was having with Billy Bach and with the Lady Blues were incalculably more fascinating to her than anything happening at Camp Marks. The exception that proved the rule was Silent Al, who had his eye upon her as always, and seemed to have some awareness of what she was thinking. She had not the faintest idea of whether Al would make a move on her anytime soon, but she had to admit that it would have been simpler, and less likely to end in disaster, than trying to be Billy Bach's girl, or Adele's friend.

"You wanted me to get noticed by Mrs. Colquhoun. I did. This happened. If you want, I can give her a copy of *Das Kapital* and a stern talking-to."

This produced a wounded look from Papa, but it also ended the conversation, which was all she wanted.

Most of her communications with Billy Bach were through letters. More and more, his concerned machinery. The movie's car chases had rekindled his interest in engines and wheels, its startlingly direct scenes in bedrooms spooked him. Machines it was, then. Armored cars and tanks were the future of the cavalry. Learning to change their oil and repair bent axles was the new stable-mucking and hoof-picking. He had been accepted for a training program. Promotions awaited. Which might be a backhanded way of telling her that he was going to be collecting a steady paycheck for a long time. If so, she ought to be flattered. But she was numb to it. Complications, obliquely mentioned in cablegrams, were delaying the tommy guns. Her riding muscles, unused for a year, hurt so much she could barely squat over a latrine. Ida wanted her shoe size, her inseam. She went to the library, the only place she could hear herself think. Bonnie and Clyde had gone to ground. Hogging the crime headlines was Pretty Boy Floyd, who had massacred a bunch of cops in Kansas City. The Brown- and the Blackshirts had a British admirer in one Oswald Mosley, who was organizing Fascists there. Some other Brit named Chadwick had discovered a thing called a neutron. Schleswig-Holstein looked to go Nazi in the coming election. Harvests were going to fail in Russia. Japanese were being vaguely frightful in the new country they had made called Manchukuo.

Dawn played an afternoon chukker with the Lady Blues. Her thighs were still killing her. Ida had not been able to round up proper boots in her size but had found some black men's boots that would do. Blacking rubbed off on opposing players' breeches and was not *comme il faut*. Patricia wore her torn pair, so it didn't matter.

Dawn had assumed that this would be her last contact with the Lady

Blues, but it turned out that their exhibition was to be played at Fort Myer, preparatory to a ball that the Third Cavalry was throwing to commemorate the 35th anniversary of the charge up San Juan Hill. Billy had already invited her to the ball. Ida now asked her to show up earlier in the day to support the Lady Blues. So over the next two days Dawn divided her energies between gun-running and trying to turn something she'd jerked out of the Salvation Army bin into a ball gown. The Sallies were of inestimable help. At Camp Marks there was no one with whom she could discuss polo, and only a few were privy to the illegal submachine gun project, but the Sallies had no trouble at all engaging with a ball gown, especially given the character of the party: both patriotic and glamorous. Efforts were made to impart a Cuban flair. It all went quite over Dawn's head.

At daybreak on Saturday, she stood on the street that ran past the front of the Salvation Army tent, dressed in jeans and boots, waiting for Ida's chauffeur. The ball gown and accoutrements were packed in a big old suitcase. Keeping an eye on her from their posts flanking the tent's entrance were two stalwart members of the Khaki Shirts: a new organization whose existence had been made public, and explained to fascinated newspapermen, by Commander Waters the day before. Following the examples of the great leaders of Europe, he was taking advantage of the unique situation into which fate had precipitated him to form a corps that would put the wasted energies of unemployed men to work in nation-building activities. Dawn hid her amusement at the way these two clicked their heels and saluted as the black car glided up to collect her. One of them stepped out to help heave the suitcase into the trunk.

Conveying twenty-four ponies from their stables around Northern Virginia to Fort Myer was a considerable project, handled by the men whom the girls' daddies kept on payroll to groom their horses and drive their vehicles. Moreover, their gracious hosts at Fort Myer had made a number of men available to the Lady Blues, and Billy had volunteered to be one of them. Nonetheless, Dawn had as much work as she wished to shoulder, managing all of the crises that emerged when ten high-strung parents, pre-coiffed for the ball, tried to get five rich girls in the saddle on unfamiliar turf while hobnobbing with whatever high-ranking brass decided to wander by and say hello. Attention was lavished upon Blanche, the number three, who had come down with female problems, described in powder-room bulletins at least as cryptic as the cables Dawn had been receiving from Chicago, and hardly less ominous than the news from Schleswig-Holstein. Number three was generally the role of the least experienced player, so they replaced the poor girl with Katherine, their understudy. Dressed as a sort of ranch hand in her desperate old jeans and a khaki shirt stolen from the Khaki Shirts, Dawn found herself in the saddle, showing Katherine a few basic moves. There was also work to be done exercising the ponies, getting them used to the new sights and scents of these grounds. As this went on she found herself under the gaze of curious cavalrymen beginning to take seats in the grandstand. Billy's eye was ever on her. That plus the natural movements of riding made it a warm morning.

The opposing side filtered onto the grounds. Fort Myer could have fielded a terrific squad and made up for it with a colossal handicap, but the game still would have been one-sided and dull. Instead they had put together a decent enough, but not crushingly formidable, team: Nunn, a colonel with a white mustache. Gatacre, a British officer, stationed here as some sort of liaison. Asquith, a lieutenant, extraordinarily well mounted. And Mrs. Pierce, the wife of a Third Cavalry officer, apparently quite the supporter of ladies' polo and a friend of the Lady Blues.

Gradually the elements of the match formed up on the grounds, and supernumerary horses and grooms retreated to the stables. Dawn found a good place to stand and watch near one corner of the stands. Remarks were made to the effect that the match was all in good fun and not to be taken awfully seriously, except for the part about fostering fresh players. The expressions on the Lady Blues' faces did not show anything like that gaiety. "Darn it!" called Lieutenant Asquith, the young man on the pretty horse. "I'd been hoping to boost my handicap!" Asquith had been quite busy during warm-ups tittupping up to members of the Lady Blues to give advice for which they had not asked. He was especially keen to show them how to hold their mallets, which called for a lot of hand-holding and arm-stroking. When not making himself thus useful he would ride over to his friends, who were sitting together, and say things to them that produced eruptions of salty laughter. They applauded and shouted whenever Asquith thought up a reason to go galloping past. Yet for all of that, Dawn did not think him a very good rider. Something was not right about his position in the saddle. His hand was stiff and heavy and likely to spoil the beautiful horse's mouth very soon if no one talked to him about it. He was not cruel in a way that would have drawn the notice of this horse-loving crowd, but insensitive in a way that, in the long run, might be more callous than beating it. She could only assume that he had brought servants with him, expert grooms who toiled to undo the damage he inflicted upon the animal's training with every moment he spent in the saddle. She thought it remarkable that his friends were oblivious to this. What cavalry could employ such officers? But then she saw it: they were the new breed, the ones who would be driving around in cars and tanks maintained by Billy. Everything in this horse world would become as anachronistic as powdered wigs, and it wouldn't matter that they did it badly.

The match was decorous enough, with outbreaks of fine play on both sides. The personalities and styles of the players began to impress themselves on the crowd and to become topics of remark, and later of emotional response. Patricia had swapped her prize mount for a pony that was nondescript but nimble. She soon made a habit of slipping Colonel Nunn's halfhearted attempts to ride her off. She didn't score—Adele did—but she did handle some balls sent her way by Adele and by the Lady Blues' back, a husky, determined college student named Irene. Irene, though, largely had her hands full guarding Lieutenant Asquith, the number two. He didn't do a lot of scoring—clearly he was under orders to hold back—but did accomplish a huge amount of dashing about. It was unclear to Dawn whether Asquith intended this as comic relief. For clues, she watched Gatacre, the British officer. He watched Asquith with an unreadable expression, but Dawn suspected that he loathed the man. Gatacre's preordained fate in the game, as number one, was to be hustled and ridden off by Irene, which he accepted with grace. It looked as if he were giving her pointers during lulls, zooming his hands about and talking animatedly while Irene watched and asked good questions.

From the way Ida and Mrs. Pierce were looking at each other, it all seemed to be coming off as they'd hoped until the final seconds of the fifth chukker. Katherine was riding after the ball. Irene was three lengths behind and in a position to receive a backhander, which she could then send up the field to Patricia, who had broken free of the exhausted Colonel Nunn. Still lacking in confidence, Katherine kept looking back over her shoulder at Irene, trying to work out the shot. But all of a sudden Asquith was there, dangerously close to committing a foul, a combination of riding too aggressively and failing to control his exasperated horse. It went all wrong; Katherine's mount stopped hard and her mallet swung short of the ball. Irene kept on coming, perhaps thinking to collect the ball on her way past. The umpire blew his whistle, whether to call a foul on Asquith or signal the end of the chukker wasn't clear. Katherine did not hear it. She tried the backhander a second time and again missed. Her mallet swung up behind her and caught Irene in the face. An audible crunch and a ghastly uproar in the stands. Irene, both hands clapped over her face, gamely steered for the clubhouse with her knees. Dawn, who'd seen worse, was as interested in the crowd's reaction as in the medical/dental consequences. She'd had her eye on a block of more senior Third Cav officers, majors and colonels. She suspected they had only come here under duress. They had looked bored in the early going. Now they'd become as excited about the game and its personalities as anyone else, and seemed quite let down about poor Irene, who had become a crowd favorite.

The verdict was that Irene might lose one or more teeth and needed to see a dentist straightaway. Katherine was almost in a worse state than Irene, and took much calming down. The interval before the last chukker was padded out to allow the Lady Blues time to regroup. A major from the Third Cavalry presented himself and asked, in the courtliest way, if he might be of assistance.

Dawn found herself in a broom closet with Ida and Mrs. Pierce.

"We can fill Irene's place with a volunteer from the crowd," Ida said, "and shall do so if needed. But—" And here, by a look, she seemed to pass the ball, as it were, to Mrs. Pierce.

"Mrs. Colquhoun says you are qualified to play," said Mrs. Pierce in an impressive Southern accent. "The matter of attire may be overlooked. I should much rather see the match played out by an all-girl side than accept a chivalrous gesture. Would you be willing?"

Dawn was willing. She took Irene's place at back. The crowd, which had started bored, then had become interested, then had moaned at the drama around Irene, was now enlivened by the appearance of the mystery girl in blue jeans. Dawn was on a bigger mount, a fifteen-hander, but well trained. She could tell she bestrode a lot of money. The only fly in the ointment was a certain skittishness; clearly this animal had grown up on a farm in horse country and never seen more than a bridge table's worth of humans together in one place. But he was fundamentally level-headed and Dawn thought he could be managed.

A chukker lasted seven minutes. She felt like making the most of it. A strong sense had overtaken her in recent days of bad things about to happen. For all she knew, she might end up in prison. The freedom and power she felt on this beautiful horse was not a thing to waste.

The opposing side treaded gingerly at first; they felt bad about Irene and knew nothing of Dawn. She was able to intercept a slow-rolling pass from Asquith toward Gatacre and turn upfield at a gallop, just shy of the sideline, shepherding the ball with dribbling strokes as she looked for Adele or Patricia. The latter was screened by Colonel Nunn, looking alive on a fresh pony. On a smaller mount Dawn might have been tempted to turn in and ride for the goal, but she was cautious of trying it on an unfamiliar horse. In any case Adele broke clear of Mrs. Pierce right in the center. Dawn turned in slightly and made the obvious pass, perhaps a bit too hard; but Adele, out in the open, was able to control it and knock it into the goal.

This elicited a cheer from the crowd. That group of senior officers happened to be just abreast of Dawn. Their cheer startled the big horse and caused it to rear. Dawn, who'd been pulling the reins for a reversal of direction, felt this coming and was able to maintain her seat with no great difficulty. Having taken note of her desire to turn around, the horse remained up on his hind legs for rather a long time, sort of tottering around to face the other way. While she was waiting for the front hooves to come down on terra firma, Dawn glanced over curiously and happened to catch the eye of the courteous major who had offered to ride in her place. The man snapped out a salute. Given that her hands were occupied, Dawn was forced to respond with a mere wink. At the other end of the field, Asquith's supporters were jeering him good-naturedly, telling him to put a bit more mustard on his next pass.

Dawn actually wanted no part of Lieutenant Asquith, but it so happened that a minute or so later she was riding after him when he swung and missed at the ball—perhaps trying to put too much mustard on it. Dawn rode in to collect it. As he was turning about he crossed her path and was whistled for a foul. His friends were merciless. Patricia took a free shot at the goal and missed by inches, so no harm was done save to Asquith's pride. He got some of it back a minute later by taking advantage of a stupid mistake on Dawn's part to score a goal. He then presented himself before his cheering section for congratulations, which they gave grudgingly, and mixed with insults that might have got them ejected from some places. The game had somehow become all about him. He was one of those men who cannot rest until he is the center of all notice, even if it is hostile.

A minute later Katherine flinched away from some aggressive riding by Asquith and left the ball sitting out in the open. Dawn galloped toward it, believing that Asquith couldn't possibly get his mount turned around in time to make a decent hit on the ball. And she was right. Hearing her approach, not wishing to let her have the satisfaction of coming away with the ball, he leaned back in his saddle and reached behind him awkwardly. Dawn came scything in off of Asquith's right fore, on course to cut behind. The ball was within her compass. But at the last moment she flicked the head of her mallet up and hooked it with Asquith's. Then she gripped the handle as hard as she could, readying herself for the shock, and leaned away from him. Otherwise the mallet would have been ripped from her grasp. Asquith lost his grip but the wrist loop caught on his hand and torqued his arm back and around behind him and pulled him clean out of the saddle. Dawn heard the thump of his body hitting the ground a moment before the astonished roar of the crowd. Though they quieted down a good deal when he did not get up and it became clear that he had suffered a dislocated shoulder. After that, Asquith received all the attention he could ever have dreamed of.

The match was then called on the grounds of there having been quite enough carnage already. Refreshments were set out while those girls who had other clothes changed into them. Dawn had nothing in reserve, save for the ball gown, and it was too early for that. So she was at loose ends. News about Asquith filtered into the clubhouse. Irene had been evacuated. Blanche was in a state of repose, wishing she could have seen it. Katherine and Patricia had no idea what to say to Dawn. But Adele marched right up and threw her arms around Dawn's neck and gave her a fat kiss on the cheek. Ida Colquhoun stood near the entrance, gripping her bag in both hands, lips pursed as if sucking wet cement through an invisible soda straw, watching Dawn as if wondering what hell spawn she had inadvertently debuted to local society. Mrs. Pierce, a bit surprisingly, seemed fascinated but kept her distance.

As Dawn had nothing to occupy the time while the others changed, she slipped out the side door of the clubhouse, went around back of the stable, and flew off on a long crying jag, her first really good one since her mother had died. A few people could see her from down the lane and so she faced the wall and let 'er rip.

Then a monogrammed handkerchief was in her sight line. She straightened and snatched it out of a gloved hand. She pressed the cool linen over her face and kept it there until she had herself under control.

"They always say to blow your nose. I don't find it helpful."

"You do a lot of crying?"

"All the time."

She took the hanky down, exposing what she was sure must be a wild red pair of eyes. As she'd guessed, it was the polite major.

"Thank you," Dawn said.

"Oh, no, thank *you*, young lady."

"For what?"

"Saving my career."

"What?!"

"I was about to go down there and assault that man Asquith."

"Oh, that? It was . . ." How would Ida say it? "It was my very great pleasure."

He grinned fiercely and terribly. "I came here to make you aware, if you did not already know it, that you are a magnificent woman. Surrounded, I'm pretty sure, by men incapable of admitting that fact."

"My pa knows." She was only joking.

"Every father thinks that. You need to hear it from someone else. If there is any way that I can help you, or repay my debt to you, only name it. My name is George Patton."

"Well, I'll have to mull that over, Major Patton. I am Dawn, by the way."

"To make a man wait is a lady's prerogative. In the meantime, I hope that you will be my guest for the remainder of the day. After the luncheon there will be a tour of our new facilities, and a demonstration. In the evening, a ball."

"Thank you, I already plan to be at the ball."

"And what young Apollo is worthy to have Diana on his arm?"

"Billy Bach."

He was disconcerted. "Private Bach! Really! Well, he seems a very decent young man. You, however, are far out of his league. And if you settle for the likes of him, the day will come when you wish you had held yourself up a little more. I do not know and it is not my business to ask what brought you to this pass, weeping behind the stables in blue jeans. But in some past life you were a princess and you would do well to keep it in mind when selecting male companions. The handkerchief is yours." He saluted, shook her hand, and strode away.

BILLY HAD EVAPORATED. DAWN HAD NOTHING TO DO WITH HER AFTERNOON. SHE ACCEPTED Patton's invitation and was thus incorporated into a group numbering perhaps one score, of whom the others seemed like rather grand Washington people. She drew one sort of attention from the women and a different sort from their men. The upshot was that none of them spoke to her, which struck her as altogether sensible.

First they sat in the grandstand and watched riders doing gymnastic tricks on horseback, a thing she had heard of but never seen. It was an easy practice to make fun of, but she could see in it a survival of tricks that knights of old must have used in mounted warfare.

They were then driven round the post for a while, seeing the sights. They ended up in a part of Fort Myer that she had not visited before: a row of outbuildings tucked behind an armory. They had a somewhat disused and out-of-the-way character, though work had been done to replace rotten wood with new blond lumber and to freshen up the paint. Patton, who until this point had ridden along in the backseat of an open car but done nothing except peruse documents handed him by an aide, now climbed down and invited the guests to remain comfortably seated or get out and stretch their legs as the mood took them. Dawn was one of the few women who elected to get out, and found Patton at the ready, gloved hand extended to help her down off the running board.

"I know I can trust all here to be discreet," Patton began, strolling toward a low building that looked to have been a stable. "The press would mangle this. Anyone who knows me knows that my love of horses is second to no *man's*." As he laid stress on this word he favored Dawn with a wink. "So I don't want you to take what you are about to see as a repudiation of the traditions of the horse cavalry. But it is a fact, ladies and gentlemen, that in the next war, men will ride to the sound of the guns on wheels." He stopped before the first stable door and let the guests form up in front of him. "We do not intend to be behindhand when that terrible day comes. Now, you might ask how such advances can be made to mesh with our way of doing things at Fort Myer—a small post embedded in a great city. Well, it's true that this is no place for a tank division. But what many civilians may not know is that armed vehicles are well suited for urban warfare also." He paused for effect, then grinned. "Urban warfare, I hear you saying, whatever can you be thinking, Major Patton? Why, this is the United States of America! Well, you might be interested to know that less than five miles, as the crow flies, from this spot, is an army of twenty thousand, many of them battle-hardened combat veterans, bivouacked in an armed camp, organized on military lines, within striking distance of the Capitol and of the White House. This organization has been infiltrated by Communist revolutionaries taking their orders direct from the

Comintern in Moscow. It is a very alarming situation, as I'm sure you will agree. What is the Third Cavalry doing about it, you might ask? Well, first of all, we have been in close touch with our counterparts in Germany, who found a similar peril in many of their cities following the war. And after some trial and error they hit on some weapons and tactics that would hit those Commies hard, and knock them down so they wouldn't get up again. And they installed those doctrines and supplied those weapons to a new corps which they call the Landesjäger—the National Hunters or the Hunters of the Nation, take your pick, German is notorious for mashing words together, they make words like they make wurst. Those Landesjäger boys were kind enough to tell us how it's done. And so when President Hoover called General MacArthur into the Oval Office and expressed his concerns about the Bolshevik threat, we knew just what was needed. Boys, show our guests the American Landesjäger."

Men who'd been waiting within now rolled the doors aside, and electric lights were switched on to reveal a row of vehicles, polished and shining. Engines roared to life up and down the line, and the machines rumbled out onto the expanse of pea gravel that had been freshly laid down in front. At least a hundred men had been lurking back there, and they came out in echelons: the drivers first, mounted cavalry with tommy guns and Browning automatic rifles and shotguns lined up on the running boards, gunners and tankers at the controls of the big weapons, dismounted cavalry marching in columns behind the vehicles, and in the back, standing at attention in the open maws of the stables, the mechanics. Dawn, who'd been wondering where Billy had run off to, could hardly bring herself to look. But at six foot three he was hard to miss. He wasn't more than twelve feet away from her, facing straight ahead but swiveling his eyes to take in the startling apparition of Dawn, the Communist's daughter, standing near Major Patton. "He cuts a fine figure, I'll give him that," Patton said, just for her.

"THIS IS WHAT I WAS SORTA TRYING TO TELL YOU," BILLY SAID INTO HER EAR A FEW HOURS later, during the first dance.

"Well," Dawn said, "I guess there are some things you just have to see to believe."

"They're real serious about it."

"I can see that."

"Major Patton says that just popping off a few rounds, scaring them away, isn't how to do it. They don't stay scared long. And when the smoke clears, well, now they've got a couple of martyrs. He says you gotta make a statement—inflict mass casualties."

She was pretty sure they were the only couple on the ballroom floor talking about mass casualties.

She had, of course, never attended a ball before. In spite of the Sallies' best efforts, her gown was rudimentary, and jewelry nonexistent, other than the Smolny Institute locket, which was the only piece she owned. Her hair and face were frankly those of a woman who had spent the day riding about on horses. She felt as though a lot of people were looking at her. Not because of how she looked but because of what had happened earlier.

"Hooking Leftenant Asquith's stick and unhorsing him was rough, verging on foul play, and contrary to the spirit of the rules and the traditions of the sport," said Gatacre, dancing with her later. "I wish I had been able to do it—and to get away with it!"

Later Colonel Nunn danced with her as well, though he didn't say much, and Mrs. Pierce came over to exchange pleasantries. Those gestures, and Major Patton's attentions, seemed to smooth things over. The sergeant at arms kept announcing new arrivals, each couple more exalted than the last. Gradually Dawn was forgotten among senators, ambassadors, generals, and heiresses. General MacArthur, the army chief of staff, was there with his aide, Eisenhower, and both of their wives. Turning around in a series of slow dances with Billy and some of the other privates, Dawn watched them all: MacArthur aloof, Patton and Eisenhower quite comfortable with each other, talking, she suspected, of tanks.

"You and I are warriors." This was Patton, talking to her ear during a dance. "This is why we recognize each other, as if we had fought side by side in some battle of old. People don't know what to do with us. They depend upon us in times of war. Between wars, we must each find our own place, or take the honorable way out."

The pattern of the dance dictated that they draw apart for a few steps. Dawn kept her eyes on Patton's. She'd known men like him before. He would keep on talking this way, taking silence for agreement. And she was silent. Not because she agreed but because his discourse was so peculiar she did not know how to address it.

"It's hard enough for me as a man, in the peacetime army," Patton went on when they came back together. "I have no idea what advice to give you as a woman. I fear we have no place for you in this civilization, and I mean that as a criticism of the civilization."

The man was barely sane. But none of this was any more surreal than the ball, the other things that had been happening. He spoke forthrightly, which she liked. And though he was a bit of a nut, his theories explained certain things about Dawn and her place in the world more satisfactorily than Papa's. Too bad he was planning to massacre Dawn and her friends.

"Don't worry about me," she said, "I know of a place where I might fit in."

"Well, that must be one hell of a place."

Patton escorted her back to where he'd fetched her from. It was a long walk, all eyes upon them. More because of Patton's notoriety than hers; she knew she was well on her way to oblivion, and she couldn't wait to get there.

"You're worried, aren't you," she said to Billy during the last dance, "that I'm going to get arrested, or get my picture in the paper, and Patton's going to find out about it, and you'll be in trouble. Well, rest your mind. He owes me a favor."

"I'm more worried that you're going to get killed," Billy said.

SHE TOOK A MIDNIGHT TAXI BACK TO CAMP MARKS. IF THE COMINTERN RAISED ITS EYE-brows, she would let them know about all the intelligence this small expenditure had bought. She had been dreading, in a schoolgirlish way, the moment of exposure when she would climb out in her ball gown beneath the stare of the Khaki Shirts guarding the entrance. But they seemed to have deserted their post. The taxi left her holding her suitcase before a dark and abandoned Salvation Army tent. Beyond it, though, the camp was alive with shouting, and bright lights were catching in the humid air above the flats. She walked through the tent, smelling the musty old books in the lending library and the perfume and mothballs on the donated clothes. Some kind of rhythmic shouting was going on down near the speakers' stand, men counting in unison: "eleven . . . twelve . . . thirteen . . . fourteen . . . FIFTEEN!"

She parted the flaps and saw the stand lit by the headlamps of cars and trucks pulled up around it. Standing atop was Commander Waters, dressed in the jodhpurs and black jackboots he'd begun wearing since the founding of the Khaki Shirts. Around him were his chief deputies. Their chins were tucked as they watched something directly below, something Dawn could not see because her view was blocked by the crowd. Roaring men counted to fifteen again, and then raised a cheer. Waters had a swagger stick tucked under his arm; he used it to point at something below, and after a few moments the counting began again. Some sort of dance or game? Men bellowed as if drunk, but no liquor was allowed in the camp. She reached the periphery of the crowd but no one really seemed to know what was happening save that it had something to do with Reds. Pushing her way closer she began to see red, all right, and glimpses of things that were horrible but difficult to make sense of.

Then finally she got a clear look and saw it all at once: six men, stripped from the waist up, wrists lashed together above their heads and tethered to the stanchions of the railing that surrounded the speakers' platform. Some of the men were black and some were white. Blood sheeted down their backs from parallel cuts and soaked the bottoms of their trousers. One of them was being lashed by a big fellow who had peeled off his own shirt to keep blood spatters off the khaki. "Six . . . seven . . . eight . . ." hollered the crowd. She saw men grinning in the light of the headlamps.

The man being whipped was Papa. She recognized the others too: Silent Al, Booker, all the men she'd been living with.

Papa was writhing and dancing below his rope like a gaffed fish. Not because of the lash-work, she knew, but because he was having difficulty breathing. She pushed toward him. "Ten . . . eleven . . . twelve . . ."

She had been thinking, during the drive home, about the moment in the polo match when some impulse had caused her to twitch her mallet up away from the ball and instead hook Asquith and unhorse him. Why had she done that? Patton had a theory. An interesting theory, flattering to her in a way. All well and good on a polo ground. But what would happen now, if she reached the big man with the whip on the count of thirteen or fourteen?

She never found out, since some man, jumping about in a kind of ecstatic dance, accidentally stepped on the hem of her gown. She toppled over sideways, heard the fabric tear, felt her knee squish into the mud. Half the skirt came away as she staggered to her feet. One shoe had gone missing. She kicked off the other and ran to Papa. Waters made a sweeping gesture with his stick and the men around him stepped up to the railing and knelt to cut the ropes with pocketknives. Papa's rope jerked free and he toppled back into Dawn's arms, his bloody back slamming into her front. He knocked her back and landed atop her in the mud, chest working convulsively. Dawn looked up into the light to see spittle raining down on them.

"THEY HAVE A MAN THERE, PATTON, AND NEVER MIND ABOUT THE OTHERS. PATTON IS A killer, and he spends long days thinking about how to mow us down. He has a gun on a truck that fires shotgun shells the size of my arm. Armored cars with machine-gun barrels pointing every which way—thirty caliber for people, fifty for buildings and vehicles." Dawn did not mention the fact that Patton was enamored of her, since it did not really go to the point and would be poorly received by this audience: the central committee of WESL, the Workers' Ex-Servicemen's League, meeting in plenary session in the basement of a derelict steam plant a few blocks from the White House. "If you go up against him and the weapons that he has, you will all be killed."

"We know of Patton," Papa said. He could only talk in a low voice, but this only lent his words gravity and forced all others to attend closely. "Why, he wouldn't even be alive now if it weren't for Joe Angelo, who rescued him out of a shell crater after he got himself shot in the ass. Joe Angelo, who's now starving at Camp Marks." The last sentence, though, was drowned out by laughter at the idea of Major Patton shot in the ass. Dawn had to hand it to Papa, he had a knack for the propagandistic wisecrack. Few of the men here had heard of Patton. None had met him. Dawn's effort to scare them had been nipped in the bud by Papa's ass joke; from now on, when Patton's name was mentioned, they would think of that, not his arsenal of 75-millimeter shotgun shells.

Papa must have read this in her face, for when the room quieted, he went on: "I don't argue that he is a killer. But the bourgeoisie do not have a monopoly on such. Think of the heroes of the Great October Socialist Revolution."

"They aren't here."

"They *are* here; their moment has not yet come round."

"They had a moment on Saturday night."

This was Tuesday. They had spent Sunday and Monday becoming human again following a helter-skelter exodus from Anacostia: six half-naked, bleeding men, a few of their sympathizers, and Dawn, barefoot in the bloody and ragged aftermath of her gown. They'd not been able to take any of their things with them. Papa had lost his jacket with the money sewn into the lining. Dawn had lost her suitcase with her jeans and her riding boots. She was now wearing men's clothing.

She had to admit, though, that the picture looked different now that they lay in the bosom of WESL. Thousands of Communists were in town. Almost all of them had chosen to respect Camp Marks's no-Reds policy and had instead taken residence in WESL squats closer to the middle of things. Papa's little cell at Camp Marks had been a lonely outpost staffed by fanatics. To Dawn it had seemed more desperate with each passing day. Why procure two dozen tommy guns for six people? But now they had been re-embraced by a small army of honest-to-God Bolshevik revolutionaries. From here the story Papa had been telling himself made more sense. She could see how men who had been living in this Red island for a few weeks, who hadn't been to Fort Myer and seen the Landesjäger, would take a sunny view of their prospects. Communists were here from Detroit, St. Louis, Seattle, San Francisco—so many of them, and such strong and vivid personalities, that her head was in a muddle just trying to sort them out. One of them, a big blond Italian from Hartford, definitely not keen on a young woman's having any role in these deliberations, broke in: "Were you thinking we had come here unaware that the forces of capital had killers in their employ, and that we would be facing them? Do you take us for children?"

LATER, TALKING IN PRIVATE TO PAPA AS THEY TOOK THE EVENING AIR ON THE ROOF, SHE tried to make him understand things: not only the danger they faced but her own frustration at being spoken to this way. Thinking back to Grisha on the truck, she said, "Nor am I a child. I have seen things these men know not of."

"And they have seen things that would be novel to you." They were speaking Russian. The day had been cool and gray, with a couple of rain showers that had left puddles on the flat roof of the building. The early evening sun was now cutting in under the clouds, shedding amber light on the Washington Monument a few blocks to the northwest, highlighting the division, about a third of the way up, where they'd paused work during the Civil War. The town was quiet. Congress had adjourned for the summer without awarding the veterans their bonus. Below them, cars' tires occasionally hissed through shallow puddles. It was a pleasant enough evening. The next day would be hot and muggy.

"We all have useful information to share," she allowed. "I wish mine were taken for what it is worth."

"The level of detail in your report was impressive," Papa said.

"Thank you."

"A skeptical listener might ask how it was that you were allowed to see so much."

This stunned her, more than anything that had happened since they had left Chicago. For a minute she was silent, working it around in her head, seeing just how the episode at Fort Myer could be—*would* be—misconstrued and teased all out of shape by a particular kind of paranoid, Byzantine Communist mind. A mind like her father's.

And she saw that there was no way to fix it. Because what had happened had all emerged from contingencies. Ida recognizing her hat. Irene taking a mallet in the kisser. Asquith falling off his horse. And Patton being a very strange man. Not just any old very strange man but that particular type most difficult for Communists to understand. Or even to take seriously.

She had told them some things about her exchanges with Patton. Not the weird stuff about reincarnation and warriors. Just enough to string together the tale of how he had invited her on the tour.

"This was all a setup," Papa said. "Patton knows who you are—where you come from. We've been infiltrated."

The problem being that if she left out the weird stuff, what was left of the story didn't hold up. In a way, she couldn't blame Papa for seeing through it.

"Anything Patton said to you was just a tactic to get you down to that garage and let you get a load of that hardware so that you could come back and scare us silly. Destroy our morale, quash the workers' revolution before it even begins."

Next he would talk about how the Cossacks and the Savages had refused to fire on the workers in Petrograd.

"Your friend Billy, those soldiers on the running boards of the armored cars, brandishing their tommy guns—they aren't so very different from the Cossacks. Imagine what those armored cars could do for us once their drivers have had their eyes opened to what is really in their best interests!"

She gave up. And like Patton, he assumed that her silence implied her consent. But it was not that at all. She knew Papa to be wrong. It was not so much that he took her for a childish dupe. That smarted. But she was used to it. To be at the receiving end of such finger-wagging lectures was a part of childhood she would relish leaving behind. The crux of it was a thing Papa would never know of and could not understand: what Patton had said to her made sense of her life and gave her a purpose she had been wanting, without even knowing that she wanted it. And to agree that Patton had only been making a fool of her was to strip herself of that dignity and purpose. She might accept the loss of a ball gown but not of that.

Papa was looking at her, trying to work out if his words had struck home. Which they had, but not as he'd intended. He looked vulnerable, and Dawn thought there was some jealousy at work too: not so much of Billy-as-beau but of Patton-as-father. Perhaps he sensed, or even knew, that he wasn't really her father at all. She smiled, reached out and crooked his neck gingerly in her elbow, and kissed his cheek.

That seemed to settle his mind. "Now," he said, "about our shipment from Chicago."

JUST LIKE ANYONE ELSE, REVOLUTIONARY COMMUNIST INTELLECTUALS HAD THEIR strengths and weaknesses. Definitely playing to the latter was figuring out how to actually transport a shipment of tommy guns a distance of four miles, as the crow flew, from Potomac Yard to the WESL squat in southwest D.C., between the Smithsonian and the Tidal Basin. The weapons had been shipped from Chicago embedded in a bale of "donated" clothes on a four-by-four-foot cargo pallet. Workers at the yard, sympathetic to the Bonus Army, were going to keep an eye on this until a Sally showed up to collect it. To that point it was perfectly routine—which was why they'd chosen to do it that way. Donations like this came in all the time.

The risk posed by that very routine-ness was that it could easily get mixed up with other such shipments. Food, clothing, and other goods came into Potomac Yard every day. These were eventually picked up by BEF sympathizers as they were able to beg or borrow trucks, and driven across the river to Camp Marks, where they were unloaded in a kind of makeshift freight depot.

No sooner had Dawn received confirmation from Chicago that the shipment was on its way than she began to have nightmares about what would ensue if some well-intentioned yard workers were to throw it on the next truck headed toward Camp Marks. Since it ostensibly consisted of donated clothes, it would end up in the Sallies' tent, where they would cut the bale open and begin sorting through it. That would be bad enough if Dawn and her group were still *living* at Camp Marks, but now they'd been exiled.

They were going to have to borrow a truck, first of all. They'd have to drive it to Potomac Yard as soon as possible after the arrival of the train carrying the goods. This, at least, played to their strengths; every rail yard in North America was infested with nomads who knew as much about the comings and goings of trains as the Asquiths and Pattons of the world knew about ponies. A bit of Communist cash, posted as a bounty, ensured that they got word of the train's arrival and the relevant boxcar's location within the hour.

And borrowing a vehicle looked to be easy. Silent Al was able to make a connection with an unemployed truck driver from Baltimore who was willing to come down on short notice and run the errand as his contribution to the movement. They just had to pay him for gas. Dawn would ride along as passenger. She had picked up a few such shipments at Potomac Yard, and so people there would recognize her and see nothing unusual in her showing up to collect a bale of donated clothing. There was still a lot that could go wrong, but it was the best plan they could improvise.

While they waited, Dawn went shopping. She'd fled from Camp Marks in a ruined ball gown. In addition, new clothes needed to be bought for the six men who had arrived bloody and half-naked. Papa had stashed some cash at a bank but he couldn't walk in there looking the way he did. So they were back to bootstrapping.

John Pace had money but had to weigh their needs against the fact that he had a couple of thousand starving Communists to feed. So it was just the kind of mess that Communists loved to argue about in eight-hour meetings. Those deliberations generally ended in deadlocks broken by assertive leaders who used raw power to do whatever they wanted.

Pace, a vigorous Detroit Communist and an ex-marine, had risen to the top of WESL following an already legendary madcap journey to D.C., dodging cops the whole way. Lately he had begun leading his men in frank, direct assaults on the White House, only to find it cordoned off, gates chained shut, Secret Service men and cops forming a picket all the way around its grounds, more cops posted on all the nearby streets stopping any man who tried to go that way.

But a respectable-looking young lady might be able to walk by and reconnoiter.

Pace had no difficulty employing women. One almost got the impression from him that, during his military career, he had been disappointed often enough by the failings of men that he was open to giving the female sex a try, and perhaps to just switching over altogether. Many of his best recruiters were female members of the Young Communists. Without hesitation he gave Dawn some money and told her to go replace some of what had been left behind at Camp Marks. This was to include a "Sally costume" for her and something that Papa would wear to the bank, where he could pick up his dollars from the Comintern and use them to pay Pace back, along with a healthy finance charge that would go to buying flour and potatoes.

Nothing was a secret in the WESL squat, and so Dawn heard grumblings about the folly of spending scarce pennies on bourgeois frippery. But a Red ex-marine was still an ex-marine and Pace was blunt, even brutal, in the way he shut the dissenters up. "Swing by the White House on your way home," Pace called after her, "and pay a call on Hoover and ask him whether he has any room on the Ellipse. This joint is getting a little crowded." And he looked pointedly at both the Camp Marks refugees and the grumblers from his own ranks.

Dressed in a borrowed pair of trousers and a man's shirt, she walked north on Twelfth Street because that was one of the few thoroughfares that would cut across the Mall. She passed by the queer little castle of the Smithsonian on the right just as the Capitol came into view beyond. Having crossed the Mall, she entered into the triangle between Constitution and Pennsylvania, a slum of mostly derelict commercial buildings that were going to be razed so that government structures could be put up. In the meantime they had become infested with homeless veterans and other squatters, to the point where Dawn would have felt uncomfortable walking there had so many cops not been out that day.

North of Pennsylvania the neighborhood began to settle down, with office buildings and such businesses as banks, drugstores, and cafés as served the people who worked in them. Dawn turned east and began heading toward Chinatown. On this heading if she walked far enough she would reach Union Station, with its tempting menu of trains going anywhere but here. Along the way, if you knew where to look, were a few thrift shops—just about the only kind of business doing well these days.

Three hours later she came out the other end of Chinatown dressed as a normal human woman of the era. From each hand depended a few shopping bags containing trousers, shirts, and underwear for Papa, Booker, Al, and the others, as well as some odds and ends John Pace had asked her to pick up and notions requested by some of the women. Slung over her shoulder was a long package she'd picked up in a pawnshop on the spur of the moment.

Her next assignment was to reconnoiter the approaches to the White House, which was a long walk back the way she had just come. She decided to cut south on Third toward the west front of the Capitol. This would get her to Pennsylvania, which would of course lead to the White House, thirteen blocks west-northwest. It would also take her right past Camp Glassford, which was Commander Waters's command post. This was situated in an abandoned Ford dealership and a derelict armory all of two thousand feet from the Capitol Rotunda. Navigating there was easy because it was surrounded by cranes with wrecking balls, visible from several blocks away. The wrecking balls were idle, since the buildings they were supposed to be demolishing had been occupied by veterans these past several weeks. Waters had surrounded the building with Khaki Shirts. As Dawn drew closer she began to feel mildly apprehensive that one of them might recognize her as the Communist who'd been kicked out of Camp Marks a couple of days previously. At the same time, though, she rather enjoyed the idea of tweaking their noses in a place where they could not enforce their brand of martial law and summary justice. As it turned out, they were too busy smoking cigarettes and bullshitting with local cops to pay her any notice. According to the latest news, Waters had worked out some kind of deal to begin evacuating at least some people from some of these condemned buildings the next day, so they had a lot to talk about.

She turned down Seventh Street to get back to the Mall, then cut diagonally across it back to the Smithsonian. Only a few blocks behind that was the WESL squat, where she was able to deliver her purchases to those who were waiting for them. Papa took delivery of a suit of clothes, used, ill-fitting, but presentable enough that he wouldn't get thrown out of a bank. He took scant notice of the delivery, though, because he was in the middle of a conversation with a hobo who had just come up out of Potomac Yard bearing news: their shipment had come in from Chicago.

IN ALL HONESTY, PART OF DAWN HOPED THAT THE WHOLE THING WOULD GO SIDEWAYS AND that the guns would end up being discovered by astonished Sallies at Camp Marks. There was nothing in the shipment traceable to Dawn, her father, or their confederates in Chicago. The weapons would most likely be turned over to the cops, and thereby be kept out of the hands of Papa, John Pace, and their company of deluded Communists.

Alas, all went perfectly. Dawn found herself in the passenger seat of a flatbed truck pulling out of Potomac Yard at 10:30 in the morning of a fine July day with the pallet strapped down in the back. It was what was described in the crime sections of newspapers as a clean getaway. Resting across her lap was a long, thin parcel containing her pawnshop purchase.

Where to go from here had almost been an afterthought. The plan had come together slapdash as Papa and the others, still recovering from the beatings inflicted on them at Camp Marks, had traded more or less harebrained versions. Listening to them, it had become evident to Dawn that they simply didn't understand how big and heavy the shipment was. A single hundred-round drum magazine for a Thompson submachine gun, loaded with .45-caliber rounds, weighed ten pounds. The gun itself weighed another ten. The shipment consisted of two dozen guns and four dozen loaded magazines. So the ordnance alone weighed over seven hundred pounds. The clothing in which it was packed weighed a few hundred more. This pallet was four feet square and six feet tall, encased in planks and plywood; it weighed at least a hundred pounds empty. None of the men in the room understood the practicalities. Obviously the shipment could not be broken down at Potomac Yard. It first had to be taken somewhere. Somewhere secret, somewhere safe, with enough room to break it open and extract the weaponry. Only then could it be taken, a few pieces at a time, to the WESL squat and handed out to whichever two dozen men Papa and John Pace deemed most battle-ready.

The only other men in that room who seemed to understand the practicalities were Silent Al and John Pace. But Pace had a couple thousand starving Communists to look after and couldn't follow the conversation for more than five minutes at a stretch. So, as much as Dawn hated to reward Silent Al for his wandering eyes, she finally made the fateful-seeming decision to actually make eye contact with this phantom who had been haunting her peripheral vision for weeks. She'd never looked straight at him before, for fear she'd be caught looking. So there was almost a palpable shock, like grasping a live wire. She feared he'd be hungrier, more of a creep. But after holding her gaze for a couple of seconds he just nodded, like a sergeant who'd been given an order, and started talking to the room. *I'll take it from here, ma'am.* She watched him as he talked and was dismayed to find that he was attractive. Bigger, more man and less boy than Billy Bach. Maybe even the kind of young man who would meet with Patton's approval.

He settled matters. For when it came to a discussion of guns and trucks, they'd only listen to a man. And Silent Al, to his credit, said exactly what Dawn would've. What she had, in fact, been saying. But he said it calmly, in a low, steady voice that brooked no argument. And the very fact that he *had*, to this point, been silent most of the time, made his words just that more potent.

And so it was that they had got word of a disused barn in the countryside just outside of Alexandria, only a few miles west of Potomac Yard. Close enough that you could walk it in an hour or so. But that wouldn't be necessary, since it was only half a mile from a rural train station serviced by three of the lines that converged from various parts of Virginia on D.C.'s Union Station. The bank had foreclosed on the farm and kicked everyone out, so all the buildings were vacant, boarded up with signs proclaiming them bank property. Breaking into the house would draw attention—the bank's dicks would be on the lookout for squatters—but they could probably get away with hiding some goods in an old barn for a day or two. They didn't want to arouse any suspicions by descending on the place in force, so it was decided that Silent Al would hike to the place on foot before dawn, jimmy the door open, and await the truck.

Which was how it happened. The crate was too heavy even for two men and Dawn to move, so once they'd got the barn door closed they pried it open and began tossing the clothes into the corner, shaking out each piece to make sure there were no small parts wrapped up in it. For some parts of the Tommy gun, such as the wooden butt stock and the receiver—a long, heavy steel rail, intricately machined—were too obvious to miss. But there were smaller bits like the slotted compensator that fitted to the muzzle and a small but very important piece of brass called the Blish lock, that could easily get lost. Layer by layer they peeled the clothes away, working by the light of the summer sun slanting in through cracks between the barn's weather-beaten planks, angling to bring gleaming metal into those blades of yellow light. The small but incredibly massive drum magazines, pregnant with lead. The front grips—beautifully carved wood with grooves sculpted for the fingers. The trigger frames where all of the small intricate levers and mechanisms were interconnected. For though they'd specified that the guns be shipped ASSEMBLED, that was something of a relative term—they had been cleaned up and packed as large sub-assemblies that could be snapped together in moments to produce a ready-to-fire submachine gun. One by one Dawn handed the parts down to Silent Al, who arranged them in rows and grids on a tarp he'd laid out on the dirt floor. They'd sent the driver down the road to the train station to get a cup of coffee and a slice of pie—there was no reason he needed to see any of this. By the time he returned, the back of the truck was bare except for the wooden pallet. He accepted his gas money plus an additional five from Silent Al and went on his way.

"I've never laid eyes on one of these before," said Silent Al, "except in gangster movies, of course." They were alone in the barn, looking at the parts—twenty-four of each. Something in the precision with which Silent Al had laid them out on the tarp spoke of an orderly mind.

"I have," Dawn said, "and I've been studying up on it. Army manuals in the Library of Congress. It's all there. And now here." She tapped the side of her head. This caused Silent Al to look at her, instead of the guns, and she found she didn't mind it. If he'd been the kind to get fresh with her, he'd have made his move by now. He hadn't. She picked up a front grip and a receiver, after just a bit of exploratory fumbling, and was able to snap them together. On went the barrel and the bull-nosed compensator with its row of neatly machined vent slots in the upper surface. Fiery gases would erupt from those and help keep the muzzle from climbing. Remembering first to pull the charging bolt back, she snapped on the trigger assembly, and the butt stock to that. After the first couple of parts went together, Silent Al picked up some for himself and began to follow her lead. In a few minutes each of them assembled a complete tommy gun. But Dawn refrained from attaching a magazine, since only trouble could come from that.

She'd almost forgotten about the long parcel she had brought with her that morning. The truck driver had handed it down to her before pulling away. She now unwrapped it and pulled out a timeworn but sturdy-enough violin case.

"You have got to be kidding me," said Silent Al.

She opened it up, removed a violin, and tossed it onto the pile of clothes.

"Apparently it's real," she told him. It was gratifying to see him so transfixed with amazement. "Not just a gag in gangster movies. You really can fit one of these things in a violin case." She laid the case open on the tarp, then picked up a wooden stock. It was the biggest single piece. If she could fit that in, she could find room for everything else. She found that it would fit neatly into the narrow end of the case where the neck of the violin would normally go. Having sorted that, she picked up a receiver and one of those ten-pound drum magazines.

Silent Al was as yet unable to make sense of this. "What are you doing?" he finally asked. "I mean, I see you're putting one into a violin case. But is it just a gag or—"

"Revolutionary discipline," Dawn said with a slight roll of the eyes. "Look, Papa has been entrusted with a lot of money by the International. Some of it's in Chicago—stashed here and there in secret places. Now, the deal is that we paid half up front for the guns and half on delivery. As soon as Papa has proof of delivery, he'll cable the boys in Chicago and let 'em know where to fetch the other half of the money. Since he can't be here to count the guns, he wants me to bring one back. A sample. Just so he can lay eyes on it. So if the International gives him any static about how he handled the money, he can tell 'em a good story. Since I'm going to have to get back to the squat on the train, I need a way to carry the sample that won't draw attention. So, yesterday, when I was out running errands for John Pace, I saw this in a pawnshop window and said to myself—"

"That's the ticket," said Silent Al with a nod.

"Exactly. Tradecraft. I can pass for a high school gal. A high school gal carrying a violin in Northern Virginia is no big deal. A gangster in a sharp suit carrying one around Chicago, on the other hand—"

Silent Al nodded.

As Dawn had been explaining these matters, she had been fitting more parts into the violin case, rearranging them as she went, jigsawing them together. She guessed a proper gangster would have custom-carved niches made to cradle the parts and keep them from rattling. She had to make do by pulling small garments out of the donated clothes pile and stuffing them into vacancies between the parts, wiggling each one to make sure there was no metal-to-metal contact. When she was finished, she had to put her whole weight on the lid to hold it closed while Silent Al snapped the latches. In the middle was a lock, just a cheap thing with a sheet-metal key sticking out of it, a dirty scrap of pink ribbon tied through a hole in the handle. With a screwdriver anyone could have pried it open in seconds. But Dawn reckoned it was good insurance against the case popping open by accident and spilling clothes and gun parts across a train carriage, so she turned the key, pulled it out, and slipped the ribbon over her wrist.

"Speaking of tradecraft," Silent Al said, "we should go back into D.C. separately."

"I agree."

"I'll give you a head start. I'll close the place up, cover the tracks. The goods'll be safe here until we can come back with a car or something and pick up the other twenty-three."

"That is all fine with me," Dawn said. And it truly was; she wanted no further part of those things.

"See you back at the squat, Dawn."

"See you."

FORTUNATELY THE VIOLIN CASE HAD A SHOULDER STRAP. CARRYING IT BY THE HANDLE wouldn't have been so bad had it only contained a violin, but with twenty pounds of ordnance crammed inside it was a beast of a thing to lug around. She slung it over one shoulder. In lieu of a purse she'd been carrying a canvas bag packed with a canteen of water, lunch, and a few other necessaries to get her through the day. She slung that over the other shoulder and began trudging down the road to the train station, which was only fifteen minutes' walk away. This was just a whistle-stop at a crossroads that sported a post office and a café. Not wanting to draw any attention from curious locals, she just settled down on a bench at the station to await the next train headed into D.C. This pulled in about half an hour later and got her to Union Station half an hour after that. She considered detraining one stop early, since that would have saved her a bit of a walk. But her route from Union Station would take her by Camp Glassford again, retracing her steps from yesterday. She wanted to see what was going on there, and possibly bring some useful intelligence back to her comrades at the WESL squat.

The street below the cranes and the wrecking balls was much more crowded today. She found herself at the back of a mob, encumbered by the violin case and the shoulder bag, wondering what was going on, and trying to piece a picture together from rumors. Waters, she already knew, had agreed to begin peacefully evacuating some buildings this morning. But this didn't look peaceful. A plurality of the rumors had it that the cops had double-crossed them and begun dragging Bonus Marchers out wholesale, and that a riot had happened. She saw nothing that answered to her idea of a riot. Those buildings had always looked like the aftermath of a civil disturbance, with missing walls exposing their rooms and staircases to the elements. Looking into those vacant cells now as she backtracked west along Pennsylvania, Dawn saw, not Khaki Shirts but blue-uniformed D.C. cops turning over mattresses and dumping out footlockers. Searching, she guessed, for Red weapons.

Her instinct was to retrace her steps from yesterday, cutting diagonally southwest across the Mall—the most direct route back to the WESL squat. But Pace had wanted information about how the police were deployed around the White House. And much might have changed in the past few hours, if cops had really been pulled away from there to quell the "riot" at Camp Glassford. This might be the chance Pace had been dreaming of to smoke a cigar in the Oval Office and hang a red banner from the North Portico. So she walked down Pennsylvania Avenue. It was slow going. Men of the BEF had begun swarming up from Camp Marks, clogging the streets. The avenue was jammed with cops, vets, press, and onlookers, and she had to fight against the flow of people. But as the crowd thinned, closer to the White House, she began to make better time, moving up between the slum on her left and the tidier district that faced it.

So it was that she had a clear view of a lone man on horseback who rode out of a gate where one of the curving roads surrounding the Ellipse connected to the intersection of Fifteenth Street—the eastern frontier of the White House grounds—and Pennsylvania, directly ahead of her. He came from the Zero Milestone. Helmeted soldiers opened the gate for him, saluted as he went past, then locked it behind. The man rode out into the middle of Pennsylvania Avenue like a knight errant. His helmet gleamed, his jackboots were polished, and his jodhpurs were crisp. In his left hand he held the reins of his white horse, a great charger, at least seventeen hands, but the reins were a mere formality, so perfectly united were the wills of man and mount. In his right hand he held a drawn saber, pommel down, tip pointed heavenward. His blue eyes gazed down the avenue toward the Capitol, a white vista smudged around its foundations by the mob that had gathered before Camp Glassford. In this attitude he rode right past her. "Miss Glendive," he said, "it is an unexpected pleasure to meet you once again."

"Major Patton," she said, "what is about to happen?"

"You of all young ladies in this city are in a position to know. Good day, Miss Glendive."

"Good day, Major Patton."

She walked the last block to Fifteenth, where she could look through the fence and see into the grounds of the Ellipse. Diagonally across rose the Lincoln Memorial in the distance, and in the greater distance the grave-sown hill of Fort Myer. From there the Landesjäger corps had arrived—no, were still arriving—drawing up in orderly ranks in the middle of the Ellipse. Pacing to and fro before them was General MacArthur in his sunglasses and his jodhpurs, shadowed by his aide, Eisenhower.

She could have seen more, but here was where she took off at a run southward on Fifteenth Street. Three long blocks took her to Constitution, where she dodged honking traffic to the Mall. Curving around the eastern flank of the hill that supported the Washington Monument she got to a little wooded park on Independence near Fourteenth, where the Communists liked to have picnics and play ball, as it was just around the corner from the WESL squat.

And a couple of minutes later, she was there—though it was hard to know what "there" really meant in a slum with a population of two thousand, divided among several buildings distributed over a whole square block.

She went to the room where she'd last seen John Pace and was dismayed but not surprised to find that neither he nor any of the other leaders was present.

On her career through the squat she had picked up a retinue who now devoted attention to her sweat-drenched hair and clothing, her heaving chest and red face. What, some of them wanted to know, had she been doing all day? Others—mostly children—were just curious. Some actually had useful things to tell her: her father had gone with Pace and most of the other able-bodied men in the direction of Camp Glassford hours ago, when they had heard about the riot. Dawn asked, "Did anyone go to Virginia?" Because asking *Is anyone fetching the machine guns?* seemed indiscreet. "Booker got a phone call from Silent Al," came the answer. "He and a couple others got in a taxicab."

She considered it.

"Evacuate," she said. "MacArthur is right over there, just across the Mall, with armored cars and machine guns and men who believe that the only way of dealing with people like us is slaughter. I don't know if they are first coming here or to Camp Glassford. Given how they feel about Communists—"

And then it was an hour, or what seemed like it, of that: going to all the separate rooms and buildings and shacks and tents to bear witness, spread the word, and argue with each little self-appointed leader. Helping to organize and pack all that these people would need to survive what might be weeks on the road. And packing herself, stuffing food, clothing, anything else she might need into that shoulder bag, now almost as heavy as the violin case.

Followed by a sudden awareness—almost a letdown—that the cavalry had not come.

Which meant that they must instead have gone to Camp Glassford. Patton had been riding that way to scout the battlefield.

She was too tired and heavy-laden to run. She alternated between walking and jogging, making her way down the Mall, the Capitol ahead of her, smoke drifting across its front from the small war going on two thousand feet northwest of it.

No, she knew as she got closer, that wasn't smoke but some kind of chemical stuff. Tear gas. And the war was already over. The Landesjäger had finished their work here and moved on, headed for Camp Marks. Patton would be riding his white horse over the Eleventh Street Drawbridge, the green Salvation Army tent coming up on his right, reflected in the gleaming blade of his saber.

Camp Glassford was even more of a junkpile than it had been a few hours ago. Cops, vets, firefighters, ambulance drivers, looters, and journalists were all ranging through its smoky, ruined buildings like armies each fighting a different war. She might have searched it for a week and not found her papa had she not noticed a waterfall of red fabric trailing from a shattered window high up on the face of the old Ford dealership. It was a corner office with a view over Constitution Avenue and the Capitol.

Papa had once dreamed of flying that banner from the Treasury or the White House. But she could clearly see him arriving here in the moment before it all went crazy. Seeing MacArthur and his cavalry coming down from the Ellipse, his eye would have flown to this window. He'd have hoisted the duffel bag onto his scabbed back and made the long, wheezing climb up the staircase—exposed by the collapse of a wall—to the top, and unfurled the banner of revolution, rallying the workers to the hammer and the sickle.

She was breathing through Patton's handkerchief by the time she reached the top floor, for the tear gas was still strong enough to choke her. A cloud of it came roiling out of the office door when she pushed it open, and she had to stand back and let it disperse.

The correct—albeit bourgeois-sentimental—response to seeing Papa's body curled up on the linoleum was tears, but she was already weeping because of the gas. A couple of the grenades had been lobbed in through the same window he'd used to unfurl the banner. They must have filled the place with gas in seconds. He'd have been blue in the face already from his run up the Mall and his ascent of the stairs. No Scarface, he was not able to retreat from the fumes, fight his way down the stairs, and face his attackers on the street with tommy gun blazing.

Dawn laid him out straight on the floor, as rigor mortis had not yet taken hold. She pulled the banner back inside and tucked it over him as a shroud.

Re-slinging the bag and the violin case across raw shoulders, she walked down the stairs, exited the building, and strode out of Camp Glassford, then south across the front of the Capitol. She was tired of walking, but she had far to go yet. Half an hour's hike took her down to the strip of parks and marinas along the channel that led to the Tidal Basin. She gazed across the water at the polo grounds, but no match was being played today. She strolled alone down the waterside promenade of Fort McNair, to Buzzard Point where Anacostia Creek came together with the channel and went round back of the Army War College to the docks where they kept the recreational canoes and the rowboats. All was in disarray there because a big steamer had put in from some base downriver, bringing troops to reinforce the Landesjäger. To make a berth for it, boats had been moved aside and beached wherever there was space for them. Dawn had not foreseen this, but it served her purposes. She availed herself of a rowboat. Distracted by events at Camp Marks, no one noticed. She pulled out into the Potomac and the current took her, trying to sweep her out to sea. Tempting as that was in a way, she put her back to Virginia and pulled hard for it, rowing due west. Her view of the Anacostia Flats could hardly have been better. The Landesjäger were rolling across it in tanks and on horseback, but the fires they had set moved faster. At the beginning of the voyage she was able to make out individual riders and vehicles, and fancied she picked Patton out of all the confusion. Farther out she could only see whole shanties as they began to steam, then smoke, then burn at the flame-front. By the time her rowboat went aground at Potomac Yards, Camp Marks was a slit of flame supporting a column of smoke that covered half the sky.

Workers had gathered at the edge of the water to watch it and were bemused to see a girl turn up in an army rowboat and climb out with a military surplus bag on one shoulder and a violin case on the other. She sensed that they were too shocked by what they had witnessed to think of anything improper. "When's the next westbound freight?" she asked them. "I'm headed for Chicago."

MAGNITOGORSK

JANUARY 1934

"I am Shpak. And you—Aurora or Dawn?" was how the man began their conversation.

The first of many, perhaps? She had no idea who Shpak was. He was dressed and groomed to seem older than he was. Very little remaining hair. Rimless spectacles. Clean-shaven, dressed in a suit and tie. He could have been a lawyer in Winnetka or an accountant in Berlin.

She had been awaiting him for half an hour in this office, which was part of a jail complex to which they had suddenly relocated her the day before. She was back in her civilian clothes. And she was well rested, for they'd put her in a little cell all her own. The darkness and isolation would be hard to take after awhile, but she'd slept like the dead.

"Aurora is the name under which I entered the Soviet Union, and by which I intend to live the rest of my life," she answered.

"Don't mistake me for a bureaucrat," Shpak chided her. "I'm not asking what you are *called*. I'm asking what you *are*. That's my job. To find out such things."

She considered asking him whether he was a psychologist—Dr. Stasova's boss, perhaps? But they wouldn't have moved her to a jail for a psychological inquiry. And a shrink probably wouldn't be accompanied by soldiers. Two of them, she knew, were out in the hallway, flanking the office's door. Seemed like overkill, but she could well imagine how useful it might be to go everywhere escorted by men with rifles.

She let her gaze wander about, searching for clues. Shpak's first act, after hanging his massive wool overcoat on a rack by the door, had been to approach the oak swivel chair behind the desk and examine it with the same wary skepticism he was now directing at her. The seat was padded by a fabric-covered cushion. Before removing his leather gloves, Shpak picked this up between thumb and index finger and tossed it onto the floor in the corner of the room. A very sensible precaution against lice. Aurora's chair was unpadded and so she was probably safe. Anyway, this wasn't Shpak's office—he had simply ejected its usual occupant—and so there was no point in trying to glean clues from it. The overcoat told her nothing except that Shpak had access to the special stores where Western goods were for sale. Back in the early days of the Revolution, Chekists had favored black leather garments because lice couldn't live in those. But those guys had been living together in squats and barracks. Shpak lived somewhere nice. People did his laundry.

They had not crossed back over the dam on the way here. They were still on the west shore of the Industrial Lake, in one of the buildings that had been thrown up a couple of years ago at the inception of the project. In due course this thing would be superseded by a new jail in one of those brick structures being hurled up in First Sector, just to the south of the factory gates. Some of those things looked to be as high as eight stories. But looming above them all was the two-story headquarters of the OGPU, for that was being constructed on a hill off to one side. It wasn't finished yet.

Sometimes the most obvious interpretation was actually correct. In this case it was that Shpak worked for the OGPU—the Cheka—and that they were using this old jail as their lockup until the new place was complete. The only part that didn't add up was that Shpak seemed important, and Aurora didn't get why someone important would bother with her. Maybe it was because she had met high-ranking American officers in Washington. Maybe her father's martyrdom accorded her some exalted status.

"This doesn't look like a psychiatric facility," she pointed out.

"It is not. You have been given a clean bill of mental health by Dr.

Stasova." Shpak reached into a leather briefcase, which he'd set on the floor next to the desk, and drew out a typewritten document perhaps ten pages long. He licked a finger and turned a few pages. But it was clear that he had already perused it. "You must understand that certain aspects of your story had struck Comrade Tishenko as bizarre, causing him to suspect some kind of mental disorder. Tishenko—" Shpak sighed. "Tishenko is loyal, energetic, fully committed to socialism, but not well traveled. Not well educated. Certain things are difficult for him to fit into his limited view of the world. Once you explained matters to Dr. Stasova, however, all became clear. We have been able to verify certain details. The existence of polo-pony ranches in the vicinity of Gillette, Wyoming. Your late father's heroic martyrdom in the streets of Washington. These hooligans Bonnie and Clyde whom you are so enamored of. The disturbance in North Dakota. It all checks out!" He punctuated this by flipping the document facedown on the desk. Turning the page. "But why? Oh, it's no longer a psychiatric question." He held his hands out, palms up toward the ceiling, and looked around, reminding her, perhaps a little unnecessarily, that they were in a jail. Not a hospital. "Why did you go to such lengths to 'kill' Dawn? And is she truly dead?" *Are you who you say you are?*

Yes, Shpak was OGPU. The Cheka, minus the black leather. The Flaming Sword of the Proletariat.

"I had to kill Dawn because of Silent Al."

It took him a moment to absorb this. He hadn't been expecting an immediate, direct answer. "The federal police agent," he said, glancing down at the report. "Who infiltrated your cell in Washington and betrayed your father."

"Yes. He knew everything about Dawn."

"If you could convince him that Dawn had died in a shoot-out, Dawn's file would be closed. You'd be safe."

"Exactly."

"Your interest in Bonnie and Clyde was motivated by something deeper than mere adolescent hero worship."

Actually, it had been adolescent hero worship. But Aurora saw where Shpak was going and decided it was best to agree. "Of course. They are just hooligans, as you said. Oh, their actions reflect legitimate grievances of the oppressed classes. That's obvious. But they have no concept of revolutionary discipline and could never contribute to an effective proletarian revolution except as agents of chaos. No, I was interested in them for the reason you have already perceived: by modeling Dawn's actions after the likes of Bonnie and Clyde, I might be able to stage Dawn's death in a way that would confirm everything that Silent Al and the other feds probably had in my file."

"And then Dawn's file would be closed. You need not fear any further investigation."

"Exactly."

"What cause did you have to believe that Silent Al was still pursuing an investigation into Dawn?"

There were two. Aurora wasn't sure whether to mention the first of them. But she had been thinking about her interrogation by Tishenko, and the way that he had reacted to emotions passing over her face. The power that it gave her. And there was something in Shpak's reaction to the mention of Silent Al.

"For one thing," Aurora said, "when you are a woman, you can tell, sometimes, by the way a man looks at you, by certain clues in his behavior, how he is thinking about you. And if it feels wrong, you know that you had better be careful around him. And Silent Al was always one of those."

"You are referring here to your interactions with this man in Washington. Before you knew him to be a federal agent."

"Yes. But that's just a woman's intuition and might not be worth writing down in an official report. The real answer is that Silent Al saw me in Chicago. He recognized me. I'm sure of it."

"Chicago."

"Yes. Soldier Field. That's a stadium along the shore of the lake."

Shpak was interested, and pleased in a way, that Aurora had broached the topic of Chicago. "It had not escaped my notice," he said, "that between your father's martyrdom in the summer of 1932 and the shoot-out in North Dakota in September of 1933 is a sizable gap. We have been able to verify the truth of your claim that you spent most of those months living in a kommunalka in Chicago. Sharing a bedroom on the third story with two other women, a Latvian and a Jew."

Aurora felt herself blushing. *The OGPU watches night and day with a million eyes. Lie to me, girl, and I'll know it.*

"You spent much time away from the house. The nature of what you were doing is unclear. You're saying you attended at least one sporting event at Soldier Field? An American football match, perhaps?"

"A balloon launch."

She now had the minor satisfaction of seeing Shpak gobsmacked.

"August of last year," she continued. "Your sources in Chicago can easily verify it. It was covered in all the papers."

"Why would they do such a thing from a stadium? And why did you attend?"

"This was not just bourgeois recreation. It was a scientific event."

"Studying cosmic rays," Shpak said with a nod. It was her turn to be surprised that he knew this. "An interest of yours?" he asked, a bit snidely.

"Of my boyfriend's."

"The same boyfriend who got you pregnant?"

"Yes."

"The father of the 'monster'?"

"Apparently."

"By the way," Shpak said, waggling a fountain pen at her, "your lurid tale about the monster continues to raise eyebrows. But Dr. Stasova confirms the, ah . . . obstetrical evidence. Seeing no other symptoms of schizophrenia, she believes that this detail will be resolved by further investigations."

Aurora nodded.

"Tell me what you were doing in Chicago during 1933."

8

CHICAGO

JUNE 1933

The buildings are crazy; the colors are crazier, and the whole is a peep into fairyland transcending in beauty the dreams conjured up by the wildest imagination.

—L.A.S. Wood, manager of the lighting division of the Westinghouse Company, addressing the Convention of Illuminating Engineers on the eve of their mass pilgrimage to the Century of Progress World's Fair in Chicago, 1933

Chicago Police Department detectives were investigating the theft, from a visiting Wisconsin automobile, of two century-old beehives filled with live bees, each containing twenty-five pounds of honey. The bee-napping was apparently a crime of opportunity committed while the thieves—who, it could be inferred, were specialists in automotive accessories—were stripping the vehicle to its axles.

Dawn Rae O'Faolain, aka Dawn Glendive, aka Aurora Maximovna Artemyeva, slept in the garret of a house two blocks from the crime scene. Even in early June, it was warm, and she left the windows open. No more than crickets did the nocturnal depredations of automobile accessory thieves trouble her sleep. But something about the keening of the lady apiarist at six in the morning brought her to a wakefulness she knew it would be bootless to oppose. She threw on a robe, scuffed her feet into a pair of down-at-heel men's slippers, and embarked on a descent to the street to find out what was the matter. First and chanciest was the shivering hinged construct, as much ladder as stair, that let her down to the uppermost of the building's proper stories. Padding along splintery floorboards and down two rude flights made for servants and juveniles, she reached the levels intended for the Gilded Age petit-bourgeois who'd had this place built. Now she treaded on cherrywood steps between a paneled wall and a carved banister, widening as it banked round to flood into a foyer. This was Tiffany-windowed where it faced the avenue. Pocket doors closed it off from the parlor where the German Communists were snoring loudly enough to drown out the trouble in the street. They had just arrived, the scent of burning books still in their clothing. These were brave men and women—you had to be brave, to be a Communist in Germany—but it was difficult to make any serious progress toward the worldwide socialist workers' paradise in a country where Communists, and even Socialists, could be kicked to death in restaurants with impunity. Which had been the case in Germany for about the past three months.

Two months ago, Himmler had called a press conference to announce the foundation of a new detention facility, specifically for Communists, at Dachau, near Munich. The men and women currently sleeping in the parlor had begun edging toward the borders of the Third Reich. In coming weeks, if they did not wander off, they would percolate higher and deeper into the kommunalka, in true American melting-pot style, sharing rooms, soap, and food with the two dozen or so quasi-permanent residents: the University of Chicago graduate students who seemed to form its Politburo, their writer and artist friends, card-carrying Wobblies who had drifted in from the Englewood yards to the west or the Illinois Central line along the lakeshore, American Communists, Russians who had come either because they supported the wrong variant of Communism or because they did not wish to starve to death, and miscellaneous comrades from all over who had been drawn to the South Side by the combined attractions of free speech, cheap rent, nubile college students, a vast and rumbustious proletariat, jazz, and lots of people in surrounding neighborhoods who could cook them the food, and speak to them in the languages, of Poland, Lithuania, Germany, Ukraine, Yugo-Slavia, Hungary, and the shtetl.

She unlocked the front door and took evasive action against the usual avalanche of newspapers in all of the above languages, some of which were mere flyers that were kept from blowing away only by the boat-anchor heft of the *Trib*. Today this sported a banner headline about the opening of A Century of Progress, which was what they were calling the World's Fair.

She paused only a moment before stepping out of doors in her robe and slippers. She had spent her early years in another kommunalka, in what had then been Petrograd and was now Leningrad. After her parents' divorce and her mother's move back to Montana, her favorite woman had been Veronika, a machine gunner by trade, a member of the Red Women's Death Battalion. Owing to some unpleasantness involving White Cossacks during the Russian Civil War, Veronika lived her life in a state of hyper-vigilance and presented a steely demeanor to the world, or at least to the street. She would not have ventured out before throwing on her Workers-Peasants Red Army greatcoat, pulling on her black boots with the hidden dagger along the right shin, and checking the action on the semiautomatic pistol on her right hip. For in those heady post-revolutionary days it had been usual for Reds to go about armed.

Since then, Dawn had grown to womanhood, and also had learned her way around a machine gun. Unbeknownst to anyone else in the house, she kept a disassembled Thompson submachine gun and a loaded hundred-round magazine in the eave space adjacent to her garret. But along the way she had learned some things that Veronika had never quite got the hang of about being a woman—a tall and noticeable woman—in a complicated urban society. She knew that, at six in the morning, when some other woman was wailing in the street, it was fine for her to go abroad in a robe thrown over a nightie, and that, just like Florence Nightingale at the front, she would go unmolested by the men, and like a nun at a wedding, unfrowned-at by the ladies. She loved Veronika, thought of her every day, and wondered whether she was still alive in Russia. But she had come to know that she did not have to be just like Veronika in every particular; and she believed that Veronika's very sternness, her ferocity, her unwillingness to feel vulnerable, had in the end made her more so.

Lacking a mother these past couple of years, she had learned all of these things from observing the women who crossed her path: not just cowgirls and Communists but, as a result of some unexpected turns, society ladies, generals' wives, showgirls, beggars, and prostitutes. She had been learning that getting respect was a matter of acting like you deserved it while pretending you didn't care; and she guessed that if she were really willing to put her money where her mouth was, she might in theory walk across the south side in her nightie without incident. It would horrify the men of the kommunalka, who, in spite of their love of jazz and political cant, were uneasy with Negroes. And it would outrage Veronika. But Dawn believed it was possible, and, as proof, looked to the Negro women waiting for the streetcars on Sunday mornings in their clean dresses and white gloves.

Before advancing to the sidewalk she gripped the *Trib* firmly in both hands and heaved it over to see if there were any below-the-fold stories about Bonnie and Clyde. Seeing only material about Hitler, Mussolini, and the Depression, she felt her chest relaxing. Her fascination with Bonnie Parker, and her daily terror of learning that the cigar-chomping gun moll had been killed in a pitched battle somewhere (or, worse yet, taken alive) was strange enough that it had led to a certain amount of introspection—or as it was styled in the house she had just walked out of, psychoanalysis. In a more properly brought-up young lady, obsessive identification with a woman who careered around the Midwest in stolen eight-cylinder automobiles spraying bullets at lawmen would have been strange, and worthy of note. But in Dawn the same symptoms were pretty banal. If she were going to be a woman of mystery with hidden contradictions, she would have to reach deeper into what passed for her psyche.

Of Clyde Barrow it was said that he had been a run-of-the-mill juvenile delinquent until he had, at the age of seventeen (Dawn's age now) been sentenced to a term at the Eastham Prison Farm, which had turned him into the most dangerous gunslinger in America, driven by a half-insane grudge against Texas, her lawmen, and her prisons. Or, in the poetry of Bonnie Parker herself:

They class them as cold-blooded killers,
They say they are heartless and mean,
But I say this with pride:
That I once knew Clyde
When he was honest and upright and clean.

Though it wasn't written up in the newspapers, the few American Negroes who got invited to take meals at the kommunalka spoke frankly about what was obvious to them—namely that young Clyde had been the victim of homosexual rape, probably repeated and sustained, during his term there and that this explained him just as (in Dawn's way of thinking) Cossacks explained Veronika.

Stretching across the front walk was a graceful crescent of dust, one limb of a dune that had appeared in the yard a week earlier, during a black blizzard. It was former topsoil from Kansas or Nebraska. Since then, the dune had been migrating gradually across the property in a blind eastward progress toward Lake Michigan. It was trodden down during the day and reconstructed, as they slept, by the west wind. Dawn stepped over it, partly because she didn't want to get Nebraska between her toes but partly because she loved its streamlined shape, its angle of repose.

A loose cordon of women in bathrobes, men in pajamas, bemused itinerants, and curious dogs enclosed one cop taking down a description of the stolen property from the boreal beekeepers and another staring, with a kind of professional admiration, at the hulk of the car. So thorough had been the work of the thieves that Dawn impressed herself by pegging the vehicle, as it were from its dental records, as a Willys Whippet.

She found it difficult to take Chicago cops with the seriousness that was probably warranted. This was because, like just about everyone else on Earth, she had seen them mostly in gangster movies. A little act of will was always needed to remind herself that they were not just actors awaiting their cue to clutch at imaginary gunshot wounds and collapse to the pavement.

Zipping like spent bullets through the crime scene were alienated bees who had apparently flown the coop during the robbery and been left behind by the bee-nappers' Clyde Barrow–inspired getaway. These drove the lady apiarist into even more operatic levels of despair as she brooded upon their inevitable doom, which was to die, but not before descending into madness and going on a pointless stinging rampage. Dawn wondered if similar things might be true of exiled German Communists.

By the time she had made it back to the kommunalka, a plenary meeting was under way in the kitchen to contemplate the preparation of breakfast. Dawn had no appetite for the food, or the political hugger-mugger surrounding its preparation. Each ethnicity had its own set of instincts around the cuisine of poverty: kasha for the Eastern Europeans, grits for Southerners, oatmeal for Northerners. All beside the point, since even these people—three dozen or so hobos, refugees, and grad students crammed into a commune—were not actually poor and hungry. Not by the standards of the wide world and especially not by those of Russia, whose silence hinted more eloquently than shouting newsreels of famine and mass death. Even in the midst of the Depression and on the edge of the Dust Bowl, there was plenty of food, if you didn't mind biscuits and gravy and beans.

Women, thrown together thus, looked to by the men to cook, jury-rigged a system of communications, or at least gestures, around food to make up for the want of a shared tongue. Most of what was being conveyed had nothing to do with "what shall we have for dinner?" and certainly not with "a dash of vinegar would go well with that!" but instead was about precedence, seniority, and respect. Some of the women were educated—wives and colleagues—but the stalwarts of the kitchen were the mothers-in-law, shirttail relations, peasant grannies, or unlettered hobo girls. It was among these that the politics of stove and pantry raged beyond all credible bounds. The drama surrounding the preparation of each meal was like a Moscow show trial: not actually what it claimed to be, but a stage on which actors could adopt stances, declaim lines, and collect from onlookers political specie. Had she really depended on that kitchen for her daily bread, Dawn might have been persuaded to take at least a bit part. Unbeknownst to the others, however, she had some money, and was not above spending it at cafés and lunch counters around the university. It was Comintern money, entrusted to her by her father before he had fallen in battle last summer, within sight of the United States Capitol. As such it was not hers to spend. Had certain men in this house known of it, they would have expropriated it, and she could not have gainsaid them. And so every Danish she bought in a coffee shop was a little sin against the Revolution. Something in her upbringing—not the Red one in Petrograd but the American one in Montana—told her that she would have to atone for each sip of coffee, each nibble of bacon. Judgment would one day be rendered in some scientific weighing of accounts in the Kremlin or the Lubyanka, where commissars, paging through massive OGPU dossiers, would draw up a register of her accomplishments and a sum of her outlays.

On this day she had breakfast with the rest of them, since going back to the house to change, then out again, seemed overly elaborate when oatmeal was there for the taking. Sitting with some of the Americans, and with a few Germans who were just trying to soak up English, she related the story of the beekeepers. She got off on the wrong foot by mentioning that they had come down from the Badger State. The Chicagoans had a visceral, Reds-vs.-Whites, Jews-vs.-Cossacks hostility toward Wisconsinites. They cloaked it in majestic robes of political discourse, but she knew it to be rooted in, or at least proceeding from the same ultimate cause as, the football rivalry between the Bears and the Packers. The beekeepers' concerns were treated in a way that Dawn found high-handed, given that they were, after all, proletarians. The fact that they were en route to display the prodigious hives at the Century of Progress—an event whose name they could speak only by enclosing it in the verbal equivalent of quotation marks—pushed her listeners from mere indifference to outright derision. The Chicagoans anyway. The German Communists just listened alertly, muttering back and forth as they debated the meaning of such unfamiliar terms as "hive"—a word apparently without a German cognate—and "Packers," trying to wrap their lips around the initial W in the name of the state to the north.

Just because of that, Dawn decided she was going to go to the Century of Progress.

It was only a few miles away. It seemed to possess a power of magnetic attraction on more than just beekeepers. One day, for example, she saw a dwarf buying a paper at a newsstand, and the next day, a pair of them on a streetcar, and then suddenly they were everywhere, as often as not dressed in miniature lederhosen and dirndls. Indian chiefs, or at least Indians with imposing headgear. Busloads of showgirls, yodelers, Civil War veterans and bathing beauties, flatbed trucks with alligators, ostriches, vintage locomotives, giant pumpkins, Frigidaires, jinrikishas, X-ray machines, and potted Florida orange trees, all went north on Drexel and did not come back. A man identified as C. C. "Slim" Williams trundled down the street behind his dogsled and his team of huskies, which he had driven all the way from his home in Copper Center, Alaska, the first 1,800 miles on snow and the balance on a wheeled contraption interposed between skids and pavement. A quarterback from Dallas strode up Drexel with a 135-pound bale of cotton on his back; he had toted it 1,200 miles so that the world would not live in ignorance of the glories of Lone Star agriculture. Not far behind him was a boulevard-filling cotton-picking machine, drawn by the largest tractor in the world (ITW), said to be capable of replacing forty-eight Negroes. All of these pilgrimages created an almost palpable gravity drawing Dawn toward the Century of Progress, though, in a funny way, what really got to her was Slim's huskies: not just pulling that sled as fast as they could but fighting and fucking each other the whole way and leaving the street half paved with redolent shit. Not to follow them seemed mean of spirit.

So Dawn let herself be entrained in that flow, using as an excuse that she wanted to show the newly arrived Germans around. As card-carrying persecuted Communists, there was little chance they'd fall for the propaganda. Anyway their kids were underfoot and their perfectly non-English-speaking womenfolk were trying to clean and organize parts of the kommunalka that, in the view of more tenured residents, could not be improved upon. Instead of which they now devoted their husky-like energies into the projected fair visit. Dawn had floated the idea of hoofing it, so as to avoid crammed streetcars and give the little Huns a chance to blow off steam. When translated into German, that took on a range of significations that were unclear to Dawn but extremely well understood by the matrons. These threw themselves into hamper-packing and knapsack-mending as if they were getting ready to be hounded over Alps by Brownshirts. These people were to going for a walk as the forty-eight-Negro machine was to harvesting cotton.

She was forced to consider the matter of attire. The only shoes she owned that were equal to the trek were a pair of men's work boots, recently resoled. She couldn't wear them with a dress unless she wanted to end up in a sideshow booth as the Amazing Montana Bumpkin Gal, so she put on jeans, a long-sleeved shirt to protect her arms from sunburn, and a straw cowboy hat to shade her face. On the Loop she'd draw stares but at the fair she might go unnoticed among midgets, quarterbacks, the Fattest Farmer in the United States, Miss Japan, Chief Evergreen Tree, and Duke Odzikuro Kwei Kuntu of the Gold Coast and his Ashanti warrior dancers, slated to perform the Golden Stool Ceremony in the Darkest Africa concession.

Somewhat getting into the Germans' intrepid spirit, Dawn opted for a less direct but more scenic route striking due east and crossing the Illinois Central sooner rather than later. There she quietly amused herself by imagining how her charges would react were she to propose that they go down to the line and hitch a ride on a northbound freight. But they were already looking uneasy about the number of hobos and the smell of their encampment, and so Dawn led them on east until they found the shore. Placing the blue water of the lake on their right hand they proceeded up the chain of parks on its shore. Consequently they saw the Century of Progress from afar and went on seeing it for a long time as they strode along swinging their alpenstocks and singing jaunty German hiking songs.

It was shockingly enormous. She was a little mortified that such a thing—all by itself bigger than most things that styled themselves cities—had been created, without her altogether knowing, out of nothing a few miles away from where she'd been living. It brought back a few memories, in a funny way, of a year ago, when she had ridden the rails to D.C. with her father, and first come in view of the Bonus Army camp on Anacostia Flats. But where that had been a stinking Hooverville, this was a glorious fairyland, or what such a thing would look like if fairies toted slide rules instead of wands and made magic of electricity. The temperature was seventy-two degrees, climbing to seventy-six during the last hour of the hike; she knew this because of the Havoline Thermometer, a two-hundred-foot-high obelisk supporting a bolt of red neon luminous enough to be read in direct sunlight. It was far from the tallest thing on the fairgrounds. That honor went to a pair of towers, steel trusswork, thrice as high as the thermometer. Cables between them supported a sky train of rocket cars. Above even that hovered the silver seed of the Goodyear Blimp and a droning swarm of aeroplanes variously towing banners or shedding daredevil parachutists. From half a mile away they could hear stentorian announcements on the largest loudspeakers in the world, relayed over the largest private telephone exchange in the world. In due course they bought the tickets—50 cents for adults, 25 cents for children—that got them through the largest and most expensive metal fence ITW and onto the Midway, passing between a pair of statues that seemed to be its household gods. Both were seated, low-slung, not posing like the idle gods and heroes of old but hunched forward at their work: on the left a bald, bearded savant peering at a test tube in one hand while running his index finger down the page of a tome in his lap. On the right a young man, powerfully muscled, enthroned on a massive gear and reaching out with both hands to control the wheel of a consequential valve.

Which put Dawn in mind of something she had read in the *Trib* within the past day or two.

Some ribbon-cutting worthy had made a speech to the effect that this fair was all based upon a great theorem—namely, that industry, manufacture, and commerce depended "almost immediately" on the pure sciences.

The temperature was eighty-two when the Havoline Thermometer disappeared from their sight line, swallowed in the clutter of Progress. Every so often it would spring into their view as they rounded some corner, the neon inexorably mounting through the eighties. From the fair's midst, getting a synoptic view of it was impossible, which probably explained the need for rocket cars and airships. Merely walking its length was half a day's journey, not so much because of the distance as the impossibility of simply placing one foot in front of the other. A troupe of a hundred women dancers in sailor costumes collided with a contingent of Mounties in a strait between a reproduction of a hillbilly shack from the Ozarks and a crowd that had gathered to watch a squad of Chicago firefighters extinguishing a burning popcorn hut; the hillbilly looked on curiously as the Mounties doffed their hats and made way for the sailor girls to squirt out through a gap between the Negro Fair Visitors' Office and a Potawatomi wigwam in which a whisky bottle once owned by Abe Lincoln was on display. Dawn seized the chance to draft behind the sailor girls. The German Communists followed her smartly. Soon they were picking their way over thrumming pipes feeding the fake alpine waterfall in the Midget Village but had to pull up short to make way for a lady lion tamer being rushed off the property on a stretcher.

For lack of any other clear goal they struggled for hours in the direction of the German-American Building. En route they passed analogous structures for Yugo-Slavs, Italians, Bulgarians, and the South Manchuria Railway (thronged because Miss Japan was in there). An echelon of well-dressed society girls, volunteering as tour guides to a horde of underprivileged children, were having difficulty keeping them from disrupting the watermelon-eating competition. Makeup running and coiffures drooping in the heat, hats askew, they struggled with the impossible challenge of maintaining decorum at such an event in a world so hungry. Fortuitously, the stately façade of the German pavilion hove into view and they made for it on the reasonable assumption that things would be more orderly there. But they stopped in a little cluster on its threshold, suddenly preferring the crowds and the ninety-one-degree air to whatever might be inside. Dawn, deeming herself immune to whatever it was that was troubling them, led them through the doors into its cool shade. After a pause for their eyes to adjust, the Germans all made astonished but happy noises. Seeing the curiosity in Dawn's eyes, Dr. Vogt took half a step toward her and allowed himself a slight relaxation of the face that was the closest he'd ever come to smiling.

"No swastikas," he explained. Which meant little to Dawn.

"Look about!" the professor explained. "No swastikas."

She must have looked uncertain still, so he explained, "In Germany they are everywhere now. Here, not a single one. Someone made a decision not to put them here. And someone else is very angry about it, I promise you."

For the mothers and children, a cool place where German was spoken, Nazis unwelcome, and beer served (for FDR had legalized it on the same day as Himmler had opened Dachau) was difficult to leave, and so they built a revetment of chairs in the beer garden and hunkered down while Dawn and some of the men made exploratory sallies. Dawn had felt something akin to nausea during their initial sweep down the Midway—some combination of heat, humidity, crowds, chaos, and the heavy scents of butter and caramel and hot grease. Sitting in the ladies' for a minute to collect herself, she remembered the embodiments of Science and Technology flanking the gates . . . and the theorem. When next she went out, she willed herself not to be distracted by the close, low clutter of all fairs: the bumper-car pavilion, the prodigious vegetables displayed on pillows like severed tsars' heads, the food stalls and the banjo pickers. She raised her sights and looked for higher and grander things that related to the theorem, and found them in plain view, rising above the Midway like colossi erected by scientific pharaohs. Save that unlike the monuments of Egypt these were never meant to endure for more than five months. Unburdened of the requirement to survive even a single Chicago winter, the fantasists—"architects" was probably the wrong word—had diverted all resources normally spent on practical considerations to the true purpose. The names blazoned on them in modern sans-serif letters were Ford, General Motors, Westinghouse, Firestone. She knew what the German Communists were thinking and what the people at the kommunalka would say, which was that this only proved that it was all just a propaganda festival for capitalism. Dawn, who had been raised on propaganda, saw that this was not the entire truth. One could easily imagine going to a party congress in the Soviet Union or a rally in Germany and finding the same buildings celebrating the same things, only the typefaces changed. As much as they might like to believe that they were competing with one another, all were a conjoined program for the theorem. When the fair closed on November 1, the statues flanking the entrance could be packed up in shipping crates and sped in streamlined dirigibles to Berlin or Moscow to inspire Nazis and Communists to do precisely the same things.

On an island linked to the streets of Paris by a curving causeway, past Hollywood, the Pabst Blue Ribbon Casino, the Horticultural Building with its pumpkin-sized cauliflowers and its cow-sized pumpkins, just to the north of the Enchanted Island, was the magnet-shaped palace of the Electrical Group. It was near the base of one of the rocket-car towers and hence, from a distance, seemed low-slung by comparison. But when they wandered closer it proved equal to any triumph of Italian Futurism, and in colorfulness exceeded any building ever made. For in studied contrast to the White City of the previous Chicago Fair, forty years ago, Century of Progress was a fair of many colors, and there was no better place to flaunt them than the humming and crackling Electrical Group with its RCA organ that translated music into fluctuating tints projected onto a screen, and the hurtling rainbow of the neon waterfall. Gaudy though it all was, Dawn—who had been raised by Reds and, during her adolescence, read of the rise of Blackshirts in Italy, Brownshirts in Germany, and last year witnessed the spontaneous eruption of the Khaki Shirts in the vet ghettos of Washington, D.C.—was happy to be in any place where more than one color was permitted. She went back to the German Building and fetched a few of the older children who needed airing out, and brought them back and let them sample the wonders of the Westinghouse Hall of Electrical Living and its Playground of Science. Her favorite exhibit was an X-ray machine that enabled her to see the bones in her hands. She went back to it several times, bending forward to press her face into a mask-shaped hood that projected from its lid, sliding her hands into a warm slot beneath. X-rays from a tube in the pedestal shone up through her hands and struck a fluorescent screen above them, which outlined all of the little bones in black against a field of spectral green.

She was amusing herself by pretending to write something, watching the way her finger bones articulated around an imaginary pen, when the "Hey, cowgirl!" guy finally caught up with her.

She knew him only by his voice. Bonnie-idolizing Red revolutionary though she was, she adhered strictly to the rule that you did not turn to meet the eye of a strange man calling out to you. But her peripheral vision, the amused reactions of onlookers, and something about the man's voice told her that he was nothing more than a pest. Finally at bay, she withdrew her hands from the machine, stood up as straight and tall as she could, and looked down her freckled nose at a man in his fifties, a head shorter, with protuberant dark eyes, a mostly bald head no longer hidden under a natty Panama, which he was doffing to her. He wore spats over two-tone oxfords that had been shined within the last few hours. He had spied her earlier in the day, and called out to her, beginning with "Why, hello!" and escalating to "Hey!," "Hey, cowgirl!," "Hey, tall cowgirl!," and, now that luck, electricity, and X-rays had brought them together, "Hey, tall, pretty cowgirl!"

"A. T. Green," he said, and, though standing well clear, bent forward at the waist in what was either a vestigial bow or an attempt to get within handshake range without dislodging his shiny oxfords.

"Dawn Glendive," she said, and, in the awkward moment that followed, took half a step forward and extended her hand. He took it and air-kissed it from a lip-to-knuckle separation of at least six inches, a gesture so peculiar as to draw uneasy chuckles from nearby fairgoers.

"You've been persistent, Mr. Green. As you can see, I am at the fair with little ones—foreign visitors."

"Oh, how lovely!"

"I've no doubt that making a good impression on them is uppermost in your mind."

This was calculated to make A. T. Green slink away. Instead he brought his heels together, drew his Panama hat to his chest, and, sweeping the other hand across his front, snapped his fingers in an almost vaudevillian gesture, like the posturing that a music-hall singer might use to segue into a number. "Why, I have just the thing!" he exclaimed.

"You do?" she said, a bit off-guard.

"Indeed. For one as interested as you clearly are in the juxtaposition of the anatomical and electrical sciences? Absolutely."

It seemed fraught with barely ponderable double entendres, but there were witnesses, and they were at a fair. In the end, she and the Germans followed him. Her mental map of the Century of Progress had become all crumpled in upon itself. They crossed a causeway beneath the taut steel spiderweb of the rocket-car line, cut across a pavilion of flags streaming gorgeously in the breeze off the lake, and diverted round the north wing of a stately edifice with a tall central tower: the Illinois Host Building. Cutting between that and a sort of pagan temple to Sears Roebuck, fighting through the crowd eager to get into the Hall of Science, they entered into the late-afternoon shade of Soldier Field, where a line of small concessions had been set up, peddling souvenirs, notions, patent medicines, film, and other sundries.

A. T. Green made no attempt to walk alongside her or make chitchat along the way but ambled along about twenty feet ahead of Dawn and her band of mystified but game Communists. Not once did he look back. In another man this might have seemed arrogant but in him it seemed naïve. She ended up following him for no reason other than that if he turned around to find them all missing he would feel that a cruel and low-down prank had been played upon him, forever smirching the character of the tall, pretty cowgirl.

He was selling shoes.

Or rather he was the proprietor of a booth in which a heavy, sweating, red-faced woman—his wife? His sister? His mother?—was selling them. Setting A. T. Green's operation apart from ordinary shoe stores were two innovations: first, that he sold only one shoe: a "sensible but trim and stylish ladies' oxford" specifically designed for walking around the fair all day. The linchpin of his business strategy was making the existence of this product known to women who had made the mistake of showing up at the Century of Progress in high heels. And second, an X-ray machine, similar in principle to the one Dawn had been using a few minutes ago to look at the bones in her hands, but configured so that it shone the penetrating rays up through the feet, enabling customers to see how the little bones in the toes were distributed around the insides of their shoes. Because Dawn was in well-broken-in work boots, her ghoul feet, seen through the machine, were surrounded by a neat picket line of hobnails, and the overall distribution of her metatarsals more or less conformed to th. c rayed on a photograph conveniently posted on the machine's lid and labeled as HEALTHY FEET. Unsurprisingly, most of the lid's real estate was given over to pictures of not-so-healthy feet, and with the exceptions of a few side-show anomalies thrown in for pure amusement (CLUB FOOT, FROSTBITE, SHRAPNEL) these were UNHEALTHY because of ill-chosen footwear. No fairgoer could do so much as scan the gallery of excruciation that was the lid without being very forcefully struck by the utter foolhardiness of the typical dame. The machine had been dragged out in front of the booth so that it literally stopped traffic. All of the Germans had a go and satisfied themselves that their metatarsals, too, were, as one would expect, sorted.

But it was not Mr. Green's purpose to sell shoes to huddled masses. He was playing a deeper game. A game hinted at by his last-ditch inclusion of "pretty" in the list of adjectives modifying "cowgirl." Dawn well knew of how she stacked up against other young women, and she knew that "pretty," while not a bald-faced lie, really meant something like "you stand out in a crowd."

The next day Dawn was striding about the fairgrounds in a conspicu-ously easy and comfortable gait, sporting sensible but trim and stylish ox-fords. At the other end of Dawn was a ten-gallon hat with a placard stuck into its band reading ASK ME ABOUT MY SHOES! She handed out leaflets to anyone who did, and some who didn't.

The cowgirl outfit came first because it was easy and obvious. From time to time she would catch sight of another tall striding girl in the same shoes, handing out the same leaflets, but dressed instead as a Grace, Valkyrie, Princess, or Angel, and generally better put together than Dawn. A. T. Green, through the mediation of Mrs. Green (so it was either his wife or his mother, but she daren't ask which), found reasonably inof-fensive ways of getting Dawn's oxfords pointed in the direction of beauty parlors, of which there were several at the fair. Thus did she find herself being evaluated and set to rights by women capable of uttering with a straight face such phrases as "the Silhouette Reform of the late Twenties" and "victory in hair beautifying." For as fair beauticians they were mis-sionaries of a sort, not preaching to the already converted sophisticates of the Loc, but grimly spreading a radically disruptive creed to downstate matrons and 4-H Club bumpkins. Dawn was going to wear a hat? Why, then it needed to be fashionably tilted down over the right eye; and in that case she required an asymmetrical variant of the Century of Progress Bob, a new style that, with a frame of fin-de-siècle curls, made a knowing wink at the styles of the previous fair while adding a healthy dollop of modern sauce.

On the streetcar home she would tone the look down a little, but the transformation was obvious, and she had little choice but to explain what she was doing and let the chips fall where they might politically.

She had literally nothing else to do. In theory she was still part of the Wobblies, but they had been split open by factional strife and then scooped empty by government action, and finally supplanted by the much more vigorous and better-financed Communist Party. She knew that working as a capitalist shoe strumpet at the Century of Progress would raise eyebrows among the same. But she had learned that she could get away with just about anything by calling it tradecraft and implying that she was gathering intelligence on the habits and vulnerabilities of the bourgeoisie.

Not just any young Red could have gotten away with it, but what Dawn had gotten up to last summer in D.C., and become somewhat locally famous for, gave her a long leash. And even had that not been the case, it wasn't clear, now that both of her parents were dead and she was not working for anyone in particular, who should be holding the end of any leashes.

More and more, it was as if last summer's events in D.C. had never even happened. She had lost contact with all of the survivors, with the sole exception of one Bob Overstreet, an engineer from Wisconsin, about thirty, now employed by a steel mill in Gary, Indiana. He was one of those fully committed socialists who somehow managed to blend in perfectly with the establishment. Short brown hair, well groomed, good manners, genuinely considerate, particularly of women. Probably homosexual, but he didn't know her well enough to confide that. Bachelor's degree in mechanical engineering from the University of Wisconsin, master's from Rensselaer Polytechnic Institute. Yes, when the management of the WESL squat had needed to send someone out to talk to cops or lawyers, Bob had always been their man.

After the debacle in D.C., Bob and Dawn had ended up in the same boxcar, along with a dozen other refugees. He'd kept an eye out while Dawn slept and she'd returned the favor. Though, if armed hobos had set upon Bob while he slumbered, her only recourse would have been to unlock the violin case, patiently assemble the tommy gun, snap on the hundred-round magazine, and stage a massacre. Still, the mere fact that she *could* gave her a kind of uncanny confidence that seemed to intimidate those men whose eyes were drawn to Bob's wallet and his suitcase while he was snoring. She wondered if Veronika had possessed such a weird power of intimidation. It wasn't as if she carried a machine gun around all the time.

Bob had invited her to hop off the train with him as it rolled slowly along a siding in Gary, and she'd done so without hesitation. He'd put her up in his house for several days, given her a chance to clean up and acquire some new clothes while he went back to his job at the steel mill as if he hadn't just spent his summer vacation fomenting a Communist revolution in the nation's capital. In the attic of his big old house in Gary there was an empty steamer trunk that had been left up there by the previous owners because it wasn't worth the trouble of wrestling it down the ladder. At Bob's invitation, and with his help, she got it down into the neat little workshop he kept in his basement and did a few simple repairs. Some Germans had apparently used this thing to immigrate to the United States fifty years ago. It had a system of internal compartments suggesting that the Bavarian carpenter who'd knocked it together had a feverish mind and a lot of time on his hands. No carpenter herself, Dawn still had enough basic farm-girl skills to modify the thing so that it would accommodate the violin case on its bottom level. On top of that went a false floor and other internal partitions. She loaded in what she'd been able to acquire in the way of garments from thrift stores and pawnshops around Gary. That left the trunk only about one-third full, but it was a start.

Bob had been telling his vigilant neighbors that Dawn was a country cousin making a brief stay during her summer vacation. Before that story had time to wear thin, he took her to the railway station and she rode a proper passenger train into Chicago, arriving in that city as a girl from small-town America, not a person of means but a damn sight more respectable than the Dawn who had ridden a boxcar out of Potomac Yard with only the clothes on her back.

Once she'd got settled in at the kommunalka, she'd found that the trunk just barely fit into the eave space next to the garret she was going to share with the other girls. This was closed off by a removable panel to stop dust, drafts, and bats. She emptied the trunk of clothes, save one set that she kept stashed in that shoulder bag, just in case she ever needed to leave in a hurry. The bag went on top of the trunk, which disappeared behind the panel, which in turn ended up mostly hidden by Dawn's bed. No one but her even knew it was there.

She arranged all of these things just-so during the two hours after she first set foot in the kommunalka. As she was doing so she was thinking that someone from the International might get in touch with her one day soon to inquire as to the whereabouts of the twenty-fourth tommy gun. For the triumphal press conference that the FBI had staged at the barn in Springfield, Virginia, a few days after the sack of Camp Marks, had featured twenty-three. Dawn had read the newspaper articles at the Gary Public Library, examined the photos, counted the weapons neatly laid out on the tarp. Silent Al had obviously put his newly acquired tommy-gun-assembly skills to use, just to provide a more menacing backdrop. Surely someone from the International had read the same articles, scoured the same photos, tallied the same numbers, noted the discrepancy. They knew where she lived. As soon as they showed up at the kommunalka asking questions, she'd hand over the violin case and the little key on its pink ribbon, which she liked to carry around with her as a frail precaution against the case's being opened by curiosity-seekers. She'd never opened it since the moment Silent Al had helped her snap it shut.

But that day never came. Days, then weeks would go by without Dawn giving a moment's thought to what was on the other side of the panel next to her bed. Sometimes the men downstairs would talk boldly of what might happen if the kommunalka were to be raided by the FBI, and then Dawn would feel an icy spike through her heart as she imagined them ransacking the garret, noticing the panel, hauling out the trunk, prying open the suspiciously heavy violin case. But that day never came either. Dawn came to understand that these conversations were all in the realm of fantasy. Refugees from Germany who really were worried about secret police raids, stoking the bloodlust of homegrown would-be revolutionaries who were bored of sitting around the kommunalka waiting for something to happen.

IT WAS BOOTLESS TO STRIVE AGAINST THAT PART OF THE FAIR THAT EXISTED TO PROPAGANdize, for everyone was doing that. It was more productive, or at least more interesting, to apply herself and attend to those parts of it that seemed universal to all propagandists in all countries. It just so happened that this was also more fun for a seventeen-year-old girl with no friends and nothing else to do. And so once again Dawn got to enjoy the somewhat delicious naughtiness that she felt when using the Comintern's greenbacks to purchase a cup of coffee and a jelly doughnut. Each leaflet that she handed out she had marked with her initials, and every one that turned up at Mr. Green's booth earned her a nickel, and so soon enough she was paying her own way. She went to the fair early and stayed late, for the work was easy and there were plenty of diversions—that being the point of a fair. Her perambulations soon made her as conversant with the place as if it were an old city, and she a native: she could direct lost visitors to the stands where the jinrikisha boys and roller-chair pushers stood waiting (rich hunting grounds for sore-footed women); the Indian Village (actually five of them, showcasing different tribes); the Largest Picture Ever Painted (a cyclorama of the Great War circumscribing a Pantheon all to itself); the Mayan Temple; the Italian Pavilion with its shrine to Mussolini; the Ukrainian Pavilion echoing to the strains of the Chicago Ukrainian Chorus some days and the Gypsy Ukrainian String Orchestra on others, competing sometimes with the Weekly Community Sing at the Hall of Science or Seth Parker and his Hymn Singing Neighbors of Radio Fame. Chatter on the loudspeaker system was cut drastically during the second week, when deafened management clamped down on amorous youths sending personal messages to their sweethearts. Dawn knew where to find Darkest Africa, featuring cannibals of the Ubangi Tribe; the Log Rolleo; the insulin checkroom, where diabetic visitors could stash their medicine in refrigerated lockers; the small but completely functional factory in the Firestone Building where you could watch tires being made for the custom automobile being built to your specs in the General Motors exhibit and drive home on them at the end of the day. Her tasteful oxfords took her down the *avenidas* of Old Mexico, over the canal bridges of the Venetian Carnival, along the Streets of Paris, where Freddie Williams's Gold Coast Orchestra—the only Negro dance band on the fairgrounds—held forth at the Café de la Paix. Her encyclopedic knowledge grew to cover lesser-known attractions: the three-foot, million-volt spark gap from MIT; the largest map ITW (a sixty-three-by-forty-three-foot relief of the United States); the largest exhibit of miniature paintings ITW; the longest soda fountain ITW, being hastily extended by panicked Walgreens executives because it wasn't nearly long enough; the Mechanical Wonderland; the African Dodger concession, aka "Hit the Coon," where you could drop a Negro into a tub of water by striking a target with a fastball; and the Midget Village, where midget drivers raced in midget cars with one-cylinder engines and midget boxers pummeled each other in a wee ring.

As they were meant to, these things drew visitors: 600 Norge salesmen on the B & O from Philly; 176 newsboys on the New York Central from Buffalo; 60 Episcopal bishops; 180 Civilian Conservation Corps workers en route to turpentine camps in the southeast; 100 Minnesota National Guard troops. Paramount Studios executives from Hollywood, Lions from St. Louis, Shriners from Fort Smith, Plymouth workers from Detroit, credit men from Milwaukee, rubber workers from Akron, rose growers from Pasadena, all rolled in on special trains on the Rock Island Road, the Santa Fe Line, the Pittsburgh & Lake Erie, the Chicago & Eastern Illinois. Five hundred employees of the National Carbon Coated Paper Company of Sturgis, Michigan, arrived on the same train as 270 members of the Jewish Socialist Verband from New York City. The New York Central line rehired 5,000 Depression-idled workers just to handle the demand for special trains. Bypassing the congested rails, an invasion force of Ohio pharmacologists packed a lake liner that steamed right up to the fair's extensive system of coves and quays, scattering a flotilla of paddlers limbering up for the Canoe Jousting semifinals. They made a beeline to the Food and Ag Building, where Aunt Jemima, a 300-pound Negro mammy, served them a flapjack breakfast. The voracious Buckeye druggists overflowed into a storage area housing 200,000 samples of canned, bottled, and preserved food products entered for competition, and some stayed long enough to enjoy an Old-Fashioned Georgia Watermelon Cutting before dispersing and mingling hopelessly with the Missouri Osteopaths, the Texas Grand Opera Association, the Chicago Cactus Club, a Postum delegation from Battle Creek, and the Brick Manufacturers' Association, all of whom were out in force. The next day it was the Association of Military Surgeons; a battalion of kids in wheelchairs from the La Crosse Crippled Children's Home; the Italian National Fascist Syndicate of Engineers; the United Typothetae of New England, New York, and New Jersey; the Braille Theater Guild; and the Anciens Combattants, a veterans' group from France.

Large as these groups were, their numbers were as nothing compared to those attending the fair en famille, coming in by train, bus, or motorcar from all over the continent. The *Trib* sent undercover reporters, disguised as typical fairgoers, to bus terminals in Omaha, Dayton, and Amarillo to rip the lid off the seamy conduct of ticket clerks who, by spreading rumors of traffic jams and parking problems, were trying to discourage would-be fairgoers from driving to Chicago. Bus-company spokesmen issued a formal apology and disciplined the offenders.

Most certainly not arriving on buses were such prominent individuals as: the English vice consul, celebrating George V's birthday at Story Cove on Enchanted Island. Prince Ludovico Potenziani of Italy, inspecting the Italian Pavilion in advance of the feverishly anticipated transatlantic odyssey of Air Marshal Balbo's air armada. George Ferris, of the Wheel. General John Thompson, of the submachine gun. Mr. Firestone, of the tires, and Mrs. Johns, the asbestos dowager. Of interest to Dawn: Princess Alexandra Kropotkin, a lineal descendant of Rurik the Varangian. She was met at the Twelfth Street Gate by mounted Cossacks, who escorted her about the fair in a wheelchair—the spawn of Rurik had sprained an ankle in Iowa. Mayor Kelly of Chicago was presented with a miniature key to the Midget Village by the midget mayor. Governor William Langer of North Dakota, Prince Iesato Tokugawa of Japan, the maharaja of Baroda, and the chargés d'affaires of Rumania and of the Irish Free State were all heralded by greater or lesser salutes from the field artillery. Lieutenant Tito Falconi, the Italian air ace famous for having flown upside-down from St. Louis to Joliet, made an inverted pass over the grounds, landed right side up, and spent a day at the fair whipping up excitement about Balbo's approaching fleet of colossal seaplanes, and a night whooping it up at Texas Guinan's Pirate Ship Cabaret, enjoying fantastical or hilarious displays of ballet dancing, stunt-skating, knife-throwing, and midgets. Jack Johnson was boxing all comers, paying $25 to any man who could go a round with him. Marchese Guglielmo Marconi showed up to tour the Radio Building and to appreciate a mechanical diorama endlessly re-enacting a shipwreck with, and without, the intercession of radio; the death toll was reduced in the latter case to a negligible figure. He spoke fluently in English without notes, but when the time came to speak, using his invention, to the people of Italy, he pulled a page from his pocket and, under the watchful eye of Prince Ludovico Potenziani, read something with frequent references to Mussolini.

Not all of the fair's visiting "royalty" were so exalted; Dawn had a brief and pleasant conversation about shoes with Miss Myrtle Suave, winner of the Iron River popularity contest. Also receiving zero-gun salutes from the field artillery were Lady Anthracite of Minersville, Pennsylvania; the Fur Queen, parading in triumph through the Streets of Paris, blissfully unaware that the French Consul had filed a diplomatic protest with the State Department demanding that the whole sorry thing be dynamited into the lake; Miss Bertha Binder, the Sugar Beet Queen of Sebewaing, Michigan; Miss Ardoth Schneider, California's Sweetheart of the Rodeo; Fannye Nutt, winner of the Georgia, and a small contingent of the winners of the South St. Paul, popularity contests. Helen Johnson, who, at the National Dairy Show in St. Louis, had been elected the Most Typical 4-H

Club Girl in the United States. The oldest living midget and the youngest amateur radio champion. The Queen of the Michigan Cherry Festival. Miss Verna Socket, elected Most Charming Girl at the bathing beach. The Oklahoma triplets.

Dawn let herself drift free on the ebbing and flowing tides of visitors, shining her oxfords twice a day, swapping them for a fresh pair each fortnight. The Century of Progress grew a collective mind of its own, which persisted even as spent visitors were replaced with fresh. The Illinois Host Building, one of two structures on the grounds equipped with an air-cooling system, became a favored refuge for tired female visitors nursing diverse womanly complaints. Its big shaded verandas, looking out over the Avenue of Flags and catching the lake breeze, gave lemonade-sipping pilgrims the feeling of being in the middle of everything and yet at a calm remove, and a modern air-cooled lounge provided a refuge for the over-stimulated and iron-poor. At the other end were reproductions of Abe Lincoln's living room and a shrine to the Emancipator, and in the middle was an auditorium decorated with murals of cows and other bucolic Illinois scenes. More or less important persons spoke there to greater or lesser audiences. It got heavy use in connection with various special Days (Luther Day, Philippine Day, Bulgarian, Utah, Jewish, American Home, and South Side Days), but Dawn had no personal interest in most of these except insofar as they drew sore-footed Filipinas or Utahans—10,000 of them every day—to the veranda and the lounge, complaining to one another of gynecological matters.

This building was but a short distance from Mr. Green's shoe booth and so was the most obvious and profitable location for Dawn and her lissome colleagues, or competitors, to troll for women who had been let down by their shoes—so much so that Mrs. Green had to resolve a spate of tiffs by posting a rota dictating which girl was allowed, and expected, to be there when. Dawn, as a rule, preferred striding about to standing still, but she enjoyed cool air and easy money as much as any capitalist, and made the most of her shifts there.

Almost perfectly useless from a shoe-selling point of view was Niels Bohr, the Danish physicist, who spoke in the auditorium one evening and drew a predominantly male audience. The few ladies in attendance tended to be far more rationally shod than average, and in any event had come specifically to hear about physics, not to wander at large about the fair. Dawn played hooky and attended the lecture, partly because she had heard of this Bohr, and partly out of respect for the Century of Progress's fundamental theorem. Like a loosely observant Christian who only went to church on Easter, she felt a nagging sense of duty to attend a free lecture by Niels Bohr as long as she was spending all her time at, and making her living from, a fair that, when you stripped away the upside-down Italian air aces, the Log Rolleo, midgets, and stunt skaters, was supposed to be about science.

Besides, no girl had ever been more perfectly turned out for an occasion. Mr. Green had caused to be made an outfit copied in every particular from a Century of Progress promotional poster now seen all over Chicago. Its central and dominating figure was a tall, lithe, yet muscular young woman standing atop a globe, her Wisconsin-sized big toe pointed directly at Chicago, throwing her bare arms up above her head to gather in a beam of radiant energy shining down out of the heavens. The iconography owed a lot to churchly depictions of virgins getting supernaturally impregnated, or at least inspired, but from the context it was pretty obvious that this was some other kind of radiance, perhaps like the X-rays that Mr. Green's machine shone through his customers' feet, except coming the other way, like cosmic rays. Anyway, the woman on the poster wore a fantastical getup: a long, diaphanous skirt fluttering prettily in astral winds, and above the tiny waist, a gleaming breastplate (approximated by Mr. Green's costumières with silver-painted papier-mâché) with streamlined steel cups over the boobs. Inscribed in the vacancy between those— for the woman's breasts were very widely spaced—was the legend I WILL in block letters. For reasons of both modesty and commerce, Mr. Green had, in the version actually worn by Dawn, appended TELL YOU ABOUT MY SHOES below it. The ensemble was completed by a headdress in the form of a young eagle spreading its wings as if to spring into flight straight from the woman's brain. Dawn and the other girls took turns wearing it. The breastplate could get a little stuffy on warm days. At any rate, she was careful not to sit directly in front of anyone at Niels Bohr's lecture. If someone were to request that she take off her hat, she would just have to leave, or go and stand at the back, since the eagle (pawnshop taxidermy) was inextricable from her hairstyle.

In any event her inspiring persona, while it drew admiring looks from many, including even Niels Bohr, did nothing to enliven the lecture. She was just as bored and crestfallen as any child who goes to Easter services expecting Jesus to descend from heaven in glory, only to find a pallid minister mumbling about Homoiousianism.

She'd read about Bohr last summer, when she'd got in the habit of spending long, hot afternoons in the Library of Congress reading world newspapers. 1932 had been a great year for physics and so plenty of ink had been spilled on the topic, much of it by reporters of the smart-alecky school who only wanted to know whether any of it could be used to beat the odds at Pimlico. Some of them seemed to understand it, though, or at least could write a decent story about it, which amounted to the same thing as far as Dawn was concerned. The big news last year had been Chadwick's discovery of a new particle called the neutron, which seemed to account for roughly half of all the matter in the universe. As such, it seemed like something whose existence ought to have been known to science a little sooner. But because of its neutrality it was apparently hard to notice. Its existence could only be inferred by solving a sort of logical/mathematical detective story whose clues and evidence must first be brought forth by doing very particular sorts of experiments. Joliot and Curie had done them in Paris and misread the evidence; Chadwick at Cambridge had puzzled out the correct interpretation, inventing or discovering the neutron in the process and confirming it with more experiments in a similar vein. The chain of reasoning, though long, wasn't that difficult to follow. It could be expressed in terms of billiard balls. The somewhat less obvious part had to do with splitting the atom. In order to perform such experiments at all, Chadwick and Joliot and Curie had to break protons and neutrons free from their prisons in nuclei, a feat achievable by so arranging things that shrapnel from the fortuitous disintegration of a conveniently unstable nucleus would bang into targets of another type and shive parts off. Which could be explained to a lay audience with analogies such as "splitting a piece of cordwood with a bullet."

The difficulty being that, in that analogy, the splits of wood didn't just fall meekly to either side of the chopping block; they went screaming off in opposite directions with more energy than the bullet had brought to the party in the first place. And this was all proof of Einstein's equation $E = mc^2$, for the energy given into the splits was accounted for by a slight reduction of the amount of mass in the log. Mass could be converted to energy, and indeed such conversions were going on all the time in stars, the fantastical amounts of energy thus produced being known to all persons by the warmth of the sun and to scientists by less obvious phenomena.

All of that could be read about in finer newspapers and, in some sense, "understood" by lay readers; it was billiard-ball physics juiced up by the matter-becoming-energy phenomenon. It was not, however, what Niels Bohr wanted to talk about. He wanted to talk about other things that had been brewing in physics during the mid-to-late-'20s and that, he seemed to feel, had been unfairly neglected by lazy journalists who found it easier to write of billiard balls and bullets. Easier because this other stuff was difficult to understand—so much so that Bohr didn't seem to think that he really understood it. The lantern-jawed Danish savant had been chatting with Einstein about it in England and Belgium, which was where Einstein had been living the past few months owing to the $5,000 price that had been placed on his head by distinguished civic leaders in his native country.

That the material was abstruse might have been all right had he explained it well. Even a sloppy explanation might have counted for something had the microphone worked properly (or, barring that, had he raised his voice a bit). But when all of these things failed at once, and a baby began crying, it became quite difficult for Dawn to convince herself that she really knew any more of these matters than when she'd walked in. The same could almost surely be said of just about everyone else in the audience—save for the boy sitting in front of her.

The boy was about her age. He looked vaguely familiar. This wasn't the first time he had placed himself in her way. He had been trying to catch her eye for a day, maybe two. Nothing unusual about that in a fair drawing millions where she had a job that consisted of being noticed by as many as possible. Boys varied in their level of persistence. It was difficult to say why some, but not others, gave her the creeps. This one didn't, despite being more persistent than many who did. Following her into a lecture on quantum mechanics was taking it a bit far, but she liked that he had taken a seat in front of her so that she could evaluate him rather than feeling his eyes on the back of her Century of Progress bob. He was wiry, with thick, wavy hair brushed back from a high forehead. He'd gone too long without a trim; excess hair, piled up on top of his head, was going curly in the humidity. He was wearing shorts, which was a bit unusual. Niels Bohr seemed to be talking about how things could exist in two different states at the same time, and she thought it well applied to this fellow whose shorts gave him an indeterminate position on the spectrum between boy and man. If there was anything to Dr. Bohr's theories, this specimen was both boy and man at the same time, and by observing him closely, performing certain experiments, she could find out which. But it was more than that; until she did the experiment, this youth would remain in the indeterminate state. It was not, in other words, a matter of her finding out whether he *was actually* boy or man, for the question, so phrased, had no meaning; she could cause him to become definitively one or the other simply by doing the experiment. Whereupon his boyhood or manhood, and her consciousness thereof, would all become part of one larger, entangled state of affairs. So she continued to observe him. The close attention that he paid to the lecture struck her as unusual. She assumed he'd only come in to get in her eyeline. She was therefore fascinated to see him reach into a skinny satchel and pull out a schoolboy's notebook. He flipped through it in a kinetoscopic blur of tabulated numbers, equations, and diagrams. He paused for a moment to gaze upon a page inscribed in a hand so large that Dawn could read it clearly:

4/33 THE MOST REMARKABLE FORMULA IN MATH
$e^{i\pi}+1 = 0$

And after looking upon it for a few moments in what seemed a reverential manner he licked his finger, turned a few more pages of equations—apparently written down in the past few weeks, since this was 6/33—and came to a blank page on which he wrote BOHR.

He must have then sensed her eyes on him, for he turned around before she could avert her gaze, and looked straight into her eyes for the first time. He had arched eyebrows and a fine, elfin face that could have seemed mischievous or even a bit wicked, but at this moment he just looked astonished, and embarrassed. Escaping from the awkward moment with an attempt at a smile, he turned back around and let Dawn watch the back of his neck and the rims of his ears turn a purplish shade of scarlet. She did not know what to make of it, but guessed that, in whatever school he attended, to play hooky from watermelon-eating contests and Hit the Coon to go to physics lectures, and to keep such notebooks, were not how to make it with girls. Dawn couldn't help but feel bad for him, even as some part of her suspected that this was at least half an act. The boy scratched down a few sentences, but a few minutes later she noticed that he had struck out the name BOHR and replaced it with an even larger BORE!!! He then began drawing sketches in the time-honored tradition of idle schoolboys, beginning with a flying vehicle that seemed to be a hybrid between the rocket cars cruising high above them on stretched cables and one of the huge Italian seaplanes that, according to breathless announcements coming in over the biggest loudspeakers ITW, were even now bending their courses south out of icebound latitudes toward eastern Canada. Below that he scratched in a few buildings apparently meant to represent the fair, and in the middle of those a high pedestal, and on it a globe, and standing atop the globe a slender, long-legged woman, arms upraised to bathe in cosmic radiation. His sketching abilities were nothing to write home about, but he had a knack for geometry and proportion that kept the rendering from being downright insulting, and as it went on he began to sneak glances back at her, furtively at first, then, when she tolerated it, longer looks that he would no doubt justify by claiming that he was only trying to do justice to her.

The last detail, added in the space between the artillery-shell breast shields, was the I WILL, which he enhanced with a string of question marks.

This was his first wrong move. It must have shown in her face, for he went red in the neck again, turned the question marks into a row of figure eights, and wrote in,

HAVE A SODA WITH DICK.

To this she was helpless to do anything but smile. Snap went the notebook. A few seconds later, having disturbed one row of Bohr-watchers on his way to the aisle and a second on his way to the empty seat next to Dawn, he was saying, "Hey, you gettin' any of this? 'Cause I can explain it to ya. And we won't need microphones or nothin'."

Dick was from Brooklyn. She knew it because she had learned how to peg accents while hanging around with itinerant veterans.

"What he's saying is—"

"Dawn."

"Dick. What he's trying to say is—nice to meet you, Dawn—that truths come in complementary pairs, and you can't have one without the other."

A lady in front of them, a downstate matron who had not caught on to Silhouette Reform or Hair Beautifying, turned around, glared at Dick through heavy-rimmed glasses, and shushed him.

Seconds later they were out on the Midway headed for the Longest Soda Fountain ITW.

9

MAGNITOGORSK

FEBRUARY 1934

"I can't believe my eyes," Aurora said. "What are you doing here?"

Dr. Oleksandr Fizmatov smiled, leaned back against his hard wooden chair, and cast his eyes briefly toward the ceiling of the room. As even Aurora knew, this was him reminding her that, even though it was just the two of them in this little chamber, they were being listened to. "I brought you some food, Comrade Battleship," he said. "Warm clothes. Some hygienic supplies. Women are not ordinarily detained in this facility and so I thought those might be lacking. The guards are inspecting these things. I trust they will be handed over to you in good order."

All of which was good to hear and warmly appreciated. But during the last part of Fizmatov's answer Aurora was staring openly at the ceiling and making broad gestures in all directions, attempting to draw her visitor's attention to the fact that they were having this conversation in an OGPU interrogation cell. What was going on here? Was Fizmatov actually an OGPU agent, living undercover as a political prisoner? How dare he set foot in this place otherwise?

"You don't understand," he said gently. "That is okay. You are assuming a more Western paradigm of crime and punishment. Oh, that does exist here—for ordinary crimes like burglary and assault. But I'm not living in the Corrective Labor Colony because I robbed a bank. This is the outcome of a deal of sorts. I must pay a debt to the Revolution. I do this by applying my skills as a scientist toward the building of socialism. The best place for me to do so is here. For what is a steel mill but a scientific experiment on a grand scale? I have no secrets from the OGPU. Nor would I wish to. Merely visiting a friend who is assisting Comrade Shpak with his inquiries is not going to get me in trouble or place me under suspicion. More the opposite. My family and I are eager to be of assistance in learning all there is to know about your fascinating story."

"Your family?"

"Oh, it so happens that Proton and Elektron have come down from Moscow for a few days to visit their old man."

"That's lovely, but . . . how would your boys enter into it?"

"Well, they are physicists!" Fizmatov said, as if it were self-evident. "There aren't many of those around here. When they came into town, Comrade Shpak had tea with them and asked them some questions."

Aurora's eyes went wide.

"Of a purely technical and abstract nature about recent developments in their field," Fizmatov continued, smiling and making a gesture with one hand as if patting her gently on the arm. "From the nature of these questions it became obvious that he was becoming acquainted with you and your story. That's how I knew you were here."

"Would it be indiscreet for me to ask what topics—what possible connection could exist between my story and recent advances in physics?"

"It sounds as though there are several connections. Niels Bohr. High-altitude balloon experiments. And X-rays. Does any of that ring a bell?"

"Those are all things I mentioned to Comrade Shpak in the telling of my story," Aurora said. She angled her face up toward the light fixture, now basically talking directly to Shpak. "I am impressed by how thoroughly he goes into these things."

"Well, of course, I have nothing more than third-hand accounts of what topics might have been discussed. But there is one detail that caused me to feel a little bit concerned about you, Aurora. About your health and well-being."

"What is that, pray tell?"

"Please forgive me for prying into matters of a personal nature. But has there ever been a time in your life when you might have been exposed to X-rays?"

"Well, they used them to treat my mother. But more recently, last year, I was exposed to X-rays all the time." She explained the fluoroscope and its use in checking the fit of shoes.

It took some doing to get Fizmatov to accept the reality of this. He simply couldn't believe that X-rays were being used in this way. But once she had explained the device in detail, he finally accepted that it must be real.

"And," he said, "once again, forgive me—am I to infer that you might have experienced some kind of unfortunate symptoms relating to your organs of reproduction?"

"How on earth would you know that?"

"Shpak asked Proton to look some things up. Proton sent a telegram to Moscow, and received a telegram back. There is recent research in this area, only published in scientific journals in the last year or two, suggesting that X-rays, as they pass through the body, can interact with reproductive tissue in a manner that can produce unfortunate symptoms."

She wasn't sure how long she sat silent. When she came out of it, though, she knew she had been weeping for a while. Fizmatov had made no move to come around to her side of the table and comfort her. But his eyes were red and he was blowing his nose.

"I really am terribly sorry," he said, when he judged her fit for conversation.

"The sorrow is all in the past!" she said, shaking her head and smiling through the last deluge of tears. "I'm happy now. Happy that I understand. The doctor in Fort Sickles told me I had given birth to a monster. They filled my mind with crazy superstitions and they filled my veins with drugs. I half believed them. But when the whole thing is viewed through the instruments of science, it all makes sense."

A DAY PASSED BEFORE SHE WAS BROUGHT INTO THE INTERROGATION ROOM AGAIN. AS usual, they sat her down and made her wait for a while. It wasn't clear to her whether this was some kind of psychological tactic or mere incompetence. This wait was longer than usual. After at least two hours, she heard cars pulling up outside, car doors slamming. Some men entered the building, soldiers' boots thumping and men's dress shoes clicking on the wooden floor above her head. Some minutes later Shpak came downstairs, talking to another man. He spoke in a mild tone. Calmly submissive. The other man said very little—just a "hmm" or "da" here or there to indicate he was paying attention. They paused outside the door while the jailer jingled his keys and turned the lock. Shpak entered the room. The other man remained in the hallway. He was not a tall man and so Aurora didn't glimpse him until Shpak stepped out of the way. Built like a fireplug. Well dressed after the Soviet fashion. Round face, receding hairline, eyeglasses with circular lenses and heavy frames. Hands in the pockets of his overcoat until he took one out to grab the edge of the door. With a warning look at the guard, he adjusted this until there was only a narrow gap between it and the jamb, through which he peered at Aurora.

Shpak sat down across from her, kicked her under the table, made a V with two fingers, and pointed to his eyes. *Look at me. Not him.*

"I know that you talked to Comrade Fizmatov yesterday," Shpak began. "He shared with you some of the recent findings about X-rays."

"Yes."

"I believe that this new information places us in a position to conclude that part of the investigation concerning the monstrosity you said came out of your womb in"—he consulted his notes—"Fort Sickles, North Dakota."

"That's correct."

"When you first alluded to this during your interview with Dr. Stasova, it naturally aroused concerns that you were suffering from a psychiatric disorder."

"Yes, I regret that I mentioned it in an offhanded manner."

"On the contrary, you should always be as forthcoming as possible."

"Yes, sir."

"Fascinated as I am by your descriptions of the Midget Village and the Pirate Cabaret and so on, today I would like to skip ahead to"—more shuffling of notes—"August of last year, and focus on this aspect of your story. Later on I will have more questions about what happened earlier in the summer, while you were still in Chicago."

"Understood."

"When did you make the decision to leave Chicago, and why did you leave when you did?"

"I had begun experiencing symptoms of pregnancy during the month of July. As I became more and more certain that I was pregnant, I came up with a plan to take the train to eastern Montana and stay with my relatives there."

"To have an abortion or . . ."

"I didn't have a clear plan in mind, I just felt a strong compulsion to get out of town before the pregnancy began to show."

"So you left immediately."

"No, I stayed in Chicago until August fifth."

"Why that specific date?"

"Dick—the boy who impregnated me—had been telling me all about this balloon launch. I wanted to see it. It was a big scientific experiment. As soon as that was over, I got on the train."

10

NORTH DAKOTA

AUGUST 1933

Through the night run to St. Paul she slept well, for the balloon launch—an all-night affair—at Soldier Field had left her exhausted. This had been followed by a long day of gathering her things from the kommunalka and saying her goodbyes. She told everyone it was just a few weeks' visit to Montana. But word seemed, somehow, to have got around that she was pregnant. So no one really expected to see her again for a year, if ever. It was fine; she would miss some of the Germans, but the rest of them were as dust to be shaken from the soles of her Century of Progress oxfords.

The Germans went with her to Union Station, taking turns carrying her trunk and remarking on its extraordinary weight. She attributed this to all of the fascinating books on Leninist theory that she had acquired. And she wasn't even lying about that, save for the "fascinating" part. Those things were hell to read, but cheap to get, and so she'd packed some in on the bottom layer just to keep the violin case from shifting around. She grew weary of listening to their lighthearted jibes. On the train, as if to prove the trunk wasn't so *schwer* at all, she manhandled it up the steps onto the pullman and heaved it up onto a rack before the eyes of crest-fallen Negro porters and emasculated German intellectuals who would gladly have helped her had she only stepped aside and been more ladylike.

As she was lifting and twisting to ram the thing home, she felt a tiny pop inside of her, so subtle that she was more aware of it in dim retrospect than in the actual moment. It had not been painful, more of an internal transition, like cracking a knuckle. But it was enough to tell her she was being a fool, so when the trunk was secure she averted her gaze from the reproachful brown eyes of the porters, went to her seat, and waved out the window to the Germans, blowing kisses as the Empire Builder began its five-day run to Seattle. She was deep asleep before the train had cleared the city limits, and awoke only once, during a brief stop in Dubuque. Morning found them in St. Paul for a twenty-minute transfer to the locomotives of the Great Northern. She might have detrained and stretched her legs in the station but did not feel like moving. The hundreds, perhaps thousands, of miles she'd logged up and down the Midway had been nothing to her at the time, but now she felt as though she never wanted to take another step.

The great train pulled out of the Twin Cities and hooted and rumbled northwest for hour upon hour, making good time and few stops as it penetrated many hundreds of miles into a flat hinterland. Late in the afternoon they crossed the Red River of the North at Fargo and then turned due north for a two-hour run to Grand Forks, then west to travel through the evening toward Minot.

It was somewhere along here that Dawn finally admitted to herself that something was wrong. She'd have put it down to something she had eaten were it not for the fact that she'd not had a bite in twenty-four hours. Hunger pangs, then. But these pains were too central, too focused, too low in the pelvis. And somewhere in the long hours west of Minot, they became too severe for her to suffer them without a certain amount of writhing and gasping.

Sitting next to her was a quick, wrenlike woman in her sixties, Blanche Baker, who'd boarded at Grand Forks en route to her sister's funeral in Havre. Not much was lost on Blanche, who had already extracted from Dawn the rudiments of her story. She might even have guessed that the real purpose of the sojourn in Montana was to serve out a pregnancy—it was a common enough sort of thing to do. Blanche sat still, eyes closed, as a sort of formal courtesy, but Dawn could tell she was not sleeping from the way her jaw tightened whenever Dawn thumped an armrest with a closed fist, arched her back, or stifled a cry of pain into a long train-brake hiss.

The cramping started to come in waves. In the respites between them Dawn began talking to Blanche. She apologized for the trouble. She could tell that Blanche was feeling—had shouldered—the responsibility, was wondering when to get up and summon the conductor. "Just a few more hours—a few more hundred miles down the line—I'll be to where my family can help me," Dawn insisted, hoping it would prevent Blanche from making a fuss. She named the stop and she named the people she deemed most likely to come out and meet her, though in truth she had no idea if her telegram had got through to any of them. She saw Blanche noting those data in a little diary she kept in her bag, Blanche being that sort of gal. Seeing the fountain pen drawing the strokes on the page, Dawn understood that matters were more serious than she'd let herself believe. During the next respite between cramps she realized she'd wet herself. Pulling the blanket off her lap for a run to the toilet, she found her skirt and her seat stained with blood.

It was later. She must have been making a spectacle of herself, for more people than just Blanche were now watching her. The whole carriage was awake, porters and conductors were on the job. The train's whistle, which twenty-four hours ago had lulled her to sleep, took on a new, urgent keening: repeated triple blasts radiating across the infinite prairie like smoke signals in the dark. It was, she well knew, a way of summoning medical help to the next whistle-stop, one of a welter of cow towns and Indian agencies in a blurred block of agate type on the Great Northern timetable, slated, for the best of reasons, to be bypassed at three o'clock in the morning. Those who lived in such places were accustomed to rolling over and going back to sleep after being wakened by the long blasts of the Empire Builder's whistle, and some could even identify the engineer by his signature. The triple blast, however, would visit their sleep as a nightmare and draw them toward the station in an unsettled frame of mind.

By such men was Dawn taken off the train on a stretcher, and only because of a last-second rolling of the eyes was attention drawn to her trunk, which was pulled down by excited men desperate to be given assignments, and slammed down on the planking of the platform next to her. A stark and simple sign read FORT SICKLES. She smelled sagebrush. The cramps came on so severely that, for the first time, she cried out in pain. She collected vague impressions of a ride on dusty wash-boarded roads in the back of a truck, but these were no more well formed than memories she had from the age of two of her mother riding a horse across a similar landscape, red hair flying behind her, and the blue of Lake Michigan, and the boat to Petrograd.

Then a white room, a woman with a white face, needles, and a hissing mask.

THE NARRATIVE CONVENTIONS OF HOLLYWOOD MOVIES, REINFORCED BY THE CENTURY OF Progress ethos in which she had been marinating for three months, and combined with the natural relief she felt at having woken up at all, all served to get her off on the wrong—which was to say, too optimistic—foot when she came around. She was lying on a cot with a lot of something stuffed into her vagina. Common sense told her not to move. Logically this ought to be some sort of hospital, or at least clinic, but the more she looked around, the more she understood just how makeshift it was. It was, in fact, a large tent, probably Great War surplus. Efforts had been made to confer the sense, if not the reality, of permanence by laying a plank floor over the dirt and stringing electrical wires about. A stern High Plains wind was rattling the canvas roof and forcing its way down a rusty stovepipe that penetrated it through a canted asbestos slab, scenting the air with creosote. Hanging curtains defined a space scarcely wider than her cot. Beyond, she could hear a few other patients snoring, talking incoherently, or calling repeatedly for one Mrs. Kidd. The smoke of their cigarettes drifted over the top of Dawn's little cell, catching splinters of light that poked in through moth holes in the canvas walls. A thumping door, and hard echoes, hinted at an adjacent structure made out of wood. Within it, hymns were playing on a Victrola. These were not the High Church four-parters of ivied northern churches but the righteous hollering of God-raging hill dwellers.

"Ooh, she's awake," said a woman's voice in the Scandinavian vowels of the high Midwest. A movement of a curtain told Dawn that someone had been peeking in on her through some gap too small for her to have noticed. A brisk, icy chiff-chiff-chiff noise receded: a pair of stout thighs encased in coarse hose and chafing against each other. Two different hoarse men's voices called out ardently for Mrs. Kidd in the accents of Oklahoma or Texas, but Mrs. Kidd was concerned with one thing only, and that was to get the attention of some man, apparently in the adjoining structure, whom she referred to variously as "Reverend Kidd," "darling," "sweetheart," and "pumpkin."

A man approached, praising Jesus, and swept the curtain open.

The infirmary contained perhaps a dozen beds, of which eight were occupied, half with Indians and half with white men. The former would be Lakota. They had been silent, so Dawn hadn't known they were there. The white men were bony and unshaven, and Dawn guessed them to be Okies who had fled black blizzards north, and rebounded from the long, hard border of Canada.

She knew this part of the country well enough to be able to guess that Fort Sickles had literally been a fort, in the military sense of that term, within living memory. Once its mission of subjugating the Indians had been achieved, it would have been turned into an agency for keeping an eye on them, and doling out such goods and services as the government was willing to send their way. Places like this were notorious for attracting people on the make, who knew that they could get away with a lot. For how often, really, was the federal government going to send inspectors and auditors out to the likes of Fort Sickles?

Reverend Kidd would forever be Pumpkin to Dawn, whose first impression was of his red face and cloud of orange hair. "Praise Jesus!" he said again, and it wasn't clear to her whether this in itself was an act of praise, or a command aimed at Dawn. He and Mrs. Kidd—a stocky woman in a white nurse's outfit, complete with white hose—approached the cot and knelt to either side, each gripping one of her hands. With their free arms they reached across her abdomen and clenched their fingers together in here-is-the-steeple mode, above her. "Lord," Pumpkin intoned, "by your grace has Mrs. Kidd cast out this girl's demon and cleansed her womb of Lucifer's pollution."

"Having fouled her with his monstrosity," Mrs. Kidd went on, "Satan reached out his scaly hand to take her soul down to hell, but by Your heavenly power acting through the healing touch of the Reverend Kidd, she was raked back from the brink of the pit. Now we pray that the poor orphan repent of her sins and be embraced into her new family. Amen!"

"Amen!" called Pumpkin, and then they both fell silent and Dawn realized that they were looking at her expectantly. A few "Amens" reached her ears from those Okies who were conscious enough to know what was going on; or perhaps for them it was like kicking out when struck on the knee with a hammer.

"How did you know I was an orphan?" Dawn asked.

THEY KNEW BECAUSE SHE HAD TOLD THEM. AND, AS SHE GRADUALLY FIGURED OUT OVER the next few days, she had told them because Mrs. Kidd had been giving her drugs: an anesthetic generally used for veterinary applications but commonly employed by Mrs. Kidd on Indians, in whom its side effects (hallucinations, amnesia, rambling speech) could be overlooked given that it was so much less expensive than drugs formulated for humans and thus helped stretch the taxpayers' money further. Mrs. Kidd employed a free hand both with it and with morphine: a more expensive compound that she was willing to spend on a white girl.

Between the hallucinogenic effects of the horse medicine and the narcotic sway of the morphine, Dawn got to understand her new situation in a piecemeal series of impressions, in its colorful and surreal way loosely comparable to being driven at high speed through Century of Progress lashed to the hood of a truck.

Mrs. Kidd, formerly Nurse Van Essen, née Trudy Larson, had been co-running the place with her late husband, Dr. Van Essen, who had killed himself with an overdose of morphine. The Office of Indian Affairs, which ran the clinic, had not yet sent out a replacement, so she was effectively the chief medical officer. Meanwhile the influx of Okies had drawn Reverend Kidd up out of Arkansas as a sort of missionary or chaplain; he had married Nurse Van Essen and made her into Mrs. Kidd. It was not clear to Dawn, from her difficult vantage point flat on her back on a cot, why so many Okies were hanging about the place, but then there was much about it that she would have been hard put to make sense of even had she been stone-cold sober the entire time. In any event, the Kidds now ran it.

All of this she collected from Mrs. Kidd during moments of near lucidity. Mrs. Kidd liked to bustle about straightening and inspecting things better left alone. She talked as she did so, confiding in Dawn as if Dawn were fully conscious; actually gave a damn; and knew Mrs. Kidd much better than was the case. Dawn, hardly able to take in the words, saw more than she heard. Mrs. Kidd dressed expensively, by regional standards. Normal, even for a reasonably prosperous ranch wife, would have been a cotton dress, no stockings, hair in a bun, lipstick on Sundays. Mrs. Kidd was somehow managing to have her hair done, and she went through white stockings and red lipstick like a burning department store.

So much for the Kidd saga. Disconcerted by the way she kept losing consciousness and waking up, Dawn tried to piece together the story of what was happening to *her*. She already knew that she had been "purged" of a "monstrosity" that was now sitting in formaldehyde in a mason jar on Pumpkin's desk, proof visible of Satan's physical presence in the world. Pumpkin kept threatening to show it to her whenever she evinced even mild skepticism about his account of the night of her arrival. After that, she had been subjected to an operation, thus far described only in King James Bible vocabulary, that hadn't gone well—presumably a dilation and curettage? Non-viable embryos happened all the time. They tended to end in miscarriages. Pumpkin had seen the results, and construed it as a demon, and thought her recovery a miracle for which he deserved credit.

She woke up and they were standing around her bed casting out her demons. Memories, fresh but false, suggested she'd been hallucinating.

She woke up underwater. Many hands were pushing her down. It was not a hallucination. Some instinct deeper than consciousness told her not to inhale. She was on her back, looking up at a ring of faces, scattered by the water's roiled surface. In the center of the ring, high above, was a shimmering white house atop a pink sandstone cliff.

One of her flailing heels struck the bottom. She gathered her legs under her and pushed up; the hands came away, letting her erupt into the air. She was standing in a river, ringed by men in suits, like pallbearers. But they were only baptizing her: a rite to which she had apparently given her consent while under the influence of some amnestic drug. They were in a cold, clear stream, at a bend where it hooked around a sandstone bluff with trees and a house on the top.

It was her second baptism, the first having occurred in a little Russian Orthodox church outside of Petrograd when she had been about seven. This one, however, happened in a place that she would always know in her bones as home. It was the landscape in which she had been born. The first natural smells she'd ever scented were in her nostrils as she drew breath now: sage, the tang of dust, cold running water, woodsmoke, pine. In some Greek mythic version of her story this would have imbued her with some autochthonous power that would have enabled her to run free of these people, but this landscape was as much prison as refuge. The winters, the wildlife, the scarcity of food, and malevolent humans forced people to cluster in camps, cabins, tipis, anywhere they could gather around a fire and share meat. And having joined such communities they found it unthinkable to leave them, and thereby subjugated themselves to those who by force of personality, strength of arms, or wealth ruled them. Dawn was as much a product of those societies as she was of the landscape. For it was in the mine heads, lumber camps, and ranches that bosses ruled, often with too heavy a hand. Men unused to rule rose up to struggle against them. Open war was fought between the workers and the hired goons brought in by the bosses. The law became involved, and out of it grew a shadow culture of Westerners who were too willful to be Communists but too political to be outlaws. Those were Dawn's mother's people. They would ride the rails to Chicago to attend Wobbly conventions, where they would thrill the Eastern factory organizers with their dash and bravado, their tales of pitched battles at mine heads two miles above sea level, and after a brief doomed romance it would all go wrong as the Easterners tried to impose revolutionary discipline on the Westerners, who would tell them to go piss up a rope. Her mother had met her father at one of those conventions and he had come west with her to see how it was and had fallen in love with her, and with here. So, emerging from the river into that landscape, shocked to full consciousness by the icy water, Dawn knew herself to be home, but knew also that home was a prison until she could get clear of communities like the one where the Kidds held sway.

Feeling much better, she politely declined her evening dose of drugs and was held down by Pumpkin and one of his acolytes as Mrs. Kidd, gazing into her eyes, slipped the needle into her arm. "There, there," she murmured. This was always the last thing Dawn heard before she lost consciousness.

She woke up in a wood-walled room, lashed to a bed. Pumpkin was sitting next to her, back half turned. His left hand was smothering her breast and his right was up to no good; she smelled hot Vaseline and saw him cringe as he ejaculated on her bedspread.

She woke up to find herself alone in the room with Mrs. Kidd and her little black bag of hypodermics. "So, how's my little Communist today?" her captor asked brightly. Mrs. Kidd was sweating with the effort of maintaining the façade of sarcastic cheer. "We should have left you by the side of the road to be et up by wolves!" she went on. "Slut—out of Chicago—show up here with your monster—ungrateful, unrepentant—and now you seduce my husband!"

She was crazy: a word Dawn had lost the habit of using as a result of hanging around with educated persons elevated through study of Freudian psychoanalysis. But it was a fine word in places like this, where—never mind what Freud might say—people, especially ones who'd found a way of getting a little bit of power, could simply go off the rails and wander off into a shadow world that was half made up, and half misseen through baroque systems of delusion. She was crazy. Crazy, and probably on drugs—most likely some kind of amphetamine. The most Dawn could possibly do was question her calmly, even meekly, in the hope of connecting with whatever part of her mind might still be sound.

"If you let me go, I will leave town."

"You'd like that, wouldn't you! To escape justice for your crime."

"What crime?"

"Jail is the only place you're going. And I'm going to keep you there until you sign those papers."

"What papers?"

"Oh, I looked through your trunk. Found your Communist books. And found your papers from the veterans. Don't you worry your pretty little head—*Aurora*."

Dawn's mind was reeling from more than just drugs. She had not heard her Russian name spoken aloud since her father had died. How did Mrs. Kidd know it?

From the papers she had found in the trunk. Her father had filled those papers out and used the name he preferred for her.

An even more salient point now came to mind: Mrs. Kidd had been rooting through her trunk. She'd delved deep enough to find some "Communist books." The violin case was below those, under a false floor of cedar planks. Mrs. Kidd must have stopped there. Or perhaps she'd seen the violin case and assumed it contained a violin. She'd have mentioned the submachine gun by this point in the conversation if she knew about it.

"I stashed those papers safe and sound at the bank," Mrs. Kidd went on.

"Bank?"

"In the vault. The banker is a close, personal friend. I see him every Monday. It's where the reverend and I keep the Lord's money."

"From the collection plate."

"Yes. The banker will keep your things safe and sound until we sort you out. And for a wayward slut like you, the only two ways out are jail or foster care in our home."

Someone was knocking on the door. "Mrs. Kidd? Sheriff's deputy."

The arrival of a law officer was a fresh surprise to Dawn. It must have showed on her face, because Mrs. Kidd now savored a triumphant few moments. "It is open, Deputy James."

Deputy James came in and enjoyed looking at Dawn for so long it even made Mrs. Kidd uncomfortable. Dawn remembered him, vaguely, from the night she'd been picked up from the train platform. "Deputy James,"

Mrs. Kidd said, "you'll remember Dawn. The girl who got pregnant and tried to give herself an abortion."

"What?!" Dawn blurted.

Mrs. Kidd was waiting for that; she slapped Dawn across the face, knocking her back onto the bed.

"Oh now, Mrs. Kidd, you didn't have to go and do that," said Deputy James cheerfully.

"She'll clean up soon enough and then you and the other deputies can have your fill of looking at her through the bars of her cage. Slut that she is, I'm sure she'll enjoy being leered at. Why, who knows what kinds of favors she will offer you in exchange for special treatment. You'll have to be strong and stern with this one." Mrs. Kidd turned to look back at Dawn. Deputy James by now had slapped a handcuff over one of Dawn's wrists and begun to untie it from the bed frame. When the rope loosened he dragged that hand over to the other and cuffed them together. Dawn's eyes were full of tears and her nose was running, which infuriated her because it wasn't that she was crying, it was just an automatic reaction to being hit in the face. "There, there," Mrs. Kidd said, "would you like another injection to calm your mood, Dawn?"

Dawn shook her head no.

"She botched the abortion, like they all do, and almost kilt herself," Mrs. Kidd told the lawman as Dawn was sitting up, waiting for her feet to be untied. "Now she's better though. Ready to be discharged. But a miscreant who's ready to be discharged is one who's ready to be held to account for her crime, ain't that so?"

"Couldn't agree more, Mrs. Kidd, and you know that the full force of the law will come down on her once Judge Hughes comes back to town."

THERE WAS NO WOMEN'S JAIL AND SO THEY LOCKED HER UP IN A BASEMENT CELL AWAY from run-of-the-mill offenders. Neither James nor any of the other deputies laid a hand on her, proving that Mrs. Kidd, in a typical thought pattern for someone with her particular brand of crazy, assumed the worst of all of them, and so laid plans doomed to miscarry. That was something.

On the other hand, going through morphine withdrawal was no picnic, and left her in a condition that the euphemism-prone residents of the upper Midwest would describe as "quite a state." That plus the overall lack of sanitary conditions probably made Dawn a lot less attractive to the jailers than Mrs. Kidd liked to imagine. Dawn had never quite been glamorous, but she'd been within striking distance of it and she had a general idea of how the magic worked, and what killed it. How anything could be less glamorous than morphine withdrawal in a basement jail cell in Fort Sickles, North Dakota, she could not imagine.

After a few days, though, the nausea and vomiting became less and she began to have long intervals of being lucid enough to take stock of her situation. Regrettably, much of that happened in the middle of the night when she'd rather be sleeping. She was still prone to twitchy legs, running nose, and goose bumps, but those at least didn't interfere with her ability to think straight.

She could not guess how long she'd been "medicated" in the Kidds' infirmary, but the number of needle marks in her arms was about twenty, the newer ones surrounded by bruises, tiny blue smudges lined up the veins like the blossoms of fireweed. Three or four weeks?

The trip from the infirmary to the jail had given her a sense of how Fort Sickles was laid out. The Kidds' clinic was on Office of Indian Affairs land just at the place where a state highway crossed the border into the Lakota reservation. A miserable cluster of shacks and businesses—mostly drinking establishments—had sprung up there, with a Hooverville full of Okies growing on the white side of the line. But the real town was five miles away on the same highway, which ran parallel to the Great Northern tracks. It consisted of perhaps a hundred small wood-frame houses, kit-built from the Sears Roebuck catalog. A river ran nearby. Some of the nicer houses were set back in the shade of the trees that grew along its course. Smaller houses swarmed a town square adorned with a cannon and a statue of Custer. A bank, three churches, a library, and a courthouse fronted on the little patch of grass. Gaps between those stately edifices were plugged with saloons, drugstores, barbershops, and the like.

The sheriff and his little jail occupied a wing out back of the courthouse. She would not have to cover more than a hundred paces to reach her arraignment, when the time came. But Judge Hughes did not come back until a week after her arrest. And that was just as well, since by the time she was finally marched into the courtroom for her initial arraignment, she'd had time not only to put the morphine behind her and get cleaned up a little but to think her situation through and make some sense of that eventful last interview with Mrs. Kidd.

Mrs. Kidd had gone through Dawn's trunk. Not all the way to the bottom. No, she'd stopped when she'd found the manila folder where Dawn kept her papers. That would include both her Soviet and U.S. passports. Dawn's father had been a disabled Great War veteran, honorably discharged, and as such entitled to a monthly benefit check. Certain benefits were transferrable to Dawn upon his death. When she had made it back to Chicago last year, she'd found all of this paperwork in his flat, and retained it.

Seeing those papers, and knowing that Dawn was a minor and an orphan, Mrs. Kidd and Pumpkin had formed a plan to adopt her. This would enable them to intercept her checks from the veterans. Dawn's papers had suddenly become valuable. Accordingly, Mrs. Kidd had taken them to the bank, which was catercorner across the town square from the courthouse/jail complex, and prevailed upon her personal friend, the manager, to store them in the vault along with the Lord's money.

Dawn could only guess at the whereabouts of her trunk. It wouldn't make sense for the Kidds to deposit the entire trunk in the bank vault. They probably had it stored at the infirmary. After she'd been in the jail for a couple of days, some of her clothes had showed up; Mrs. Kidd or someone must have taken those out of the trunk and had them delivered.

When the deputies had fingerprinted her, they'd confiscated some of her belongings, including the key to the violin case, which she'd got in the habit of wearing around her neck. Mrs. Kidd, of course, had noticed this, and asked about it, then supplied a useful answer: "Is that the key to your diary, sweetheart?" It seemed as good a lie as any and so Dawn had answered yes, then improvised an explanation: she must have left the diary on the train on the night of her hectic arrival in Fort Sickles. "There,

there," Mrs. Kidd had consoled her, "perhaps it was the Lord's way of help-ing you forget all those old memories and start a new life."

Why had she been thrown into the slammer, and how did that figure into the Kidds' plan for that new life?

When the judge showed up, they were going to charge her with crimes related to abortion. That much was clear from the conversation between Mrs. Kidd and Deputy James when the latter had come to the infirmary to arrest her.

Women had miscarriages all the time, though. How could a judge really determine whether such an event had been spontaneous, or the re-sult of a criminal act?

In the absence of direct witnesses, it would have to come down to the testimony of qualified medical professionals. They'd be able to examine the patient and render judgment as to whether the loss of the pregnancy had been an act of God or of man.

The only medical professional who could conceivably be called as wit-ness was Mrs. Kidd.

Why go to all the trouble of having Dawn arrested and arraigned, though, if the goal was to adopt her so that her benefit checks could be intercepted?

Because Dawn, as a seventeen-year-old, would have some say in the matter. She'd have ways to fight the adoption. They didn't want her to fight it. They wanted her to go before the judge and meekly consent to becom-ing a foster child of the Kidds. In order to make her do that, they had to have something they could hold over her. Which they did; a few words from Mrs. Kidd on the witness stand could put her away for years.

WHAT TROUBLED DAWN MOST ABOUT THIS SCHEME WAS THE SHEER LEVEL OF DESPERA-tion and baroque harebrained-ness it involved, and what that implied about the states of mind, and the financial straits, of the Reverend and Mrs. Kidd. More particularly the missus, since Pumpkin was so hapless. His inability to keep his hand off his cock when he was in the same room with Dawn must have been noticed by Mrs. Kidd, who had realized she had to get Dawn out of the infirmary, and away from the reverend, without letting her slip away altogether. So she was having the judicial system act as her jailer—much easier anyway than keeping Dawn restrained and drugged.

This was the bad side of the high plains: communities so remote that people could get away with anything, and, lacking contact with settled places, could wander far down strange thoughtways from which there was no route back to sanity. The Siberian taiga, the Australian outback, the interior of Brazil, must all have towns, and people, like this. Acting as fuel, or as accelerant, were the Indian agencies, bringing in unsupervised government money to establishments like the Kidds' infirmary. Mrs. Kidd's pharmacopoeia had unquestionably been paid for by taxpayers, and if she even bothered to cook the books, she would claim that all of those drugs were being used to relieve the suffering of the Lakota people.

THE WHOLE CAST OF CHARACTERS WAS THERE IN JUDGE HUGHES'S COURTROOM. THIS SESsion was a cattle call for every man, woman, and child who had run afoul of the law since his previous appearance, as well as family members, victims, witnesses, and curious spectators. Perhaps three dozen were in the place, including Reverend and Mrs. Kidd. Pumpkin averted his gaze but Mrs. Kidd gave Dawn a cool, searching look as the bailiff led her to a spot on a bench reserved for prisoners, off to one side, at right angles to the pews where free people sat. As soon as Dawn had sat down, Mrs. Kidd chiff-chiff-chiffed up the aisle, smiling sweetly for all to see. She bent over the rail, put her face so close to Dawn's that her powder got up Dawn's nose, and whispered: "I hope you have had time to consider our generous offer to take you in as our foster child. A simple nod will suffice and then all of this will be behind you."

The calculation, though odious, was not a difficult one. Refusing the offer would bring down Mrs. Kidd's false testimony. This would lead to prison time. Worse, there'd be an extensive paper trail that might be noticed, somewhere down the line, by Silent Al. Accepting the Kidds' offer, on the other hand, would mean a release from chains and bars and a different style of imprisonment in the home of the Kidds. The latter would be much easier to escape from—and one opportunity to escape was all she required.

"What did you do with all of my things?" Dawn asked.

Mrs. Kidd smiled. "Honey, don't you worry your pretty little head about that. We've already moved your trunk to our house. It's waiting for you in your new room. All you need to do is say yes and you'll be out of this nasty jail before sundown. You can settle into your new home with all of your things and it'll be just fine."

"Gosh, what kinda house is it? Is it real nice?"

"It's *so* nice, sweetheart, so much better than the places you've been living. Dr. Van Essen, may God rest his soul, bought the land above the crick. Pumpkin and I built the house back in the woods there. We sit on the veranda and listen to the birds singing and the water running in the crick. You're going to love it there."

"Thank you, Mrs. Kidd, it sounds very nice."

Noises back in the corridor indicated that Judge Hughes was about to come in. Mrs. Kidd chiff-chiff-chiffed back to her seat.

A cowboy seated in the back of the room let out a fart.

Everyone looked at him.

His big hat had been over his face as he'd dozed. Awakened by his own flatulence, he now nudged it back, then took it off to reveal his face.

It was a familiar face to Dawn. It was her mother's half-cousin Reggie Walker, who in his forty or so years had pursued a wide range of occupations, some of which had been legal.

By what miracle was he here?

Blanche Baker. The woman on the train. She must have sent a telegram from Havre, letting Dawn's kin know that the girl had been taken off the train at Fort Sickles, in distress.

Having got her attention, Reggie crossed his arms insouciantly over his chest with his thumbs projecting up. He glanced over at Mrs. Kidd, then turned back to look Dawn straight in the eye.

He shook his head no.

She did not make any particular response.

He raised a hand up lazily and drew it across his throat. Then he dropped it into the crook of his other arm and pantomimed an injection, his thumb depressing an imaginary plunger. Just in case he wasn't making himself clear, he looked back at Mrs. Kidd. Then his eyes rolled back in their sockets, his tongue came out, his head fell back, and he sprawled in an imitation of death.

"YOU FORCED HER TO COMMIT PERJURY," REGGIE SAID TO HER LATER. HIS TONE WAS ADmiring, congratulatory. He was *proud* of her.

It was visiting hours at the jail. What had just happened in the courtroom made it clear that Dawn was going to be here for a while. She made no answer.

"She testified you gave yourself an abortion. That's a lie, I figure."

"Sure is. I wouldn't have done it on a train."

Reggie nodded. "Well, that's gonna make her sleep poorly—a respectable woman and all."

"You really think so, Reggie?"

"Oh, I *do*. Don't matter how rotten she might be on the inside, or what she done in secret. To get up in front of those people and swear to something that ain't so, that's a big step. Bigger than killing someone."

"What did you mean by that?" She imitated his pantomime from the courtroom.

"She killed her first husband. The doctor. Maybe kinda-sorta by accident. Not that he hadn't been dipping into the ol' medicine cabinet. He was. For a long time. Everyone knew it. That's why it was a good way to get rid of him. They found him with the tube around his left arm, the needle in the vein, his heart stopped. Only problem being that he was left-handed."

"Was there no investigation, no—"

Reggie shook his head. "She is a respectable lady hereabouts. At least, among the kinds of men who conduct investigations." He turned and stared into Dawn's eyes, his mustache drooping, his blue eyes sadly expectant. "You're probably wondering why I showed up in that courtroom. Did what I did."

"I reckon it did arouse my curiosity a bit. You seem awfully well informed for a man who doesn't even live in these parts."

"I been here for three weeks. Ever since your kin received a certain telegram. Been buying drinks and asking questions. I was going to visit you at that clinic, but once I started learning about the Kidds and their racket I decided against it."

"Why didn't you come say hi when I was in the jail?"

"Didn't want to let the Kidds know I was onto what they were planning."

"Making me say yes to being their foster child."

For a completely uneducated and illiterate man, Reggie had a certain way of reacting when the person he was talking to was just being impossibly stupid. He broke eye contact. One corner of his mouth twitched back.

"Dawn Rae. She would've just killed you."

"Oh."

"Same as she did her ex-husband. They'd have sunk your body in the crick and collected your benefit checks forever."

Dawn was knocked back for a spell. Partly just by the sudden and absolute knowledge that what Reggie was saying was true. They'd have held her down in her nice new bedroom at the Kidds' house. The last words Dawn would have heard would have been "There, there."

It *had* to be true. Like one of Dick's mathematical proofs. Mrs. Kidd had ejected her from the infirmary because of Pumpkin's wandering eye. To bring her into their home would create a much worse temptation, one that could only be dealt with in one way.

Also leaving her scatterbrained and off-balance for a bit was shock at how stupid she'd been not to have seen what Reggie had seen. She'd come so close to saying "yes" in that courtroom.

But there was another thing too. It had come to her when Reggie had mentioned that the Kidds would sink her body in the crick. She had a memory from when they had forcibly baptized her. They'd pushed her under. Drugged, she had come awake and looked up through the streaming water of the crick and seen the ring of people around her, the hands holding her down.

But above them, high on a sandstone bluff, there had been a white house with a veranda.

The silence had become long enough that even Reggie felt awkward. "Better for you to be in jail," he insisted. "Hell, we can get you out of that."

"Yes and no."

"How you figure?"

"I got in trouble with the feds, Reggie."

"Mmm."

"They know my name. My Russian name. I never used it anywhere else. But Mrs. Kidd found it on my papers. Now it's on the arraignment. The case documents. Eventually the feds will get wind of it and Silent Al will come to get me."

"Who's that?"

"A G-man I crossed paths with in D.C. Knows too much about me. Way too much."

Reggie chewed on it for a while, like a twist of tobacco.

"I might need help from more than just you," Dawn said. "Not that you ain't terrific. But some jobs take more fellers."

"You're real special to me, Dawn, because of your ma, who was like a sister to me, and helped me through rough patches when I was drunk and crazy. I would do anything for you. But the kinds of fellers I judge you're featuring are thin on the ground. It's hard to get 'em together anymore, and pointed in the same direction. It takes an incentive is all I'm saying. Your feminine charms might go part of the way, but—"

"I got more to offer than feminine charms."

"Let's have it then."

She was tired and lonely and her strongest emotion was to do nothing at all. To accept what was coming to her. This had been the case for a while, and was made more obvious now by her sitting across the table from Reggie Walker.

He was the kind of man to whom you could say anything, but once you had said it, it could not be unsaid. It would set in motion consequences as implacable as emptying seven hundred cylinders of hydrogen into a balloon. It was just his way.

She balked before saying what had been on her mind. He waited patiently, for it was in the nature of a man like him to do so, knowing that the consequences of speech could be of no small moment.

What came to her during that wait, strangely, was General Patton. It was not a particular set of words that Patton had spoken to her. It was rather the way he had looked at her, the feel of his eyes upon her when she had ridden her horse and danced with him at the ball, the regard he had shown her and the appraisal he had made of her as a warrior, one for whom there was no place in civilian peacetime society. One who would have to find her own place. If she failed in that, she would be guilty of letting herself down in the eyes of Patton and would never again be worthy of the regard he had shown her with his gaze. For to have earned his respect once and let him down later was a far worse thing than never to have earned it at all; it was the kind of respect that brought with it terrible responsibilities.

Reggie was still waiting, as a gun waits for its owner to pull the trigger.

"They told me my second arraignment is coming up in a week. That's the one where I can enter a plea."

"I am somewhat familiar with the process."

"I can also post bail."

"You got that much?"

"Well, I don't know how much they're gonna ask for, Reggie. But the answer is probably no. Even if I did, the Kidds took all my stuff. It was in a trunk. The trunk's at their house. But I had papers too. Passports and such. Mrs. Kidd took that to the bank and put it in the vault. A big safe-deposit box where she and the reverend keep the Lord's money."

These words had roughly the same effect on Reggie Walker as insertion of a fresh dry cell into an electrical toy. He took his boots down off the adjoining chair and sat up straight, then reached down unconsciously with one hand to touch the top of his cowboy hat on the table, adjusting its angle slightly. "Bank vault, you say. Been awhile since I seen one of them from the inside."

"Yep."

"What's she mean by the Lord's money?"

"Collections they take from their flock."

"Their flock is a sorry-looking bunch."

"Maybe because they give all their money to the Lord."

"Maybe."

"Reverend Kidd came up from the South. He seems like a man with a past. Maybe he brought some of the Lord's money with him. Maybe some of his flock down there got wise to his schemes."

Reggie nodded. "They got a nice house over yonder. Nicest house in town, people say."

"White house on a bluff above the riverbend?"

Reggie nodded, watching her alertly.

"On the other side the ground's flat. You can drive right up to the water's edge. They go there and baptize people."

Reggie didn't want to venture into this new topic of baptisms. "Folks say that Reverend Kidd bought that lot the day he showed up in town. Cash on the barrelhead. Hired some people to build the house. Always paid cash."

"He brought money up from down South," Dawn said. "Probably fleeced a bunch of Okies and got run out of town."

Reggie said nothing for a while, just gazing off into space. Then, finally, he met Dawn's eye.

Dawn said, "Get me some fellers like you said, Reggie, ones who feel as you do about banks."

Reggie was nodding.

"Only thing is, Reggie?"

"Yeah, Dawn?"

"That house has to burn. Dawn has to die."

11

MAGNITOGORSK

FEBRUARY 1934

"This has, in some ways, been the most vexing investigation of my career," Shpak announced. He was seated on a leather armchair, placed on a Persian rug directly on the ice covering the Ural River. He wore that heavy wool overcoat, but there was not really a need for it; they were sheltered in a spacious ice-fishing shack, almost a dacha on skids, and Shpak had stoked its pot-bellied stove until it glowed. Aurora could feel its warmth on her exposed skin from two meters away. "Oh, not because of you, Comrade Aurora. You've been cooperative, if somewhat rambling. But that's in the nature of your story—you really have been all over the place."

Aurora was doing her level best to make eye contact and pay attention, but circumstances were making that difficult. She was flat on her back, stark naked, on an old steel bed frame, to which she was being lashed down with bedsheets torn into strips.

"I am being pressed to deliver results quickly—far more quickly than I consider to be good practice. When we began our series of conversations, I assumed that I would detain you for months, perhaps years. Instead, results are demanded within *days*. Hours, even! Important visitors are in town. They want this all wrapped up before they leave."

Shpak was being assisted by two men and a woman. At the beginning the men had been involved in holding Aurora down to the bed frame. Once she had been partially immobilized, they had turned their attention to other tasks. The woman was still circling around her, pulling strips of linen out of a sack and using them to lash down an elbow here or an ankle there. But one of the men was operating a handsaw, using it to widen the hole in the ice while the other was fussing with a block and tackle. Having satisfied himself that this was firmly anchored to the ice house's roof beam, he began to fashion a Y-shaped arrangement of ropes connecting it to the corners of the bed frame near Aurora's shoulders.

To either side of Shpak's chair was a low table fashioned of cedar planks in a rustic style. The one on his left supported all of his notebooks. The table on the right was for his pipe, ashtray, and tobacco. As well there was a pocketknife with its blade exposed.

"These are the kinds of men who simply will not believe in the veracity of a report unless technical methods have been used," Shpak continued. He was stuffing some loose tobacco into a pipe, but glanced up from that for a moment at the block and tackle. "All quite normal. Easily done. But there is a complication in your case, which is that, in the unlikely event it does not culminate in your summary execution, you're to be delivered unblemished, in the full glory of your young womanhood. My instructions as to that could hardly have been more explicit. So I had to ask myself, what is a technical method that is severe enough to lend credibility to the report without inflicting visible damage?" He struck a match and spent a few moments puffing fire into his pipe. "I hope you appreciate the ingenuity I have shown in finding a way to meet all of these requirements: speedy results, extreme rigor, no marks."

The woman seemed to have too much time on her hands, or perhaps she was worried that if she didn't do her job thoroughly enough Shpak would use technical measures on her. Aurora's wrists were already strongly bound to the bed frame, but now the woman was winding strips of linen between her fingers and lashing those down too.

"What is it you want to know?" Aurora asked. "I've always answered all of your questions."

A curious feature of ice-covered lakes in winter was that they emitted noises: groaning, rumbling, and even cracking sounds as the ice slowly heaved. It was distracting—even alarming—at first and then you got used to it. Shpak paid as little attention to Aurora's question as he did to the sounds of the ice. He was being interrupted from time to time by the men working on the rigging, who wished to draw his attention to certain details or to make sure everything was being done to his satisfaction.

In a strange way, the situation actually became boring once she could no longer move.

Who were these important men—men Shpak was obviously afraid of—who wanted results within hours?

During his visit to the jail last week, Fizmatov had mentioned that Sergo Ordzhonikidze would be visiting town in a few days. The head of the People's Commissariat of Heavy Industry, and the ultimate boss of Magnitogorsk, unless you counted Stalin himself. Like Stalin, he was a Georgian. He was in the habit of swinging through Magnitogorsk from time to time to inspect the facilities and pin medals on hero workers.

Important visitors are in town. They want this all wrapped up before they leave. Shpak had definitely been speaking in the plural. It wasn't just one visitor. There must be other people traveling with Ordzhonikidze. Including at least one person who would actually care about Aurora and her story—care enough to put pressure on Shpak. But why would anyone care?

The preparations were nearing completion. No one did so much as glance at Aurora for about a quarter of an hour as everything was squared away. The man who had been doing the rigging pulled on the rope that snaked through the block and tackle, taking up slack until the bed frame began to rise up off the ice. Aurora felt herself angling up to vertical. Finally the foot of the frame lifted off and she began swinging free. She pendulumed once, twice across the gaping hole in the ice and then came to a stop directly above it as several hands reached out to check the swinging. Then she began to spin around as the rope unwound under her weight. While she was coming into equilibrium, the rigger fussed with a final detail. A hand-cranked winch had been crudely lashed into place atop the massive table to Shpak's left. He got the end of the rope fastened to it and then devoted a few moments to showing Shpak how the device worked: how to crank rope in, raising Aurora higher toward the roof beam, and how to let it out, dropping her toward the black water below.

Then all of the assistants tromped out, leaving Shpak and Aurora alone together. "Another great advantage: privacy," Shpak said. "My office, the interrogation rooms, the holding cells below, those are all bugged. Not this place. No wires, no electricity, no connection to anything save the ice on the river."

He set his pipe down on the ashtray, then reached out and casually picked up the pocketknife. He twiddled it between his hands for a few moments while eyeing the stretched rope coming out of the winch. "Usually the *vysshaia mera* is a bullet to the head," he said. The Supreme Measure of Social Defense. "I needn't even waste a bullet on you. A single swipe of the blade and you simply disappear."

"What is it you want?" Aurora asked. "All you have to do is tell me. None of this is necessary."

"I'll be the judge of what's necessary," Shpak said sharply. He slapped the knife down on the table and began turning the crank. The bed frame sank until Aurora's legs were immersed in the water up to the knees. The pain was nauseating.

"How," Shpak asked, as he slowly turned the crank and the water climbed up her thighs, her belly, her breasts, her neck. "How did you know that we were so interested in balloons?"

That final word was the last thing she heard before her ears went under the water.

12

CHICAGO

JULY 1933

"Like, suppose I'm Momentum and you're Position," Dick was saying. "Or I'm Energy and you're Time."

"Position . . . Time . . . why do I always have to be the boring one?"

That shut him up: something of an achievement.

"Okay . . ." he began, playing for time.

"It's all right," she assured him, "momentum and energy are good quantities for you."

His concerns eased. "Well then! As I was sayin'—though it's a lot easier to say with noncommutative algebra—tryin' to peg one of us all alone just don't work as good as treating us like a complementary pair."

The sun had found the western skyline during Bohr's talk, and a Dust Bowl crepuscule was now adding its profound colors to the neon spike of the Havoline Thermometer (79 degrees) and the iridescent-paint train derailment of the fair at large. Ahead of them the soda fountain was a horizontal slit of sanitary white light, now extending all the way from Indiana to Wisconsin, stippled with the high-energy glow of germicidal lamps.

"If you stood still, like the statue gal—"

"Talking about Position again?"

"Yeah, then I'm bouncing around all over the place. And likewise if you show up at a certain time for a date—"

"Who said anything about a date?"

"Settle down, sweetie, this is just a *Gedankenexperiment*."

"I know what it is," she said ambiguously.

"Anyway, if we know everything about Time, we know nothing about Energy."

"So if I'm to know anything about you, Dick, I need to be as mysterious as possible?"

"Why, yes, that's exactly right!" he exclaimed, then added, weakly because too late, "And vicey-versey."

She allowed him to buy her a root-beer float; and true to his theme, as soon as she fixed her position on a stool at the soda fountain, he began fidgeting, frequently catapulting himself, with a vigorous pelvic thrust, from a stool to prowl up and down the counter scavenging straws, towels, saltshakers, and other objects useful in diagramming atomic structure and modeling incident wavefronts. The only way she could get him to sit still was to stand up and move around herself, for example to the ladies', which caused him to settle on one of three or four nearby stools he'd been laying claim to at various moments in his perambulatory flirtation-cum-physics-seminar.

"This is quantum seating," he shouted when she came back from freshening up, "and that is classical." He pointed to a booth along the wall, framed between benches newly upholstered in Walgreens-red stuff fresh from the pleather tanneries of Naugatuck and redolent of synthetic chemistry. "On a bench you can choose any position you want and snuggle up next to your sweetheart like those two lovebirds back there in the corner. But here you have to sit on one stool or another, they're bolted to the floor, and they keep you in separate orbitals."

"If you are suggesting that we move to a booth, that is fine, as long as I can sit across from you."

"Oh, I didn't mean anything by it!" he assured her too hastily. "We can stay here in the quantum section and the Pauli exclusion principle will keep us from occupying the same space." Probably meant to be reassuring, this remark led to an awkward silence. That was fine with Dawn, who was beginning to feel a bit overstimulated. She sucked on her straw and watched him sliding the tip of his index finger around in a puddle of spilled water on the zinc counter. He was, she realized, doing science. At first she thought he might be drawing more of his math symbols. His finger was too restless for that, though. It would noodle about in one area and then shoot across the counter, drawing a trail of water in its wake, striking smaller outlying pools, shattering or merging them according to the whims of the surface tension that held them together. Another girl might have pouted over his having forgotten she was there. The man in him had forgotten his date and the boy had forgotten his banana split. But she enjoyed the respite and the opportunity to watch him. It wasn't just that Dick wanted to get to first, second, and third base with her as soon as he could. He most certainly did want that. But he also just liked being with a girl. He needed the steady complement of his crazy energy and veering momentum.

It was a peculiar kind of flirtation. Back in the auditorium, when he'd understood that she'd spied his notebook, he'd been embarrassed. But she had not recoiled, which had emboldened him, and led him on to further gambits.

She was not used to just sitting there being the girl. Her exploits of last summer, on polo fields and urban battlegrounds, had obliged her to act more in the role of lone, dusty Amazon, more Bonnie Parker than Fay Wray, and she expected that there'd be more of that in her future. Her height, peculiar looks, and most of all the extreme irregularities in her personal background meant that chances for soda-fountain courtship of this wholesome and conventional style would be rare in her life, occasioned only when she met a boy as weird as Dick, which happened just about never. So she sipped it slowly through a straw rather than tossing it back.

His eyes fixed on the purple glow of a germicidal lamp. "Thing is that when transitions happen, energy gets emitted, or absorbed," he said. He slid off his stool and moved to one farther down the bar. "I just soaked up energy, now I'm in a higher state."

The soda jerk, squirming a towel around the inside of a parfait glass, eyed Dick curiously, then looked at Dawn. "Your date soaks up any more energy, I'll buy you a Pepsi."

"Won't happen," Dick said, "'cause I can emit radiation and jump back down to the lower orbital." He sat next to Dawn and glared at the soda jerk, who was twice his size.

"The Bohr atom," Dawn said, "that's what you're getting at."

"See? If the great man had just come here instead of that auditorium with the paintings of the cows, he coulda explained it easy, just like you."

"It's old science. Even I know about it."

"The ultraviolet catastrophe," Dick said, his eye wandering back to the lamp. "There's mercury in that tube. The filament excites the electrons. Mercury's a big, heavy nucleus, the orbitals are way out in high-energy land—when an electron drops down a few notches," and his eye traced a little jump from one stool to another, "the light that comes out is high energy. High enough to kill things. Like germs."

"Why doesn't it kill us?"

"It just kills stuff on the outside, that it can reach. Stuff that grows back."

"Like skin?" Her mother had died of melanoma.

"Like skin. Your cornea. Right now it's killing cells in my retinas."

"Let's go somewhere else."

They walked up the Midway bathed in nonlethal wavelengths from a fairyland of neon tubes, painted bulbs, and gel-tinted spotlights. Dawn had been around enough that she was inured to its particularity, as if every cell in her retinas had been fried, but Dick was new to it, and continually distracted. In spite of this they had something approximating a real conversation. Dick was not from Brooklyn, as she'd guessed, but Far Rockaway, which was technically a part of Queens—though he seemed to feel that this was about as meaningful as saying it was in North America. He was here with his mom and dad and his kid sister, Joanie. They'd loaded up the family car and found a way off of Long Island and joined in with the Chicago-bound torrent of fair-going motorists undeterred by the gloomy slanders of Greyhound ticket clerks. Just now the rest of the family was cooling their heels at a nearby hotel, giving Dick an evening to do as he pleased.

"Well, thank you for spending it with me," she said.

"I was going to spend it with Niels Bohr," he returned injudiciously; then, recovering, "but you're prettier—and he just wanted to talk philosophy."

"Where do you draw the line between science and philosophy anyhow? I think that's what he was trying to get at."

"Okay, yeah. But I mean he wanted to say something that could be written up in the *Trib* without any equations." And it was quite clear how he felt about science without equations. "Millikan was there tonight. Compton. Levi-Civita came all the way from Italy—and he oughtn't to go back, if he knows what's good for him."

"I don't know them."

"Neither do I, to be honest," Dick admitted. "I mean, I haven't read all of their papers yet. But I have an idea what they do. Levi-Civita helps Einstein get his math right. Millikan: local talent, but runs Caltech now. Nobel Prize. First guy to call cosmic rays cosmic. Compton: also local, also Nobel, argues with Millikan about where those cosmic rays come from."

"The cosmos, surely?"

"Yeah, but why and how? That's why these guys are forever going up in friggin' balloons."

13

MAGNITOGORSK

FEBRUARY 1934

After dunking Aurora a few times, Shpak began to refine his technique. His hand rested lazily on the winch's crank. He had noticed that he could raise her up just to the point where her eyes came out of the water, but her nose and mouth were still submerged. She could then blink the water out of her eyes and focus on that hand, willing it to move just a few inches forward and lift her nostrils into the air. In the meantime she could thrash against the restraints and try to jerk her head upward just enough to draw in a scrap of air. But the woman who had lashed her to the bed frame had done her job too well. Struggling against the restraints only deepened her oxygen debt. She must force herself to be still—nearly impossible at the beginning of a session when she had strength in her, almost inevitable later, when her lungs were half full of water and the world was narrowing and shading gray.

Judging just how long he could make her wait before she suffered irreversible damage had become a kind of scientific inquiry for him. Her brow tended to knit up when she inhaled water, and that was a signal he had learned to recognize. Sometimes then he'd give the handle a shove, yanking her entire head out of the water, and let her puke and breathe. This in turn led to further refinements as he got the timing down. The first thing she did, of course, after expelling water from her lungs, was to suck in the deepest breath she could, and if he dropped her back down in the middle of that it added pain to panic.

All of this curious experimentation meant that the rest of her was spending a lot of time fully immersed. So every few minutes he had to hoist her out and let her dangle in the air, fully exposed, soaking up the warmth from the red-hot stove, lest she perish from hypothermia. Or maybe he didn't care if she died but just wanted her fully conscious for the next round of dunkings.

Anyway, "technical procedures" were probably more effective when they included a carrot—the exquisite warmth of the stove—as well as a stick.

As well as a third element: the bullet to the head, or the threat of it. This was the pocketknife. One gesture with it and the rope would snap, she would drop, the weight of the bed frame would drag her down into the river's current, and she would be swept away beneath the ice. Fish would eat the flesh from her bones and no trace of her would ever be seen.

For the first few minutes after being pulled out she existed in a hazy dreamworld. Then riotous shivering consumed her whole being as her body temperature passed up out of the near-fatal range. During that time it was impossible to think. But as this subsided she had a few minutes of something like sleep as the warmth of the stove suffused her and her body relaxed. During these breathers Shpak would smoke his pipe and do paperwork. He had spread documents all over his lap and the tables flanking his chair. Whenever she regained awareness, Shpak was there, smoking his pipe and sifting through his notes, reading glasses down on the tip of his nose.

"For all you have told me, I feel we are only getting started!" he exclaimed. "It is a shame that my comrades from Moscow are so insistent on an answer today. 'Shpak, we need to know,' they say, 'is she safe to use?'" He gave the crank a spin and lifted her a few inches higher. "'Or did you liquidate her?'" He picked up the knife and slid its edge against the taut rope, watching curiously as a few threads popped loose. "Either answer is perfectly acceptable—further delay is not."

"I would not have come back to the Soviet Union of my own free will unless I were a sincere revolutionary."

"Or a spy, of course."

"God. It's like talking to my father." He did actually look so fatherly, sitting there with his pipe and his pen.

This remark had at least brought a trace of amusement to Shpak's face. "How so?"

"I told you. He sent me to Fort Myer to gather intelligence. And when I came back with intelligence, he accused me of being Patton's dupe. A vector of misinformation."

Shpak paged back through his notes, shuffled documents. "You find Patton abhorrent. And yet you agree with his appraisal of your character."

"A better way of putting it is that I agree with his appraisal of the United States. That there is no place for me there. But here it's a different matter."

"Oh, I like that better." He clenched his pipestem in his teeth so that he could strike out a line in a document, scribble a note. "You see? The advantages of privacy. I can change the wording. No one will know but us."

Something told her not to say yes to this. It was so difficult to remain alert. So easy to mistake this for an actual conversation. "That sounds like a trap," she said.

"How so?"

"If I agree, it's proof that I am practicing deception. Slash, splash. Please put it all in."

The beginning of this conversation with Shpak seemed like years ago. A few significant details were floating just below the surface of her memory. Trying to recover them was like bobbing for apples. No, that was the wrong analogy—too much the wholesome American pastime. It was like bobbing for chunks of ice in the Ural River. Or just trying to catch fish with your teeth.

He'd mentioned that important men were in town for a few days. The ones who were pressing him for answers.

Magnitogorsk was too primitive and too new to have real newspapers. But in each place where people gathered there was a Red Corner where something like a newspaper was tacked up to a wall. If you were literate you could stand there and read it. If you weren't you could ask someone to read it for you, or just look at the crudely retouched photographs of Stalin and steel mills. In the last days before Aurora had been made prisoner, all the news had been about the 17th Party Congress in Moscow. Sergo Ordzhonikidze was there, naturally, as head of the Commissariat of Heavy Industry. His friend and fellow Georgian Vissarion Lominadze, who basically ran Magnitogorsk, had traveled there to take part. Aurora had lost count of the days, but perhaps the congress was over now? Perhaps some of those men had come down to Magnitogorsk to make inspections? Was one of them the strange man who had peered at her through the crack of the door?

She was brought back to the here and now by the squeal of the pulley above her. Rope was moving through it. She opened her eyes to see Shpak's hand on the crank. "No," she said. She was too exhausted to beg or scream, and so it came out in a conversational tone. "You don't have to do this. I'm telling you everything."

"How did you know?" Shpak asked. "Who told you that we were so interested in balloons?"

14

CHICAGO

JULY 1933

"Take it from the top, Dick."

"Okay, but then I gotta start from the bottom." Dick paused for effect and stomped the earth of the Midway, pounded to fir-like consistency by a billion footfalls. "Under the ground. Elements decay and send out radiation. It comes up through the soles of your feet just like the X-rays in your shoe-fitting machine."

Dawn hid a smile. She had not known that Dick had tailed her back to the shoe stall, but she was not surprised.

"How do we know that? Because scientists detect more rays closer to the ground, fewer as they climb higher—air absorbs 'em, see."

"Then why 'cosmic'?" Dawn already knew, but it was fun to provoke Dick.

"'Cause if you keep going higher—like in a balloon—you again start seeing more and more of 'em." Dick reached into his satchel, pulled out his notebook, and began flipping through it. She was mildly worried he'd try to make her digest a slab of equations until he stopped on the last page: the picture he had sketched of her, arms outstretched, bathed in radiance from above. "Put you on your X-ray machine and that's the full picture. Rays from above and below. The ones from below created by decay. Annihilation. Millikan hates that."

"Why?"

"He's a Christian. Has theories about God and what He is up to, what is His master plan, how is He gonna keep the universe from running down the way this midway will when November rolls around. Now. Go up. In a balloon. At first, fewer rays. After that, more and more, coming down from the cosmos. What made 'em?"

"I don't know, more atoms decaying in space?"

"If the rays are protons and electrons—and I guess we gotta include neutrons now—then yeah, the annihilation hypothesis wins, and Millikan's pissed off, pardon my French, and has to have a little talk with God. But that's what Compton thinks."

"What does Millikan think?"

"That they are light."

"Light?"

Dick shrugged. "High-energy light, like your X-rays, but more so. Caused by lighter elements fusing to make heavier ones—ones heavy enough to make physical bodies. Like you and me, Dawn."

They kissed. It happened so spontaneously that she was not sure which of them had started it. They backed away from each other, Dawn reaching up to stabilize the eagle, which was threatening to pitch forward off her head and pounce on poor Dick. It seemed to have been the right, the natural thing to do, to celebrate the holy fact that light elements had long ago fused in glorious showers of penetrating radiance to form the elements that made their lips and the warm blood rushing through them.

Dick was a moment getting his equilibrium back but then seemed to think that to keep talking was the best salve for the awkwardness. "Praise the Lord," he blurted, and she knew it had been his first kiss.

"Amen," she returned. Straightening her headdress had made her aware of how conspicuous she was in this getup. She looked around to see if any children had noticed. As a living avatar of the Century of Progress, she needed to keep up appearances. Some people were looking at them, but the place was full of unique exhibits, and a boy kissing a girl was nothing on the Smallest Bible ITW or the twitching dirndls of the *Mädchen* in the stein-carrying contest.

"Compton doesn't buy it, huh?"

"Nope, he's an Annihilation man."

"Not a Christian?"

"Different kinda one, I guess."

"How about you, Dick?"

"Jew. You, Dawn?"

"Communist." There was a little thrill in exposing that much of herself even though—especially because—she didn't have to.

"Not the kind of Jew that goes around wearing the little hat," Dick went on.

"Obviously."

"Atheist, Ethical Culture Society and all that. What kind of Red are you then?"

"Oh, long story."

"We got all night."

Somehow they ended up walking toward the shoe store, as if drawn thither by the green glow of X-rays. They held hands, occasionally wiping them on their garments as they slickened in the humid heat of the Midwestern summer, then shyly rejoining.

"Compton got his Nobel for X-ray stuff," Dick remarked.

"I thought those were old hat."

"He solved a riddle, a quantum riddle. Showed that they were particles as well as waves," Dick said, "particles called photons." He enjoyed pronouncing that word.

The little door in the back of the shoe stall was padlocked, which Dawn looked on as barring entry unless they were prepared to unleash revolutionary violence. But Dick borrowed a pin from her headdress, dropped down on one bare knee as if to tender a marriage proposal, and went to work. In a minute or so the lock snicked open and they slipped inside. That it hadn't been closed for long was suggested by the lingering scents of Mr. Green's pomade and Mrs. Green's powder, and the warmth still emanating from the X-ray machine, which they had dragged inside for safekeeping. As if he owned it, Dick removed the access panel at the bottom, allowed a lead slab to whomp into the ground, and exposed the glass tube that made the X-rays. With un-Dicklike caution he eased the hairpin into a chaos of fat asbestos-braided wires, then jerked back with a cackle as it shot sparks at him. "Still some juice stored up in those condensers," he explained, "had to get rid of it before it got rid of me."

Once their eyes had recovered from the lightning, they went to the machine's power cord and tracked it across the floor to its plug, lying there in the dirt with its two gleaming blades like an equals sign. It was safe. Dick had the tube out, a blown-glass contraption about a foot long, sternly and wackily Victorian. "A filament there, like in a lightbulb; but electrons get boiled off of the metal and go flying over this-a-way, to this thing, which pulls 'em in with a positive charge. Did you know opposites attract?"

"Heard it somewhere. What's your point?"

"They slam into the target like bullets from a tommy gun flying into an Irish bar, and whack electrons out of it. Other electrons drop down to fill the holes in the orbitals and—"

"Emit."

"Yeah. X-rays they emit."

"Of a certain frequency."

"I never have to tell you anything twice, Dawn—"

"You've told me about a hundred times, but thanks."

"If you could see 'em they'd be a color. Not a mess of colors like a sunset but pure color like a neon tube. And what Compton observed—well, hang on, that's not true, others observed it but he explained it—was that if you shone X-rays of one color on matter, why, X-rays of another color—a different frequency—would come outta it. They would come out at an angle, like they had been deflected, and the angle of the deflection predicted the color."

"Proving—?"

"That light is made of particles. Or at least that it acts that way sometimes. It's as if you took green light from a neon tube and shone it through a piece of cellophane and it came out red, and bent. You can't explain that if the light is a wave. The math just don't work. But if it's a photon? Easy-peasy! The Compton effect, voilà."

Dawn found that all quite interesting but did not really understand why picking the lock, breaking into the shoe store, taking apart the machine, and waving the actual tube around had been necessary parts of the explanation. The mental image of a neon tube shining through cellophane had been sufficient.

Another remarkable fact was that, in the privacy of this shuttered stall, they could quite easily have started making out, perhaps even had sex. Not that she necessarily wanted to, not right away. But it seemed like the sort of detail that Dick might have noticed, given that he'd had an erection about fifty percent of the time she had known him. But he had been blinded to it by the penetrating light of science.

"See, this is about as far as we can go!" he said, missing a possible double entendre, holding up the X-ray tube like a chalice, or whatever holy object secular Jews reverenced at the Society for Ethical Culture. "This is some gizmo! A lot of energy! See those fat wires it's hooked up to, those coils? You can only get the energy levels so far apart, working with the heavy atoms, way out in the M orbitals, where the transitions are huge and the X-rays are hard. Then you just hit a place where you can't get any more energy, any harder rays, any more violet photons, just by making electrons hop around. To go beyond that, you gotta give up on electrons—on chemistry—and go to the nucleus. This here"—he gave the tube one more shake—"is fascinating, but it's a dead end and that's why they are mass-producing 'em in Schenectady and using 'em to sell shoes."

He left her to ponder all of that while he knelt again and reassembled the machine. She had unconsciously sidestepped around so as to get between him and the door, just in case that erection put in an appearance.

"Better test it," he muttered, and plugged it in. Then, as an afterthought, he got his fingertips under the edges of the lead slab and heaved it back up into its place, hiding the tube, which had begun to glow as its filament warmed up and began machine-gunning electrons at its heavy-metal target. Since the machine had failed to blow up or catch fire, the next phase of the test consisted of examining various found objects and body parts on the fluoroscopic screen, and peering sidelong into the foot slot to see whether blue light could be seen leaking out of it; for he had the idea that, at certain angles, Compton scattering should manifest itself as colored rays visible to the naked eye. But it didn't quite work. He became frustrated and opened his notebook to make calculations.

"I should be getting back," she said.

His head bobbed up. He looked not so much guilty as disoriented. "Sorry. I forgot Compton's formula, so I'm just re-deriving it real quick."

"That's fine but I have to go."

"I should walk you to the streetcar," he intoned, as if he had forgotten manners and was having to re-derive them from first principles.

"That would be lovely but I can take care of myself."

"No, I'll do it. Any chance I can get back in here for more experiments?"

"All you need is a bobby pin, Dick. I could give you a whole box." She was a little shocked to find herself going all pouty, all self-pitying. Dick didn't really like her. He only wanted her for her X-ray tube.

"For some kinda experiments we would need the both of us," he said, advancing.

That was more like it, but it was too soon. "Perhaps tomorrow," she said.

He shook his head. "Hate to say it, but Dad got tickets to the Wild West roundup. A must-see." His eyes wandered over the stacked shoeboxes as if they were squares on a calendar. "Next day though—big stuff happening. First thing in the morning."

"What?"

"Meet me at dawn, Dawn. I'm taking you to Navy Pier."

STARS DID NOT SHINE IN THE SKY OF DAY, BUT THESE DID. IGNITED BY THE LATE-AFTERNOON sun—for Dawn, Dick, and several thousands of others had been standing on Navy Pier since before the air armada had lifted off from the waters of the Rivière du Nord before Montreal—silver flares emerged from the haze above the lake. They arranged themselves into a rectilinear constellation that, as it passed high above Chicago, resolved itself into the letters ITALIA. Profoundly emotional men swept off their Panamas, placed them over their hearts, and sniffled into their neatly waxed mustaches.

Taking a more analytical view was Dick. "There's more ι.
four of 'em!" he announced. "Three dozen easy. No, more!" She knι
well enough to know that he had not actually counted the stars, but figuι
it out some other way, some geometrical logic telling him you couldn't
spell ITALIA with twenty-four points only, not if you put the crossbars on
the I's. "That's gotta be the escort. Those are Uncle Sam's, not Il Duce's."

The announcer, who all day had been updating the crowd by loud-
speaker and the people of Chicago by radio as Air Marshal Balbo had
dodged storms over Ontario, spat out the news that this was an Army
Air Force group, three squadrons from near Detroit that had picked the
Italians up as they'd roared over Lake Saint Clair and escorted them over
U.S. territory.

The anticlimax produced a lull and a last-chance mobbing of the pier's
gruesomely overtaxed sanitary facilities. But in that silence could be heard
the juicy rumble of forty-eight Fraschini motors, eighteen cylinders each,
powering twenty-four planes low over Chicago on the final leg of their
7,000-mile argosy. Balbo, it seemed, had doglegged over the Century of
Progress, where 60,000 awaited his Roman triumph in Soldier Field and
further tens of thousands had swamped its electrical iridescence with
acres of green-white-and-red banners.

In their eagerness to look south down the shore, the Navy Pier crowd
surged toward its southern edge, pressing Dawn against the railing hard
enough to leave a welt. Navy MPs blew whistles and shoved them back. A
rescue rowboat scuttled across the slack water to extract a luckless specta-
tor who'd fallen in, taking a long stretch of green-white-and-red bunting
with him and leaving his hat bobbing on the lake like a bubble. The surge
relaxed anyway as the air armada tacked west over the city, disappearing
behind the rampart of stately buildings on Lake Shore Drive, and made
a pass up the Loop. Its progress could be guessed at by observing the reactions of the thousands who had gathered on rooftops; arms waved like
cilia and Italian flags stirred the sky in languid infinities. Finally the rumble broke out into the open as the planes rounded the northern end of the
Miracle Mile and banked east over the lake. The tops of their wings were
banded with the three colors of Italy and the black of the Fascists. In two

stormi of twelve each they came, each *stormo* comprising four arrowhead-shaped flights of three.

When seen from above or below, the Savoia-Marchetti was identifiable as an aeroplane because of its huge single wing, so fat in the middle that the crew actually rode inside of it, looking forward through a row of portholes set into its leading edge. But from the front it looked like a pair of teardrop-shaped boats: two bullet-like hulls, with accommodations for passengers and cargo, suspended below the wing where they did double duty as pontoons. From the side the view was dominated by the engines, mounted back-to-back on a rakish gondola thrust high above the center of the wing, a pusher prop at its aft end and a puller to fore, stubby exhaust pipes like rows of spines on a dinosaur's back, spurting an endless cyclical tattoo of gas-scented exhaust. The empennage of rudder and tailplane was dragged behind it at the end of some spindly pipestems, stiffened by a few cables; from a distance these were invisible, making it seem as if the tail was a separate, smaller aeroplane flying in close formation behind the wing/hull/gondola contraption. It seemed incredible that such constructs could get up out of the water at all, much less fly for thousands of miles, but none could doubt the proof of their being here. The strangeness of the design seemed to call into question the whole direction of American aviation.

The *stormi* banked in a vast turn south over the lake, curling west toward the city again and then north as they descended toward the yacht basin. The tips of their wings were blazoned with white rondels, each scored with three parallel black stripes. As they came closer it could be seen that each stripe had a little hook to one side of it, for these were stylized *fasces*. On the side of each hull was a more fully realized rendering in brown, showing the bundle of rods with the axe head peeking out. The lead plane of the lead flight of the lead *stormo* also sported a black star, the insignia of a general officer, marking it as the flagship of the armada. As this came in on its final approach, a wayward pleasure craft passed in front of it, to furious, palpable horn-blasting from a navy launch stationed there just to prevent such enormities. From Dawn and Dick's point of view, looking almost straight-on into the portholes of the cockpit, it seemed a nearer thing than it was. In truth it was more embarrassment than hazard. The boat's operator, putt-putting around the lake, alive only to the mundane hazards of shallow water and flotsam, perhaps wondering if he might profitably cast a line and hook a lunker, was infuriatingly and yet all too recognizably blind to the unheard-of, unprecedented prodigy of the greatest air armada in the history of the world bearing down upon him. He was a stand-in for all of the Midwest, and as such for all of America, making everyone blush from the shame to which he was so oblivious.

Balbo's ship and its two flankers plowed a broad lane through the anchorage, and Dawn imagined she could feel a warm gust as everyone on the pier exhaled. Revving its engines back up to reclaim a bit of speed, Balbo's flight veered, howling and smoking, round the end of the pier, accepting a salute from a Navy destroyer tied up at its end, and idled to a triad of green-white-and-red buoys recently placed there for their use. It was just to the north side of the pier.

A hatch opened. A swagger stick, then a cigarette, and finally a stocky, swarthy, bearded man emerged, followed closely by a sword. He was in a handsome blue-and-gray uniform, belted high at the waist. His chest and shoulders gleamed with medals and golden eagles. Puffing on his cigarette, he began to strut up and down the giant wing as his sailor-airmen made the ship fast and tended to the engines.

This, as all of Chicago knew, was Air Marshal Italo Balbo. The lengthy run-up to his exploit and the several days of its execution had given the newspapers plenty of time to rake over his biographical details. He was one of the four Blackshirt quadrumvirs who had led the Fascist march on Rome eleven years ago, inspiring Hitler to the decidedly less effective Beer Hall Putsch a year later. If anything bad happened to Mussolini (a consummation devoutly to be wished by everyone in the kommunalka), Balbo would probably succeed him as dictator of the Italian Empire.

Doing their utmost to make him feel welcome was a contingent of young locals in new black sateen shirts, black neckties, pinstriped trousers, and meticulously oiled hair who forced their way to the brink of the pier, snapped to attention, and gave him the Fascist salute while making a strange noise in their throats that Dawn guessed must be some manner of cheer or battle cry. Balbo turned his head to look, then returned the salute in a more casual style, swinging his hand out from his chest, pausing for a moment at full extension, then letting it swing wide and down, as if he were only waving.

The proceedings became dull and tense. All of the Savoia-Marchettis had to touch down, taxi, and be made fast before Balbo would consent to board the destroyer at the head of the pier, where a menagerie of Chicago pols, archbishops, debutantes, radio announcers, polo players, industrialists, Italian princelings, diplomats, movie stars, and admirals waited to subject him to some grueling program of salutations. Less exalted VIPs had been relaxing all afternoon in a shaded grandstand at the end of the pier, but groundlings such as Dick and Dawn could only stand, wait, and sort of tread water in the hot stew of the crowd, trying to stay together as those trapped in the center tried to force their way to the edges for a peep at Balbo or a breath of fresh air. They heard and felt the nineteen-gun salute as Balbo finally boarded the destroyer, and heard its band playing, and saw the smoke from its stacks as it cast off for the short cruise down the lake to the next echelon of greetings at Century of Progress, where more Blackshirts waited to salute the hero at the Italian pavilion and the sixty thousand were listening to staccato narration over the loudspeaker system at Soldier Field.

Balbo's departure set off further turbulence in the Pier crowd, which had no plausible way of getting out of this place other than lake steamers. Ever since the fair had opened, a fleet of these had been shuttling between Navy Pier and Century of Progress on half-hour schedules. Now they were out in force and taking on passengers as fast as they could, the MPs blowing their whistles and pushing the crowd back from the gangplanks just as soon as they became fully loaded. The crowd surged in the direction of each looming smokestack, only to stall as the approaches became choked. Dawn, simultaneously vexed and bored, found some entertainment in watching Dick, who was neither; she could tell he was trying to make sense of the crowd's movements, tantalizingly on the verge of some insight that would enable him to stand in just the right place to be squirted aboard the next steamer, not by forcing his way past others but by letting himself be entrained in their natural flow. Once or twice, it almost worked; picking up some weak signal in the postures of those around him, Dick would reach out for her hand, she'd give it to him, and he would lead her into a slim rivulet of pedestrians making inexplicable progress toward a gangplank.

They came within yards of a place where people were flooding aboard a lake steamer, only to be frustrated by a thin screen of downstaters too well behaved to take the opportunity given. She could sense by Dick's posture that he was just going to play the New York card and force his way between them, pulling her along in his wake. Then they were cut off by a flying wedge of Blackshirts. Dick tightened his grip on her hand. She sensed he was getting ready to leap in behind them.

She was knocked off balance by a man, and then a second man, stepping in from behind her, exploiting an almost nonexistent gap to their left, like a couple of linebackers spearing in through a seam between the guard and the tackle. They moved, but scarcely looked, like ruffians; their hair, beneath the brims of their snap-brim hats, was short and freshly cut, and sweat ran down the clean-shaven backs of their necks to dampen white collars that had been crisply starched that morning. The one in the lead was twice Dick's size, and the one behind him was bigger yet; as Dick made to sidestep through the same gap, the first one shrugged him aside. In the same moment the larger man was body-blocking Dawn out of his path.

"Hey, Joe Palooka, what's the big idea?" Dick protested. The first of the two men was already past him, and past caring. Dick put his hand on the shoulder of the second man, who, in a graceful response, without really breaking stride, turned to face Dick, allowing Dick to get a look at his barrel chest, then peeled back one side of his suit jacket to reveal a brass credential. Then he was past them and hustling across the gangplank, and Dick, forgetting his indignation and seeing his chance, lurched into the space that they had made. Dawn's mind was telling her not to get on that boat, but her legs had not yet got the message. She tried to let go of Dick's hand but he had got her by the wrist already. Her trim, stylish oxfords took her in a scattered and disarranged gait over the boards and they were on the steamer, no hope of going back as people were piling on behind them, the two palookas still right in front of them and the Blackshirts, having formed a sort of phalanx, forcing their way up a stair to an upper deck where they could see the air armada. Dick seemed inclined to follow those guys, but Dawn pulled back hard, diverting him around the base of the stairs and off-balancing him so that he had to follow her for a moment. The two of them banged into a life preserver. An instinct was telling her to seek out quiet, close spaces, to go belowdecks.

Above them the Blackshirts made their war cry again, and she heard it better: something like "*Eja Eja Alala!*"

"Hey, that guy had a badge and a gun," Dick remarked. "He's some kinda special agent or something. Hey, where we going, Dawn?"

Away from the special agent with the badge and the gun, Dawn was thinking. *Away from Silent Al—before he recognizes me. And forgets about the ridiculous Blackshirts. And decides to slap the cuffs on a real Communist.*

She'd been very lucky: Al, focused on the Blackshirts, had only seen her from behind. She was a distinctive looker in lots of ways, but the Century of Progress bob was as different as it could be from the braided ponytail she had worn most of the time Al had known her last year in D.C. So she had not been recognizable from that angle. But Silent Al had spent a lot of time, in those days, looking at her, to the point where people had noticed, and guessed he must be sweet on her. Which maybe he was. Either way, if he saw her face-on, he'd know her.

They were in a steel corridor belowdecks. She tried a hatch, found that it opened, went into a dark space beyond, a sort of closet full of pipes and valve wheels. Only when she'd closed the door behind her did she feel safe.

"Hey, we're not supposed to be in here!" Dick said. She could not see the puckish look that must have been on his face, but she could hear it in his voice.

"Like you care about that, Dick!"

"What's going on?" he asked.

There were only two possible answers that would pass Dick's logical filters. One was that she was a wanted, fugitive Communist in immediate danger of being recognized and arrested by a Division of Investigation agent who'd spent much of the previous year following her around.

The other—

She groped out, found his shoulders with her hands, followed them up his neck to his face, and drew it in to hers.

15

MAGNITOGORSK

FEBRUARY 1934

Sometimes during the lulls between the dunkings, Aurora would be vaguely aware that words were coming out of Shpak's mouth. She would ignore them. Not because she didn't care—he was obviously the most important person in her life, and during the last hour or so he had grown more and more fond of playing with his jackknife, teasing her by letting its bright, honed edge play along the thin strand of rope that was keeping her alive. No, she ignored him because her mind simply couldn't follow what he was saying. Her mind couldn't really do much of *anything* except stumble around in an attic of dim hallucinations and memories. Maybe Shpak knew as much and was just talking as a way to find out whether she had regained consciousness to the point where further interrogation and more dunking would be worth the effort.

But on one such occasion, as she was coming to, she started to get the increasingly firm and definite impression that Shpak's words were interspersed with another man's voice. Her eyes were closed but there was a faint scent of gasoline in her nostrils, as if a car had pulled up outside.

Yes, she could hear its engine idling. Then she heard the door of the ice house open and close. Boots crunched on snow. The car's door slammed. But the car stayed where it was, engine running to keep it warm.

She opened her eyes and looked into the face of the man who, the other day, had peered at her through the cracked-open door in the jail. He had taken Shpak's place in the chair. He was leaning back, knees spread apart, in an attitude that struck her as so informal as to border on tasteless. He was gazing at her through the round, heavy-framed lenses of his eyeglasses. Not making much eye contact though. So she was able to study him for a bit before he noticed—or perhaps before he cared—that she was awake. His hands were plunged deep into the pockets of his overcoat. Which was fine with her; they couldn't operate the winch, or the knife, in that position. But then she realized that under the coat he was playing with himself. It was one of those coats with slits behind the pockets that made it possible for the wearer to reach through and gain access to his trouser pockets. Which this man had done, and then some. She could see the bulge of his hand moving rhythmically.

He looked into her eyes and knew that she knew.

"You needn't worry," he said. "You're too old for me."

She couldn't think of a comeback to that.

"I was just imagining you a couple of years younger," he said dreamily, "getting fucked by Patton. Yes, getting fucked up the ass."

"He didn't fuck me."

"I like to think he did."

"Don't get me wrong. He's abhorrent. He killed my dad. But he wouldn't have done what you're imagining."

"Oh, let me guess," the man said, "it would go against his *honor*. His sense of bourgeois propriety."

"Exactly."

He rolled his eyes up to the ceiling. "Ah, that makes it even more delicious! Him debasing himself—and you—in one act. In the stables, I think. With all the horses watching. Stallions too. With their big, hard—"

He closed his eyes and made the noises, and the expressions, that men make at such times. Then he let all the air out of his lungs. Then drew in a deep breath. After a few moments, he began to stir. He snapped a handkerchief out of his pocket with the hand he hadn't used, and did some wiping up. When he was done he found himself holding the maculated cloth out at arm's length, pinched fastidiously between thumb and index finger, trying to decide what to do with it. His eyes passed across Aurora's midsection and she flinched, wondering what ideas might be going through his head. But in the end he squatted down in front of the potbellied stove, opened the door, and tossed it in there. For a moment it cast bright-yellow light on his face as it flared, and his eyes became amber disks as the lenses of his glasses caught it. He rested his forearms on his knees for a few moments, staring into the flames contemplatively.

"You know what river this is?" he asked.

"The Ural."

"Yes. Still fixated on the flames, he pointed one direction with his left hand. "To this side, Europe." His right. "Asia. We're right on the boundary. It's one of the things that makes us different—culturally, spiritually different—from Europe. I was thinking about it when I was reading Shpak's report. What you had to say about Chicago and how it was on a similar boundary between the eastern United States—more of a European kind of place, I gather—and the west. A big place. Full of savages and savagery. Making America different too. In a similar way perhaps to Russia."

He seemed to remember now, even through his post-ejaculatory reverie, that his interlocutor was naked and lashed to a steel bed frame. "I'm satisfied," he announced, slamming the stove's door shut.

She didn't think he was talking about satisfaction of the carnal kind. "Of what?" she asked.

"First of all that you're not crazy. Though that issue hasn't really been in doubt since I talked to Proton."

"What did Proton Fizmatov have to say regarding my sanity?"

"What you had was a genetic birth defect caused by X-ray exposure during the early stages of pregnancy. Not a monster."

"And?"

"Oh, secondly? That you are not a plant. Not a spy. You must understand that the fact that you are too perfect—too good to be true—aroused suspicion."

"Perfect for what?"

He ignored the question. "But your story is too idiosyncratic. Not what they would have concocted. You are too"—he let his eyes travel down and up her body, beginning and ending with her face—"conspicuous. They'd have picked someone more bland. Given her a less remarkable story. And they wouldn't have sent her to Magnitogorsk." He snorted. "Who the hell goes to Magnitogorsk?"

Both of us, apparently, she might have said.

The man checked his watch. "I'll have them cut you down. We're going to be late for dinner!"

16

CHICAGO

LATE SUMMER 1933

Three days later the Generalissimo of the Skies flew his armada to New York, and Dick, in the backseat of the family automobile, began traveling in the same direction. She saw him one more time. It wasn't so much that he was avoiding her (though he might have exerted himself a little more) as that she never knew when Balbo would make another visit to the fair, attracting Blackshirts, who drew bureau agents. Reading about the quadrumvir's official schedule in the paper wasn't foolproof, since he liked to come incognito when he wasn't attending polo matches in posh suburbs or high mass at the Cathedral of the Holy Name. So she told the Greens she was taking a few days off. She spent them in a cheap hotel. She could afford a place of her own now—could have done all along, to be honest—and her surprising encounter with Silent Al had put her in mind of what ought to have been obvious, which was that living with a bunch of known Communists was a bad idea. Her backup plan of packing up the tommy gun and going to enlist in the Barrow Gang seemed impractical, given that neither G-men nor Texas Rangers could establish their whereabouts.

Her last contact with Dick was another soda-fountain date at a time when she knew Balbo and his supporters to be at the Dante Alighieri Society fete. This was pleasant enough, but she knew she was losing his attention, and small wonder since he was about to leave and they'd never see each other again.

She did not regret it. She'd satisfied her curiosity as to sex. It had not been as bad the first time as some said. Dick had satisfied his, and seemed to find it altogether a fine thing. They ended up doing it again in the shoe stall after closing, Dawn sitting atop the dormant X-ray machine with her skirt around her waist and the flat heels of her Century of Progress oxfords digging into Dick's skinny, clenching butt as he stood there on the fluoroscope. This time, he had come prepared with a rubber. Like the suitor who forgot the bouquet on the first date but brings it out with a compensatory flourish on the second, he produced this with a certain degree of ceremony, and donned it with a single clean stroke of the fist, suggesting he'd been practicing on inanimate objects. The first time, in the machine room on the boat, he'd murmured something about protection while she had been throwing herself on him. She thought well of him for it. Her biggest regret, perhaps a little strangely, was not getting to meet Dick's parents, for she thought that they had brought Dick up not so much well (as that was usually defined) as artfully. For anyone could be made polite with enough beatings. But Dick had a knack not often seen for combining rude horniness with always putting out some effort to be mindful of others, all the more affecting for being so self-conscious.

The next day Dick, and Balbo with his hundred dashing aviators, were gone, within a few hours of each other. The latter's departure was, as usual, more dramatic, consisting of a parade up Michigan Avenue, lined ten and fifteen deep with spectators airing out the green-white-and-red banners one last time and women holding babies above their heads calling out, "This is for Mussolini!" After taking in a polo match at Fort Sheridan, Balbo then jumped into his Savoia-Marchetti and blasted off at the spearhead of his *stormi* for New York, passing, somewhere en route, Dick's family car, which had slipped out of town that morning sans cavalry escort, Fascist salutes, brass bands, or polo exhibitions.

Dawn wondered whether it was smart to stick with such a conspicuous job. Safest would have been to go far away. But how far was far enough? Home to Montana? Seattle? All the way to Russia? And how great was the risk really? She had never been arrested. There were no mug shots of her, no fingerprint cards. Silent Al had no doubt entered a description of her into his report, but he was the only cop, as far as she knew, capable of recognizing her. He did not know her real name; she did not even *have* a real name. And now that Balbo was gone, there was no particular reason for a G-man specializing in foreign-influenced subversives to be wandering at large around Century of Progress.

The oddest notion came to her, which was that she would be safe if Silent Al were dead.

She did not act on this. Despite owning a submachine gun, she wouldn't have had the first idea how to go about finding and slaying a G-man. But the mere thought of it affected her thinking as magnets torqued the tracks of cosmic rays. It brought her in mind of the Soviet Union, where such calculations were made, and acted upon, all the time. As if the doings of the Cheka and the OGPU produced a signal that, like Marchese Marconi's marvelous emanations, traveled invisibly round the world and resonated in some crystal that had been planted in her young skull when she'd seen, but not understood, the purges in Petrograd. And just as nearby frequencies would interfere with each other on the radio, she heard a little of Bonnie and Clyde when she was listening to that transmission. Red-baiters in the States liked to say that the people running the Soviet were little better than gangsters. Dawn could hardly gainsay them, given that, last year, she had, at her father's direction, bought guns from gangsters. But when she re-read Bonnie Parker's poem, she saw it more and more clearly as a revolutionary document, a protest against prison camps as bad as any in Siberia or Germany. It was not so much that Bonnie, and the Soviets, were interfering with each other's broadcasts as transmitting on the same frequency.

She went back to work as if nothing had happened. It might be a foolish invitation to revolutionary martyrdom, but she somehow felt a little bit safer with every person who saw her face, as if hiding in plain sight were the best trick of all. And a lot of people saw her face. The fair welcomed its ten millionth visitor. There were only 125 million people in the whole United States. Then just a little later it was fourteen million. Or perhaps time was passing more quickly. The place felt altogether different to her. On that first day she had paid her 50 cents and walked onto the Midway fully armored against what she knew to be a barrage of propaganda, and had ended up liking it nonetheless—delighting in its absurd vanity and drawing vim from its stupid, relentless pep. Now it all seemed a bit much, a bit forced. The exhibit of barking sand from Kauai, the armless and legless painter from Canada, the Swedish singers from Sioux City, the exhibits of men's collars, of purple wood from Costa Rica, of a beating replica of a human heart, of a piano with two keyboards, of the Sultan of Sulu's personal Koran, the oldest Czechoslovakian bible in the United States, demonstrations of scoutcraft, the gorilla impersonators from Hollywood in their yak-hair suits, they all now seemed as if they were reaching for something of what the Century of Progress had genuinely had in its early weeks.

She kept perambulating back to a gag in the Westinghouse Pavilion: $20 in gold coins, and a plate of cookies, displayed in an open window. Whenever someone reached for them, their hand would break an invisible ray, casting shadow on a photoelectric cell, and a barrier would rise up to close the window. Dick had talked to her about it, and explained the photoelectric effect and told the story of how Einstein had figured it all out thirty years ago—and now here it was being used in an automatic machine to keep children away from cookies! He had found it amusing, albeit old hat in the same way as the shoe-selling Jules Verne X-ray tube. Dawn, as the summer wore on, saw it more and more as a metaphor for everything about the fair—including Dick himself. She had made love to him in the full knowledge that she was interrupting an invisible ray, triggering the descent of a barrier. He would leave and forget about her. Perhaps she had been emulating her mother, who had fucked the outlaw Jim O'Faolain to get pregnant with Dawn. Perhaps she was putting revolutionary ideals around sex and morality into practice. Perhaps she was just putting her body on the line for the thrill of the physical risk, as a Komsomol boy might have enlisted in the Red Army and gone to fight Cossacks. But as July gave way to August her mood changed, and she remembered the look that her mother had used to get after the cancer had gone to her brain and she would reminisce about Jimmie, and the lamentations of the women in the kommunalka in Petrograd when they had been fucked and abandoned by men given official leave to do so by Soviet theoreticians.

It became clear that the climax of the Century of Progress had been the arrival of Air Marshal Balbo's flying armada, and having sex with Dick. Everything after was just a slow dwindling.

Except for the thing in her belly, which was unquestionably growing.

She had certainly missed one period and was overdue for another. The changes in the way she saw things and reacted to them might have been put down to simply being tired of the fair, or changes in the fair itself, or the natural alteration in perspective that came of being a grown woman who had Done It with a Boy, but as weeks went by with no menstrual flow she began to think it was actually a result of changes in her body, and her mind, resulting from pregnancy.

The shoe store—in the evening anyway—was literally in the shadow of Soldier Field, and so she was among the first to be aware of it when the usual round of athletic competitions was suspended and the great stadium's entrance ramps and loading docks were claimed by trucks blazoned with the trademarks of Dow Chemical, Goodyear Rubber, the United States Navy, the University of Chicago, and Union Carbide. Not twenty feet from where Dick had picked the lock, a meteorological station was hoisted from a flatbed truck to the roof, its anemometers and vanes stirring in the eddies alee of the stands until they caught the unsullied air. A caravan of trucks rumbled in, each carrying on its open bed a phalanx of steel cylinders stenciled HYDROGEN. For a whole day the empty stands resounded with the trundling noises of them being rolled down ramps to the ground, and when the work was done, seven hundred of them stood in a great horseshoe round the edges of the field where Tunney had once bested Dempsey in the Long Count.

Dawn had grown used to the stadium's east front looming over the shoe stall, but she had not actually gone inside until now. It was only a few years old but made to look ancient, like a Roman ruin before it had become ruined. Not so much Colosseum as Circus Maximus, with long Doric colonnades ranking above the east and west sidelines, terminated at each end by tidy little temples. Below them, acres of plain fir benches terraced down to the field. Dawn picked her way up and down those vast, splintery ramps as the days passed, seeking the shade of a neoclassical pediment or making a foray for a discarded *Trib*, hiking up when the meteorologists were prepping a weather balloon in the colonnade, down when Arthur H. Compton was holding forth for a cluster of journalists. She wondered what Italo Balbo must have made of it, flying all that distance from Rome to find a Roman stadium bigger and better than any in the Old World.

Three busloads of sailors went over the field on hands and knees, plucking away every twig and pebble. Next came a pair of trucks laden with nothing but white drop cloths, which were spread out on the gridiron as if it were an operating table being prepped for surgery on a Titan. Then a giant truck all covered with tarps, which when peeled back revealed infinite convolutions of cream-colored fabric. With maddening deliberation this was unpleated by the navy men and spread across the white drop cloths under the eyes of clustering officers, executives, and scientists on the field, and a few curious spectators who'd begun to gather in the stair-stepped plane of fir, and radio announcers sharing the high places with meteorologists. Dawn was there when a special flatbed rolled in bearing the sigil of DOW, and supporting a spherical object seven feet in diameter in a padded, halo-shaped creche. When the tarps were flung off to a spattering of applause, the words CENTURY OF PROGRESS could be seen painted on the whitish metal of its lower hemisphere, where they'd be visible from the ground. On the upper were eight mooring points where ropes would be attached. All about it were tiny windows.

To non-scientifically-minded onlookers it might now appear that everything, save actual balloonists, was in place for a launch. But sorting out the details seemed to be much more engrossing. Another whole day passed. Arthur H. Compton, a big, handsome man and a magnet for journalists, was given to standing before tables strewn with scientific-looking junk and gesticulating, occasionally raising his hands on high, prompting his interlocutors to stand up straight and squint into the radioactive sky.

Dawn would sit there on her breaks, sipping lemonade, scribbling her initials on shoe flyers, and watching the scientists. Discarded newspapers blowing around the stadium informed her that the sphere was made of a wonder metal called magnesium, electrically produced from a special brine found only at Midland, Michigan, and that it was an eighth of an inch thick. Seemingly quite valuable and delicate contraptions were ferried out to the magnesium sphere by junior scientists, then brought back when they'd failed to fit, or to work.

Dawn, in her current state of mind, could not rid herself of what was admittedly a very obvious and sophomoric comparison between the perfect silver sphere and an egg making its way down the old fallopian. If one were resolutely to prosecute that analogy, then the scientists clambering into its hatch with their dark nests of apparatus, all a-dangle with disconnected wires and tubes, were the sperm; but a more visually pleasing sperm analogy lay in the nimbus of vertical steel hydrogen cylinders, which seemed to be spreading out to envelop the target.

The more time she spent watching the scientists, the fewer flyers she handed out at the fair, and the less money she made; but she was finding it difficult to care about that, the weather was fine and hot and she felt lazy. Mrs. Green sensed that something had changed—probably had sniffed out the pregnancy through some arcane female power. She gave Dawn penetrating looks but did not trouble her—probably wouldn't until she began to show. Dawn learned from more derelict newspapers that some of the instruments had been shipped in from Caltech by Dr. Millikan, and understood that this flight was to be a sort of eschatological showdown between Millikan's theory that cosmic rays were the birth cries of new matter, and Compton's annihilation hypothesis. Her own delicate condition inclined her to the birth-cry view, but she found it interesting that Millikan entrusted his instruments to a rival who wished to prove him wrong. She wondered if Compton weren't tempted to sabotage Millikan's contraptions, but reckoned it would violate some sort of gentleman's code. A code stiffened, come to think of it, by the fact that any lie would out in the due course of scientific progress and its perpetrator put down in the logs as not just a villain but a fool.

The aeronauts—a Swiss named Jean Piccard and an American, Lieutenant Commander Thomas G. W. ("Tex") Settle of the U.S. Navy— arrived the day before the flight and, after a round of press interviews and posed photographs, set to work checking the balloon's controls. Inflation commenced that evening and carried on into the night. Dawn sent word to the German Communists and saved some good seats. They arrived just after dark, as banks of portable lights were thudding on all around the field, and balloon-watchers beginning to stream in by the thousands. The Germans had come victualed to hike all the way to Hudson's Bay should need arise, which was why Dawn had invited them. Suddenly ravenous—for she was not one of those pregnant girls who felt sick all the time—she inflicted so much damage on one of their hampers as to draw keen looks from a German crone who had probably sussed out the whole thing, gazing straight into her uterus with X-ray vision.

They fashioned a nest of blankets and a battlement of hampers and sat together deep into the night, drinking 3.2 beer and watching the bulge of hydrogen swell and rise in the slack folds of the balloon. The clanking of the cylinders as they were moved to and from the filling point, the hiss as they were discharged into the balloon, made a music that lulled her. For a while she was kept awake only by the MPs patrolling the stands to prevent people from smoking, and the jostling of nicotine fiends making their way to or from the exits. But eventually the old German lady made a little gesture and drew Dawn's head into her lap and stroked her hair with her leathery hands, and then she was out, just like that.

She woke from a jumbled dream of fire and fear. Sensing she'd been asleep for some hours, she sat up and pulled her loose, wild hair out of her face to see a smooth orange bubble rising from Lake Michigan, as if the magnesium factory over there in Midland had gone up in a terrible spitting flare of burning metal. But it was of course just the sun rising in a mostly clear sky, striped by the stolid entasis of the Doric columns. Answering it on the fifty-yard line of Soldier Field was a giant sphere of gas straining to be free of the slack pleats of the great balloon. The lower cone of it, converging toward the magnesium pellet, was striped by the shadows of the colonnade, but the smooth dome rose far above the highest reaches of the stadium's enclosing roofs, an orange-yellow ball that Compton had drawn up out of the sod to answer the one God had hung in the sky. Twenty thousand people were in the stadium to watch America venture into the stratosphere, higher than humans had ever gone, but they were rapt like churchgoers, not raucous like a football crowd. And no wonder, since the balloon was so huge and so close and seemingly balanced on such a tiny ball bearing. All normal intuition warned of its toppling over into the stands. Dawn knew now why her dreams had been troubled. Part of it was the orange sun shining through her hair, making it the color of fire. But more than that was the tone of the men's voices below. She could make out few words but they sounded like men responding to an emergency. And so they were—but it was an emergency they'd willingly and with forethought created by emptying seven hundred cylinders of buoyant flammable gas into a bag surrounded by twenty thousand men, women, and children. The balloon was too big for the stadium, the tension in the bar-tight mooring ropes was palpable. For those who knew anything about the properties of hydrogen, the possibility of a colossal fireball, the immolation of tens of thousands, was obvious. Releasing the balloon was as much a desperate measure to avoid catastrophe as it was a planned and orderly start to a scientific expedition. The crowd wouldn't have had it any other way; they'd come to be near the danger and the power, as the spectators on Navy Pier had gone to feel the rumble of the Fraschinis in their bones and bellies.

It went up in an explosion of silence. Air rushed down toward the center to replace that voided by the rising balloon, entraining cigarette papers, ticket stubs, peanut skins, and human hair, all bright in the light of the sunrise, a chaos of litter when you were amidst it but intelligible as a system of flows and vortices when viewed across the gridiron. Born from the stadium, the bald baby jumped straight up a few thousand feet, caught an upper-atmosphere breeze, and began to drift away from the lake. And Dawn began to think in a serious way of what she was going to do now.

They were getting updates over the loudspeakers. Scientists, meteorologists, and aeronauts were taking their turns at the microphone as they bided their time waiting for radio updates from Piccard and Settle. The general strategy was to vent gas, stabilizing altitude, and soak up heat from the sun for a while. Dawn, still coming awake, drifted between listening to their commentary and pondering her situation.

She had money for a train ticket. She wouldn't have to travel hobo-style; she could ride in a pullman to Montana and go to ground.

She could find someone to give her an abortion in Chicago, but she well knew the dangers of placing herself at the mercy of an illegal practitioner, the infection or scarring, or both, that could leave her infertile or dead.

No, if she wanted that she should go to the Soviet Union, where she could get it done for free, by a real doctor. She could get there by going east, but the old familiar way for her was west, to Seattle, thence Vladivostok.

She would buy a ticket on the Empire Builder today and go to Montana and see how matters stood there, whether the loose network of cousins and uncles and aunts would have her, and maybe she would stay and have the baby, and maybe she would keep right on going to Vladivostok.

She was brought back to the here and now by a gasp from the crowd. All were shading their eyes to look up at CENTURY OF PROGRESS hanging in the dawn light a mile above them, drifting slightly to the west. She had missed an announcement—a dire one. The Germans were demanding a translation. She heard it said that a hydrogen vent had got stuck open. Gas was rushing uncontrollably from the balloon. It was on its way down. It was coming back.

The stadium was emptying out. The marines were piling into troop carriers, rolling out onto the streets. Spectators with vehicles began to pursue them; but the marines knew no better than anyone else where the balloon was going to crash. All one had to do was watch it. And it was coming down so nearby—headed for the adjoining railyard—that vehicles were of little use. People were swarming fences and fanning out across the tracks. Appearances had deceived them—it landed a good two miles away—but that was only a few minutes' good run. Impelled by the curious magnetism of the crowd, Dawn and the Germans crossed a trampled-down fence and reached the site a bit late. The first spectators to reach it had descended on the flaccid envelope with pocketknives to cut away souvenirs. Marines had then arrived and driven them off with rifle butts, leaving the creamy fabric marked with arcs of blood. What Dawn and her party found was a cordon of marines with fixed bayonets, dense around the dented magnesium sphere, where Tex Settle and Jean Piccard were being stethoscoped under the eye of the local and international press corps, and sparse around the piled envelope of the crashed balloon.

Dawn was on the Empire Builder that night.

17

MAGNITOGORSK

FEBRUARY 1934

None of these men ever bothered to introduce themselves—a failure of manners irksome to whatever was left of Aurora's "sense of bourgeois propriety." She tried to put it all in perspective by reminding herself that a couple of hours earlier they'd been torturing her, and so if she were going to get indignant about something it should probably be that.

Shpak had told her, at the beginning, that he'd been ordered to leave no marks on her body. She had to give him credit for the successful completion of that task. When they'd cut her free from the bed frame there had been red wrinkles wherever the torn bedsheets had been wound around her limbs, but by the time the car had delivered her to Magnitogorsk's Central Hotel, these had faded. When she inspected herself in the mirror after a hot bath she saw practically no sign that anything had happened, other than red eyes that she could have concealed with makeup, had there been any makeup. Her throat and lungs felt as if she had gargled battery acid, but no one could see those. Her voice would be hoarse for a while.

A private room with a bathtub was a luxury she had not enjoyed since entering the Soviet Union. Someone had packed up all her stuff from the cottage where she'd been staying in Berezka and moved it here. She could have just sat in bed for a day, enjoying the solitude, but the man with the glasses had been insistent that she show up for dinner, and she got the clear sense that she belonged to him now. So she did what she could with her hair, put on a skirt and blouse, and went down to the hotel's restaurant. No one was there. But in the back was a private dining room where pre-dinner drinks were in full swing.

Seated around one end of the long table were three men smoking cigarettes and speaking in an alien language. She recognized one of them from photographs as Sergo Ordzhonikidze, the head of the Commissariat of Heavy Industry for the entire Soviet Union. Across from him was Vissarion Lominadze, who reported to Ordzhonikidze; never mind his official job title, he ran Magnitogorsk and everyone knew it. She had seen him a few times around town, but even if she hadn't, she'd have guessed who he was based on his fatness, which was infamous. He was indeed the fattest man she had ever seen. If the Workers' and Peasants' Revolution got crushed by the forces of capitalism, he'd be able to get a job as a circus freak. In Magnitogorsk, what passed for powerful, important men revolved around him like electrons around a massive nucleus, and he was accustomed to being the dominant man in any room. But here he cringed and fawned before Ordzhonikidze.

Seated between those two at the head of the table was the man with the round eyeglasses.

She knew that Ordzhonikidze and Lominadze were, like Stalin, Georgians. So the language they were speaking must be that. The man at the head of the table was speaking it too. Also a Georgian, therefore. But he must be of higher rank even than Ordzhonikidze, for he was at the head of the table, and anyway it was clear from clues in how they treated him that he was the top dog. But of course he wasn't Stalin.

This man had to be Lavrentiy Beria. She'd heard of him but hadn't recognized his face, since he generally didn't appear in papers.

Seated next to Lominadze—therefore, given Lominadze's girth, rather far down the table—was Shpak, stuffing tobacco into his pipe and gazing inertly into a glass of water, since he had no idea what the Georgians were saying. He avoided meeting Aurora's eye—as well he might. She didn't imagine this kind of situation was covered in Emily Post. It must happen a lot, though, in the Soviet Union: bumping into persons who had tortured you or murdered members of your family.

Speaking of family: at the foot of the table was Dr. Oleksandr Fizmatov. Flanking him were two young men. These had to be Proton and Elektron. Proton, the older brother, though only a bit taller than Aurora, was broad-shouldered and handsome, straight out of a Komsomol poster. Elektron wasn't a complete disaster to look at but suffered by comparison. He better fit the profile of an unathletic youth who spent a lot of time squinting at his slide rule. Where Proton had green eyes and neatly brushed, honey-colored hair, Elektron was brown on brown, his hair hanging down over his ears and brushing the collar of the ill-fitting jacket he'd thrown on for the occasion.

The gist, socially, was that two parties were going on at this table: at one end the three Georgian bigwigs, making the most of the opportunity to smoke and drink and converse in their own language, and hardly deigning to acknowledge that Aurora was in the room. At the other, the Fizmatovs, soft-spoken and polite. In the middle Shpak, the odd man out. He was seated with his back to a row of triple-glazed windows supplying a view over what would one day be Magnitogorsk's town square. The sun had set hours ago, but she knew what was out there: a squat plinth in a sea of rutted and frozen mud, awaiting a monumental statue of Stalin. Behind that, the factory gates—a mere formality, since most of the material and the workers came in from the other direction. Rising up beyond that were the blast furnaces and the rolling mills, leaking orange heat and dense fumes into the winter night.

Aurora was no closer to understanding what was, and wasn't, considered bourgeois than she had been when she'd stepped off the boat with Engineer Overstreet in Vladivostok. It seemed that one of the few forces in the world that could rival the power of Marxist-Leninist thought was men's craving to be respected. And, to be fair, women's. For hadn't she just spent half an hour fussing with hair and clothing in front of the mirror in her room? In Magnitogorsk—less a city than a city-sized factory infested by humans—it was de rigueur to dress like a worker. A few days earlier, when she'd first laid eyes on Shpak with his suit and his overcoat, she'd known he was important. Not because he was dressed as a bomb-throwing firebrand but because he wasn't. He looked like every other man in a suit. Lenin and Stalin could get away with distinctive proletarian-inspired clothing but Beria, only one notch below Stalin, wore a suit. The Fizmatovs had gone out of their way to look respectable—even Elektron smelled faintly of pomade—and they were defaulting to bourgeois, pre-revolutionary etiquette. Perhaps it was the case that when you were Dr. Oleksandr Fizmatov, a slave in all but name, liable to be shot at any moment and looking right down the table into the bottle-bottom glasses of the man who would give the order, it simply didn't matter.

Some social conventions had to be observed. It hardly mattered which. So Aurora shook the hands of Proton and Elektron and said how pleased she was to meet them. Proton announced he was *enchanté* and Elektron bobbed his head in the manner of one who had read old novels in which men were described as bowing. They waited for her to sit. In the corner of his eye she could see Oleksandr trying to communicate wordlessly with Elektron, urging him to assist the young lady by scooting in her chair like a proper gentleman, but Elektron was oblivious. In the end Proton and his father just exchanged an amused look with each other and took their seats in turn. Proton reached across and filled Aurora's water glass from the provided carafe.

Both of the Fizmatov boys were studying at Moscow University and so this provided grist for the conversational mill in the early going. You could always ask students how they liked their classes. It seemed they'd been warned not to ask difficult questions about what Aurora had been up to in the past few days. She caught the father's eye when he was studying her, and he gave a look expressive of immense relief.

Her arrival was apparently the signal for the kitchen staff to begin bringing food out, and so before long Beria was dinging his mother-of-pearl caviar spoon on his crystal vodka tumbler and calling the dinner to order. They toasted Comrade Stalin. They toasted the recently concluded 17th Party Congress. They toasted the People's Commissariat of Heavy Industry, represented by Ordzhonikidze. The Magnitogorsk Metallurgical Complex (Lominadze). The Sword of the Revolution (Shpak). The Mining and Metallurgical Institute (Dr. Fizmatov). Our comrades in America (Aurora). The future of Soviet science and technology, as embodied by

Proton and Elektron. The City Dining Trust and the City Food Processing Complex, which were providing dinner. And when that was all done and Beria looked like he might actually sit down and let people eat, Ordzhonikidze flung his napkin down, scrambled to his feet, and made them all toast Beria. Aurora was completely exhausted, and had no wish to pour grain alcohol down her scorched throat, so she faked it by dumping some water into her vodka glass. Shpak had got his pipe going and the smoke was wafting toward her. She knew that for the rest of her life she would associate its fragrance with what had been done to her on the ice of the Ural River.

There was small talk through soup and salad, mostly about the younger Fizmatovs' studies, but when the meat was trundled out, Beria finally let them know what the real agenda was. The reason he had brought all of these people together to break bread around a table: balloons.

Fucking balloons again, Aurora thought, and made an effort not to shake her head. As the only woman here, people tended to look at her when they had nothing else to look at. Even Shpak met her eye for a moment.

"I believe that some of our guests share an interest in this topic," Beria said, once he'd broached it. "Comrade Artemyeva was present in Chicago for the launch of the failed American probe, and Proton and Elektron are engaged in similar work in Moscow—are you not?"

Elektron was already nodding vigorously enough to make his lank hair swing over his cheek, and even risked a curious glance at Aurora. Proton looked like he was choking on his beef—given its toughness, not an unrealistic scenario. His father reached out and rested a hand on his forearm, then stared at Beria quizzically.

"My compliments to the Fizmatovs," Beria said, "for being mindful of the correct security precautions around this sensitive topic."

Elektron audibly gulped and stopped nodding.

"Please know," Beria continued, "that Comrade Shpak and I have recently concluded a thorough investigation of Comrade Artemyeva's background and issued the necessary security clearances. You may speak freely in her presence on this topic."

In spite of herself Aurora blushed, pleased to have been made aware of this—though some clue should have been detected from the fact that she was sitting here eating caviar instead of being gnawed by fish at the bottom of the Ural River. Sensing Shpak's eye on her she glanced across the table at him, to be met by what she could only describe as a murderous glare.

He'd been overruled. Beria had pulled rank on him.

"Perhaps the young lady might share her recollections of the Chicago probe and why the Americans expended so much on this debacle," Beria continued.

"Of course," Aurora said through raw vocal cords. She faltered for a moment, still a bit distracted by the realization that Shpak wanted her dead. That Beria, the pervert, had saved her life. Looking at Beria helped a bit. Looking at Proton helped a lot. He was looking back, that was for sure, and with more than merely scientific curiosity. "The Fizmatovs will know more than I," she began, "but I did happen to make the acquaintance of a physics student there who tried to explain to me the experiments performed on these balloons and why they are of such interest to the capitalists. I can try to relate that to you if you like—the Fizmatovs can correct my mistakes, of which I'm sure there will be many."

"Please proceed!" Beria said with the satisfied air of a polo player showing off his new prize pony.

"Well, everyone knows about radiation—the experiments of the Curies and Joliot in Paris and so on. It comes from heavy elements like radium that are out at the end of the periodic table. Apparently when the nucleus gets too big it's unstable. When it flies apart the rays come out. As scientists created better devices for detecting radiation, they began to see very powerful rays whose origin was mysterious. They were not produced by radium or any of the other heavy elements. What could explain these rays? They are present everywhere, all the time, passing through us without our knowing it. Some supposed they came from processes deep in the earth. Others that they came from space. Experiments performed on mountain peaks showed more of them, suggesting a cosmic origin. They are attenuated by the atmosphere. The higher you go, the more there is to learn. The highest mountains in America are only a few thousand meters above sea level, and in inaccessible parts of the country. A balloon, properly outfitted, can go much higher, and can be launched from anyplace that is convenient. Soldier Field is only a few kilometers from the University of Chicago, and it's right in the middle of Century of Progress—the world exposition where Niels Bohr spoke last summer. So they made such a balloon and launched it. But it failed because of a defective valve."

At Beria's prompting she went on to supply more details: the seven hundred steel cylinders of hydrogen gas, the magnesium sphere, the folds of rubberized fabric.

The Georgians, who up to this point had merrily ignored everyone else in the room, listened to all of this with an intensity that Aurora found a bit unnerving. "You're saying," said Ordzhonikidze, "that all of this effort and expense was just to put up an airborne laboratory. An observatory for these rays?"

Beria said something in Georgian and then added "*Kosmicheskie luchi*," cueing Aurora as to the Russian terms.

"Yes," Aurora said. "At those altitudes it is intensely cold and there is not enough oxygen to breathe, so the gondola containing the aeronauts is a sealed capsule, pressurized with air. Inside it are certain instruments, such as 'cloud chambers'—I don't know what they are called here—"

"*Kamera Vilsona*," muttered Elektron.

"*Kamera Vilsona*, thank you—that the aeronauts can use to study these rays when they are drifting along at the outer limit of the atmosphere—the threshold of interplanetary space."

"But it failed?" Lominadze asked. "The Americans did not obtain the knowledge they were seeking?"

"That is correct, Comrade."

"In a few days, though, we're going to steal a march on them, aren't we, Comrade Proton?" said Beria.

"Indeed we are, Comrade!" said Proton. "We are making preparations to launch a more advanced balloon that will succeed where the Americans failed. I have the very great honor of being one of the aeronauts."

After a brief pause, this elicited a round of applause and a raising of glasses. Proton blushed in a way that Aurora, even through all of her exhaustion, found ridiculously fetching. Of course they'd have chosen this magnificent boy to be one of the aeronauts.

"It is all a fine testament to Soviet science and engineering," Ordzhonikidze said, "but I am a bureaucrat who builds steel mills. Can anyone explain why it matters? Or do we do it simply because the Americans couldn't?"

"Scientifically—" the elder Fizmatov began, but Ordzhonikidze silenced him with a wave of the hand.

"Scientifically, I know how a blast furnace works. By stripping oxygen away from iron oxide to give us pig iron." He extended one arm in an Ozymandian gesture toward the colonnade of glowing blast furnaces marching off into the night. "Pig iron begets steel, and from steel we make rails and tanks. These cosmic rays you're talking about—can they give us something like this?" Waving his arm again and nodding out the window. "Or is it like collecting butterflies?" Silence fell, and he added, "Collecting butterflies is perfectly fine, by the way. I just need to know."

For some reason Proton and his father both turned to look at Elektron, who had been staring fixedly at his half-eaten meal through all of this. Aurora wasn't the only person in the room to notice it. Though he didn't look up, he seemed to be aware that attention was on him. After clearing his throat he said one word: "Neutrons."

"The word means nothing to me," Beria volunteered after he and the other Georgians had exchanged baffled glances.

"There's no reason it ought to," Elektron reassured him.

Shpak threw him a look. Oleksandr Fizmatov saw it, and stepped in: "Lek is talking about a new kind of elementary particle that was only discovered in the last year or so," he explained. "Outside of university physics departments, there's no reason anyone should ever have encountered this term."

"Lek" nodded.

Lominadze didn't mind playing the clown. "For those of us who are not even within a thousand kilometers of such an institution, what's the connection to balloons?" he inquired. His tone was all forced merriment, but he was casting nervous glances at Beria and Ordzhonikidze.

Elektron ran his hand through his hair, combing it back from his face. He looked to be wrestling with the weighty problem of trying to explain these matters to steel makers and secret police. Watching him in some bemusement was Proton, who put in: "As Comrade Aurora has very clearly explained, radiation of extremely high penetrating power enters from above into our atmosphere. The upper atmosphere is the best place to study it."

"Does it come from the sun?" Ordzhonikidze asked.

"These rays are observable at *night*," Elektron said, "and during *total solar eclipses.*"

Silent chewing for a few moments. Aurora, not unwilling to play the dumb blonde, said, "Oh, I see. When the Earth or the moon is in the way—blocking any rays that might originate from the sun."

"Obviously," Elektron said. Not unkindly. Just pointing out that it was obvious.

"So, by process of elimination, it must come from astronomical phenomena farther away—stars, galaxies—"

"Supernovas, probably," Elektron said. "Where elements are forged. There's your blast furnace. When smaller atoms are smashed together in a star to make heavier nuclei, amounts of energy are released that are so far beyond that"—he waved dismissively at the industrial colossus outside the window—"as to be beyond comprehension. Supernovas spray these heavy nuclei into space, where they condense into planets like droplets of water from steam. The really heavy elements like uranium slowly sink to the bottom and decay—the energy they release in doing so keeps the Earth's core hot and churning, sometimes bringing a trace of uranium or radium to the surface. We live in this intermediate layer of medium-sized nuclei that are stable enough to form complicated molecules that support life. Below us, massive nuclei are decaying in a hellish sea of lava. Above us, light nuclei are combining to make starlight—but every bit as hostile to life. To know more we have to dig down or fly high—getting just a tiny bit closer to those terrible places of energy release and radioactivity.

Flying high is easier." He nodded deferentially at his brother. "Which isn't to suggest it's easy, or safe."

"My compliments, Dr. Fizmatov," said Beria, looking down the table. "The boy speaks well once he gets warmed up. Like starting a tractor's engine on a cold morning. But what's this about neutrons? That was the first word that came out of his mouth, was it not?"

"You are very kind," Fizmatov said. "As might be guessed from the names of my two boys, protons and electrons were all we knew about just a few years ago. In those days there was no way to measure the mass of a nucleus. More recently that has become possible. But then a problem of arithmetic reared its head."

"Arithmetic? I should have thought that was settled in the days of the ancient Greeks!" Lominadze said jovially.

"We know," Fizmatov said, "that hydrogen has but one proton. It must therefore have but one electron as well, to balance out the charge. One positive, one negative, sum zero. Helium has two of each. So you would think helium would have double the mass of hydrogen. But it does not. In fact, the helium nucleus weighs *four* times as much hydrogen. Since electrons weigh practically nothing, the only way to account for this is to assume that helium's nucleus has *four* rather than *two* protons. Yet we know that its electrical charge is only two."

"It does seem like a large discrepancy when you put it that way!" Ordzhonikidze blustered. He had been stung a little by Elektron's dismissive attitude toward the energy output of his blast furnaces, and was now inclining more and more to the view that these physicists were all just butterfly collectors.

"The Curies and Joliot looked at it at the Institut du Radium in Paris. Rutherford and Chadwick in England. Compton and Millikan in America. Fermi in Italy. Hahn and Meisner in Germany," Fizmatov said. The Georgians all directed their gazes on him, and Aurora perceived something, which was that they were all afraid that the Soviet Union would fall behind. Fizmatov understood as much. And he knew that by playing upon that fear he could force their hand—prevent these powerful ignoramuses from dismissing him and his boys out of hand. "There were theories that a couple of extra electrons might be hiding inside the nucleus somewhere, for example. But Rutherford has proved, and others have confirmed, that this third particle, the neutron, really exists."

"It was hard to see," Lek said, "because, lacking charge, it passes through matter undetected."

"What is its significance?" Ordzhonikidze asked, "other than making the arithmetic work out?"

"It's the key to everything," Lek said.

"Can you be a little more specific?" Shpak asked sharply. At last his skills as an interrogator were finding some practical application here.

"Alchemy," Lek said. "What the ancient alchemists merely dreamed of is happening now. In Cambridge, Paris, Chicago."

"He means transmutation of elements," said Proton, looking at his little brother with a mix of concern and affection.

"Until now—right now!" Lek said, slapping the table. "We believed it could only happen in two ways. In the interior of stars—not very useful! Or simply by waiting for a nucleus of uranium or radium to decay. But Curie, Joliot, Rutherford, Fermi—they are finding that when neutrons are directed at ordinary nuclei, transmutation happens easily."

"I thought you said it passes through matter undetected," said Shpak, ever alert to contradictions in a story.

"Because we were looking in the wrong place. We should have been looking in the nuclei themselves. The neutrality of this particle is what gives it the ability to strike home and re-order a nucleus—turning it from one element to another."

"And what does that give us?" Ordzhonikidze demanded, "other than an arithmetical curiosity?"

"Energy," said Elektron, "the power of stars."

At last they had the attention of Sergo Ordzhonikidze. And so keen was his interest that the elder Fizmatov felt the need to moderate it: "Many of these same authorities—at least in their public statements—are saying that it might never happen on the surface of the Earth. To engineer just the right set of conditions to bring about these alchemical transmutations in an industrial facility might be physically impossible. Perhaps the cores of planets and the interiors of stars are the only places in the universe where conditions are right."

"*Can ever* be right," Elektron said. "Even in theory. But my professors at the university are saying that, every month, Joliot-Curie or Fermi or one of those others is finding some new isotope that they can produce simply by exposing everyday substances to neutrons. There are hundreds, probably thousands, of them waiting to be discovered."

Drawing Ordzhonikidze's eye, Proton said, "It is as if a few scientists discovered a new continent with thousands of hitherto unknown species of butterflies. Catching them all and drawing pictures of them is going to take awhile. But the possibility exists that at least one of them might be a magic butterfly that gives its discoverer powers we thought were reserved to wizards and gods."

"That's the *unsaid* bit," his father emphasized. "Talk to any of those scientists and they'll pooh-pooh the 'wizards and gods' bit and insist they're just butterfly collectors."

Whether or not it was the case that Oleksandr Fizmatov was really being that clever—that devious—the fact of the matter was that this sort of explanation jibed perfectly with the way men like Beria and Ordzhonikidze were wont to view the world. Namely that the outward pretenses maintained by important men—scientists, in this case—concealed subtle and hidden motives, and that to understand as much was to be sophisticated and therefore strong. They exchanged a few words in Georgian and it was obvious from their tone that in their minds it all added up. Shpak watched them impassively, but it seemed to Aurora that even he was buying it.

"Well," Ordzhonikidze said, after lighting a cigarette and blowing out a long plume of smoke, "it is all a good way to enjoy some conversation over dinner. But if you had any idea of the shit we have to put up with just to make a blast furnace—"

"Dr. Fizmatov knows," Aurora put in. "We know. We have volunteered for Workers' Shock Brigades. We have been up on those things. Seen people die."

"Good! Then you'll understand that even if this is all as important as you say, it will never be a matter for the Commissariat of Heavy Industry. At least, not during my tenure."

"I agree," Beria said. "My suggestion, Comrade Ordzhonikidze, is that you build your steel mill and leave the butterfly collecting to me." And for some reason he looked at Aurora.

18

FORT SICKLES, NORTH DAKOTA

SEPTEMBER 1933

Dawn had declined the State of North Dakota's generous offer to supply her with a public defender, and signed papers to the effect that she would be acting as her own lawyer. To his credit—and to her surprise, for she was new to this sort of thing—her adversary, the local prosecutor, had tried to dissuade her. He had spelled out the gravity of the charges and listed all of the ways in which even the most poorly trained and inattentive public defender might be able to reduce her sentence or conceivably even talk a jury into returning a not-guilty verdict. Dawn was gratified that this man had identified her as a young woman of some intelligence, even promise. He was trying to talk to her as one reasonable, educated person to another; perhaps a rare sort of encounter in his line of work. One that he found worth putting some time into. Dawn had tried to cut the conversation short by announcing that it was her intention to plead guilty at her arraignment, and she didn't think she needed a lawyer for that. Even then the prosecutor had persisted, explaining that a lawyer might be able to find some hole in his, the prosecutor's, case that would render a guilty plea a foolish mistake on her part.

It was all quite interesting from a standpoint of understanding the legal mind, but Dawn suspected, and Reggie confirmed, that the prosecutor was doing it not because he really wanted to help Dawn but because he needed to make sure that all the rules were followed so that the conviction would stick.

As far as Dawn was concerned it was neither here nor there. She needed for the arraignment to take place on a predictable schedule, and soon. A lawyer might just create trouble by filing motions and causing delays.

Reggie paid her more visits during the week leading up to the arraignment. There was no place in the jail where they could really talk in private and so they spoke obliquely, with Reggie making frequent reference to an upcoming family reunion that would be attracting brothers, uncles, and nephews from all over the West and Midwest. Many of the details of what he was getting ready for, though they were obviously of interest to Dawn, were really none of her concern and best left unsaid. She had only a few specifics that she wanted to get straight with Reggie. First of all, that this really was going to happen on a specific date and time. Secondly, that she needed to get her trunk. And third, a detail that came to her late one night as she was thinking the whole thing through: she needed a hundred feet of rope. This last item was difficult to say outright, but important, and so she wrote it down on a scrap of paper and snuck it into Reggie's hand when none of the guards was watching. He couldn't read, but some who had already filtered into town for the "family reunion" probably could.

That settled, she had nothing to do but wait for the big day. She was the only occupant of her cell. Reggie had brought her a book—a dime-novel western—but she'd already been through that twice. As bookmark she'd been using a newspaper clipping consisting of a story about Bonnie and Clyde. This had been mailed to her, care of Reggie, by a second cousin in Montana, a pen pal of sorts who knew of Dawn's interest in the doings of the Barrow gang. Most of the story was a poem, written by Bonnie Parker herself, and apparently typed up in some moment when Bonnie had got access to a typewriter and some carbon paper. It was entitled "The Life and Death of Bonnie and Clyde," though, as far as anyone knew, they were still alive. Either way the poem seemed worth studying. On the night before her arraignment, Dawn perused it one last time before the jailers turned out the lights. Tomorrow at this time she'd be dead or alive, that much was for sure. If alive, she'd be on the run, just like Bonnie. If dead—well, then it hardly mattered.

Some day they'll go down together;
And they'll bury them side by side;
To few it'll be grief
To the law a relief
But it's death for Bonnie and Clyde.

She wondered if that made it any different—dying next to your boyfriend. Being buried next to him. She'd been raised not to believe in God or an afterlife, but she still found it affecting that Bonnie loved her Clyde so that she believed that death would somehow be different if her corpse was buried next to his. Dawn's father's voice sounded between her ears, pointing out that it would make a difference to the living, politically. The grave would become a monument, visited by the masses. A rallying point. But Bonnie didn't seem to have much political consciousness beyond disliking cops.

If they try to act like citizens
And rent them a nice little flat,
About the third night
They're invited to fight
By a sub-gun's rat-tat-tat.

Bonnie had a lousy sense of meter, that was for sure. Dawn tried to make excuses by supposing that the whole poem had been written in the backseat of a Ford jouncing down a potholed country road, its V8 straining to stay one gunshot ahead of pursuing lawmen.

Bonnie's devotion to her Clyde, her placid expectation that she would die next to him, was fascinating but completely alien to Dawn. There'd been three boys in her life. Billy Bach. But Patton had pointed out his unsuitability, which was completely obvious the moment he'd said it. As if to underscore that, Billy had then fallen in with the Landesjäger. Dick for his part was charming enough, but look where that had got her. And then there was the curious case of Silent Al. And as she lay on her cot in the dark of the Fort Sickles jail the night before her arraignment, staring up at the ceiling, she had to admit that—if you ignored the part about how he had deceived her, betrayed her, and been a key figure in a government operation that had put her father and friends to death—he'd really been the best match for her in a lot of ways.

She drowsed off to sleep while imagining something pretty naughty involving Silent Al and handcuffs. If he tracked her down, and got the drop on her, and put her in shackles, would it be in her power as a woman to make him break that iron self-discipline? Hands behind her back, powerless except for her face and her words, could she break him? And what would it be like if she did?

WHEN SHE WOKE UP, THOUGH, HER THOUGHTS WERE ON A FOURTH MAN WHO HADN'T entered into last night's drowsy reckoning because he was homosexual. Bob Overstreet, the clean-cut Wisconsin engineer who had sheltered her for a spell at his house in Gary. During the subsequent year she'd kept in touch with him through the mail. In his most recent letter, posted just a couple of weeks ago, he'd mentioned that the steel company had sent him to San Francisco to build some sort of bridge. Bob hadn't come out and said so directly, but she understood that he was offering her a bolt-hole if she needed one.

The notion of going, not just to the West Coast but all the way to Magnitogorsk, had apparently come to her in some already-forgotten dream, for it was just there, fully formed in her head, when she opened her eyes. It was obvious. She had to do it. Dawn would die today. Aurora would somehow get to San Francisco and begin a new life in the Soviet Union. A better life by far than the outlaw road described by Bonnie:

> The road was so dimly lighted;
> There were no highway signs to guide;
> But they made up their minds
> If all roads were blind,
> They wouldn't give up till they died.

The road gets dimmer and dimmer;
Sometimes you can hardly see;
But it's fight, man to man,
And do all you can,
For they know they can never be free.

There was just the inconvenient detail that she was locked up in a jail cell in Fort Sickles. But a plan to fix that had been set in motion and there was nothing she could do now either to stop it from being carried out or to abet it.

She sat there on her cot for most of the day, just waiting. They'd expected it would all go down in the morning, but—as far as she could discern from scraps of information filtering down from the courthouse—there'd been delays. The westbound train carrying the judge had arrived hours late. The judge had been drawn into some last-minute conferences in his chambers. Several other cases were on the docket before Dawn's. These had become unexpectedly complicated. It was time for lunch. Lunch was running long.

Dawn began seriously to entertain the possibility that it was all going sideways. The bank closed at three. The gang—no point in calling it anything else—was awaiting a signal from Reggie. He wouldn't give that signal until Dawn had been unlocked from her cell and led into the courtroom by the bailiff. At that point the robbery of the bank would commence, with a lot of shooting. This would be clearly audible from the courthouse. Most of the cops in that building would head for the bank, leaving a skeleton crew in the courtroom. Reggie and two of his confederates would be there, with pistols in their pockets. They could easily spring Dawn at that point. They and the bank robbers would head for a rendezvous outside of town: a certain house above the river where Dawn had a trunk she needed to collect.

But if the court proceedings were delayed past three o'clock, the bank would lock its doors. Rather than miss that opportunity, the bank-robbing contingent would probably just go in guns blazing shortly before the hour. If Dawn was still locked in her cell at that point, then that was where she would certainly remain.

She heard the bells in the church across the square ring two, then two thirty. She was sitting on her cot, eyes closed, mentally composing a little statement to the judge, requesting a public defender after all, when she heard keys rattle in the lock and looked up to see the bailiff. "You're up, young lady," he announced.

She got to her feet. The blood fell out of her head and she became light-headed. She drifted unsteadily out of the cell. The bailiff grabbed her by the arm and frog-marched her around a corner and down a row of men's cells. Then through another locked door, up some stairs, along a connecting passage to the courthouse. She sat for a few agonizing minutes in a sort of anteroom before finally the door to the courtroom was opened. The bailiff marched her in. She found herself in the defendants' dock, which was surrounded by a low, basically symbolic wall. The judge sat on a dais to one side. He was facing out over a courtroom with a seating capacity of perhaps fifty. No more than a dozen onlookers were there, and one of those was just in the act of stepping out the back. This drew her eye to the back row of seats. Reggie was sitting there next to one of his confederates. The other had just stepped out—he was going to signal the boys waiting near the bank. It was all going to happen now.

The courtroom was silent except for a faint rustle of papers from the judge's dais as he opened the relevant documents. Dawn was able to hear, quite distinctly, a man's voice emanating from a row of seats near the front. Three men were seated together. Well groomed and well dressed by the standards of Fort Sickles. Out-of-towners, clearly. Ranging in age from mid-twenties to mid-thirties. The one in the middle spoke up clearly. "That's her," he said to his comrades. "I'd know her anywhere." He aimed his index finger at her. Dawn stared up it, like the barrel of a revolver, and directly into the eyes of Silent Al.

He stared back. Their eyes were locked together for a spell.

Finally he looked away, though, distracted by the sound of a Thompson submachine gun being fired down the street.

THE COY STYLE IN WHICH DAWN AND REGGIE HAD CONVERSED DURING THEIR MEETINGS meant that Dawn had only a general notion as to the plan. She had got the sense, though, that even if they'd been able to meet privately and talk for hours, Reggie might not have had much more to say as to the exact order of operations. In that, some might have seen reckless disregard. Until the summer of 1932, Dawn would have been one of them. But everything she'd seen in D.C. had made her skeptical of plans in general, and complicated plans in particular. From time to time, reviewing the events of that summer, she would shake her head in dismay at the sheer amount of time and mental effort that those Communists had poured into the framing of plans. They had even planned their planning, setting up schedules of meetings at which planning was to take place. Guys who had actually done stuff, like the riotous marine John Pace, showed polite but absolute lack of interest. Pace's attitude seemed to be that the sole benefit of plan-making was that it kept the plan-making sorts out of his hair.

It was through this lens that Dawn had conducted all of her subsequent research into the publicized exploits of Bonnie and Clyde, Pretty Boy Floyd, Baby Face Nelson, and other "public enemies" as they were styled in the press and denoted in stern G-man press conferences. Bonnie's poem, in which she likened their life to a dimly lighted road with no signs—a road that might turn out to be a dead end—didn't seem like the work of a dyed-in-the-wool master planner. Reggie, while he had not achieved the headline-grabbing notoriety of a certified public enemy, had been in enough scrapes that he had a general sense of how these things were likely to play out, and was apparently not one for making plans either. Life was not *entirely* a crapshoot—there were a few commonsense things you could do to stack the odds in your favor—but as soon as the shooting started, only the most brute, elementary plans were of any use. Which might say as much about the human brain and how it reacts to the sound of gunfire and the sight of blood as it does about the plans themselves.

In this case, the plan was "the courtroom and jail will have a lot of cops but they'll be drawn to the bank robbery and then something something something." To the extent Reggie had made any plans at all, in other words, they had not included three presumably armed G-men in the courtroom—G-men who had apparently come here specifically targeting

Dawn and who, unlike the bailiff standing behind her in the defendants' dock, knew her to be something more than a wayward orphan who'd experienced a spot of female trouble on the train.

But in a sense it didn't matter. That was the beauty of the Reggie approach. A plan can't go awry if it doesn't exist. Whilst appreciating that, Dawn thought it might benefit Reggie and his two confederates if they knew more.

The sound of multiple submachine guns being discharged a hundred strides away at the bank, interspersed with shotgun blasts and revving V8s, had the paradoxical effect of causing the courtroom to become absolutely quiet as everyone listened excruciatingly, wondering if this was really what it sounded like. Everyone, that is, except those who'd been expecting it. An amusing detail here was that the church bells were beginning to ring three o'clock.

A windowpane popped, developing a hole and a system of cracks.

"Reggie," Dawn said—speaking up clearly, but there was no need to shout—"these three right here are G-men."

"I know," Reggie said, and shot one of them. Not Silent Al. The one on Dawn's right. "You're in my line," he added with a demonstrative nod.

This put Dawn in mind of a new and important topic: what *she* ought to be doing. It was all well and good to be part of a gang—as she now was—with a propensity for shooting first and making plans later—or *never*—but it did require that she get in the spirit and actually *do things*.

She'd vaguely expected that she would sit demurely in this box until all of the lawmen ran off to deal with the bank robbery. Reggie and his friends would then pull bandannas up over their faces, draw pistols, approach the front of the courtroom, and disarm the bailiff. But the presence of the G-men had already thrown a monkey wrench into that plan. Now, as Reggie was pointing out, she was creating a problem for him by being downrange, from his point of view, of his targets. This hadn't discouraged him from getting off one meticulously aimed shot. But she did need to move.

She glanced back at the bailiff. His job was to keep an eye on Dawn. He was failing at it, to a degree that almost made her indignant. Much more interesting to him at the moment was a federal agent exhaling blood and sinking to his knees. Dawn braced both of her hands on the railing of the dock and vaulted over it. It was a good thing no one was looking at her, because this went poorly. She was wearing a skirt, for one thing, and her internal organs were still in a bit of a state from Mrs. Kidd's surgical intervention of a few weeks back. She *did* make it over the rail but ended up lying full-length on the floor in no small amount of discomfort. This was a good place to be during what, to judge from what she was hearing, was now a full-on gunfight.

Papa and other vets had told stories about being trained by the army to crawl on one's belly under barbed wire, using elbows and knees, and of putting that skill to use in the no-man's-lands of the Great War. Dawn now began to move in that style laterally across the front of the courtroom, right in front of the judge's dais, because that was where she needed to be heading in order to put distance between herself and the last observed position of the G-men. Being handcuffed by Silent Al no longer seemed like an opening to romance. Even that amount of planning turned out to be wrong, though—the two surviving G-men had moved to take cover behind the dais. One of them even vaulted over Dawn on his way there. Shards of marble hit her in the face. She risked getting up to a low crouch. In that attitude she scurried over to the box where the jury was supposed to sit, then headed down the side aisle toward the back of the room.

Suddenly a man was right in front of her, down on one knee, firing a revolver. But this must be one of Reggie's. The one who'd ducked out of the courtroom to give the signal. He'd re-entered through another door and put the G-men in a crossfire. He'd pulled a red bandanna up over his face. Recognizing Dawn he waved his arm vigorously toward the back, as if she were a vexatious horsefly he wished to expel from the room. Dawn stayed low until she was well past him, for the G-men were returning fire. Then she got up and ran out.

Looking across the square to the bank as she ran down the court-house steps, Dawn was a little taken aback to see that the robbery was still very much a work in progress. Several cops had taken up positions behind cars or the corners of buildings. Perpetrators inside the bank—a suitably fortress-like piece of architecture—shot at them when they showed themselves. So it was a standoff. How long did it take to ransack a bank? she wondered. Had they found the Lord's money yet? Then she reflected that probably no more than one or two minutes' time had elapsed since the signal had been given. Everything inside the courtroom had happened very fast. Faster than thought.

A car pulled up in front of the courthouse as Dawn, pursued by Reggie and his two henchmen, was running down the steps. Red Bandanna was hopping on one leg, not making very good time. Reggie and the other fellow, who was wearing a blue bandanna, were covering for him, moving very much in the style of men who were expecting to get shot, at any moment, from the building's interior. Reggie only turned around long enough to shout at the driver of the vehicle—who, given that he, too, had a bandanna pulled up over his nose, seemed to be part of the operation. "Get them to the drop-off and come back!"

The driver reached back behind his seat, stretched across, and shoved the rear door open a moment before Dawn reached it. She was of a mind to dive in, but that amount of haste didn't seem warranted, and she was still feeling a little stiff. So she entered the vehicle in reasonably ladylike style and scooted across to sit behind the driver. He, though, had already exited and was running up the courthouse steps toward the one who was limping.

Reggie and Blue Bandanna had found cover behind the stonework and were engaged in the curiously meditative procedure of reloading their revolvers. Pounding directly up the steps, the driver bent low, tucked a shoulder into Red's body, and picked him up in a fireman's carry. As he was stomping back down the steps toward the car, gunfire sounded from a courthouse window. Reggie and Blue returned fire immediately. The driver bent forward and pitched Red in the general direction of the front passenger-side door. Red managed to crawl halfway in while the driver was running around and getting behind the steering wheel. As they went into motion, Red's legs were still outside the car, dragging on the pavement, but he was able to pull himself all the way inside during the first couple of blocks that they put between themselves and the action. After that, the driver stepped on it. Dawn had prostrated herself on the rear seat, as she'd heard a few alarming noises suggestive of the car's being shot at. Whether by G-men inside the courthouse or cops surrounding the bank she couldn't guess.

They were at "the drop-off," as Reggie had called it, no more than sixty seconds later. It was a city park. Or it would be once the settlers found time and money to populate it with parklike structures. For the time being it was just a stretch of wooded floodplain with a sign in front. Smaller trees and scrub had been cleared away and the ground planted with grass. Bigger hardwoods had been permitted to stand, creating a transition between the town and the lower, more heavily wooded river valley farther back. The driver simply jumped the curb and drove straight across the open grassy part, slaloming around trees, until he came to the verge of the woods. Several horses, saddled, were grazing there under the eye of a boy of perhaps thirteen.

Dawn during all of this had sat up straight in the back again, the better to hold on for dear life during the jouncing drive over open ground. She was gripping the driver's seat. Before he had even brought the car to a halt he turned around and barked, inches from her face, "Get out! And get you gone."

FROM FORT SICKLES IT WAS OPEN PLAINS IN EVERY DIRECTION FOR HUNDREDS OF MILES. But there was this river that ran through the town, and its valley was cut deep into the sandstone bedrock that underlay the thick pelt of prairie soil. The town had been built entirely to one side of it, since bridging it would have been expensive. For though the stream itself was only twenty feet across, the valley was half a mile wide. All of it was forested. Running from the cops in cars across the prairie would have been a purely automotive competition—a question of which cars were fastest and which gas tanks were fullest. You could see for miles. Getting away clean would require pulling so far ahead that they could turn at some rural intersection without being observed.

Running from cops in the valley of the river would be a different matter altogether. Visibility was limited to a few yards. And the cops wouldn't be expecting such a gambit. They'd have to go back and get horses to even begin a serious pursuit. And the type of men Reggie had recruited would be able to ride circles around them anyway.

They didn't seem to have been pursued. The scene here at the edge of the woods was so placid compared with what was happening in town that Dawn would have been of a mind to dawdle, had the driver not been so keyed up. She approached the lad who was looking after the horses. Part Indian, she guessed. No, all Indian, but short-haired, and dressed after the fashion of a ranch hand. "Which one, do you reckon?" Dawn asked. For the saddles and other tack made it obvious that most of the horses belonged to specific men, and she'd no sooner touch one of them than steal a man's car.

"Posey," said the boy, turning his head to nod at an Appaloosa mare shyly grazing off to one side. "You're big," he said, sizing Dawn up, "but the other fellas is bigger, most of 'em, and Posey'll take care of you just fine in the woods."

"I don't suppose you have any spare jeans or chaps?"

"No, ma'am."

"Can I borrow a knife then?"

The boy produced one from a sheath on his belt and Dawn used it to slit her skirt halfway from hem to waist, fore and aft, so that she could at least get her legs over the saddle. "Thataway," the boy said after helping her up. He made a blade of his hand and squinted into the woods. "About a mile."

"I asked Reggie for—"

"A hundred feet of rope. Got it here." The boy walked over to a place where various supplies had been arranged on bare earth around a big old oak. Dawn and Posey got to know each other a little in the meantime. Posey got the idea that Dawn wanted her to follow the boy, and she did. A few strides away from them, the driver had been performing some kind of makeshift first aid on Red Bandanna, who was lying spread-eagle on the grass where he'd dragged himself out of the car.

The boy handed her a hank of manila rope, neatly coiled. Dawn hooked it over the horn of her saddle, got Posey turned around, and rode into the woods. It was the first time in a long while—years at least—that she had been alone, moving at will through wild country, and in spite of the bad things she was leaving in her wake and the uncertainty of what was to come, she found that it was like going home.

ON THIS SIDE OF THE RIVER THE FOREST RAMPED GRADUALLY ABOVE THE LEVEL OF THE stream. In two places, tributary creeks snaked down from above, each enfolded in its little ravine. Dawn found it easier to ride along the river's bank or even have Posey wade knee-deep than to negotiate those obstacles. Most of the way, the land to the right, on the opposite side of the river, was every bit as steep and densely wooded as on the left. But shortly after she made it past that second creek, the river commenced a big, sweeping turn to her left, almost a full horseshoe bend, as it dodged around an outcropping of pink stone. This was too steep for most horses, and so it was at that point that Dawn forded the river. The right bank rose quickly to a lip—nothing Posey couldn't scramble over—but beyond that it was as flat as the left one was steep. An expanse of sand and gravel, too coarse to be called soil, stretched for fifty feet or so to where the woods resumed. Some combination of bad soil and frequent flooding prevented the growth of any trees thicker than Dawn's wrist. Much of what did grow had been hacked away or smashed down by the wheels of cars and trucks. For this was the place where Reverend Kidd baptized people. Dawn knew that if she put the river to her back and rode toward the woods she would find a tunnel through the vegetation, arching over a dirt track—just a pair of wheel ruts left by the comings and goings of the Kidds' parishioners, and of others who came here to drink beer and catch fish. Farther away from the river this connected to a gravel road that led eventually to the Indian reservation. It was along that road that Reggie's gang would later be making their escape. No getaway vehicles were here yet though.

Discarded bottles and the cold craters of fire rings were strewn about. Dawn rode Posey to a place where there was at least a little bit of tall grass to munch on, and draped her reins over a feeble sapling. She took the rope from the saddle horn, slung it over her shoulder, and walked to the riverbank, following the track worn into the loose earth by the Kidds and their flock. As she knew from experience, there was a pocket of deeper water just below the bank. Her skirt inflated and went inside out, almost covering her face as she sank into that. She whooped in a sharp breath at the coldness of the water and stifled a bit of panic as her feet lost traction and the current swept her along for a few yards. But she'd already crossed the deepest part of the channel. With every bit of floundering progress she made toward the opposite bank her footing grew more secure and the current got slower. There were a few more stumbles as her feet came down on unseen rocks, but before long she was striding up onto a sandbar in water only knee-, then ankle-deep. Then she was on bedrock, looking directly up at the Kidds' house.

They'd hired men, and paid them with the Lord's money, to construct a deck out over the brow of the stone outcropping that supported their house. It did not extend more than a yard past the brink, but Dawn could see its underside and the row of posts that held it up as she followed a somewhat devious course up the rock. This looked like a cliff from a distance but when you were up close you could find ways to scale it by traversing this way and that to take advantage of natural folds and ramps.

Suddenly she was at the top, crouched under the deck, full in shadow as the low afternoon sun would be striking the opposite side of the house. She uncoiled the rope, letting it tumble down the face of the bluff. She passed one end around a post—a creosoted four-by-four set in a crude concrete footing that the workers had poured directly on the bedrock. She began pulling the other end up toward her while letting the first end snake its way down. When she could see that the two ends were about even with each other, just a couple of yards above the river, she stopped. By grabbing both ropes, anyone could use this to climb up or let themselves down. Pulling on one end, though, would take the other up and around the post and allow the whole thing to be retrieved without leaving any trace.

During this whole time she had heard no sound from the house. She knew the Kidds well enough to be confident that they would still be at the clinic. Or, perhaps, since the job had run so late, on their way back. But they weren't here. That was all that mattered. She found a little flight of steps that got her onto the deck. Part of it was open to the elements but the rest was a roofed and screened veranda. From this an unlocked door led her into a pantry. Beyond that was the kitchen, and then she was in the house proper.

It would have been interesting to wander through the whole place looking at their family photographs and so on, but she didn't have time. She went upstairs and found the bedroom where the Reverend Kidd kept his wardrobe. No shortage of black suits here. She swapped her ruined skirt for a pair of his trousers. The waist was too big but she threaded a necktie through the belt loops and cinched it tight. She was wearing a cream-colored blouse. She pulled a blue denim work shirt on over that and then a black suit jacket. The smell of the Reverend Kidd made her gag. Worse, the smell of Mrs. Kidd was all over her collection of scarves, but Dawn picked out the darkest ones and arranged them around her neck and over her hair.

Down the hall was the bedroom that had been promised her—the place where Mrs. Kidd would have jabbed the fatal overdose into Dawn's arm. But the trunk wasn't there. Of course not. It was heavy and awkward. Why bother bringing it upstairs?

Dawn found her way to the basement. This was low-ceilinged, with an uneven floor—just a layer of dirt over the bedrock. On the river side was a hatch giving way to the crawl space under the deck. That seemed valuable, and so she left it propped open and dragged some obstructions away from it.

On the other side of the basement, toward the front of the house, was a set of steps leading up to a sloping cellar door. At the base of those steps her trunk was just sitting there on the dirt. She opened the lid and saw mostly Communist theory and propaganda, since her clothes had all been removed. Tossing those aside she exposed the false floor of cedar planks. When she levered that out of the way, there was the violin case, just as she remembered it.

It was still locked. The jailers had confiscated the key when they'd booked her. She didn't expect to see that key again. This basement was too cramped to serve as a workshop, so there were no tools. She carried the violin case up the steps to the underside of the cellar door and shoved it open. Emerging into the side yard she spied a detached garage only a few strides away. She entered that through an unlocked side door and found an oil-stained plank workbench along one wall. Pumpkin was clearly no handyman, but he had a few screwdrivers and a couple of hammers on a pegboard. With those Dawn was able to make short work of the lock. She opened the lid to find all the parts of the tommy gun precisely as she had last seen them in the barn in Virginia, more than a year ago, when Silent Al had helped her close the lid.

She made a couple of wrong guesses early in the process of reassembly, but the parts would go together only one way, and soon the whole thing made sense. She got it all together, heaved the drum magazine up, and slid it into the side of the trigger assembly, doubling the weapon's weight. Angling it into a ray of low red sun coming in through the door, she operated the charging handle and satisfied herself that a cartridge had been fed correctly into the breech.

The thing was a real bear to carry around. She stole a few yards of stout twine and threaded it back and forth through the lugs at either end of the weapon, creating a makeshift shoulder strap. With the fully assembled and loaded weapon thus slung over her back, she began looking around the garage for things that would burn vigorously. Of this there was no lack.

SHE'D READ ENOUGH NEWSPAPER CRIME STORIES TO KNOW HOW THIS ONE WOULD BE written up. After a standoff at the bank, the gang, protected by a withering barrage of covering fire from tommy guns, surplus Great War hand grenades, and Browning automatic rifles, piled into a couple of stolen vehicles and made a break for it. One vehicle was soon abandoned at a local park. Its occupants got clean away by riding horses into the woods. The other car, pursued hotly by local police, stiffened by a couple of federal agents who just happened to be in town, headed out of Fort Sickles but soon lost their way on unfamiliar local roads and made the mistake of going up a dead end. It was a dead end because it led to a cliff, and a river. The last structure on it was a fine house owned by the Reverend Kidd, an independent preacher, and his wife, a nurse who worked at the nearby Indian agency. Fortunately these decent and upstanding citizens were not at home when the stolen vehicle roared into their front yard. The bank robbers, finding their retreat blocked by a fleet of pursuing law enforcement vehicles, piled out and sprinted into the safety of the house under a hail of gunfire. Trapped in the building, they made a desperate stand, shooting out of shattered windows with every weapon at their disposal, shouting imprecations at the police during lulls in the action. Amid the volleys of taunts and curses a woman's voice could be heard, leading to speculation that the perpetrators might be none other than the Barrow Gang. A woman clad in black was glimpsed popping up in one window, then another to deliver bursts from a tommy gun. The standoff continued through the hours of dusk. At some point a stray bullet apparently touched off a fire inside the living room. Within minutes the house was fully engulfed in flames. The screams of the trapped gun moll were interspersed with sporadic reports of ammunition cooking off. A grenade detonated—someone committing suicide rather than be burned alive? After that, the woman's voice was heard no more.

Not until the following morning was it possible for law enforcement to approach the smoldering remains of the house. Some members of the gang were suspected to have escaped out the back by jumping off a cliff into a river. If so, and if they had survived the jump, they had gotten away clean.

The Reverend and Mrs. Kidd could not be reached and their whereabouts were unknown.

THE REAL STORY, AS SEEN BY DAWN, WASN'T FAR OFF FROM ALL OF THAT, SAVE THAT IT WAS like an opera as viewed, not from the audience but from backstage.

They waited until it was nearly dark to slosh the gasoline on the floor and strike the match. By that point most of the gang had already gone down the ropes and across the river to meet up with the horseback contingent; cars awaited them there. Reggie pulled the pin from the grenade and underhanded it up the flaming stairs into the master bedroom. Before it even exploded he and Dawn were running downstairs to the cellar. The fire above was sucking a river of cold air in through the hatch beneath the deck. They could have found it with eyes closed. Dawn went down the rope, then Reggie, and when he'd made it to the river he pulled on one end of it until the other end came loose and fell into the stream. The cops had got wise to the fact that some were escaping out the back, but down on the opposite bank, men with long rifles discouraged anyone trying to creep around the side.

They drove the cars up the dirt track through the woods, working their way up out of the valley to the intersection with the gravel road. Headlights, but only a single pair, were approaching from the direction of the Indian reservation. Everyone piled out of the cars and took cover in the trees, unslinging and unholstering weapons, cocking hammers and chambering rounds.

The car came recklessly close before it stopped. "These ain't no cops," someone chuckled.

The passenger-side door opened and someone got out. Dawn heard the chiff-chiff-chiff of the stockings before Mrs. Kidd came round into the beams of the headlights, radiant in her white nurse's uniform.

Dawn stood up and stepped out onto the road, swinging her tommy gun's muzzle around. "I'll handle this," she said.

19

MAGNITOGORSK

She had never been in an airplane before. This, combined with the mere fact of still being alive, made her fascinated and giddy during the first hour of the next day's journey. Extraordinarily silly of her, given the circumstances: being for all intents and purposes abducted to an unknown destination by the head of Stalin's secret police and one of his expert torturers.

The other Georgians were left behind in Magnitogorsk to build their blast furnaces. Proton and Elektron were supposed to be going back to Moscow but were apparently deemed unworthy of being given seats on an airplane—even though there was room for them. Their father, of course, still had years left on his sentence and would be going nowhere.

The knock at Aurora's hotel-room door had come hours before dawn. And normally when Lavrentiy Beria sent someone to knock at such an hour, it signaled the beginning of a very bad day. But in this case it was just a polite notification that she needed to be down in the lobby in half an hour.

Twenty-four hours would not have been long enough for her to get out of bed and feel human. The previous day's hours of uncontrollable shivering, the straining against her bonds, the gasping for air, had wrecked every muscle in her body. When they'd finally freed her and summoned her to dinner she had felt paradoxically fine, almost like she was back on the morphine. Maybe she *was*. Maybe they'd slipped a dose into a vein while she was semi-awake. But by morning everything hurt and she moved like a hundred-year-old woman. It was fortunate that all she had to do was put on clothes and crawl down to the lobby. A car was waiting, a nice black Mercedes. She dozed in the backseat and was only vaguely aware when Shpak and finally Beria climbed in, followed by some aide of Beria's, a younger Georgian man. Twenty minutes' jouncing and skidding along roads paved with soot-blackened ice took them to the airfield north of Magnitogorsk. And there waiting for them in a pool of light was the plane. It was a beautiful object, much more so than the ungainly contraptions of Italo Balbo's air armada. Perhaps it had to be beautiful in order to do its job. The wings and so on probably had to be shaped in a particular way for such a thing to work at all. A streamlined fuselage rested atop a pair of broad wings. There was a single engine up in the nose, and it looked like the pilot sat right on top of it in a narrow glass cupola. The better to keep an eye on oil levels and adjust the carburetor in flight, perhaps. Back close to its tail was a little door in the side.

There were young men in uniform all over the place. Nice uniforms, clean and new. One of them opened the car door on Aurora's side and extended a hand to help her out. Normally she'd have scoffed at the bourgeois courtesy but in this case she took it in a death grip and hauled hard, only to topple into him once her feet were on the ground. He offered his arm and she took it, then walked in small, careful steps across tamped-down snow to the plane's door. He and another soldier helped her up and in with a firm shove on the backside that probably would have looked like out-and-out kidnapping to anyone watching from a distance.

There were six seats, three on each side. In the front row Beria was already sitting across from his aide. Shpak sat behind the aide in the second row. Aurora opted to sit on the other side, Beria's side, in the back. She was afraid Shpak would attempt to make conversation with her. But when the pilot started the engine it became clear she needn't have worried. Conversation was going to be impossible as long as that thing was running. Aurora, strapped into a seat, no longer being asked to get up and move about, no longer under the gaze of these men, could simply look around and take it in. And—strange as it was to think this way—enjoy it. The plane was made of wood, but more like a boat than a house, since everything was curved. Out the window she could see the hinged vanes on the wings' rear edges, moving up and down as the pilot fiddled with the controls. Those looked to be made of cloth stretched taut over elaborate wooden frames. The engine's roar became even louder and the plane began to roll forward and swing round, feeling its way over ruts smashed into snow and frozen mud by terrestrial vehicles. Then the ride got smoother and it swung around to a new heading. She could not see forward, but off to one side was a windsock, and people watching. After a ceremonious pause the engine began to roar louder yet and they accelerated forward. Very soon she was going faster than she'd ever gone, even in the getaway car when they'd been speeding away from Fort Sickles. Suddenly the ride became perfectly smooth and the ground began to fall away below them. A spike of orange light hit her in the eye and she looked out the window into the dawn.

AFTER A WHILE THE NOVELTY OF IT WORE OFF AND SHE WENT TO SLEEP. SUDDEN IMPACT OF landing gear on frozen ground awoke her. They had stopped somewhere. Just to refuel, as it turned out. The men got out to smoke. It was recommended she use the toilet, so she got out and did that. Apparently they were in a place called Kazan. She had learned to expect the very worst where Soviet toilets were concerned, but she was beginning to get the picture that some parts of the country made the leap from medieval to modern without passing through any of the intermediate phases. Any facility related to air transport jumped the queue and straightaway got flush toilets in centrally heated bathrooms. She was able to do her business and return to her seat in the airplane without being exposed to the horrors of outdoor privies in the Russian winter. In a few minutes they were airborne again, Aurora gazing out the window at the sun glinting off the frozen Volga and some nice old churches and fortresses. She was thinking about how a few simple items could transform your experience of the world. How rapidly one could come to expect the conveniences of air travel and warm toilets, how desperately one would long to have them back if they were taken away, the lengths one would go to, to preserve one's access to them. For all that Beria and his ilk had soldiers, police, and torturers at their beck and call, their ability to give or take mere conveniences must, in the aggregate, confer more power by far.

It seemed that Kazan had been the flight's halfway mark, for a couple of hours later the plane landed outside of Moscow. The center of the capital had been in sight, some miles distant, when the plane descended and the view out the window was cut off by white birch and black pine lining the airstrip. This was not a proper airport but a single-runway field in the countryside. During the final approach she'd glimpsed a few houses in the woods. Big ones, widely spaced, abutting patches of cleared ground where it looked like vegetables or even flowers might be cultivated in the summer. Now of course they were just blank lakes of snow, and even though it was only midafternoon the long shadows of trees were beginning to reach across them. A car awaited. Warm, engine running—another of those little conveniences people would probably kill to keep, once the Berias of the world had seen fit to dole them out. They drove for no more than fifteen minutes before slowing down and turning off onto a driveway flanked by stone pillars supporting massive wrought-iron gates. A short drive through a slot between tall black conifers took them to a compound, anchored by a big house, with a large stable off to one side—by far the biggest of the estate's several outbuildings. The car stopped before the house's main entrance just long enough for staff members to unload luggage from the back—even including the tiny valise that now contained all of Aurora's possessions. Then the car pulled forward and approached the stable, which was large enough that they simply drove into its central aisle and parked. Barn doors were pulled closed behind them. This didn't make things any warmer but did prevent the wind from whistling through. A few high clerestory windows shed some light into the space but it still took a few moments for Aurora's eyes to adjust when she climbed stiffly out of the car.

What she had observed in the last few minutes had powerfully drawn her mind back to some of her earliest memories: the years she'd spent in the city that was now called Leningrad but that had been built by the tsars under the name of St. Petersburg. There was a style of building and decoration particular to that era that she'd forgotten about during her adolescence in the States. It was all over the place here, though, and it called to five-year-old Aurora, riding on Papa's shoulders before the Winter Palace or clinging to the skirts of Veronika's greatcoat on her way to school. She knew what this compound was, or rather what *sort* of place it was: a dacha, which meant a cottage outside of town, a second home in the countryside. But the word literally meant a gift. For these properties had been handed out, in the old days, by the tsar to members of the ruling classes who had somehow earned his favor. As such this one—particularly the gates on the carriageway, and the house itself—had the look of the fine old buildings she remembered in St. Petersburg. Though apparently one was expected to cultivate a woodsy and rustic aesthetic at the same time. That was certainly on display in this stable. Whoever had been given this dacha by some grateful tsar must have been a cavalry officer. A general, no doubt. The number of stalls was sufficient to accommodate two polo teams, with room left over for workhorses and riding horses. The open space in the middle was much broader than what would be needed merely to lead horses in and out—it approached the scale of an indoor arena, though the space was interrupted by a double row of columns, consisting of whole tree trunks, necessary to support the roof and bear the weight of winter snows.

Alas, not a single horse was now in the building, and it seemed that work was under way to convert it into a motor pool. To the extent you could smell anything in this cold, it was metal and petroleum, not leather and manure. She was reminded strongly of the former stables at Fort Myer that the army had converted into a depot for the Landesjäger.

But that was mostly in the future here. Perhaps they would get to work on it as the weather warmed. Today the only activity was a fire burning in a steel drum, next to a table covered by a blanket. Standing around the fire were four soldiers, all in their winter greatcoats, carbines slung over their shoulders, pistols holstered at their hips. As the new arrivals approached, they moved away to make room. Three of them took up stations across the width of the stable's central way. The fourth moved only a little, and yet there were subtle cues in the style of that movement that this person was a woman.

She turned around and met Aurora's eye.

It was Veronika.

Once she had recovered from her astonishment Aurora's first impulse was to go to her. To embrace her, even. But Veronika—after holding her gaze just long enough to be sure she'd been recognized—flicked her eyes toward Beria, then back to Aurora just long enough to say, *Absolutely not.*

Then she turned directly toward him. "Yes," she said, "it has been a long time, Comrade, but this is unquestionably the same girl."

"Very well." Beria was approaching the fire. He drew his hands out of his pockets to warm them. The flames were reflecting in the lenses of his eyeglasses, just as they had in the ice-fishing house on the Ural River. But Aurora could tell nonetheless that he was looking at her. "Only two more tests remain, then, before I can be sure of you." He nodded at the table. "Take a look at what is there."

Aurora stepped to the table and peeled the blanket back. Arranged there neatly were the components of a Thompson submachine gun, including a straight magazine.

"It's getting a bit dark in here," Beria said, "but if your story is true, you should have no difficulty assembling it." He turned his head in Veronika's direction. "Comrade, perhaps you could find a few small items that could be set up for target practice." He nodded down the length of the arena, which would indeed do service as a shooting range if one didn't mind a few bullet holes in the barn doors at the far end. The same thought seemed to occur now to Beria. "Shpak," he said, "do us a favor and get those big doors open."

Shpak seemed a bit put out by this request, and glanced meaningfully at the three male soldiers, but then seemed to understand, from the intensity with which they were staring at Aurora, that they were here not to open doors but to provide security for Beria. So he and Veronika both stalked off in the same direction, Veronika presently dragging a sawhorse into the middle of the space at a range of perhaps twenty yards, Shpak going all the way down to the far end, where he began to decipher an old wrought-iron latching mechanism.

Conscious of being watched alertly by the soldiers, Aurora began to repeat the procedure she had first only read about in the Library of Congress, then performed for the first time in the barn in Springfield under the gaze of Silent Al, then again in the Kidds' garage outside of Fort Sickles. It went quickly. She wondered how badly she would have to fumble this for Beria to nod at the soldiers and have her shot out back of the stable. But it didn't matter. She had it together in short order, no mistakes.

When it was all in one piece, she reached out and picked up the magazine. It was heavy with lead. She cast an inquiring look at Beria.

"But of course," he said. "How else can you pass the third test?"

She was conscious that one of the soldiers had come up right behind her, and she heard the muffled pop of his holster being unsnapped. If she were to move the wrong way she'd get a bullet in the head. So with great deliberation, facing squarely down the length of the arena, she snapped the magazine into place and drew back the bolt to chamber a round. Veronika had stood up three pieces of cord wood on the sawhorse to serve as targets and gotten out of the way. Shpak had got the barn doors open and was most of the way back to joining the group. Accordingly she kept the weapon aimed at the floor, waiting for everyone to get on the near side of the firing line.

"Kill him," Beria said in a quiet yet perfectly audible voice.

"I beg your pardon, Comrade?"

"Kill Shpak."

Her relatives in Montana spoke often about guns and the relative merits of different ammunition. It was boring to her, but she couldn't help absorbing some of it. Long weapons were usually rifles, the entire point of which was to fire bullets great distances, and so the cartridges were more powerful. These had a propensity for going all the way through soft targets and passing out the other side, like needles. The tommy gun was something of a novelty because it fired what were normally pistol rounds. Fat and slow, these hit hard and often stayed in the body. They weren't called slugs for nothing. This was more punching than stabbing.

Shpak was only the second person Aurora had ever machine-gunned, but it went the same as it had with Mrs. Kidd. Maybe if you shot someone with a revolver there would be enough of a delay between successive rounds—supposing you even bothered to use more than one bullet on them—that they would feel that first shot, and know its effect, and develop a fear of the next. But taking a dozen rounds in the space of a few seconds must be different. Like being run over by a car. Aurora had learned to fight the climb of the muzzle, and fought it especially hard now, because she wanted to show her prowess. Especially in the eyes of Veronika. But also because she didn't want to hit Shpak in the head too early. She wanted him to know she was killing him. Before long, though, the sheer impact of all that flying lead had thrown him onto his back and the slugs, if they didn't go into the ground, were basically entering his groin and traversing the length of his body and hitting his head anyway.

She set the gun down on the table and raised her hands. She spoke loudly, wanting to make herself heard over Beria's laughter. "Do you believe my story now?"

20

MOSCOW

FEBRUARY 1934

If Scott Gronsky hadn't been such a straight-arrow all-American, Aurora would have looked askance at his handwritten order—delivered to her flat by a messenger at 9 P.M.—telling her to meet him the next morning at 10:30 at a bathtub. But she now had two weeks under her belt in this job: pretending to be a translator for foreign press correspondents in Moscow while actually spying on them for the OGPU. She'd come to know the bar they frequented, the special stores where they bought bread, butter, and sausage in exchange for *valuta*—hard currency—the rooms in the Soviet Press Office where they submitted their dispatches to the censors, and the back room in the Central Post Office on Tverskaya Street where they sent cables to London or New York or Chicago in advance of their newspapers' deadlines.

And the bathtub. For most of the foreign press corps lived in flats lacking any such convenience. Russians generally bathed in communal *banyas*, where the wait could be long and the conditions rugged. Rumors flew of high-rent apartment buildings where superintendents had installed showerheads in secret basement rooms and would let tenants use them in exchange for bread or sausage. But one of the New York papers had actually managed to rent a flat that included a functioning bathtub. And as a professional courtesy they were willing to let reporters from other papers use it. You had to schedule a thirty-minute slot weeks in advance. Thanks to a last-minute cancellation, Scott Gronsky had secured the 10:30–11:00 berth tomorrow. It was his first opportunity for a proper bath since he'd come to Moscow two months ago, and he wasn't going to let it go to waste.

So first thing in the morning Aurora dressed and coiffed herself in a manner consistent with her cover story: a tall but mousy ex–Moscow University student named Svetlana. She'd dyed her hair dark brown and framed her eyes in heavy-rimmed glasses. No cosmetics. That was a game there was no winning. You'd be looked down on if you didn't make the effort. But store shelves were bare of makeup, perfume, and silk stockings, so women who craved such things had to resort to elaborate schemes to procure them. The job of "Svetlana" was to translate for *valuta*-bearing Western expats like Scott Gronsky. If she showed up looking fancy it would be assumed that he had traded luxury items to her for "favors." Better, and more consistent with her cover story, was to be as frumpy as possible. So in her frumpy, bootlike shoes she walked down five flights of stairs from the flat she shared with four other OGPU informants likewise pretending to be translators. She took a clanging and careening tram to Theater Square, walked round back of the Metropol Hotel, and ascended five flights of stairs to the Soviet Press Office, where she gathered the morning's batch of official press releases plus fresh copies of *Pravda* and *Izvestia*. Another tram ride took her to the flat with the bathtub. This was on the ground floor of a nice apartment building with a courtyard and a lobby. It no longer looked like, nor functioned as, a residence. It had been emptied out and converted into a newspaper bureau with a stenographer, filing clerk, and an office manager who appeared to devote about fifty percent of her working hours to juggling bathtub appointments. There was also a steady traffic of messengers and attendants coming and going on various errands, and a custodian who just sat in the lobby smoking and waiting for the bathtub to malfunction. All of the employees except the correspondent himself were Soviets, though from a wider than average range of backgrounds: a Jew, a Lett, a Ukrainian of German extraction, and an Englishwoman who had perhaps somewhat rashly torn up her British passport and gone full-blown Soviet. Any or all of these might be filing reports with OGPU, so Aurora was always careful to maintain her cover as Svetlana and to affect a Russian accent when speaking English. As far as Scott Gronsky or anyone else knew, Svetlana was from Rostov-on-Don, orphaned during the Civil War, raised in a state school, sent up to Moscow in recognition of her academic prowess, opted out of an otherwise promising academic career to put her weird proficiency with languages to work helping foreign journalists spread the good news about the completion of the Five-Year Plan.

Her tram had been delayed. In what she'd come to recognize as typically Soviet, the reason for the delay was as prosaic as it could be (a fender bender in an intersection down the line) but was treated as a state secret of the highest order, not to be spoken of or even noticed. Consequently Scott was already five minutes into his bath by the time Aurora walked in. Probably just as well. Like half the other rooms in this country, this one was partitioned into smaller ones by blankets suspended from the ceiling, making it possible for non-bathers to enter and use the toilet without awkwardness.

"Svetlana" perched on the toilet's rim. The seat had been removed for "safekeeping" and could be rented from the custodian for cigarettes. She greeted Scott in her fake Russian accent and he bid her good morning in the flat vowels of an upstate Bears fan. His voice always made her wish she'd never left Chicago—until, that is, she reminded herself why she'd had to. He smelled like good Western soap, which was hardly surprising. Svetlana and the other girls in her flat, when not masking it with perfume, always smelled faintly of kerosene. They all had beds. But the building was infested, and the only way to prevent bedbugs, cockroaches, and lice from crawling up the legs of the beds during the night was to plant each leg in a bowl and fill the bowl with kerosene. The scent of kerosene, slowly evaporating from all those bowls, permeated clothes, hair, and even flesh. Aurora wondered if half an hour in that bathtub would be enough to get rid of it, or whether it had penetrated so deeply that it would well up to the surface again, like crude oil coming out of the soil in Azerbaijan?

She had to vacate the room once to allow a correspondent from Manchester to use the toilet (he was next in line for the bathtub, in the 11 A.M.

slot) but otherwise spent the time reading the news to Scott, translating the Russian on the fly. She was aware of many infelicities or downright mistakes in her own work but trudged ahead anyway, like a kulak behind the plow, dodging rocks and tree roots in marginal soil. She had listened to the work of some of the other girls. They got away with howlers. Beyond a certain point she began to summarize, or skip over, sentences. Then paragraphs.

Even with a blanket hanging between them, she could sense Scott's boredom slowly rising to exasperation. These articles were the same shit every day. Everyone knew it: the shills who wrote them, the party bosses who told the shills what to write, the translators like "Svetlana" and the foreign visitors like Scott. To a point, a worldly man like him could amuse himself and flaunt his cleverness by pretending to winkle out hints as to what was going on inside the Kremlin, but that was a parlor game that for him was already wearing thin. Aurora could hear the hydraulic sound effects as he heaved in the tub. Or nothing at all as he just lay still in the lukewarm water letting the will to live drain out of him.

Speaking of drains, the knock on the door came, letting him know that his time was nearing its end and he needed to make room for the man from Manchester. Aurora briefly thrilled to a skin-crawling possibility, namely that they re-used the bathwater. But the rattle of a chain and the gurgle of a drain told her that Scott had pulled the plug. She rose, gathered up her newspapers, and left the room so that Scott could get dressed.

"Let's walk," he said. He was a big man, a former left tackle with the facial damage to prove it. But after college he'd gone to Princeton and got some kind of advanced degree. He shrugged on his gigantic camel overcoat and helped "Svetlana" on with hers: a well-worn but still substantial garment that had been issued to her by the OGPU, still smelling faintly of cigarettes and imported cologne.

"To where?" she inquired, but Scott shook his head and rolled his eyes to say it didn't matter. So it was one of *those* walks, common in Moscow, the purpose of which was to have a conversation that would not be overheard.

But. Scott was no dummy. He knew perfectly well that "Svetlana" was reporting to the OGPU. So what was the point of privacy?

He wanted to keep a secret from the other reporters.

He pulled on an astrakhan hat so that his wet hair would not instantly freeze to his scalp. They stepped out into a formerly prosperous boulevard.

"The *Trib* is gonna send me home," he announced, "so I figure I might as well go out in a blaze of glory. I have three weeks, give or take."

If she'd really been Svetlana, orphan girl of Rostov, she'd have had difficulty with these idioms. But Aurora understood almost too easily.

"Why are you being sent home?" She would actually be sorry to see him go. Some of the other girls had to work with men much less agreeable.

"I keep on writing the wrong shit."

"What is wrong precisely?"

"I write think pieces. Abstract. Inside baseball. Doesn't sell papers."

"What would sell papers?"

"Oh, you know. Human interest. Man on the street. Interesting characters, personal adventure."

"Blaze of glory?"

"Yeah. So, most of the others"—he turned to look back—"they're coloring inside the lines because their press pass is their meal ticket. They don't want the commissars to yank it and send 'em packing." He turned sideways to appraise her. She got the nervous sense that he was onto her. Or at least that he had suspicions. Could she follow all of his Americanisms? "Coloring inside the lines." "Meal ticket." If so, it cast doubt on her cover story.

Was he a spy?

Or had she spent too much time around people like Shpak and Beria? Paranoid. Overthinking everything.

"Anyway," he continued, "my point is, my days are numbered. So I'm going to Ukraine."

"Ukraine? Why?" But she knew perfectly well. Everyone knew.

"To see what's actually happened there. The censors will never let me cable that story out of the country, but I can take it home up here." He tapped his giant furry hat.

They walked a few more paces through enormous clouds of their own condensed breath.

"You know your way around," he said. "You're from Rostov."

"That is not in Ukraine," she pointed out.

"But close."

"Close," she agreed, trying to remember the map the OGPU had showed her. She had not imagined her geographical knowledge would be tested so soon.

"I need a translator."

"I could get in trouble."

"With OGPU."

She didn't respond. He took that, correctly, as agreement. "I'm going to do it anyway," he said. "I can get on a train anytime I want. Unless they arrest me. For what? Thinking about getting on a train? They're not gonna do that. So, I get on the train. If you're with me, then it's okay."

"How is it okay?"

"'The naïve, overconfident Westerner thought he was pulling a fast one on us,'" said Scott, adopting a hilariously bad Russian accent, "'but we were onto him from the beginning. He was shadowed every step of the way by our girl Svetlana, who provided a full report.'"

Aurora found herself nodding.

"I'll spring for soft class," he offered. It was a reference to the quality of the seats.

She shook her head. "You want hard."

He nodded. "So I can see how ordinary people live?"

The real answer was that the soft seats had lice in the cushions. But she nodded. "Yes."

THEY WERE ON THE TRAIN, SITTING ON HARD SEATS, LESS THAN TWENTY-FOUR HOURS later. Aurora had explained matters to her nominal boss at OGPU, a woman named Katerina, who reported to one Zhirkin, who reported to

Beria. Katerina was not happy. But Aurora knew that there was nothing Katerina could do about it. As Scott had pointed out, they couldn't prevent him from boarding a train short of preemptively arresting him—an act that would be seen as a major provocation and an admission that they had something to hide. And since he was being sent home anyway, the threat of expulsion had no force.

As for "Svetlana," her conduct was above reproach. She'd reported the conversation to Katerina immediately. The most they might have done was to forbid her to get on the train with Scott. But better to have a faithful OGPU informant shadowing him every step of the way than to have him go alone.

And there was another thing somehow factoring into all of this, difficult for Aurora to see beyond its blurry penumbra, which was that she had some kind of special status in the mind of Lavrentiy Beria. She was his prize catch, his protégée. Or at least one of them; for all she knew, he might have a hundred. This stint as "Svetlana" was just a way of breaking her in. Showing her the ropes. He had bigger plans for her. Katerina somehow knew it.

DURING THEIR BRIEF WORKING RELATIONSHIP, "SVETLANA" HAD PERSONALLY SUBJECTED Scott to hours of press statements from the People's Commissariat of Railways extolling the pace at which new roadbeds were being laid across steppe and tundra. If he'd paid any attention whatsoever, he was probably expecting new lines stretching across vast distances, stations few and far between.

The journey south and west from Moscow was anything but that. Railway lines, most of them decades old, covered the landscape like a finely drawn web of steel. In the thousand-mile expanse between Moscow and Odessa there were few places more than twenty miles from a railway line. Getting from Moscow to—where, exactly? Somewhere in Ukraine that Scott would accept as typical?—entailed making a lot of decisions. It was evident from the worn-out, yellowed maps and inscrutable timetables spread out on their laps that every station they pulled into was going to present them with choices. Seven lines radiated from Bryansk, six from Gryazi. Eight converged on Kharkov. "Shit," Scott exclaimed after they'd been on the train to Bryansk for an hour, "there'd be a million ways to get where I want to go—if I even knew where that was."

He had heard tell, from more seasoned correspondents, of a big hydroelectric project in Ukraine that had been the site of a massive press junket last summer. Until he came up with a better idea, that seemed a good place to aim for. He could go there and follow up on the story, explain how his colleagues had been duped. But it was just a pencil smudge on a map that was too out of date to show the new line that the Soviets had constructed to haul steel and cement to the site.

As it turned out, almost all of the choices implied by the maps and the timetables were ruled out by circumstances and so they just opted for whichever trains seemed to be headed in the right direction reasonably soon. The farther they went, the emptier the carriages became. Few people, it seemed, wanted to go toward Ukraine. At the same time there was a marked upward trend in the rank of the railway personnel pacing up and down the aisle, pretending to do things. The Soviet Union as a whole seemed to divert a lot of its productive capacity into uniforms, badges, and medals. The foreign correspondents hanging around the bar at the Metropol made fun of them for it, then went back to their fleabag hotel rooms to write think pieces about what it all meant. If you couldn't pay, feed, or house the masses you could at least make them feel like they were part of something by giving them uniforms and awarding them ranks. Anyway the sleeves and collars of even the lowliest railway workers all bore the hammer and sickle as a matter of course, but pretty soon they began to collect little red chevrons, and when there was no room left for those they switched to red dots. When the collar became crowded with those they were replaced with red stars. There was room for maybe four of those, raising the obvious question of just how many four-stars dwelt in the most exalted ranks of the responsible Commissariat. On this journey, they observed no stars at all, but chevrons and then, increasingly, dots were more and more in evidence the farther south they went.

Guessing from the map, they were now very near, perhaps actually in, Ukraine. The carriage was otherwise empty except for one middle-aged man in a suit who had been pretending to read the same copy of *Pravda* for seven and a half hours. When they approached stations, railway workers with lots of dots appeared at either end of their car and—as could be inferred easily enough—discouraged new passengers from entering.

It was at one such stop that a woman approached the train holding up a bundle. This was little more than a whistle-stop, consisting of a single platform between the southbound and northbound tracks. A snatch of roof on stilts sheltered the platform from direct assault by the elements. Built into that structure was a stairway-and-bridge contraption giving access to the platform from the road side, which happened to face east. The west side, on their right as they pulled into the station, gave way immediately to open fields. These, of course, were covered with snow. No matter how assiduously Scott stared at them, he could glean no hints as to the true current state of Ukrainian agriculture.

It was from that side that the woman approached. Some attempt had been made to fence the station off, but you couldn't fence off an entire railway line. The woman was picking her way over the ballast—the linear heap of crushed stone in which the railroad ties were embedded. All she could see from that low vantage point would be steel wheels and undercarriage. When she tilted her head back, exposing her yellowed face to the overcast sky, she'd be looking at the windows of the passenger carriages above her head. But Aurora got the idea that she couldn't see inside. The panes of glass were reflecting too much light from the sky. Clearly she wanted to get the attention of passengers inside the carriage, to show them what she was carrying. She was making her way down Scott and Aurora's side of the carriage, gazing up toward each window in turn—windows that had no people on the other side of them.

Their *Pravda*-reading minder, down at the other end of the carriage, was seated on the platform side, oblivious. Scott and Aurora exchanged a look, but no words. The woman was approaching, faltering on the frozen ballast and the protruding ends of the ties, but indefatigable in the true peasant way.

"Selling produce?" Scott guessed. "Onions? Turnips? What grows here?" The guess was reasonable. He'd been in Moscow long enough to know of the unsanctioned street markets where people from the countryside sold vegetables to city-dwellers.

Aurora shrugged. "Jars of honey?"

Faint thumping could be heard through the shell of the carriage. The train might be completely empty for all this woman knew. Pausing beneath each window she pounded on the wall with her mittened hand, trying to get someone's attention.

Scott glanced sidelong at their minder. The whistles and gesticulations of the railway workers with the chevrons and the dots told that the train was getting ready to pull out of the station. Their minder hadn't yet twigged to the existence of the woman trying to sell her turnips or whatever, but pretty soon the thumping was going to give her away. This was Scott's first, and might be his only, chance for a face-to-face encounter with an actual Ukrainian—a bit of personal experience that would satisfy his editor in Chicago.

He stood up, excused himself past Aurora, stepped into the aisle, and sauntered—he didn't want to tip off their minder by moving too decisively—two rows up to the place where the woman was thumping on the side of the carriage. Entering the row he got a knee on the hard seat closest to the window and began fumbling with the latch. Their minder looked up from *Pravda* and stared at him, then threw "Svetlana" a hard look.

She rose and stepped quickly up the aisle to where Scott was just now getting the window open.

As she sidestepped into the row, she caught a glimpse of the woman outside thrusting her bundle up toward them.

Scott recoiled from the window and, like an offensive lineman putting a spin move on a defender, almost flattened Aurora. She saw him coming just in time to dodge out of his path but tripped over his foot and sprawled toward the window. Not wanting to smash her hands through the glass she reached for the frame instead and caught herself, arms high and wide, face so close to the window that it fogged instantly from her breath. But in that moment she saw what Scott had seen. Then she was glad the pane was misted over. The train shrieked and began to move.

Railway workers with many red dots, supervised by a one-star, moved down the length of the carriage pulling all the blinds down over the windows and securing them with twists of wire. Their efficiency was proof that they did it all the time. The next time Aurora got up to use the toilet, she saw that the same thing had been done in adjoining carriages as well.

Passengers were not allowed to look out windows of trains passing through Ukraine.

Scott and Aurora were both silent for half an hour, avoiding each other's gaze. Her purpose in going to the toilet had been to throw up. She wondered if he could smell it on her.

"Do you think it was dead?" Scott finally asked.

Aurora's gaze swam in his direction.

"She didn't unwrap it—*expose* it—until she saw me in the window." His eyes focused. "*Him.* It was a boy."

In this picking over of words Aurora saw him beginning to write the story that he would carry into the West in his head. She envied him that ability to step back from it. To file the story and move on.

It seemed important to him that she be a part of this conversation. She nodded. "I was wondering why it was exposed."

"He."

"That shocked me. Would she have exposed a living baby to the cold?"

"Well, maybe. As a way to show how emaciated he was. But he wasn't moving." How was he going to write it up for his three million readers in Chicago? He could say that the baby was alive or that it was dead. He could change any detail he wanted. Nobody would gainsay him. It wasn't like the *Trib*'s fact-checkers were going to track "Svetlana" down before they ran the story.

"If the kid's dead, then the lady's just crazy," Scott said.

"Maybe not crazy. Maybe she's just trying to communicate."

"If the kid's alive, then she's just a beggar." It was clear from Scott's tone that a mere beggar was a less potent story than a lady trying to say something to the world about what was going on here.

For her, though, there was a layer to this that she could never explain to Scott. Never talk about to anyone.

Scott went silent. He crossed his arms over his barrel chest and stared straight ahead, unfocused, for a while. Composing the story in his head. From time to time, though, she caught him looking at her curiously. She had been second-guessing herself since that last exchange. She was almost certain that in her shock she had forgotten to use the fake Russian accent. She'd blurted out at least a few words in mid-American English. Had he noticed?

The train eased into another stop. Conductors blew their whistles and shouted up and down the platform, unseen on the other side of those window shades. No one got on or off. Aurora practically jumped out of her seat as a muffled thump-thump sounded through the wall of the carriage. A moment later it had moved on to the next window.

The thumps were sounding from more than one place now.

The baby, with its tiny, wrinkled body and its huge, swollen head, had looked like an embryo floating in a jar.

THE TRAIN'S WHISTLE SOUNDED IN A WAY THAT DID NOTHING TO STEADY HER NERVES. IT came to a stop, more harshly than when it was gliding into a station. The staff were surprised. Even Scott could have guessed as much from the tone of their voices. One of them opened the door at the end of their carriage and climbed down to the ground. Dry snow was squeaking under boots outside the windows.

If there was anything to the map, they were in the middle of nowhere, still on flat land but headed into some hills that, Scott speculated, wrapped around the artificial lake behind that big hydroelectric project. At such a juncture it would be normal to pause while additional pulling power was added to the train to help with the uphill grade, but nothing seemed to be happening.

Half an hour went by. The conductors were showing no urgency at all about getting back on the train. Indeed, more and more passengers were getting off. Aurora leaned forward and strained to listen. "They're actually asking people to detrain," she said.

"Well, that's all I need. Shall we?" Scott stood up and heaved his overcoat off the hook, then helped "Svetlana" on with hers. Both of them were tracking their minder in the corners of their eyes but he made no move to interfere. It was a delay. Delays happened. Whether the foreign visitor experienced it from inside the sealed carriage or outside would make little difference in how he wrote it up.

Aurora was, to be honest, terrified that the train would be swarmed with people holding up dead or dying babies. But the map didn't lie. They were well and truly out in the middle of nowhere. No one was around. Just here the two tracks were running straight across level ground between snow-covered fields. Half a mile ahead, though, the ground began to rise. Not so steeply that the railway couldn't manage the grade, but the twin lines did curve to the right seeking a more gradual ascent. Something had gone wrong up ahead, near the beginning of that curve. Other passengers were issuing in ones and twos from carriages. Train staff were exhorting them, with sweeping arm movements, to move up the line.

Aurora was beginning to wonder if they should go back and fetch their baggage, but none of the other passengers seemed to be doing so. Scott's attention was fixed on the ground. The snow was deep in the ditch beside the line and so they, like all the other detrained passengers, were moving in single file along the strip of exposed ballast next to the rails, trailing one hand along the flank of the train for balance.

"New ties," Scott observed. "Maybe a couple of years old. But the ballast."

"What of the ballast?"

"It's mostly sand." Scott used the toe of his boot to scuff at it. Sharp fragments of crushed stone skittered into the snow, exposing loose sand.

Aurora, despite all the time she'd spent on trains, was a little unclear on the significance of this. But it meant something to Scott. Ballast was the heavy, loose stuff that they poured over the ties once the rails had been spiked down. Once the ties were so embedded, they couldn't move. Seemed like any heavy stuff would do the job, but Scott didn't think so.

She might have asked for a more complete explanation of why it was bad to use sand, but this soon turned out to be one of those cases where words weren't needed. Ahead of them, only a few yards ahead of where their locomotive had screeched to a halt, another locomotive, facing the other way on the other line, rested askew. It was listing to one side at a forty-five-degree angle and pitched nose-down into the earth, as if it had been driven into a pit of quicksand. Its weight and momentum had simply driven the rails and the ties to which they were spiked down into the earth. Behind it, half a dozen boxcars had derailed and flopped over onto their sides. The rising terrain made it possible to see the whole length of the stopped train. Scott paused to count the cars.

A repair crew had preceded them in a little train equipped with a crane, spare rails, ties, and tools. They hadn't been here for long. They were still looking at things and arguing. But it was possible to guess at their strategy. Those boxcars had toppled to the other side—away from the uphill-bound track. So they weren't blocking Scott and Aurora's train. The only thing that stood in their way was the locomotive, and the mess it had made of both tracks when it had foundered in the morass of bad ballast. The affected section of track was no more than a hundred feet long. The southbound line was intact. The rails themselves hadn't been damaged. Those rails were simply in the wrong place—passing too near the marooned locomotive, which wasn't going to move for a long time.

So they moved the track. The workers from the repair train, bolstered by volunteers from Scott and Aurora's train, drove prybars into the ground next to the rails and heaved, dragging and bending the whole line sideways away from the downed locomotive. This effort, which seemed almost Pharaonic in its scope and ambition, took surprisingly little time once the ties were free of the sandy ballast. They didn't have to move it that far. It was just a matter of getting enough volunteers heave-hoeing in unison. And they had plenty of volunteers once a grizzled one-star conductor had made it plain in the most stark and profane language that they were all going to be stuck here until this got done. Scott was the most enthusiastic heave-hoer of them all, his ruddy face showing actual joy. Only Aurora knew why: his editor in Chicago was going to eat this up.

The ineluctable laws of geometry dictated that this sideways diversion of the line created a gap. The rails weren't long enough—the unbolted ends didn't quite meet. Fortunately, there were extra rails on the train, fresh from the rolling mills of Magnitogorsk. They only needed to be cut to the right length to fill the gap. Unfortunately, there was only one hacksaw blade. So the rapid and glorious victory of the sideways-rail-bending operation gave way to a manual hacksawing project that was obviously going to take hours. Perhaps longer as the blade got duller.

So Scott began to wander around, if for no other reason than to stay warm. Aurora followed him. All semblance of order had dissolved. No one was keeping an eye on them. Lavrentiy Beria could not be everywhere. Scott had spied a farmhouse on the opposite edge of a field. It was perhaps a quarter of a mile away. He had got the idea—which in Illinois would have made sense—that a farmhouse had to have a basic complement of tools; that among these were hacksaws; and that if a hacksaw could be borrowed, or rented, the rate of rail-sawing might be doubled.

So he trudged across the field, followed by Aurora. They got to the house. No smoke came from the chimney, no chickens or livestock were in evidence. They pushed at the door, which was ajar, and found a family of dead people. There were no signs of struggle or violence.

They walked back toward the derailed train. Scott had forgotten about the hacksaw.

Up to this point they'd seen very little police or military presence, however there were half a dozen men in Red Army greatcoats and ushankas standing around the toppled boxcars, pacing desultorily back and forth, rifles slung over their shoulders. Apparently the cargo in those things was valuable, and they'd been posted there to discourage pilfering.

Yet none of them seemed to mind when Scott Gronsky, with that air of self-assured entitlement that both awed and annoyed Aurora, strode between them and walked right up to a boxcar. Aurora hung back. But when no one leveled a rifle at Scott, she hurried to catch up.

The boxcars were literally just boxes, made of planks bolted to a steel frame. Upon impact many of the planks had splintered, and the frames had bent, but they all still retained their boxy shape and performed the function of boxes—namely to contain things.

What they contained was people. Some of them were still moving.

"WHEN WE ASSIGNED YOU TO THAT JOB," BERIA SAID, "OUR ONLY OBJECTIVE WAS TO AC-quaint you with the procedures for managing foreign press correspondents. That was accomplished in a matter of days. It is simply not that complicated." He paused and looked up at her through those round, heavy-framed lenses. "We could not have anticipated that you would go into Ukraine and see the things that you did."

He paused to rearrange a few papers on his desk. Nikolai Zhirkin—Aurora's boss's boss—the OGPU official who seemed to be in overall charge of the program of which Beria spoke—sat as still as it was possible for a living, presumably breathing human to sit. During the first ten minutes of this meeting he had unlimbered a few preliminary gambits, feinting in the direction of scolding, denouncing, praising, or merely educating Aurora whilst keeping his gaze fixed on Beria's face. Beria, though, had given no hints as to which way the wind was blowing. Aurora guessed that Zhirkin was now replaying those ten minutes in his head imagining all the ways he had gone wrong.

It all hinged on what Beria was going to say next. Beria knew as much, and was enjoying the moment. Here was a man who really liked what he did for a living. Aurora ought to have been anxious to the point of hysteria, but after all she'd seen and lived through in the past year she could not bring herself to feel very much. She knew that as long as she lived in this country, within reach of men like these, she'd be dangling above that hole in the ice, the knife on the rope. With a word Beria could kill her. The only point was that he wanted her to know that.

"However," he went on, "it is actually a good thing that you went to Ukraine. Fortuitous."

"May I ask—did Gronsky write the story?" She had parted ways with Scott in Kyiv, and he had got out of the country by way of Odessa.

"Yes. He filed it from Zagreb." Beria glanced at a document.

"Did the *Chicago Tribune* print it?" Zhirkin asked. Not his job to know that, apparently.

"No," Beria said. "Nor will they. We have a friend in that company who can recognize vile anti-Soviet propaganda when he sees it."

"Fortunate," Zhirkin said, with a none-too-friendly glance at Aurora. "I will see to it that in future—"

"I am not here to talk about Gronsky or any of that," Beria said. And it was clear that a lot of time would pass before they heard Zhirkin's voice again. Beria's attention was on Aurora. "Now that you have seen what you saw in Ukraine, a young woman of your intelligence will immediately understand the importance of the task I have entrusted to Comrade Zhirkin here. Namely, the shaping and molding of how our story is told beyond our borders, in a way that best supports our national strategy. It is every bit as important as tanks and airplanes."

Aurora nodded. "Especially now. Because of . . . Ukraine."

"I of course do not believe in miracles," Beria said, "yet it is a kind of miracle that no one knows. Do you have questions about what you saw? It would be natural to have questions."

If she said no, she'd be lying and he'd know it. "Well, it's obvious that there have been food shortages. And . . ."

Beria nodded, looking serenely and pleasantly sad. "Some increase in mortality from diseases related to poor nutrition."

Starving to death. But she made a note of that phrase.

"My only other question, then, Comrade, would be about the people in the boxcars."

"Kulaks," Beria said. Then, perhaps seeing some trace of skepticism on her face, he shook his head and lifted his hands slightly from the desktop. "Why else would they have been put in boxcars?"

Aurora nodded. "On their way to . . ."

"Being relocated to parts of the Soviet Union where they can do some good. It is regrettable that the train derailed, but such mishaps are a known hazard of rail transportation. Just ask yourself, if they had not been on that train, what then would have been their fate?"

"I suppose they would have been at very grave risk of diseases related to poor nutrition," Aurora said.

Beria's face took on a bit of the proud-uncle aspect it had worn when he'd watched her tommy-gun Shpak. He glanced at Zhirkin as if to say, *You see?*

Aurora wondered if Zhirkin knew about Shpak. If Zhirkin was afraid of her. Because that was how it worked. Beria was at the center of a web of people who were all afraid, for good reason, of being killed by the others.

"Now that you have a perfect understanding of these things, we must put you to work without further delay on a more challenging and consequential task," Beria said. He nodded to Zhirkin. Zhirkin nodded back, reached into the briefcase next to his chair, and drew out a fat manila envelope sealed with string. This he handed to Aurora. She tried to ignore the block-letter imprecations stamped on its front, promising death to any who opened it, as she unwound the string. She drew out a folder. This was stuffed with loose documents—photos, newspaper clippings, typed reports—to a thickness of about half an inch. A name had been written on it in Cyrillic, which didn't quite scan, but once she opened it and glanced at a few of the documents—which were mostly in English—she saw that the subject matter was one Owen Crisp-Upjohn, a British journalist. Or perhaps "writer" was a better descriptor.

"This man is coming to the Soviet Union?"

"He's been here for ten days," Zhirkin said.

Ten days. Long enough to have overlapped for a bit with Scott Gronsky. Aurora found a loose photo of Owen Crisp-Upjohn standing next to a polo pony. She'd seen him before, probably on the day he'd arrived in Moscow, in the bar at the Metropol, downing gin with a vengeance and saying hilarious things to a circle of admirers. Foreign journalists could be a jealous and back-biting lot, but they seemed to see in him a refreshing novelty, not a competitor.

"You would like me to serve as his translator?" she asked.

"He's already gone through two of those. Number three seems to be holding her own," Zhirkin said.

Beria added, "You may consider yourself as having been awarded a promotion to a higher grade than mere translator."

"Are you asking me to fuck him?" It was a risk saying that. But Comrade Stalin himself had recently stated that the act of sex was a routine natural function, no different really from taking a shower. Zhirkin, an older gentleman, stiffened in a way that suggested he might not yet have come round to Stalin's point of view. Beria seemed to appreciate the simple candor. But he deferred to Zhirkin, who, after taking a moment to compose himself, said: "Based on the man's reputation, we had assumed, going in, that the strategy you are alluding to would be simple, quick, and effective. But life is full of surprises and it has not worked out that way. One thing that is now certain is that, in the wake of failed attempts by some of your, er . . ."

"Sisters in revolutionary struggle," Beria cracked.

"Yes, Mr. Crisp-Upjohn will now be very much on the alert for any such direct approach—anything obvious, heavy-handed."

"However," Beria added, "should the opportunity present itself, by all means take advantage of it."

Her eye fell to another photograph of Owen, an eight-by-ten glossy, shot through a long lens at the Metropol, still redolent of darkroom chemicals. Compared to most of the Metropol crowd he was young, fit, and well put together. The idea was not inconceivably disgusting.

"If that was all we wanted," Beria went on, "we'd have given the job to someone else."

"Someone prettier?"

Anyone else would have blanched. Not Beria. "Someone more his type."

"What is his type?"

"Going in, we were told redheads," Zhirkin said. "Based on copious empirical evidence. But at this point it's anyone's guess."

"Does he like boys?"

"*No!*"

Zhirkin spoke this one word with a finality indicating they'd tried it. Combined with an exasperation and world-weariness that caused a whole story to appear in Aurora's mind about an expensive, madcap, ham-handed effort to put a likely boy in Owen's way, culminating in failure.

"Do we know—does he have any fixed plans here?" she asked. But the thing about the boy was stuck in her head and now she was getting the giggles. At the end of this question her voice rose to a squeak as she tried to suppress it. Had anyone ever got the giggles in Beria's office? It seemed unlikely. Beria's deadpan face made it impossible to tell whether he had noticed, but he didn't seem to mind. Was that a wry twist to his mouth? It was. The fact that he could find humor in such things only made him seem more deadly. What did it say about her?

"Other than drinking at the bar at the Metropol, he has no plans that we know of," Beria said, then glanced at Zhirkin for confirmation.

She was about to ask why this man was so important to them. But newspaper clippings kept falling out of the dossier, skating to the carpet of Beria's office like leaves, and this was enough to give her a general idea. This man Owen wrote for British newspapers. Of late he wrote exclusively for *the* British newspaper, the one that would be read, every day, by everyone who mattered in London. And a glance at some of his ledes was enough to tell her that he was no Scott Gronsky. Owen Crisp-Upjohn was never going to be upbraided by his editor for writing abstract think pieces. He was a personal-adventure man all the way. The anti-Gronsky.

A thought occurred. She gazed, unfocused, at a clipping that had ended up between her feet. Owen with the polo pony.

She looked up and discovered that Beria and Zhirkin had both been staring at her. Partly, of course, because they were men and she was a woman and that was how it was. But she'd learned from Shpak and others that this was even more likely to happen when she was thinking, and they didn't know what she was going to say next. "Polo," she said. "But at this time of year—we'll have to wait." She considered it some more. "Is there such a thing as a Red Army women's polo team?"

Zhirkin was saying "Don't be ridiculous!" but Beria spoke over him: "Would you like there to be?"

An awkward silence then as Zhirkin had been elbowed out of the way by this remark of Beria's that might have been a joke.

"Does he know about the balloon launch?"

Aurora knew about it because sometimes she had tea with Proton and Elektron, who were working on it. It was the day after tomorrow.

"He ought to," Zhirkin said. "We circulate a daily briefing to make all foreign correspondents aware of such opportunities. But it seems unlikely that a man of his tastes and interests would—"

"He'll go," she predicted, "if other correspondents are going, and if it seems . . . sporting." She said the last word in English, with an English accent, but they knew what it meant.

ZHIRKIN HAD BEEN A BIT RUFFLED BY HER CONFIDENT PREDICTION. WHAT WOULD A GIRL like Aurora know of the mentality of a man such as Owen Crisp-Upjohn? A fair question, but what he didn't know, or had perhaps forgotten, was that Aurora had once been Dawn, and Dawn had spent her adolescence on a polo-pony ranch in Wyoming. Men like Owen went there all the time. During their stay, which was rarely less than a week, they inevitably posed for photos in cowboy hats. They took potshots with six-shooters at bean cans on fence posts. They gawked at buttes and teepees.

Owen was the second of three brothers. A remittance man, living off payments from his late father's estate. Very little about the thoughtways of such men made any sense at all to the kinds of people who worked on ranches in Wyoming, but one thing they'd all learned was that they could be talked into anything if it were couched as a sporting proposition. That, sex, and drinking were what got them out of bed in the morning.

The balloon was to be launched from a military base in the suburbs of Moscow, lately expanded to include an aerodrome. Weeks ago the balloon project had taken over a hangar. Days ago the Soviet propaganda machine had, in turn, taken over the balloon project. Zhirkin's operation was only a small cog in that apparatus.

"Svetlana" was too new to the job to have witnessed it in action, but she'd heard stories from some of the other girls about the spectacle that they'd staged a few months ago to celebrate the completion of the Five-Year Plan. It sounded as though every singer, dancer, musician, and lighting technician still alive within the borders of the Soviet Union had been pulled away from their duties digging canals and chopping down forests, and mobilized. The result had been to stage productions that were to Broadway extravaganzas what Magnitogorsk was to steel mills. What the other girls ended up saying, after repeated, failed efforts to put its scale and magnificence into words, was that you just had to have seen it to believe it. "Svetlana" nodded and wished she could have been there. But Aurora cast her mind back to the Century of Progress in Chicago and knew she'd seen its like. And according to Scott Gronsky, who had spent some time in Germany, the National Socialists there were throwing their own spectacles to match.

The balloon launch was, of course, a different sort of affair. Turning it into a staged spectacle would have undercut the message: the Soviet Union was neck and neck with the United States in the race to send aeronauts to the threshold of outer space. In fact, they were going to succeed where the Americans had fallen flat on their faces. Proton Fizmatov and his comrades were going to return from the edge of the void with scientific data that would crack the code of the universe. They were going to settle questions that had bedeviled the world's greatest scientific minds. No amount of peripheral singing and dancing could improve on that. On the contrary. The infamously cynical and jaded foreign press corps would find in it reasons to cast doubt on, even to lampoon, its pretensions. So, though busloads of fresh-faced Komsomol youths had been brought in, and the Soviet Union's strategic reserves of lipstick and pomade had been broken open, it was all in the service of the science to be done and the feats of engineering needed to do it.

Owen was there. She caught sight of him climbing out of a big car in company with three other Metropol regulars. A smaller car behind them disgorged its bevy of translators. Unseasonably cold weather was outstaying its welcome, and a balloon launch by its nature was an outdoor event, so everyone was bundled up. Someone had procured the requisite ushanka and thick boots for Owen. He and his colleagues, already blowing into their hands, were greeted by a highly presentable Komsomol tour guide who waved in the direction of the athletic field where the balloon was being unrolled and spread out, then got them into the hangar—which was a few degrees warmer than outdoors—before frostbite could set in.

Aurora shadowed him at a distance. She was still in the Svetlana getup. She wanted to observe him before he noticed her. The density of the throng made it easy enough for her to hide in plain sight. For the first fifteen minutes or so he dutifully looked where he was told. Aurora could have stood directly behind him and never crossed his eye line. But after that he became restless, even irritable, as he grew tired of being led around. Aurora put a little more distance and a few more bodies between herself and Owen and watched from a distance as he climbed down into the spherical gondola that was going to take Proton and his comrades into space. She saw him peering out through one of its tiny, thick portholes, made of special glass that wouldn't burst from internal pressure.

She was thinking about Dick. Seeing it all through his eyes. She had no formal education in physics but she'd learned from talking to him, and to Bob Overstreet, and more recently Elektron, that certain things were physics incarnate. Bridges, blast furnaces, aeroplanes, and balloons all looked the same in every country. If you had an eye for it you could make them more stylish, like the Golden Gate Bridge, but the form had to be the same. She knew everything about this Soviet balloon before she saw it, because she'd learned about the American one they'd launched from the fifty-yard line at Soldier Field. And they had to obey the same physics. Two spheres, a huge one of rubberized fabric to hold the hydrogen and a tiny one of thin-walled metal to hold the air that would keep the people alive. A cone of shroud lines connecting them. Compressed gas and ballast to make it go up and down, controls and contraptions for actuating those from inside the capsule. Some of the English-speaking reporters were already muttering that this was just a copy of the American one, but Aurora doubted that Dick would have agreed.

She felt that she was more than halfway to being Proton's girlfriend. Close enough that she ought to have been entitled to wish him well, maybe even give him a kiss on the cheek for good luck. But that was ruled out by circumstances. Things happened fast. The days were still all too brief and the launch was behind schedule. Abruptly the hangar doors were hauled open, letting in a fanfare of bleak sunlight and a fist of cold air. A truck towed the gondola, which was mounted on a trailer, out to the field where the balloon was beginning to mound up. It moved at no more than a walking pace, so the crowd went with it. But everyone who wasn't a scientist, engineer, or aeronaut was diverted onto a wedge of bleachers rising from the edge of the field. During the walk she had almost come close enough to Proton to call out his name, but she wasn't sure he'd even recognize her in the full Svetlana disguise, surmounted by winter clothes. What ought to have been hers—the wishing him well, the kiss on the cheek—was taken care of by some fake girlfriend issued from the ranks of the Komsomol. Then he saluted to some important people who'd come out from the Kremlin and crawled through the capsule's tiny circular hatch. This was bolted into place. Various pre-flight checks and tests happened, making sure that the aeronauts could breathe. The whole time the balloon just kept getting bigger, peeling itself off the ground and growing to a size that would have astonished her if she hadn't seen one like it before.

And then at some point physics took precedence over story and the thing just sprang into the air. What had seemed so huge became tiny over the space of a few minutes. For a while it was a white star in the northeastern sky. Then it rose up through a veil of high, icy clouds and disappeared. By that point Owen and a few other handpicked journalists had long since piled into their cars and roared off in pursuit.

THE FACT THAT PROTON AND ALL THE OTHER AERONAUTS WERE DEAD WAS NEVER AN-nounced, but they did get an excellent funeral. Aurora had now been in the Soviet Union long enough to understand. A big, splashy balloon launch made for excellent, upbeat propaganda. A big funeral made for sad, but still excellent, propaganda. The in-between part—the actual announcement that the balloon had crashed and killed everyone aboard—did not make for such great propaganda and so it was simply omitted. Beyond a certain point you were just expected to know that all of those aeronauts were dead. Naïve persons—foreign visitors, say, who had only just arrived—might think, *I must have missed the announcement,* and flip back through the last couple of weeks' back issues of *Pravda* looking for an article—perhaps squirreled away on a back page, but at least still *there, somewhere*—stating that the balloon had crashed with the loss of the entire crew. But people in the know wouldn't even bother. They would just know. And the sooner they knew, the more well-connected they seemed.

His captors in Magnitogorsk gave Dr. Fizmatov a week's pass to travel to Moscow for the funeral. Aurora was able to have tea with him in the lobby of the Metropol. Elektron arranged it and sat there with them. It was all complicated because the parents were divorced, and not in a very friendly way, and poor Lek wasn't good at navigating such situations—he'd always relied on Proton for that kind of thing.

After all the trouble it took Lek to arrange the get-together, they didn't have a lot to talk about. But Aurora had already seen enough of death and funerals to understand that it was always thus. You didn't go to a funeral to break new ground in a friendship. You just showed up, made small talk, nibbled on things, and went home. It was really just a way of taking a census, a head count of who was still alive.

Dr. Oleksandr Fizmatov, Ukrainian metallurgist and political prisoner, normally wouldn't have been welcome in the Metropol, but he was still dressed in the getup that had been provided him for the funeral—a massive procession across Red Square, complete with warplanes flying overhead. So, just this once, they let him sit there and take tea. He had apparently got updates from his sons as to what Aurora was up to, so he didn't have a lot of questions. For her part, she could have asked him how things were going in Magnitogorsk, but the answer would have been forgotten as soon as heard.

She got up to use the toilet. When she emerged, she noticed, from across the lobby, that a man had come over to chat with the Fizmatovs. He was standing with his back to Aurora. Young, upright, well-dressed. As she came closer she realized that it was Owen Crisp-Upjohn. She turned away and found a place to sit at the other end of the lobby, in a high-backed chair around which she could peek from time to time to see if Owen was still there. He stayed longer than she expected—fifteen minutes or so—then went on his way. Only then did Aurora go back and reclaim her place.

"What did *he* want?" she asked.

She recalled, now, that prior to the launch, in the hangar, Owen had spent time talking to both Proton and Elektron. He'd have recognized Lek in the lobby. Perhaps even made the reasonable guess that the older gentleman next to him was the bereaved father.

"That is a very courteous and well-spoken young man," said Dr. Fizmatov.

"What language were you speaking?"

"French."

Lek shrugged. Not a French speaker himself.

"There are a lot of ways to say you're sorry in French. He knows some of the better ones," Dr. Fizmatov continued.

"You talked to him for a while," Aurora observed.

"He was there. At the site of the crash. He wanted us to understand that death was instantaneous." Dr. Fizmatov was strangely impassive, clinical, as he said this. But then tears filled his eyes faster than he could blink them away. "Of course in a sense that's true when you hit the ground at very high velocity. *Then* death comes before you can feel it. But *before* then . . ."

"They were falling for a long time," Lek said. "Minutes." His eyes rolled up and to one side. Aurora realized, fascinated, that he was performing the calculation in his head. How long, to the decimal point, had his brother known he was about to die?

"This Owen chap is a sophisticated man, and he knows it's all just words at this point. But he also knew that it would mean something to me to talk to one who was there." Dr. Fizmatov wiped his face with a white linen napkin and threw it down. "Aurora. Walk with me."

One of *those* walks. They left Elektron Fizmatov in the lobby to calculate.

It was as if the crash of the balloon had precipitated a change in the weather. Winter was over. Tires were hissing on streets that were wet for the first time in six months. The conversation wasn't long, and didn't need to be. They just made a quick turn around Revolution Square.

"I can guess well enough what they have you doing," Fizmatov said. "I saw it all taking shape around that dinner table in Magnitogorsk. I won't say the obvious things. You can't possibly have any illusions in your head as to what kind of man Beria is—what he's capable of."

"Certainly not."

"You must do what is necessary to survive. I understand this. We all do it."

"Thank you." She meant it. Though she hadn't really dwelled on it, there'd been this voice in her head recently. The voice of Dr. Fizmatov. Approving or not.

"This business that we talked about at that dinner . . ."

It took her a moment. "You mean neutrons? Alchemy?"

"Yes."

"What of it?"

"It's important, Aurora. It's very important."

21

POLOSTAN

MARCH 1934

It was a matter of drainage. In the spring, half a year's precipitation suddenly became liquid and the world became mud and you couldn't play polo on mud. But it turned out that there was a place south of Moscow where a river made a big, lazy bend. It had been depositing sand on its floodplain since time immemorial. The sand couldn't hold water, which made it useless for agriculture. But in the spring thaw it became a decent enough riding surface as soon as the snow had melted away. Slower than turf, of course, but they weren't trying to hold the world polo championship here, just getting some exercise for the mounts and the men.

And now women. Aurora came down a week in advance, dragging a massive trunk containing Owen's entire literary output, the three different English dictionaries needed to fully decipher it, several Red Army uniforms (men's and women's), a sewing machine, leatherworking tools, boots, jodhpurs, and red hair dye. The cavalry, which of course consisted entirely of men, was already pitching camp on the site, and trailering ponies to makeshift stables. It was clear from the manner in which they received her that they'd been given a stiff talking-to from someone of whom they were terrified. The fact that the Red Army women's polo team was utterly factitious (an Owen word, there) was neither here nor there. Separate tents and sanitary facilities had been set up for them. Like so much else in the Soviet Union these looked to have been thrown together in a day by men with guns to their heads. But it wasn't much worse than where the men were going to stay. Aurora told the men where to put her enormous trunk. She got the stove lit and then sat down to ponder as the place warmed up.

More than once she'd replayed in her head that exchange in Beria's office. Like a censor airbrushing a disgraced commissar from a photograph of Stalin, she had simply edited Zhirkin out of the recollection.

Is there a Red Army women's polo team?

Would you like there to be?

It was both a simple ask and a way of Beria saying, *What would you do if I allowed you to have that much power?* Part of her shrank from that, but after a couple of sleepless nights (they'd given her a new flat, the bowls of kerosene were no longer necessary) she understood that from here on there would be no steady state, no day-to-day job into which she could settle. She was going to have to keep advancing.

She remembered her father taking her to a seafood market in Seattle, close enough to the waterfront that you could hear the waves pounding the piers, where they had a big aquarium full of live Dungeness crabs. They never stopped climbing over one another. Occasionally one would get high enough to thrust one claw up out of the water and hook it over the rim of the tank. It seemed plausible for a few moments that it might heave itself over the edge, fall to the floor, and scuttle out the door, making a break for the cold, murky waters of Elliott Bay. But any crab that ascended to that height was immediately grabbed onto by others below and dragged back down. Young Dawn had always sympathized with those aspirant crabs—the climber-outers, she called them—and instinctively loathed the grabber-onners. The ones who just sat motionless on the floor of the aquarium, waiting to die—the giver-uppers—she scarcely noticed. She wondered if any of the climber-outers had ever made good their escape. She wondered, too, how much craft the builders of the aquarium had put into making it seem escapable, but in reality an Alcatraz for crustaceans. In sight of freedom. But if you attempted it you'd learn the physics were against you. You were no different from Proton, bolted into a metal sphere, experiencing zero gravity and knowing what it meant.

Anyway, she was a crab in a tank. Beria had already figured out that she was no giver-upper. By posing that question he was trying to find if she was a climber-outer or a mere grabber-onner. After some consideration she'd said yes, she wanted such a polo team to exist.

It helped that the idea wasn't purely ridiculous. The Soviet Union had an army—the largest in the world, at the moment. Like all armies, this included cavalry. Like every other cavalry, they played polo. As could be attested by the likes of Veronika—a minor celebrity in her own right—the Red Army was second to none in incorporating women into its ranks. This team only needed to be willed into existence. The men here already had the physical apparatus: the ponies, the stables, the grooms, the tack, mallets (Brits called them "sticks"), balls, and goals. All that was really needed was three women, in addition to Aurora, who were good riders. In some inscrutable way these had been extracted from the Soviet military. One of them, a Tatar from Bashkortostan, had arrived a couple of days ago. Two more—a Zaporizhian Cossack and a Belarussian—showed up the next day. The only thing they had in common, other than absolute bewilderment, was that they were experienced riders. None of them had played polo, of course. The Tatar had never even heard of it. But having arrived early, with no orders, she'd watched the men play and got the general idea.

But they weren't claiming that this was a crack polo team. Just that it was a new one—which was no lie. Some of the girls were better than others with needle and thread, but over the course of a few evenings they were able to pull together what passed for uniforms. Secondhand gear from the men's team was adequate—anything nicer would have looked suspicious. Ponies, of course, were abundant. The men didn't mind letting the women borrow some of the smaller ones. Aurora rode full-sized mounts. This was resented by some of the grooms and lower ranks, but those were overruled by obviously terrified officers. When it came down to it, the only thing that really mattered to these men was the horses. They didn't want these carefully trained mounts spoiled by bad riders. Once they saw that the girls were good riders, they settled down.

So it only remained to teach the girls enough basics to make it look like they'd done this before. A tall order in the few days they had. But if you knew how to ride, and you were on a mount accustomed to the swing of the stick and the crack of the ball, this boiled down to smacking a thing with a hammer. The camp already had a polo pit—a wooden horse surrounded by an embankment. It was the usual way to teach the basic strokes to beginners. From there they moved on to practice on an old, very calm mount, legs protected from errant strokes by leather boots. They watched the men practice and rode with them to get a sense of how the game flowed, where you did and didn't want to be on the ground. They learned some basic tactics—the fact that even if you never struck the ball you could assist your team by interfering with the opposing back. And as twilight fell on the evening of Owen's arrival, they all rode out in their uniforms and played a chukker against some of the men.

"Polostan!" Owen dubbed it, a few moments after he'd climbed out of the car that had brought him and a couple of other Brits down from Moscow. He kept turning his head from side to side trying to estimate the distance separating the goals, which seemed almost to sink beneath the curvature of the Earth.

The witticism went untranslated by his interpreter. But the joke was the same in any language. His hosts, mostly high-ranking cavalry officers, didn't get it. Oh, they understood that he'd slapped the Central Asian suffix "-stan" onto "polo"—that much was obvious—but the whole concept of clever wordplay for its own sake just didn't belong to their world. Banterers they were not.

Aurora was ready for it though. By now she'd read everything Owen had ever published. She'd even learned a new word, "persiflage," which accurately described ninety percent of the man's literary output. His capacity for it was why important—which was to say, educated—Brits read his stuff. His wit was now therefore a strategic asset. His only rival—for there was always a rival—was Christian Audsley, Viscount Rocksborough, who'd gone to the same posh school as Owen and was even more disgustingly young and precocious. But the rivalry was like a wheel spur digging into Owen's flank. It was the only thing saving him from his own indolence. It was why he had bothered to drag himself out of bed this morning, shave, dress, and endure a three-hour drive south to the windswept and chilly floodplain that was now and forever Polostan.

And it made for good watching, as far as Aurora was concerned. Notwithstanding the Bonnie Parkers and Amelia Earharts of the world, it was just the case that men did and women watched. Some watching was more fun than others. Watching a delectable young man like Owen trying to outdo his rival by going out into the world and doing rash, stupid things made for some of the best watching ever. It was why they had cheerleaders at football games. Not just there as entertainment, but to be entertained.

And that was just from reading his words on the page. He wrote in an arch, flagrantly clever style that made his sentences impenetrable to more academically trained Russians. Even for Aurora, a native English-speaker, it took some getting used to and some looking up of words in dictionaries. She'd been looking forward to seeing him in the flesh, in more ways than one. The only thing that had troubled her about the Owen assignment at first was Proton: the only boy she'd met in the Soviet Union she might actually like to date. But she couldn't cheat on a dead boy.

Owen's companions were a diplomat from the British embassy and a journalist from Edinburgh. Both were old and podgy and wearing trousers. Owen had worn jodhpurs, meaning that he intended to ride. The junket had been billed as an opportunity for him to have a bit of fun, seeing how his favorite sport was played in the unique circumstances of the Soviet Army. The article practically wrote itself. Aurora could easily imagine high-and-mighty men of the British Empire chortling over their milky tea and runny eggs as Owen described the sandy immensity of Polostan and the primitive ways of Communist equitation. And yet beneath the funny surface layer they'd be learning a few things about the state of the Red Army in general and its cavalry in particular.

His minders had been instructed not to mention the existence of a women's team. It had to be something that Owen *discovered*. He had to spy it, to be intrigued by it, maybe to push through some minor show of resistance to learn more—making it an achievement for which he could congratulate himself. Accordingly, Aurora and her team began to conduct a visible but unobtrusive practice off to one side of the main polo grounds during the sixth chukker of a match between two of the men's teams. The vast size of Polostan left plenty of room for that. There were no fences, no demarcations. Owen had been provided with a good pony. He'd watched the army teams play from the vantage point of the saddle, restlessly riding up and down the edge of the grounds to follow the action or help chase down stray balls.

When the whistle sounded terminating the sixth chukker, Owen cantered directly across the field toward the women, pursued by a minder who, if he was doing as he'd been told, was insisting the whole way that there was nothing to see there. But Owen, like a stallion who'd caught a whiff of a mare, came straight on. More men began to approach in his wake.

Aurora's experience with the girls' polo team in Virginia provided her with a template for how she knew this was going to go. The men would be amused by the novelty—the cheek, really—of women trying to play their sport. They would tolerate it at first, if for no other reason than that they enjoyed looking at the shapely bottoms of healthy girls in tight-fitting breeches. Most would not advance much beyond that. But a few, as Patton had done, would begin to take it seriously once they understood that the *women* took it seriously. This was surprising. A separation would occur. Men who did not like being surprised—stupid men—would turn away and mutter rude things. Men who rather liked being surprised—and she was pretty sure Owen was one of those—would find in it something to take them out of their ennui.

He'd outridden his interpreter. Aurora turned her mount with her knees and a gentle shift of her weight, a detail she knew he'd savor, and rode toward him. She had red hair now. The transformation had startled her teammates, who had been told only that they were here to form a polo team and couldn't make out what hair color had to do with that. But as with so many other inexplicable happenings in the Soviet Union, they knew better than to ask questions. She knew from Owen's dossier that he'd now be suspicious if she presented with a radiant waterfall of red hair and so she'd put it up and tucked it under her helmet, except for one stray lock that had "worked loose" during her exertions. Demurely she tucked it back as she drew closer. "Katya," she said, placing her hand on her sternum. "I speak some little English. Not them." She waved her stick in the direction of the other girls. "You are Angliskii? Americanskii?"

"The former," he said, "but fear not, I'm not here to invade you. Unless you want to be invaded." He muttered the last bit under his breath, looking around for some other chap who might appreciate the double entendre, but no one was there.

"You like to play? It seems you do," she said, turning her mount so that she was facing in the same direction as Owen, a length ahead. He was obliged to catch up. "Is new sport for us. We try to learn. Good riders. Bad polo players."

"Well, there's only one thing for it then," Owen said, "and that is to play more! From what I've observed, all you ladies lack is experience."

"So give us experience, former."

It took him a moment to get it. Then his head snapped sideways to look at her.

She had him.

He led the women onto the main ground and galloped about, handpicking three other men to form a scratch team. They went at it. Not hard, at first. But Owen had chosen his side well, picking men who'd play seriously but with restraint. He shouted at them in English, of which they spoke not a word, but he did it with a combination of zeal and humor that they understood well. If "Katya" was nearby, she attempted to translate. Once they had all got used to one another and the horses and the humans had come to a shared understanding of how it was going to be, they just played. They played with the joy of children and the intensity of warriors.

The only really competitive play was between Owen and "Katya," whom Aurora already knew was going to be written up in Owen's next dispatch as the tall, mysterious redhead whose riding skills were a match for any Englishwoman's and who bantered with him in an effective but hilariously crude approximation of English. She played back, meaning that she was the last defender, and he played number one, providing many excuses for contact. If his number two was mounting an attack, he might come galloping down the field to ride her off. If he was the sole attacker, she would head him off and get in his way. So there was a lot of body-to-body contact between horses and players. For the final chukker she selected a big mount that could handle it. He understood the challenge and came at her hard, and frequently. The incredible size of Polostan sometimes led to the two of them finding themselves virtually alone.

She had not planned on what she did next. Had not even imagined it. But she saw that this was her moment to climb out of the aquarium. She spun her mount round to face him and said, in American English, "Owen. This whole thing was a setup."

Owen was having so much fun—he was so ridiculously infatuated, with both her and the game—that this took him as much by surprise as if she'd smacked him in the gob with her stick.

"The OGPU wants me to sleep with you."

He got a thoughtful look on his face, clearly seeing this as more of a good than a bad outcome. Yet understanding the gravity of the situation.

"I need your help getting out of here," she said. "Sure, I'll sleep with you if you want. I'd enjoy it, and I can't get pregnant. But you have to know what this really is."

There was now a slow but unmistakable transformation that came over him, beginning with his mouth and propagating through his face and body to a degree that even his horse noticed it. She found it fascinating to watch, precisely because she had no idea where it was going at first. At its beginning he was just a fop trying to have a good time. He could have gone on as such without end, and probably would have found that a lot easier. She'd ruined that plan. How, then, was he going to respond? A damsel in distress had thrown herself across his path. He could easily have hurdled this obstacle and galloped on without a look back. But at some level even the most selfish and degenerate man knew what was expected of him. You never knew when you were going to be tested. It was what you did in such a moment that told what kind of man you were. He did not make his choice easily or without misgivings. But after those first few moments of uneasy consideration, an alteration came over him that reminded her in some way of the balloon being slowly filled with hydrogen.

At first just a flaccid sack, supine on the field, but by the time it was over, inflated and shapely with power.

"How may I be of assistance, young lady?"

"Fall in love with me."

"Done. Will there be anything else? Is there some acceptable pretense under which I might see you again? I should like that more than practically anything else my feeble mind is capable of imagining."

"Someone will make that happen if you continue to show interest."

"That much, Katya, will be quite easy for me. But you must know I've been called away. I'll be leaving the country very soon."

"Write me letters."

"Which . . . will be read by OGPU."

"Of course. Go around the world and do what you do. Eventually they'll send me out after you."

"Then I'll see you out in the world." He wheeled his mount and rode back into the fray. She galloped after him.

ACKNOWLEDGMENTS

Expect more comprehensive Acknowledgments in later volumes as the shape of this thing becomes clear. But it all started with Seamus Blackley sending me a text message in 2013, inviting me down a rabbit hole that he had already discovered and begun to explore. Other than that, the most important contribution that I am bound to acknowledge is the patience shown by my editor, Jennifer Brehl, during the years that have repeatedly put this project on hold to write other books!